INSECTICIDE
A REPUBLICAN ROMANCE

INSECTICIDE

A REPUBLICAN ROMANCE

DOUGLAS ROBINSON

WITH RESEARCH ASSISTANCE FROM BILL KAUL

atmosphere press

Contents

Prologue

A New Republic of Texas

High above New York City, balanced on the parapet encircling the balcony outside his employer's boardroom, James Percival fished in his breast pocket for his hankie. Even in the chill, gusty November wind that now threatened to topple him back over onto the balcony, now down into traffic forty-five stories below, he was soaked with sweat. He dabbed at his forehead and cheeks, carefully lowered his hankie-clutching hand to his side, and thought:

I bet Prescott Bush could stand here all day without teetering.

He, James Quincey Percival IV, fifty-three years old next Tuesday if he lived that long, had worked for Harriman Investments for twenty-five years. Prescott Bush, surely not many days over thirty, had worked for Dogsbody Harriman just under three years. When Prescott lost all his money in the crash two weeks ago, Dogsbody quietly made up his losses. When James lost all his money in the crash two weeks ago, Dogsbody sailed past him down the hall in a great hurry, his feet hardly touching the carpet, his insectile gray head barely even acknowledging his presence with a nod.

Who was Prescott Bush, anyway? His father was an iron manufacturer in the Midwest—Ohio, James thought, or some ghastly place even further west. Richer than God, to be sure—but who *were* they? The Percivals had been a powerful force in New York banking since the Revolution; now, this new breed had come out of nowhere to seize control and subtly but inexorably push the Percivals and their ilk off to one side.

This stock market crash? Dogsbody Harriman's doing. James was all but sure of it. If only he could prove it! Though, of course, even if he could, he couldn't *prove* it. No one would take his word over Dogsbody Harriman's. Nobody. Not even his own father. Not even his older brothers, though they, too, had been ruined by the crash. They would all say, horrified, in a shushing voice, flicking their eyes around the room to see who else had heard him airing this heresy: "You're accusing Dogsbody Harriman of *what*? Are you out of your *mind*?"

But he *knew*. He had worked with Dogsbody all these years. He knew how Dogsbody's mind worked. He knew that Dogsbody Harriman had no compunctions, period. None whatsoever. About anything. He would do whatever he had to do to enhance his position. *Whatever*. It occurred to James, in fact, that Dogsbody would quite calmly destroy the world if he could, if it was in his power, and if, in doing so, he could make a killing.

Killing! Ha!

Thirty years ago, nobody had heard of Dogsbody Harriman; one day, he appeared out of nowhere and started making money and amassing influence with uncanny grace and speed. Suddenly, he was the President's best friend, was already in on every deal in the making the day before those in the know knew, had his secret sweetheart arrangements with everybody who was anybody—and then, gradually, inevitably, with only those somebodies *he* chose. His business partners became fantastically, unimaginably rich seemingly overnight, seemingly without great effort or forethought. Those he ignored were soon ignored by all and dropped out of sight. Those who fought him were utterly and irrevocably crushed.

Like James himself now, teetering on this parapet. Not that he had fought Dogsbody. But it had occurred to him more than once that Dogsbody Harriman somehow *knew* his suspicions, knew that James was contemplating sharing those suspicions with others. Insane paranoid fears, of course. Dogsbody was no god, no descending angel, no superior being who could read his thoughts; he was just a man. An extraordinarily talented man, yes, but just a man.

Still, sometimes James wondered ...

A sudden upward gust rocked James back on his heels. Following the gust up the wall came a man, a man in a business suit, his hands crooked up under his chin like the long, spindly front legs of a praying mantis, holding a briefcase—

"Mr. Harriman!" James blurted like a boy. "How—"

"Hello, James," Dogsbody said coolly, hovering there briefly, no sign of propulsion, his expensively shod feet drooping down below slack legs a few inches above the parapet.

"D-did you just—" James stammered. "Did you just *fly* up here?"

"James," Dogsbody said in the same even tone, still hovering, "you're weak."

"How did you *do* that?" James' mind reeled. Sick waves of vertigo washed over him. Suddenly, he no longer knew which way was up. Suddenly, he hardly even cared.

"You were too weak to hold onto your money," Dogsbody said, "and now you're too weak to jump. Can I give you a push?"

James panted, beyond all rational thought. He hardly even heard the question.

"Well," Dogsbody said, "make up your mind, James. And be quick about it. It's bad for business to have our executives dithering on the parapet."

And he flew across the balcony and through the open French doors into the ballroom.

James thought to himself, with a wild glance over his shoulder:

Something just happened.

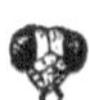

Inside the boardroom stood Prescott Bush, seemingly at his ease, his right hand resting on the back of Dogsbody Harriman's soft beige calf-leather chair. Dogsbody flew in, spotted him there, emitted a quick guttural cry, but made two quick passes around the room, his shiny black shoes only now and then dragging along the hardwood floor before coming to hover before and just above him.

Almost instantly, Pres was overrun with shiny green beetles. Body, face, hair. They clicked and scurried over him as over a hillock. He paid them no attention whatever.

"Ah, Pres," Dogsbody said with something like a smile. His mouth clacked a little as he said it. False teeth? Pres did not let his imagination run wild on such things.

"Welcome back, Mr. Harriman," Pres said.

"Call me Uncle Dogsbody," Dogsbody said.

"Yes, sir," Pres said, "Uncle Dogsbody."

Dartingly, expertly, Dogsbody touched him ten, fifteen times on the head and chest and shoulders. Every place he touched, he deposited a glob of some gluey substance that trapped a beetle or two. Their little feet continued to wriggle impotently in their little prisons.

"Pres, I have a job for you," Dogsbody said, picking a beetle off Pres's lapel and popping it in his mouth. Crunch, crunch. His jaws moved sideways on the beetle, like mandibles.

"I am at your disposal, sir," Pres said. "Of course."

"I want you to create a country for me," Dogsbody said.

"A country, sir?" Pres said.

"A country," Dogsbody said. "Well, a fortress, really. A country-sized fortress. A safe place for our people that looks and talks and acts like a country."

"There is some danger, sir?" Pres said.

"There is always some danger," Dogsbody said, "if you know where to look."

"Will this be a new colony, Uncle Dogsbody," Pres said, "or an existing place that I should begin to convert to our values?"

"An existing place," Dogsbody said, popping two more beetles in his mouth and crunching them sideways. "Texas."

"A new Republic of Texas?" Pres said.

"If you like," Dogsbody said. "So long as it is a republic in name only."

"Of course," Pres said.

"You and your family will need to relocate there," Dogsbody said. "Sorry."

Pres shrugged. "We have made sacrifices before," he said.

"Good boy," Dogsbody said.

"Do you want me out in the open, sir," Pres said, "as President, or behind the scenes, as you've been proceeding thus far in Nazi Germany and the Soviet Union?"

"Behind the scenes," Dogsbody said, "as in Europe. Recruit local politicians; put them in positions of power. Win the Texans' trust that way. They won't support a rich Yankee financier."

"Yes, sir," Pres said.

"And I am increasingly convinced that we do need their support," Dogsbody said, "for this sort of enterprise. I swear, though, if I live another ten thousand years, I'll never fully understand you mammals with your herd instincts."

"Yes, sir," Pres said. "I assume you'll be running interference in Washington and New York?"

"Don't you worry about that end of things," Dogsbody said.

"I won't, sir," Pres said.

"Good," Dogsbody said and pried up four or five more beetles, pasting them to the palm of his hand like a biology project. "Now, I assume you and your family have some packing to do."

"Yes, sir," Pres said.

Out on the parapet, James Percival made up his mind with a sudden cry and plunged to his death below.

"Who was that?" Pres said.

"Nobody," Dogsbody said. "Now go."

Pres went.

Prescott Bush drove his red 1928 Studebaker through the Oklahoma night. Under the supervision of his efficient, orderly wife, Dottie, who could have been a famous general (had women been designed for such things), the servants had packed his household in less than a week, boxed it up, carted it to the train station for cross-country transport. He and the family drove ahead to purchase an estate outside of Houston.

The rest of the family slept. It had been an exhausting three days and nights, driving straight through, Pres stopping only for brief catnaps two or three times a day. A difficult way to travel, but Uncle Dogsbody had stressed the importance of getting on the ground early, so he had pushed them, his wife and children, pushed them hard, and as usual, they had responded with the requisite obedience and discipline.

"Dad?"

One of the boys in the back seat stirring in his sleep, no doubt. Pres Jr. was eight, George was five, and Nancy was a toddler, seventeen or eighteen months. Pres drove on in silence.

"Dad?"

"Go back to sleep, son."

Pres half-turned. It was George, whom his wife had started calling "Poppy." He, Pres, was Big Dog. Pres Jr. was Little Dog. Little George was Poppy. Awake at this time of the night. Five years old and still couldn't talk right. Not right in the head, their family doctor had whispered to Dot when Pres wasn't there. Pres had mentioned this casually to Dogsbody Harriman, and the doctor had ended up relocating to Toronto three days before the AMA revoked his license. Bushes did not have problems with their heads.

"Dad, when we're get gonna go there?" George said.

"We'll get there when we get there, son," Pres said. "Now sleep."

"Dad," George said, "why can't I look in the lox?"

"Box, son."

"Box, Dad?" George said, as if continuing his previous question. "Why can't I book in the box?"

"Look in the box, son."

"Why can't I book in the lox, Dad?"

"Because it's a box for grown-ups," Pres sighed. Pres Jr. had been better spoken at three than George was at five. "Sleep, now."

"Will I be able to fook in the fox when I grow up?" George said.

"Yes," Pres said. "You'll be able to *look* in the *box* when you grow up, George. But you're not going to grow up at all unless you get some sleep. Close your eyes now, and sleep."

"Yes, Dad," George said.

Pres drove on, half-listening as his son's breathing grew heavier and more even.

An hour later, he found the Fort Sills access road and turned in.

At the entrance to the cemetery, he stopped the car and got out. His family did not stir. He reached back in and carefully lifted out the ancient carved box, set it on the roof of the car. He walked around to the back, where the beetles still swarmed. He waded through them to the trunk, brushing them aside in the air, crunching a few underfoot. Stuck his key in, opened the trunk lid, and felt around until his fingers closed on the flashlight. He switched on the beam, found the shovel and the crowbar, slung both over his shoulder. He stepped back to the driver's door and gently hoisted the box under his left arm.

Uncle Dogsbody had impressed upon him the vast holy power of this box.

This fox, he thought, was not to be fooked with.

Pres walked through the graveyard, flashing his light on the gravestones till he found the one he was looking for. He set the box down carefully and set to work.

It took him two hours to dig down to the wooden coffin, another half hour to shovel all the dirt off the lid and pry it open with the crowbar. There it was: the exposed skeleton, after twenty years, only a few scraps of clothing still clinging to it. The skull had rolled to one side. He lifted it with both hands, stood, and reached above his head to set it up top, next to the box. He replaced the coffin lid and climbed out of the grave. He wiped his hands as best he could on his pants, lifted the box lid with reverent fingertips, and set the skull inside. The skull was surprisingly clean: he had expected to soil the box's red velvet lining with the skull's dirt, but there was no dirt on it at all. He closed the box, set it to one side, then set about reburying the coffin.

As he tamped the dirt back down on top, he flashed the light one last time at the gravestone:

GERONIMO
Friend of Atlantis
1829–1909

Clem Hauser shifted his considerable bulk over onto his right foot. He had just shifted it over onto the left thirty seconds before, so he was not exactly overwhelmed with relief. Two and a half hours to go on his shift. He had to get some better shoes.

Or a better job.

But as his wife always said, he was lucky to have this one. It wasn't exactly back-breaking labor. It didn't require much in the way of intellectual effort. He mostly just stood there waving cars and trucks through the border checkpoint. Easiest job in the world, really. If they'd just let him park his fat ass on a stool or something. But no.

10

But while it was true (he reminded his wife) that his wasn't the busiest border checkpoint between Texas and Oklahoma, it wasn't exactly the slowest, either. It was a responsible job. It wasn't like being a night watchman in a warehouse. You did have to use your head and keep your wits about you and your eyes on the traffic. Anything suspicious, blam, you were the man. Nobody else. No backup. Call on the phone, and somebody might drag their asses out here in a couple of hours, maybe. You had your six-shooter and your car and your judgment. When to ask a driver to get out of the car, open his trunk. When to make a more thorough search.

Not that Clem made such searches very often. Or, well, if you came right down to it, had made one even once. But still. He could. It would be up to him. He would be the man. He would be Johnny-on-the-Spot.

His wife just laughed when he talked like this. She came from up north. A good Texan wife would never laugh at her husband the way his wife did at him. He imagined his mother laughing at his father like that: ha! Never happen. The very thought was so absurd he could hardly imagine it. A Texan wife respected her husband. Just what possessed him to go after a Yankee wife, he had no idea. Temporary insanity, probably.

He was reflecting on this regrettable lapse on his part for perhaps the ten thousandth time when he spotted the car approaching from the Oklahoma side, raising a dust cloud the likes of which he'd never seen.

As that dust cloud came closer, he stared hard at it, trying to figure out just what was so strange about it. It wasn't a light dusty tan color, for one thing. It was dark, even sort of dark-shiny, but of course, that couldn't be. He'd probably just been out in the sun too long. And it didn't fan out to the sides. It stretched out straight behind the car, like a long tail, whipping from side to side a little, exactly like a tail.

As the car approached—a red late-model Studebaker, he noted, with Connecticut plates—he held up his hand. "Stop!"

Exercising his judgment. A man's got to do the job the state hired him to do.

The car slowed. And now he saw that what he thought was a dust cloud was actually—imagine!—some sort of swarm of insects. Insects! What if they were poisonous? What if they ate crops? Some kind of Biblical scourge or plague, like locusts! He could feel his whole being go on red alert. The State of Texas paid him to protect citizens from just this sort of intruder!

The car pulled up. Thirtyish well-dressed man and his family. Wife and three little kids. Two boys in the back, baby girl in the wife's arms up front.

"What's the problem, officer?" the man said.

"You realize you've got a swarm of some kinda bugs trailing behind you, sir?" Clem said.

The man held up his right index finger and waved it back and forth.

"Never mind about the bugs," the man said.

"Ne—" Clem started but suddenly forgot what he was going to say.

Then he noticed a strange-looking carved box on the front seat between the man and his wife.

"Whatcha got in that box, there, sir?" he said. "Mind if I have a look?"

"You don't want to look in the box," the man said.

Clem's mind sort of went blank. What was he thinking again? What was his plan here? Why did he stop this car?

He thought about it for a moment but couldn't think of a single reason to detain these nice people.

"Everything seems A-OK here," he said with a smile and waved them through.

"Thanks, officer," the man said and drove off.

As the strange-looking bug-swarm tail followed the Connecticut car off down the road, Clem suddenly twitched, as if waking from a light sleep.

"The bugs," he said, narrowing his eyes a little. "I stopped that there car cuzza them bugs."

He strode over to his little booth, squeezed through the narrow door, and picked up the telephone mouthpiece to call in.

Before he could even ask the girl to patch him through to headquarters, though, a strange thing happened.

Suddenly, the entire booth was overrun with shiny, clicking green beetles. Including the phone and his arm that held the mouthpiece. Clem dropped the mouthpiece in shock and disgust, brushing beetles off his clothes with a panicky gasp as he backed away.

What the hell?

Mutt Rider saw the roadblock up ahead, downshifted, and downshifted again. He'd been driving since eight this morning; it was almost that time in the evening now, and he was ready to be home with his wife's voice in his ear and a hot home-cooked dinner on the table. He was carrying oranges from Florida, 560 boxes. He'd pushed it a little yesterday in order to be within driving distance of Humble today. And now here he was, could probably see his roof if he climbed on top of his truck, and—what? Something. Some delay.

He crept forward slowly, tickling the clutch, his left calf by now almost as tired as his right. The cops were turning everybody back. Every car that reached the roadblock was turning around and driving back. A fist of annoyance grabbed at him from inside.

Maybe these were all out-of-towners? Maybe they'd let locals through?

No: there went Sam Browning, back the way he came, with a shrug and a rueful face for Mutt. On his way back from the big emporium in Houston, probably, picking up fabric for Nell.

Damn.

Texas Rangers: not the cops, the Rangers. Mutt pulled up to the Ranger who was turning everybody around, and he rolled down his window.

"So what's the problem?" he said.

"Quarantine," the Ranger said.

"Quarantine for what?" Mutt said.

"Small pox," the Ranger said.

"What, who's got it?" Mutt said.

"Gas leak," the Ranger said.

"Huh?" Mutt said. "Which is it, small pox or a gas leak?"

"Move it along, buster," the Ranger said.

"Wait a minute, my wife's in there; tell me what's going on," Mutt said.

"I'll tell you what's going on," the Ranger said. "You're either moving your truck right now or spending the night in jail; that's what's going on."

"So when can I go home? Tomorrow morning?" Mutt said.

"Watch for further announcements," the Ranger said.

"Watch what?" Mutt said.

"You gonna move that truck," the Ranger said, "or do I have to handcuff you to it?"

Mutt had a very bad feeling about all this, but he shrugged and put the truck in low. Started pulling it ahead and around to the left. This gave him an unobstructed view of the car behind him, a red late-model Studie with what looked like a middle-class family in it, being waved through the roadblock.

"Hey!" Mutt yelled out the window, "what the hell is *that*?"

He stopped his truck, opened the door, and jumped out on the running board to yell at the Ranger some more. The Ranger pulled his gun and was about to aim it at Mutt when two things happened.

First, a huge buzzing swarm of shiny green bugs swooped through the roadblock between Mutt and the Ranger.

And second, some kind of weird flying saucer came flying in *over* it, maybe twenty feet wide and a hundred feet in the air.

The Ranger and Mutt both stopped to gape.

Right over the town, the flying saucer stopped and hovered. A hatch opened up, and a tall, thin gray man in a business suit climbed out, clutching a briefcase up by his chin. Without wings or anything, he flew off the saucer and into town. The saucer shot up into the air as if on springs.

"And what the fuck was *that?*" Mutt yelled at the Ranger. "Fucking *Superman?*"

Now, the Ranger leveled his gun at Mutt. "I'm going to ask you one more time to move your truck, sir," he shouted, "or you are going to be one very sorry dead motherfucker, sir!"

Mutt shook his head in disgust but climbed back into his cab, pulled the door shut, and drove off.

He was going to have to drive to his sister's place in Houston; that was clear. And he didn't much like his sister's cooking, or her pushy husband, Mac, or their snotty little kid, Bryce, or Bruce, or whatever the hell the kid's name was, or their yippy little dog, or the way their house stank of dog piss.

But what really got his goat in all this was that, when he did finally make it home, tomorrow or the next day or next month, when he finally rolled up in front of their house, his wife was not going to believe a damn word he told her about it. Flying saucers? Flying men in suits? She'd fucking laugh in his face. So he'd have to make something up, and she'd think he had a girlfriend, which he didn't, or that he'd been drinking, which he hadn't, and she'd yell and cry and carry on, and all because there was no way in hell he could tell her what he'd just seen.

Ross Sterling was as tough as they come—he'd fought ornery oil rigs in hundred-and-ten-degree temperatures, all covered in oil and sweat; he'd mixed it up with roughnecks who'd had a few too many to drink; for three decades, he'd done whatever it took to get the job done—but it was taking every ounce of his toughness not to bail on this one.

He could take extreme heat. He could take extreme physical exertion. He could take extreme violence. He could take just about anything an oilman could have thrown at him.

He was about three seconds away from admitting he couldn't take being swarmed over by shiny green beetles.

Even if it did mean being elected Governor of Texas and becoming the man of the hour, proclaiming the resurgent Republic of Texas and himself as its first President.

Even then.

"Just ignore them," this fucking butter-won't-melt-in-his-mouth upper-crust Yankee errand-boy Prescott Bush said, noticing his discomfort. Bush was covered with the fuckers, too, of course. "You'll get used to it."

"You think?" Ross said, trying to sound as calm as this man looked.

"Absolutely."

"Can I brush them off or anything?"

Tightly: "I, uh—I wouldn't recommend it."

And it wasn't just the beetles. It was that weird, tall, thin gray fuck up by the window, buzzing up against it like some kind of fucking fly, his hands crooked up by his neck. Dogsbody Harriman. Some kind of fabulously rich and powerful Yankee financier. They all acted weird, Ross had heard that; they weren't like ordinary folks down here in Texas. But this was fucking ridiculous. This was fucking out of control.

"Is he okay?" Ross said, jerking a beetley thumb up at the window.

Bush made a big show of turning up to the freakshow by the window.

"Uncle Dogsbody, are you okay?"

Buzz, buzz, buzz: "Proceed."

"Now," Bush said, "let's think about your declaration of martial law."

Hal Welch loved these mornings out on Lake Houston with his dad, just the two of them out in the boat, not talking, their lines in the water, the early morning mist still on the lake like a veil. Still sort of sleepy from waking up at four in the morning, riding out in his dad's truck in the dark, the sky turning slowly lighter as they approached the lake, the trees emerging out of the night like dark sentries along the road ... then, the lake itself, full of promise, the promise of catching a fish, sure, that primal combat between man and beast played out across the mystical barrier that was the water's surface, but the promise of something else as well, adulthood, perhaps, manhood, the world of driving a fishing truck out to the lake with your son and initiating him into the ways of nature.

Hal couldn't have put any of this into words. He was ten, eleven next month. But he *knew* it.

Then, the strike: his dad's rod bent double into the water.

"Dad!" Hal shouted.

His father grabbed his hat and came wild-eyed up out of his daydream.

"Reel it in, Dad!" Hal shouted again.

He loved it when a fish struck his line. Of course. Then it was all up to him. Then his dad shouted encouragement, and he, Hal, had to show his father what he was capable of.

But he loved it almost as much when one struck his dad's. Any strike was a major event. Any strike was a goddamn holiday.

But this fish didn't run with the line. At first, they thought it was a snag, but it kept coming up. His dad kept reeling, slowly, laboriously.

"What the hell, son?" his dad said, his voice strained. "I think we're reeling in a sunken log here."

After ten or fifteen minutes, they began to see a glimmer of something rising up from underwater. Hal got the net without having to be told and held it ready with a brimming sense of expectation and importance.

But when it finally broke the water, it was—a hat.

A fancy black top hat, like the fancy gentlemen wore in that movie his dad took him to in Houston last month, *The Career of Katherine Bush*, about this office worker who became a lady.

No way a hat could put *that* kind of drag on the line!

But it kept coming, and under it rose a man's head, with Hal's dad's hook in his lip.

And then further: it became a whole man sitting on some kind of weird cow, with wide horns and burning red eyes. The man was dressed in a long black suit, white shirt, and black bow tie. When the bull's haunches were above the water, the pair stopped rising, and the man *turned* to Hal and his dad.

He was *alive*. They both were. This man and his cow rose up from the bottom of Lake Houston, and they were *alive*. The man looked exactly like Abraham Lincoln. *Exactly*.

But while Hal was pondering this, without warning, four or five fish jumped into their boat and started flapping about. He and his dad looked down from the amazing thing that had just risen up from the depths of the lake at their feet, and somehow, the fish flapping around down there were the most amazing thing of all.

They went fishing.

They caught Abraham Lincoln or somebody who looked *just like him*.

The fish they were supposed to be catching jumped up into their boat.

Whoa.

Slowly, methodically, the man reached up and pulled the hook from his lip. It didn't bleed. He didn't wince with the pain. His lip looked sort of rubbery, like a fake lip or something.

"Gentlemen," he said.

"Mister, uh—President," his dad said, and touched his hat. So his dad was just sort of assuming that this *was* Abe Lincoln?

But wasn't Lincoln President like, a hundred *years* ago?

"The Welches, am I right?" the man said. "John and Harold?"

"That's right," his dad said.

"I go by Hal, sir," Hal said.

"Hal, yes," the man said. "I want you to listen up, son. You listening?"

"Yes, sir."

"Some day you're going to grow up and meet a girl named Jenna Hawkins, Hal. Marry her."

Marry? A *girl*? Gross!

"Listen!" the man rapped out sharply.

"Hal!" his father snapped nervously.

Hal hung his head. This was a time to be polite. Be grown-up. Not show how much you hate pukey girls. He nodded.

"Marry her, Hal," the man said. "This is important. The future of the entire world depends on it. You and she will have a daughter. Name her Laura."

"Laura, sir?" Hal said.

"Good boy," the man said and started sinking back into the lake.

"But—" Hal started.

"Remember," the man said. "The *entire world*."

The man kept his eyes on Hal as his face went underwater and bubbles started coming out of his mouth.

For a while after he was gone, father and son sat there dumbstruck.

Finally, Hal's dad began bashing the fish in the head that had jumped into their boat and packing up to go home.

"Dad," Hal finally ventured as they were loading the boat into the back of the truck, "was that—"

"I don't know, son," his father said wearily. And somehow, Hal knew not to lean on that button any more.

On the road back, they spotted a new notice on a tree. Hal's dad slowed the truck down and squinted over at it, but couldn't make it out.

"Run, go read me that sign, boy," he said.

"Yes, sir," Hal said, and, as soon as his dad stopped the truck, hopped out and ran over.

"It's some kind of announcement!" he called out. "It says: 'Attention! By order of the President and Congress, Republic of Texas: All labor unions—' "

"Louder, boy!" his dad yelled.

He stepped it up a notch: " 'All labor unions are hereby dissolved. All schools are closed until further notice. The borders with Mexico and the various United States are closed. Drug possession or use, including the excessive use of alcohol, is punishable by death. Prostitution is punishable by death. Spraying fields with insecticide is punishable by death. All males over the age of fourteen must wear a handgun in public. Females unescorted by males are prohibited in public without special permit; violations are punishable by public flogging. Public displays of affection will be punished by public displays of ridicule. All persons will report to a public hygiene clinic for health-and-wellness evaluation within the next three months; failure to do so will result in imprisonment, deportation, or death. Further instructions will follow.' "

He looked over at his dad to see what he wanted him to do next. His dad motioned him back. He ran back and climbed in.

His dad put the truck in gear, looked over at Hal, and started driving.

"Well, son," he said finally, "there goes our liberal pie-in-the-sky paradise, I reckon."

Ross Sterling crossed his right leg over his left and leaned back magisterially in his chair.

No beetles now. He had made it. And it had been worth it. Had it ever.

To the interviewer, who'd only been shaving for a month or two, looked like, this wasn't just a story. This was the opportunity of a lifetime. He, Ross Sterling, a poor wildcatter who made his millions off oil, founded the Humble Oil and Refining Company, then Sterling Chemical, then bought up railroads, newspapers, a bank, and so on and so forth, he was rich; he was used by now to a certain deference in the people around him—but nothing like this. Nothing like being President of the Republic of Texas.

"Could you explain for our readers, Mr. President, just why you found it necessary to declare martial law at this time, only a few months into your presidency and the creation of the new Republic?"

"Why, I'd be happy to, son," Ross beamed back. "You see, we got us a little problem here, and the problem is called *too much oil*. Oil production is up from ten million barrels a year in 1920 to three *hunnerd* million last year. That's too damn much. F'r instance, you may know that over those same ten years, the price dropped from three and a quarter dollars to fifty cents a barrel. This summer, somebody's drilled a oil well somewhere in Texas almost every damn hour, round the clock. Before I declared martial law, almost a half million barrels a day was being pumped out of the East Texas field alone, and the per-barrel price dropped to *five cents*. Now, see, *nobody* can make a profit on five cents a barrel. So I did what I had to do, son, to bring oil production down to some kind of workable levels. That answer your question?"

"Yes sir," the boy said, "thank you sir. Now, if you don't mind, I have just one more question."

"What's that, son?"

"President Sterling, what would you like to tell Texans who are reporting Abraham Lincoln sightings?"

"Say what now?"

"What would you like to say to Texans," the boy said, "who are saying Lincoln wasn't killed in Ford's Theater but snuck out before the end of the play and moved to Texas and is alive and well and living at the bottom of a lake somewheres with his devil-water-cow? And that he's some kind of Lemurian diving beetle from outer space?"

Well now, Ross thought, if that don't beat all, I don't know what does.

He chuckled appreciatively, as if at a good joke.

"As far as I know," he said, still smiling, "Lincoln has been dead since April 1865. And he never lived in Texas, nor, as far as we know, ever even visited it. And this whole insect thing, well! He was a flesh-and-blood human, just like everybody else, except, of course, Yankee."

"Well, I surely do thank you for your time, Mr. President," the boy said, and both of them rose to their feet. Ross motioned for an aide to show the boy out.

"Always happy to speak to the press," he said.

When the boy was gone, Ross was startled to find a lone beetle crawling up his pantleg.

A shiny green beetle. Oh shit.

These fuckers never traveled alone.

Sure enough, two seconds later, that weird Yankee Doodlebug Dogsbody Harriman flew in through an open window, and President Ross Sterling was overrun with the damn things again. He grimaced and squirmed. The President of the Republic of Texas shouldn't oughta have to put up with this shit.

"What?" Ross said, perhaps a bit snappishly.

"Find Abraham Lincoln," Harriman said in that nasty gray voice of his.

"Find who?" Ross said.

"You heard me," Harriman said. "Find him. Hire divers. Make them drink one quart of cod liver oil every day for two weeks before diving for him. Scour every damn lake in Texas. Find him and tell me where he is. Under no circumstances should your men approach him. He's a predaceous diving beetle and my ancient nemesis. He is extremely old and extremely dangerous, and could bring everything down about our ears in two seconds flat."

"Down about our ears?" Ross repeated, somehow failing to take all this in.

"Insecticide," Harriman explained and flew out the window.

Ross sighed. Why exactly did he sign on for this gig, again?

Documents

Interviews with Ordinary Texans
(August 24, 1931)

[handwritten note:] auditions closed, all roles filled; filming begins Tuesday

(1) EXT. RURAL TEXAN VEGETABLE GARDEN - DAY
A MAN (50s) stands in his garden with a hoe, obviously having just stopped hoeing a very dusty row.

INTERVIEWER #1 (O.S.)
Can I get your feelings about President Sterling declaring martial law, sir?

MAN
Martial law? I say it's about damn time Texas growed a damn backbone.

INTERVIEWER #1 (O.S.)
Backbone, sir?

MAN
Texans have went soft. Too much comfort. Too many luxuries. Gotta kick us some Texan butt, I say. Toughen us up. If it takes martial law to do that, hell, I say, more power to 'em!

(2) INT. COUNTRY STORE - DAY
The OWNER (40s) stands behind the counter, keeping a vigilant eye on his customers.

Across the store, a CHICANA (30s) and her THREE CHILDREN shop.

OWNER

I just think the niggers and wetbacks and Injuns and all them other half-wit half-breeds has ruined this country long enough. Texas was settled by good God-fearin' white folks and needs to get back to its roots. All these damn muddy-faced foreigners is just breedin' like bunnies and makin' stupid babies to take the bread off the table of good, hard-working, intelligent Texans.

INTERVIEWER #2 (O.S.)

So what would you suggest we do?

OWNER

Send the niggers back to Africa and the wetbacks back to Mexico and the Injuns back to India. Let's have us a real Texan republic here for once.

(3) EXT. BANK - DAY
A middle-class MATRON (40s) comes out of the bank.

INTERVIEWER #3 (O.S.)

Ma'am, excuse me?

MATRON

Yes?

INTERVIEWER #3 (O.S.)

I wonder whether I could ask you what you think about all this trouble we've been having lately?

MATRON

Trouble?

INTERVIEWER #3 (O.S.)

Yes, ma'am. All the riots and arrests all across Texas.

MATRON

Well, my husband says the trouble's all being caused by liberal agitators from the United States. I think he's right. The sooner we get rid of them, the better, I say. They just stir up trouble for good, loyal, right-minded Texans. Chuck 'em in jail and throw away the key! Deportation's too good for 'em!

(4) EXT. URBAN SIDEWALK - DAY
A young MAN (early 20s) stands self-confidently in the middle of the sidewalk, legs spread, thumbs in belt.

MAN

Time was a Texan stood on his own two feet, just his wife and kids to back him up. Now we got these freeloaders out here everywhere you look, holding their hand out for a free ride. Self-reliance is like some kinda cuss word or somethin' these days. We got liberals who LAUGH at self-reliance, like it's a BAD thing. Yes! We do! I ain't lyin'! But see, the thing is, I kinda noticed, you know, liberals hate Texas. HATE it. And we don't need folks around hatin' Texas to gum things up. Put the freeloaders to work and shut the mouths of the damn liberals. Permanently.

INTERVIEWER #4 (O.S.)
Permanently?

MAN

Okay, it's a harsh solution! But we're a simple, pragmatic people, Texans. We don't prevaricate for years and years about a thing. We shoot first, ask questions later. If at all. If—at—all!

For Immediate Release
(September 30, 1931)

The newly formed Republic of Texas Food and Drug Administration announced today that all farming and eating in Texas will be rigorously organic, based on the hygienic purity of traditional pioneer living. Pure living for a better world!

Not only will no synthetic fertilizers or insecticides be used; no biologically derived insecticides will be used either.

The decision was hailed by environmentalists around the world but provoked some questions among Texas farmers, wondering how they were going to protect their crops against what they called "pests."

Special Texas Farm Reeducation Camps have been set up to accommodate the farmers asking the questions. Students at the camps will be happily spending several months learning new farming techniques that do not endanger the country's precious insect population.

Among the new substances that will be made available to Texas farmers is a biological fertilizer made of dead fish. It is anticipated that the smell will keep the insects at bay. Better living through chemistry!

Bloodline

(Poppy, May 13, 1934)

We're all out playing baseball in our big field. Outside Houston a little ways. Our family's been here a few years by this time. Used to be some big, huge, rich person's estate. Now it's ours. Don't know exactly who it used to belong to, some Texas patriock. Dad bought it when we moved here. Famous battle fought out here somewhere, 1836. Can't remember which one. Right here in this field, maybe. Good place for us boys. Plenty to do. Games to play, horses to ride, places to explore. Bullet pacings, Indian echoheads. History. Very important, history. Gotta know it. Gotta remember it.

I'm nine. I'll be ten in two months.

Every Sunday afternoon, we play baseball. Mom and baseball, no apple pie. No sangamon sticks. She organizes the games. Organizes most things in our family. Dad's sort of the Big Boss but diggerates. Mom loves games. She's always arranging them. Everybody has to play. Everybody has to play to *win*. You don't play your hardest, you're not her son. Well, you are. But. Gotta play hard to win but be sort of unchalant about it. What Mom calls class. No pushing the other guy out of the way. No goating about winning. Just winning and being sort of pretend-modest about it.

Doesn't matter what we're playing, still have to act like that, or she yells at you. Ticklywinks. Parcheesy. Blackgammond. Football, baseball, basketball. Checkers, chess. The Weezer board.

Whoever spells out the future first is the big winner, has to be a *good* winner. No crying over spilled beings. Buck up, play harder next time.

I'm kind of scared of her. Also love her. Of course. She's my mom. Came out of her tummy. Owe her my *life*.

Poppy is her ninkom name for me. We're all dogs in my family. Dogs and dots. They make poppies out of opium over there in China. Opium's a drug. Learned about it in school. Very bad. Very bad drug. Only cerebropates take it. Cerepobrates. Cerealplates. It's illegal in the Republic of Texas. If they catch you doing it, they kill you. Cut your balls off and kill you. Or something. But mostly only if you're poor, I guess. Rich people don't get their balls cut off. They just get killed straight off. Or usually not. It's usually better to be rich than poor. Those Americans, they coddle their poor. We don't coddle our poor down here in Texas.

Not real happy about the baseball game today. Stuck out in right field. Right field! Position for losers. Where the worst player always plays. I'm *good*. Mom says a really good player knows how to play every position. Won't let me pitch or play first base or shortstop every time. Gotta play the field. Gotta get experience. Experience very important. No whining about it. First sign of a sour look on my face, and her whole body freezers up. Then, something freezers up inside me, too.

So I'm standing out in right field, feeling a little bored, trying not to look bored. I look bored or indifferent, and she yells at me. "Pay attention, Poppy! No slouching around in right field! Somebody steps up to the plate, you crouch down, get ready to run for the ball! I don't care if it *never* comes to you; you get ready to run on every play!"

And so on.

And then a miracle happens. Big brother Pres steps up to bat and connects with the first pitch, and it comes out to me. He's right-handled, but he stepped into it and pulled it hard to right. Guess he wanted to give me some action out here.

It's high and long. I start running back the instant it leaves his bat, looking up at it over my shoulder, as my mom's taught me. But it's way over my head. Can't get to it. It drops maybe thirty feet beyond me. Feel myself flash all over. Going to cash a tongue-latching for this one. I run harder, but the ball's got legs. Just keeps rolling and rolling. Am I running downhill?

I'm chasing the ball so hard I almost run into him. The tall, thin man with gray eyes. I've seen him around now and then, talking to Dad. No idea what he's doing out here in our field, tossing our baseball up a few inches with his right hand and catching it again.

Pull up short. Rub the back of my hand across my forehead: "Excuse me, sir, may I have our ball back?" Pres must be rounding third by now. Homer for sure.

"Sure, George." He tosses it to me. "Throw it back in and walk with me."

"I—I can't, sir. I have to get back to the game."

"Never mind about the game. The others will understand."

Hesitate a little. Get in for big trouble if I go for a walk with this guy in the middle of the game. Who's going to play right field? I mean, sure, they could just close right field, but. You know. Mom never one to let us cup cornels.

But I throw the ball in, and when Pres yells at me to come back to the game, I can hear Mom slushing him, sort of fiercely, like she was *ashamed* of him for yelling that. Suddenly realize this is a Big Guy. Even my mom's afraid of him.

Well, maybe not *afraid*. Hard to imagine her afraid of anybody. But respects him. Does what he wants. He wants to pull me out of the game, she lets it happen. Even the game comes second to this guy.

The tall, thin man introduces himself to me as Uncle Dogsbody. Says he's a business 'sociate of my father's. His eyes as gray as ashes. He's not the kind of uncle whose lap you want to climb up on his lap to for a hug.

We start walking, slowly. The grass is kind of high out

here, and I have to lift my feet up over it. Uncle Dogsbody seems to glize through it. I mean, glime. Grime. Like, sloat. Slat. Slit. Like a sloader. Without bobbling up and down like me. Just going sort of straight across, like a line.

It sounds like a bus station. The grass, I mean. Or something moving in the grass. Like a far-off conservation. Concertation. Like a concert or something. Like people talking, down low. Almost wistering. Rustering. I've never heard the noise before. I keep looking around to see where it's coming from, but everything looks pretty normal.

Uncle Dogsbody starts asking me about my ancestors. He has false teeth, I think. They clack a little. When he talks, his mouth sort of reminds me of insect mangibles. Magnibles. I saw pictures in my biology book at school.

"What's your father's name, son?"

"Prescott Bush."

"Full name."

"Prescott Sheldon Bush."

"Good boy. And his father's name?"

"Samuel Bush."

"Do you know his middle name?"

"No, sir."

"Prescott."

"Oh. Same as my father's first name."

"Right. And do you know where your father's middle name comes from?"

"No, sir."

"Your paternal grandmother's maiden name."

"Paternal —"

"Your dad's dad, Samuel Prescott Bush, married Flora Sheldon. They named your dad Prescott Sheldon Bush."

"Oh."

"This is important stuff, George. Names."

"Yes, sir."

"Your grandad's parents were James Smith Bush and Harriet

Eleanor Fay. And it's the Fay line I'm interested in. It goes back in a direct line of descent to King Edward I of England, in the thirteenth century."

"Wow."

"And it doesn't stop there. King Edward's father was Henry III. King Henry's father was John, who signed the Magna Carta. King John's father was Henry II. That Henry's father was Geoffrey of Plantagenet, the founder of the Plantagenet line."

We walk on in silence. Getting a little discant for me. Sounds imprehensive, but what does it have to do with *me*?

"I could step you through all the generations, but never mind. Your direct bloodline proceeds back through the sixth-century emperor Clovis to Constantine, the Roman emperor who converted the empire to Christianity in the early fourth century. His ancestors, and yours, include Marcus Aurelius, the Herod who had Jesus Christ executed, Cleopatra and Marc Antony, Alexander the Great, and Philip of Macedonia. Other branches of the bloodline include the Merovingian kings and their ancestors down through Charlemagne to Louis I, II, VI, VII, VIII, IX, XIII, XIV, XV, and XVI, and that last Louis's wife, Marie Antoinette, also of the same line; the de Medici family in Italy; King Ferdinand of Aragon and Queen Isabella of Castile, who drove the Jews and Arabs out of Spain; George Washington, Thomas Jefferson, John Adams, John Quincy Adams, and every other President of the United States, right up to Franklin Delano Roosevelt; the Windsor royal family that now rules England—Mary Stuart, King James I, King George I, II, III, Queen Victoria, King Edward VII, King George V and VI—and Kaiser Wilhelm of Germany, our recent 'enemy' in the Great War."

"I was named for my mom's dad."

"That's right, son. George Herbert Walker, who was named for the seventeenth-century English metaphysical poet George Herbert."

"Oh," I say. I didn't know there was a poet.

He lets me think about this for a while. We walk and walk. His hands are clasped under his chin. He looks a bit like a praying mantis dressed in a woolen charcoal pin-strike suit.

"The bloodline goes back to the pharaohs of ancient Egypt," he says, "including the thirteenth-century-BC pharaoh Rameses II, the greatest pharaoh of them all. His name can be found on almost every ancient shrine. The gold mines of Nubia made him rich beyond the human imagination. Beyond Rameses, the bloodline runs back to the extraterrestrial-human hybrids who ruled Sumer, Babylon, Greece, and Troy, and beyond them to the Atlanteans who still today rule the world."

"Extraterrestrials, sir?"

"Of course. Didn't you know that the ruling families in every white country in the world are connected by blood to extraterrestrials?"

"No, sir." I feel a little ashamed, not knowing a thing like that. Especially since the whole point of this bloodline theme seems to be that I'm one, too. Descended from extraterrestrials.

Destined to rule, I'm starting to think.

I feel my arms and stomach, wondering whether the guts inside me are different from that of ordinary humans.

"Uncle Dogsbody, sir?"

"Yes, son?"

"Are you really my uncle?"

"No. I'm not actually related to you."

"But I thought—"

"That I was a member of the ruling bloodline too?"

"Well. Yes."

"That I was descended from extraterrestrial-human hybrids?"

"Um. I guess." It sounds horrible, the way he puts it now.

"I'm not a hybrid, son."

"You're not?"

"No."

"Then ... you're a pure-bred human?"

He laughs quietly, mirthlessly. "Whatever gave you that idea?"

"Can I ask you a question, sir?"

"You can ask me anything you like."

"Why are you telling me all this?"

"It's a great responsibility, being born into this ruling bloodline. It places certain demands on its members."

"What sort of demands?"

"Remember I told you that every President of the United States had belonged to it?"

"Yes, sir."

"Well, the fact is that in every U.S. presidential election ever held, the candidate with the most royal genes has won."

"Oh."

"And now, with some help from me and some other friends of ours, your father has set up a new country. The Republic of Texas. You're a citizen of a brand-new country, boy. And you have a significant role to play in its future."

"I do?"

"Yes, you do. Your father is going to be President. So are you. So is your son."

"Really?"

"Really."

"When?"

"Never mind when. It'll happen when the time is ripe. Not for many years yet."

"Oh."

"In the meantime, you need to be preparing yourself."

"Preparing myself, sir?"

"Yes. Getting ready. Studying hard."

"You mean, like at school?"

"At school, too, yes. But I meant generally. In everything you do. These games that your family plays, for example. They are not for 'fun.' "

"They're not?"

"No." He smiles a little. "*Are* they fun for you?"

"Sure. I guess."

"Good boy. What makes them fun?"

"Winning."

"Right. Good answer. Being better than the others."

"Yes, sir."

"When I say they aren't *for* fun, I don't mean they can't *be* fun. I just mean that their main purpose is to prepare you to rule, not to give you frivolous pleasures."

"Yes, sir." We walk along in silence for a while. Then something occurs to me. "Uncle Dogsbody, sir?"

"Yes, son?"

"If I need to ask you something, like in the future some time, will you be somewhere I can find you?"

"Good question, George. And the answer is yes. I'll always be here."

"Always?"

"Always. I mean that literally."

"Even when I'm President?"

"Always means always, George. Even then. Even when your son is President."

"Okay."

"And now I must go, son."

"Go?" I look around, puzzled. Where is he going to go, from this place in the middle of nowhere? Does he have a car slashed somewhere on our property?

"Yes, go. Turn around, George. Start walking back. Don't watch. It's for your own good."

I do as he says. I start walking back. From behind me as I walk, I hear the flapping of giant wings and a low shrieking sound, like a fork being dragged across rusted iron.

Documents

Legends of Modern Texas
(Texas Roundup Magazine, October 23, 1936)

"Man-eating devil-water-cows live here," claims Porter "Chop" House of Weatherford, Texas. "I seen 'em. One of 'em chased my best bird dog into the swamp and dang near ate her."

"Hell, yes, there's a family of woolly mammoths out there in that swamp. Aliens put 'em there back in 1897 when they visited. I ain't seen 'em do it 'cause I was busy that day, but I *heard* 'em out there," says Polly "Tater" Wogg of Aurora.

"First, I figgered it was just some drunk high school boys, but now I understand that mindless zombies who have risen from the grave are actually responsible for all these half-eaten corpses," says Sheriff Bud "John" Wise of Garner, Texas. "Or it could be those eight-foot alien stick bugs. I dunno. It's hard to separate fact from fiction around here."

Devil-water-cows? Aliens? Mammoths? Zombies?

What's going on in rural Texas?

Some say it's just the ignorance of country folks who are steeped in folk superstitions. Others say they are well-educated Texans, graduates of Rice Institute and other prestigious schools, and they have seen things too.

"I'm a neurosurgeon for the Department of Public Hygiene. I'm a scientist. Naturally, I don't drink or take drugs, either," says Dr. Rance "Chaps" Burger of Austin, "and I've seen things around Weatherford and Garner that I simply can't explain. Weird things. Giant bugs wearing business suits. Guys that look like Abraham Lincoln riding glowing creatures that look like hippopotamuses, only dappled."

Texas Roundup asked Dr. Burger to elaborate on his experience in and around Weatherford and Garner. What follows is our exclusive interview, the last one he gave before his untimely death last week. (Dr. Burger fell to his death from the parking tower at Austin Public Sanitation General.)

TR: Dr. Burger, what have you seen out there in the lakes and swamps around Weatherford? Can you describe them?

RB: Well, I was fishing with my friend, Dr. Rollcot of Dallas, when all of a sudden, something hit real hard on a big trolling lure we had in the water, bouncing the bottoms. I played it toward the boat, figured it was a big catfish, but when I tried to bring it up to gaff, I saw it wasn't a fish at all.

TR: What was it?

RB: It was a huge hippo-type thing with long horns, glowing red, and on its back was a tall man who looked very much like Abraham Lincoln.

TR: This sounds very unlikely. How many Lone Stars had you and your friend consumed?

RB: None! I realize that this story is hard to believe, but you asked.

TR: Well, what did you do after that?

RB: Turned out the line was wrapped around Lincoln's neck, and the devil-cow-thing had the hook in its mouth. Neither of them looked very happy. I cut the line after the initial shock, and they sank back to the bottom of the water.

TR: Have you seen anything else?

RB: Yes. Giant bugs.

TR: Excuse me? Giant bugs? What do you mean?

RB: Have you ever seen a praying mantis?

TR: Sure. Spooky bugs. Especially close up.

RB: Well, imagine seeing one about almost seven feet tall, dressed in a topcoat and hat and carrying a briefcase.

TR: You saw that?

RB: Yes, I did. I was driving through the country near Garner when I saw this giant bug come down out of the sky and land in the middle of the road. At first, I thought it was a log falling off a tree, so I swerved, but then it moved, so I swerved again. That's when I realized it was a giant praying mantis-type thing dressed in men's clothes. I sort of freaked out, lost control of the truck, and went into the ditch. The impact must have knocked me senseless, because I came to with the little plastic Jesus that had been on the dashboard stuck in my mouth, and I was dazed. Then I remembered where I was and looked around. That damn bug was looking in the window at me! Its jaws were working, chomp chomp chew, and that felt hat on its head was just creepy. Its grabber claws were trying to get through the window; it was clearly planning on eating me. Well, I pulled Our Lord out of my mouth, cranked the truck, and drove straight on into the woods. Couldn't get back on the road, didn't care.

TR: And then?

RB: The damn thing started following me through the woods trail. It flew in front of the truck, in back, landed in the bed, and began trying to crack through the window again. It was making cracking and hissing noises. Reeaaal creepy. I was scared shitless.

TR: How did you get away?

RB: Well, let me tell you, it was getting dark, and I wouldn't have gotten away at all, except that just as I was running out of trail, nowhere to go but in the lake, with that damn bug cracking my windshield and clicking his mandibles, out from the top of a tree came the biggest bat I ever saw, and snatched up this mantis-type bug by his topcoat, and flew off.

TR: Giant bat.

RB: Yes. Just clean snatched up this mantis and flew off. The bat was marked with hieroglyphics, too, Egyptian stuff. Weird. Anyway, I guess he took that mantis off and ate it.

TR: Uh-huh.

RB: Well, you asked.

In a later interview with Sheriff Bud "John" Wise of Garner, *Texas Roundup* followed up on some of Dr. Burger's statements:

TR: Good morning, Sheriff. Nice of you to agree to this interview.

SW: My pleasure, Tex. I have great respect for the fifth estate.

TR: Recently, we interviewed a doctor from Austin who claimed he'd been attacked by a giant mantid dressed as a businessman and had only escaped with his life after the mantid was carried off by a giant bat marked with Egyptian hieroglyphics. He claimed that the mantid looked like a praying mantis and was trying to eat his flesh. He further claimed that he had caught a devil-water-cow with Abraham Lincoln riding on its back while fishing.

SW: Yeah, I know about all that. And the high school zombies, too. Not to mention them goldarn alien mammoths and John Wilkes Booth wannabes.

TR: So you believe him? These things really exist in and around Weatherford and Garner?

SW: Well, it's mighty hard to tell fact from fiction around here, you know.

TR: You've seen these things, then?

SW: Shoot. I had to send a whole passel of them high school zombies back to the grave after they started eating local Baptist families. Set 'em on fire with Sterno. Only way to kill 'em. Then they got me out to Aranasville on a call that John Wilkes Booth had just robbed a gas station while riding a woolly mammoth. I got there, and sure as hell, there he was, and he wasn't alone. There musta been a dozen mammoths there, all crowding around the combination gas station/feed store, all of 'em with a John Wilkes Booth on its back, shootin' off pistols and hollerin' stuff.

TR: Like what stuff?

SW: I don't know. Wasn't Texas talk. More like Spanish Indian er somethin'.

TR: What'd you do?

SW: Heck. I shot all them bastards.

TR: Did it work?

SW: Worked fine on the John Wilkes Booths, they fell right

off dead, but it didn't even slow down the mammoths. Every time I'd shoot 'em, they'd just bellow and run in circles. And I shot 'em a bunch of times. I finally figgered they was aliens. Can't kill aliens with bullets, y'know. They figgered all that out back in 1897. Naw, only way to kill 'em is with heavy-duty bug spray, and that stuff's against the law these days in Texas, pain of death.

The final interview was with Mrs. Polly "Tater" Wogg of Aurora. Mrs. Wogg is a semi-retired schoolteacher and gardener whose passionate hobby in recent years before the founding of the Republic of Texas was the development of stronger and stronger bug sprays. Her family has lived in the Aurora area for over 125 years; she claims to have been present at the "great UFO invasion" of 1897 and to have witnessed "herds of steamin' furry elephants comin' off them spaceships, along with tons of giant bugs." To this day, she will tell anyone who asks the full story of "woolly mammoths in the swamp."

We caught up with her at her small farm just outside of Aurora on the edge of the Big Boggy Death Swamp. Mrs. Wogg was 87 years old at the time of the interview. A tart and peppery woman, she claims to be fond of reading and watching Texas Educational Television.

TR: Thanks for agreeing to talk to us, Mrs. Wogg. I know you have trouble getting around, hearing, and seeing these days.

PW: I hear just as well nowadays as I ever did, you weteared pup! Mind your manners.

TR: Sorry, I just meant—

PW: Yes, that's mint. Now, don't step in it. Just sit down here, young man. What do you want to buy? Melons? Tell your fortune? Hope you ain't lookin' for no heavy-duty bug spray; they outlawed that stuff. I don't have no truck with contraband.

TR: Actually, Mrs. Wogg, I wanted to ask you about the woolly mammoths—

PW: Yes, love of worldly mammon can lead to no good, as you say, young man, but that wasn't why I started mixing my own bug spray. It was to kill the aliens.

TR: Aha. Aliens.

PW: No, not mammalians. *Aliens*, mostly insectile. They're hairy, all right, but I suspect that's because they've been breeding with renegade Negroes from the state farm. They live in the Big Boggy over there. That's where they breed. Them damn spaceships put 'em in there back in '97. 1897, that is. My grandma, God rest her soul, tried to stop 'em. Shot at 'em. Threw rocks. Sprayed 'em with a hellacious mixture of tobacco juice, moonshine, and lamp oil. Nothin' stopped 'em. Well, use to was folks around here'd know to buy my extra-heavy duty bug spray if they was going to the swamp. It was the only thing that worked. Now, hell, you're on your damn own with them aliens. Can't make it, can't sell it. No sir. There was that doctor from Austin; he come 'round after seeing a alien, wanted to buy a whole case from me. Poor guy, he was really shook up. Practically screaming like a girl about some giant bug wearing a suit. But I couldn't help him. I obey the law.

TR: Yes, that was Dr. Burger. From Austin Sanitary.

PW: Of course it's not sanitary! Bugs wearing suits? How could that be sanitary? And them woolly mammoths? Downright disgusting creatures! They smell like a nickel whore. And the way they slobber. Gives a body the creeps just thinking about it, the way they run around in the swamp with them renegades, up to God only knows what ...

TR: You certainly have a spicy vocabulary for an elderly Christian lady.

PW: Now see here, young man. I won't tolerate folks coming here from the city and spoutin' off foul language and sex talk around decent women! You can take your "crimson laddie" and just scram. Go on, now. Git. 'Fore I spray you with some of my Ultra-X.

Wise County Crime Report
(October 18, 1936)

Arrested, tried, sentenced, and executed for manufacturing and selling insecticide: Mrs. Polly Wogg of Aurora.

Aliens in Weatherford
(TBI Tape, January 1940)

Pres—check this out. TBI just passed it on to me. They're still trying to figure out who the voices are. They're just marked Voice 1 (V1) and Voice 2 (V2). You said you wanted a copy of everything pertaining to DH or AL. Ross

(V1) The aliens? They want to control our minds, a course, kid. That's what this whole new Texas Republic is all about. Ain't that just fucking plain as day? Aliens trying to take over the world, starting right here in Weatherford!

(V2) Take over the whole fuckin world?

(V1) I wouldn't lie to you, kid. Take that there Bugsbody Harriman, f'instance. He's a alien. Some kinda giant bug from outer space. Ten, fifteen thousand years old, that fucker. Use ta live in Atlantis; now he's here. And Abraham Lincoln, who lives out in the swamp? He's a alien too, a giant diving beetle or some such, who use ta live in that there Lemuria, under the sea in the South fuckin' Pacific. Course, now, I think Lincoln's on our side, basically.

(V2) Who's "our"? I mean, who's us?

(V1) Humans, kid. He's trying to help us. He's got a plan to stop ole Bugsbody from taking over. I ain't making this shit up, kid. This is *real*.

(V2) I dunno, mister. This is just too weird. This is like outta some kinda scientifiction novel, or somethin'.

(V1) Just you wait, kid. When them aliens come after us, and put us in pods, and cart us off to the fuckin stars, I'll be there goin', "See? See? I told you so, kid. I fuckin told you so."

(V2) Whatever, mister. Now, are you gonna crack open that bottle of moonshine, or are you savin' it for ole Abe Lincoln?

Welch-Hawkins Wedding Disrupted
(Midland Reporter-Telegram, January 30, 1944)

The wedding of Harold Welch, 31, and Jenna Hawkins, 22, both of Midland, at St. Mark's Cathedral was disrupted yesterday when the Rev. Dr. Michael Tooley, who was conducting the ceremony, exploded. Wedding guests later reported that, just before the explosion, Rev. Tooley's skin rippled violently like a burlap bag full of angry cats. Then, with a wet swish, his skin ruptured, and hundreds of live fish came bursting out of it, flapping madly through the air in all directions, some as far as fifty feet. What remained on the floor when the fish had flown resembled a shredded ectoplasmic Hallowe'en costume.

Two elderly wedding guests, Mrs. Gabriel Toke and Mrs. Arnold Smackery, both of Odessa, later insisted that the fish sang a Baptist hymn as they flew, but Mrs. Toke claimed the hymn was "Blest Be the Tie that Binds," while Mrs. Smackery was sure she heard "Bringing in the Sheaves."

Other guests said they thought the fish were mumbling the multiplication tables or the Gettysburg Address.

"I think they were bass," said Mr. Welch, a building contractor and an avid fisherman. "Though if you're wondering what sea bass were doing this far inland, well, you got me."

After some confusion, the Rev. Larval Brine Fly, a distant relation of the groom, kindly offered to finish the service, and in the end, the young couple was married. The newlyweds will be honeymooning in a cabin on Pecks Lake—and, the groom hopes, doing a lot of fishing.

2

War Hero

(Poppy, September 2, 1944)

Flying off the USS *San Jacinto*, *Huh*-cinto, not *Juh*-cinto. Some kind of Mexican name there. Not much of a psychoanalyzer, but I guess they know what they're doing over there in Houston, in the War Department, giving these light aircraft carriers Mexican names. I mean, Texas beat Mexico best two out of three, didn't we? Back in whenever. If Mexico had of won, we'd all be speaking Mexican and have dark greasy hair and swarthy skin and be rapers and murderists, and San Juan down there by Brownsville would be pronounced San *Hewin*, not San *Jewin*. So, but if we won and they lost, how come this carrier's got a Mexican name?

We Navy boys mostly call it the *San Jack*. Sounds lots more Texan.

Flying a TMB-3E Avenger torpedo bomber. We torpedo Jap ships from the air. Swoop in close, drop our payload, get out. Drop our torpedoes in the water, aim 'em at the ship. Try to avoid AA fire off the ship. The big ugly towers of flak climb up at us like fart bubbles in the bath, and I take evasive action, slight adjustments of the stick, whoop, whoop, whoop. Barbara II responds easily, glides through the sky with a minimum of fuss. Named her for Barbara, my Barbara, Barbara Pierce, back home. She'd be making a lot more fuss, probably. Fussy Barbara. Not really. Just like saying that. Feisty girl, but she'll be a good wife. Quiet, submissive, a good wife. Wide hips.

Nice rack. Like that word, *rack*. She'll give me a son or three. George Jr. Name 'em all George : George I, George II, George III. Like those British kings there. Ancestrals. A man's home is his castle.

Going in after a radio transmitter on Chichijima today. Four Avengers from the *San Jack*, escorted by Hellcats, and some planes from the *Enterprise*. They're Americans, over on that *Enterprise* there. I'm in the Barbara II — did I mention that? Lost the Barbara I back in June. Lost oil pressure and had to ditch. Leo and Jack and I. Leo's my gunner, Leo Nadeau; Jack's my radioman-tail gunner, John L. Delaney. Got our raft inflated and bobbed around on the sea for a couple of hours there before getting picked up by a destroyer. Leo's not flying with me today. Rear-seat gunner today's Ted White, Lieutenant Junior Grade William Gardner White. A good man, a Yalie and Bonesman like my dad, hopefully, like me too someday, if I make it back from this war. Though, of course, in the Texas Yale, not that other one up in Connecticut. His dad was my dad's classmate at Yale, at the other Yale, in his 1917 Bones Club. The Texas Yale didn't exist back then when my dad was coming up. Ted doesn't have the experience Leo does, but they said there'll be no Jap planes to shoot down today, so Ted'll do fine, I'm sure.

Jack and Ted ride along quiet as a couple of wives, too. Submissive as wives. Good solid men. Behind me one hundred percent. They do their job; I do mine. They know my style: quiet and competent. Get the job done. Get in, drop the bombs, get out. No excess chatter. No patter. Flak to starboard, flak to port, Poppy flies on, calm, calm, calm.

Poppy. It's been my family nickname forever. I've decided to make everybody call me that. Makes me sound old and wise and like a man of the people. No harm sounding like that. Like some kind of old country geezer. I'm too, what's the word for it, too something. Patricia? No, that's a girl's name. Aloof? Sounds like a haymaker in the gut. A-*loof*. Bloodless? Whatever.

Somebody named Poppy isn't bloodless or whatever else. He's crusty, cankersorous, curdungeonly. A character. Corn-cob pipe. Button nose. Two eyes made out of whatever. Sitting on the porch somewhere, some broken-down shack. Somewhere in West Texas. An old roughneck. Poppy. A tough, wised-up son of a bitch. Poppy won't take no shit offa ya. You don't fuck with Poppy. Sittin' there smokin', takin' long pulls from his jug. Moonshine. Moonshine. Like the sound of that. Tough guys drink moonshine. Rotgut. Rot your guts. You don't fuck with Poppy, no sir.

Up ahead of me, I can see Ski in the machine-gun turret of the next Avenger up in the VT-51 formation. Chester Mierzejewski, Doug Melvin's tailgunner. What a name. Sounds like he's a Jew, but with a -ski name like that he's probably a Polack. Polack Jew? Jewski. We just call him Ski.

Intelligence was right: no Jap planes. But the sky ahead of me is thick with angry black clouds of AA fire. That's anti-aircraft. AA. Sounds like we're all a bunch of drunks or something. Hi, I'm Poppy, and I'm a pilot.

Pushing Barbara II's nose down into a thirty-five-degree dive. Feels like we're headed straight down. Got the target map strapped to my knee. See the target area up ahead. Headed straight for it. No more invasive action. Gonna nail that sucker. Black splotches of gunfire all around me.

Then, and I swear this is what happens, swear on my mother's voice, *Abraham Lincoln* comes flying up at me out of the water. It's just like in the movies. I mean, fast like that. I mean, not that the movies are fast, but *fast*. Like in the movies. You know what I mean. When the movies go fast. He pops up out of the ocean on some kinda big, ugly longhorn steer or something and flies straight up at me like ack-ack fire. And it's like he was shot out of a cannon. Water coming off him and that steer like off, I don't know, a steer and an ex-President coming up out of the water really fast. I think I'm going to hit them. They're right there in my windscreen. All of a sudden.

Like a flock of birds, except fewer and sort of more condensed into a guy on a steer.

And then it's over. They go sort of up and over my plane. I don't think I hit them. I can feel the steer's hooves on my fuselage, rat-a-tat, like machine-gun bullets. And they're gone. Up and away and gone.

And then Barbara II coughs and splutters. I'm hit. Or else— maybe Abraham Lincolned? Fish-fried? I've heard the legends, same as anybody else. Never believed them till now.

Barbara II is still coughing, almost stalling. I'm still in my dive. She stalls now, I'll crash into the target. I release my four bombs and fight the stick. Pull up! Barbara II responds sluggishly, but finally, her nose comes up. I just clear the target by inches and head toward water, Barbara II ready to die on me any minute.

And now I notice the fish. Down by my feet. Four or five of them, flapping around. I kick at them a little, but where are they going to go? And *where did they come from?* This is how it starts, I know: the fish-fry.

And then the little buggers are trying to jump up in my lap. Flapping really hard against the floor part. One flops against my leg and falls down. The next one lands in my crotch, turns to face me.

"Don't do it," it sort of whines at me. Oho, now it's starting. "Don't clone the boy."

Talking fish in my cockpit?

Don't do what to what boy?

I slap the fish across the face, and it falls to the floor.

Now, a whole fish chorus starts up from down on the floorboards.

"Take 'er down, Poppy! You're hit bad! The cockpit's full of smoke! Ted and Jim are dead!"

Oh my god. Ted and Jim!

"Ted! Jim!" I scream into the radio. No answer. Oh my god, they are dead. "Ted! Jim! You all right?" There's two inches of steel between me and Jim. Can't turn around and look to see if he's all right. And Ted's in the tail turret. Maybe. If the flak didn't just punch it out, drop him out into the air. "Jim! Ted! Come in! You guys all right?" Still hoping. But it's hopeless. They're dead. My guys are dead.

"Told ya so!" the fish chorus continues. "Told ya they were dead!"

Can't think about that now, though. Shut up, fish. Got to get back over water. Got to get far enough away from the Japs to survive a bailout. They'll come after me if I'm too close. Barbara II's laboring bad. No smoke yet, but coming soon. Imagine the cockpit filled with it. Hack, hack. Damn smoke, can't see a damn thing. Imagine myself going down. Going through my head: "My daddy's a war hero, my daddy's a war hero." Get out over the water far enough, level off, turn the plane to starboard to take the slipstream off the door near Jim's station, sing out over the radio one more time, telling my guys to bail, and hit eject. Then I'm out, my chute opens, and I'm in the air, floating down, looking for the other chutes, but there's nothing. They're dead, I know it. Those fish weren't lying. My poor guys never had a chance. So much promise, so much potential. Watch the plane come down, thloop, into the sea. And then into the sea, wet as a fish myself, fiddling with my raft.

Then, whoosh, the raft inflates and I climb in. No easy task. I'm a big guy, and soaked to the skin. You try it if you think it's easy.

And now it starts again. The fish. All around the raft, they're bobbing to the surface and talking at me.

"They were alive, Poppy."

"We lied to you."

"You killed your guys, Poppy."

"When we said 'take her down,' we meant a water landing, Poppy."

"You fucked up, Poppy."

"That plane woulda stayed afloat for two minutes, Poppy. You coulda saved 'em."

I know that's not true, though. They're trying to mess with my head. That's all it is. That Abraham Lincoln with his nefertarious schemes. Finally I just plug my ears and start singing loudly: "Hail Britannia! Britannia rules the waves! We will never never never be enslaved." Over and over. I'm still singing it when the American sub surfaces near me and the fish scatter. The sailors load me into the belly of their fish and take me back to my carrier in red pajamas.

I'm a little worried about the report. What am I going to tell them? Do I say Abraham Lincoln got me? Fish-fried me? Did Ski see Lincoln from the plane in front of me? He must have. Did he put Lincoln in his report? He must've been back for hours now. If he doesn't say anything about Lincoln, how's it going to look that I bailed?

But it turns out I've nothing to worry about. Uncle Dogsbody's there to meet me on the flight deck. Puts his long arm around my shoulders and walks me to the bridge. On the way, we pass Chester Mierzejewski. He looks a little green around the gills. I mean, not really. He doesn't have gills, really. But he looks afraid. Not of me: of Uncle Dogsbody. I see his eyes. They flicker a little as we pass. Up at Uncle Dogsbody's face, then down, quick.

The very next week, my C.O. calls me in and congratulates me. I've won the DFC. The Extinguished Flying Cross. For valor in battle over Chichijima.

And then it hits me. No sudden revelation of what I want to do with the rest of my life, or anything. But a kind of an awakening. No question that underlying it all are my own religious beliefs. Gotta be some kind of destiny, and I was spared death and dishonor for something on Earth. To lead? To read?

Documents

Memoirs of the Director of the Department of Social Hygiene
(August 1946)

To the Future Generations,

I have written these memoirs as some small documentation of what I know to be the greatest achievement in modern medical and social history—the Republic of Texas Department of Social Hygiene. Since the early development of the modern eugenics movement, many have looked forward to the day when social and medical programs would be implemented that would strengthen the human race through genetic manipulation and social selection. I am proud to say that, in Texas, we have achieved that goal. We are a strong, productive, and efficient race of people. This is evident in our gross national product and standard of living. These achievements in business would not be possible without the work of this department.

Allow me to digress and introduce myself. The world knows me as Dr. Heinrich von Lugen, the architect of the finest public health programs in the world. However, the name I was given at birth is Dr. Josef Mengele, a name that unfairly continues to receive bad press. I hope that at the time chosen by Mr. Prescott Bush or his heirs or designees to reveal my true identity, this document, and the achievements of my department that it demonstrates, will restore the good name of Mengele to its rightful place in the world of science.

When, after the war, Mr. Dogsbody Harriman personally recruited me for this position, I had to accept it under an assumed name, naturally. It was never openly discussed who I was, although the very facts that recommended me to the position made it quite obvious, I'm sure. In addition, the Bushes had personal reasons to know me, as I will reveal. However, the work I oversaw at Auschwitz had subsequently come to light and garnered a certain amount of negative media attention, and it was felt, rightly perhaps, that an unwholesome fixation on the more gruesome aspects of that work might impair any progress I might be expected to make as Director of the Department of Social Hygiene in Texas. And, for the record, let me say that I never personally enjoyed those gruesome aspects. Certainly I never took any perverse "satisfaction" in them. Essential as my work at Auschwitz was for the future of the human race, it was ultimately dirty and dreary. However, the genetic improvement of our species requires certain sacrifices. It was my great love for humanity that steeled me to make those sacrifices, to take the actions necessary for the future evolution of our kind.

I had been at work in the field of eugenics long before Auschwitz. Few people realize the years of dedicated effort I contributed, not only in Germany, where our successful eugenics program was well established by 1940, but also behind the scenes in the Republic of Texas, where I had acted as an advisor to the then-directors of this department.

Mr. Prescott Bush and Mr. Harriman were quite familiar with my work, of course. They had been following with interest and with substantial financial incentives not only the business opportunities in Europe before and during the war but also the mechanics of our successful economic revival, as well—our use of labor pools, our identification of both talent and its opposite, and elimination of the latter. Naturally, I was happy to share these developments and, for many years, organized and attended eugenics fairs in Houston and at Yale University of Texas, as well as advising the department.

When I arrived on the scene last summer, after the debacle in Europe, the Republic of Texas Department of Hygiene (as it was then known) was, despite my earlier advisement, in a rather sorry state. It was inefficient, for one thing. It was also far too worried about public relations. Texan public health administrators went so far as to stage popular votes on issues of public health, for example. They attempted to hide selections and eugenics procedures behind a cloak of "clinics" and "hospitals." I suppose this was understandable, given their proximity to the United States and its somewhat hysterical emphasis on "human rights," and given as well the subversive efforts of Abraham Lincoln and his fishy friends to undermine Texans' efforts to put society on a rational footing. There was always the possibility of a counterrevolution.

In addition, there were certain religious aspects of Texas society that argued for a cloak of secrecy. Abortions, for example, were officially outlawed, and yet, as we all know, they are often necessary for various purposes, serving the greater good of society. Thus, a cloak must be thrown over certain aspects of our work, out of deference to the unscientific among us, those whose genes are fully human and yet still salvageable.

However, having said that, my arrival as director of the department rang in a new era of efficiency, and my firm hand instilled a certain ruthless and goal-oriented drive that was badly needed. When I took over operations, there were still well over 250,000 genetically unfit and unsterilized citizens in Texas, draining valuable resources from those equipped to handle life in a country that is truly run like a business. Today, only one year later, the only unsterilized and reproducing genetically unfit persons in Texas are a handful of renegades. The purification of virtually the entire population of Texas in a single year was a Herculean effort that would not have been possible without political support at the very highest levels. Prescott Bush's support has been unwavering. He is truly a man of steel. His directive to me was: "Public relations is my job. Your job is to engineer the most efficient work force this world has ever seen. The business of the Republic of Texas is business, and we can't afford a bunch of sickly slackers draining from the bottom line. You make it happen."

And I did. Many of the slackers and unfit had fled across the borders early on, unable to adjust to life in an orderly, ruthlessly fair, and efficient society, and were now the problem of the United States and of Mexico, two fish-fed nations that cannot stand the test of time anyway. The leaders of this country had invited many of the more superior types to settle in Texas, and many had responded. Thus, a certain balance was already being achieved. There were those whose allegiance to—as they called it—the "real Texas" caused them to foolishly remain behind and defend "the honor of real Texans." These were the ones, along with an unacceptably large group of citizens too soft-hearted for the common good, who were the ongoing problem. I am glad to say they have been dealt with. Although a small group of uncontrolled and breeding renegades still operates within our borders, they pose no threat to the general well-being and will eventually be dealt with.

We have had a cloning program in place right from the start. I had raised the possibility back in Hitler's Germany, but we had only just begun to explore various technological solutions to the many problems cloning poses when the war turned against us and we had to curtail our research activities. Before we knew it, the Soviet troops were closing in on our KZ installations all across Eastern Europe, and operations were dismantled. When I arrived in Texas, then, this was one of my primary areas of interest, and Mr. Harriman encouraged me in it greatly. We had a certain amount of success with lower mammals and then stepped up to lower humans, largely taken from the Mexican, Negro, and Indian prison populations. Human cloning presents a whole new magnitude of difficulty, of course, and we had many monstrous births, infants born with three eyes, three arms, three testicles, three nipples, three hearts, etc. Several sets of Siamese triplets. Mr. Harriman himself donated some cells to our research, but those infants were even stranger, many with wings and protruding mandibles, and all of them emerging from the womb absolutely covered in Texas scarab beetles.

We did finally work out all the bugs, however, and after a dozen or so successes with lower humans, Mr. Harriman suggested we try cloning a member of the royal bloodline. Then-Vice President Bush, in particular, was eager to offer himself as a guinea pig, but Mr. Harriman suggested that we convince the Vice President's young, newly married second son, George Bush, to participate instead. He and his wife were less than enthusiastic, but they did, in the end, acquiesce, and last month, on July 6, Barbara Bush gave birth to their first son, George Walker Bush. To all outward appearances, he was normal; unfortunately, there were subtler problems with his genetic structure, which manifested as an almost complete physical, emotional, and motor dysfunction. Fortunately, I had been working on some devices similar to those used by Dr. Delgado in the bull experiments. These devices are the now-common neural implants used to control unpleasant thoughts and emotions in some citizens. Back then, they were new and novel. I implanted one in the Bush infant to allow intelligent handlers to put thoughts in his mind, since it was clear that he had been so damaged by the genetic impairment that he could not operate on his own without outside input. Fortunately, his genetic strength allowed him to survive the operations. Had he been a simple human, he certainly would not have survived. There were unavoidable undesirable effects, of course. He will never be able to smile; he will only ever smirk. He will be prone to fits of anger caused by the stimulus of the implant. He will often seem slow or stupid, and his speech and spontaneity will almost certainly be affected, as he will have to wait for the "suggestions" to enter his brain through the implant before he can articulate them. In adolescence, he can be expected to begin partaking excessively of alcohol and amphetamines, the result of some unintended stimulation of his "binge" complex near the hypothalamus. He will only be able to achieve sexual arousal when outside agents stimulate his libidinal centers through the implant. His emotions, aside from anger and feigned sincerity, will always be flat unless externally stimulated.

These are minor problems, however, and in time, I think we will see that he can function effectively as President. And our implant technology will continue to improve. By the time he is ready to ascend to the high office, it may very well be that we have overcome some of these deficits and his social operations will be much smoother.

Monster

(Poppy, October 5, 1946)

"Mom, what," Bar says, "where are you going? What's this all of a sudden? You're packing, without a word?"

My mother-in-law. Pauline Robinson Pierce. Bar's mom. She's been here with us since the baby was born, three months ago now, back in July. Bar just walked into her room and found her packing, looking grim. She keeps on packing. Ignores her daughter's questions.

"Mom!" Bar says.

Finally, she stops. "What?"

"Aren't you going to talk to us, tell us what's wrong?"

"Nothing's wrong. I'm leaving, that's all."

"Nothing's wrong, but you're leaving? Mom, that isn't rational."

"*Rational*?" she says. "We're in *Texas*, and you're talking about *rational*?"

"Moms," I say, "you don't like Texas?" I call her Moms. She likes it. She's an American. From America. Up there in New England. I didn't marry a Texan girl. Dad found her for me. And boy, did he ever find a winner.

"Not like Texas?" Moms says, a kind of hard, angry look in her eye. "What's not to like about Texas? It's hot as hell, and it stinks of oil. The streets are unpaved, which is a blessing in disguise because they soak up the moisture when the locals spit in them. Fancy dress is cowboy boots and your best jeans.

A night out on the town means a burger and a malted down at the Circle K Drive-In."

"It's not New Haven, Connecticut, is it, Moms?" I admit this sort of ruefully. When Dad arranged for the opening of a Republic of Texas campus of Yale University, he didn't have much choice in the matter. There was only the one New Haven, Texas, and it wasn't much. It'll grow, though; Dad and I are sure of that much. It'll feed off the world-class university we're building. Hiring like mad, Dad says. Smart men coming back from the war need a job; hire 'em to teach history or math or biology at Texas Yale. Get a top-notch football program going; that always brings in the best teachers and students. Look at Notre Dame! It was nothing before Knute Rockne created a winning football team, Dad says. Once we get the music department up and running, we'll have simuphonic music in town. A theater department will do Shakespeare and Milton and all those other great Christian classics. We'll get the streets paved. Streetlights put in. Bring in new businesses, maybe the aerospace industry. Dad says that's likely to be big in the next few years. Dad's a whiz at this sort of stuff. He knows all about it. He knows all the big divestors. He knows how to put a package together. A package, like the sound of *that*. What kind of package, ha ha. Don't know what it means, exactly, but sure do like the sound of it.

Moms is going on and on to Bar. All about Texas. How much she hates it here. Been keeping all this in for months, I guess.

"But, Moms," I finally break in. "What about *us*? Your family? Your daughter, your grandson? *They* need you!"

"Need me? Sure, they need me. Bar needs me to tell her what to do, that's obvious. How to clean behind the fridge. How to dust the Venetian blinds. How to heat the baby's bottle."

"Sure, see? That's how important you are around here! How's Bar going to manage if you up and leave on us?"

Bar's giving me some look, but I pay her no mind. This is

for her mom's sake. Moms just plows on as if I hadn't opened my mouth.

"How to darn your socks. How to cook your toast. Where to put your John Thomas on your wedding night."

"Mom!" Bar is bright red. So that's how she finally found out: she called her mother.

"Well, you needed to know. How's a sweet, innocent girl like you going to learn these things if she can't ask her mom?"

Okay, okay. We did need a little advice on the sex part, at first. We had no idea how to do it, how to set it up, where to put things. Imagine! It was almost months before we figured out where things went, and then what to do once they were there. Fortunately, around then, my dad asked me to parciprocate in that science experiment old Dr. von Lugen was running. Made our Little Georgie Porgie. Right out of cells Dr. von Lugen excrapted from my body. Croned me, he said. Crowned me, like one of those kings of England. Something like that. Stuck a needle in me and pulled out some cells and did something to them, and poofto changeo, Little George. Well, they put him up inside Bar's parts there first. Let him grow up in there for the regular three months or whatever it is. He's a cute little devil. Little George. Sometimes, we call him Georgie Porgie.

Still, it was good to get that whole sex thing going, too, even so. Just in case, you know. In case the croning didn't work or whatever. Didn't take. But I had no idea Bar had gone to her mom for help! I just figured she'd asked a girlfriend or something.

Not that she knew anybody here in New Haven back then. I got back from the war on Christmas Eve, 1944. Bar quit Smith at the end of the fall semester of her sophomore year, and she and I were married January 6, 1945, in the Rye, New York, Presbyterian Church. At the precise moment we were tying the knot, I figured out later, the U.S. Third Fleet was bombing the holy bejesus out of Luzon, getting ready to invade that sucker. Boom! Wish I coulda been there. Not really, but sorta. After the ceremony, we had a lovely reception for three hundred of our families' closest friends at the Appawamis Country Club. Black liveried servants. I think their dark skin looks so striking against their white uniforms, don't you? Like an expensive chocolate. Might as well wrap those boys in gold tinfoil. We hopped on a train that night for The Cloisters on Sea Island, Georgia, four days of swimming, tennis, and golf ... and then the spring and summer months in the Pacific, where we kicked some serious slant butt until they surrendered. Demobbed straight back to Texas so I could start up at Yale. Bar flew down to meet me. She'd been staying with her mom and dad while I finished out the war. She cried and cried. When she got to Texas, I mean. Girls always do when they have to leave their mommas and go live with their husbands. Bar didn't like Texas any more than her mother did, back then. Said a lot of the same things Moms is saying now, how hot and smelly and dirty and uncouth everything is. Well, it's Texas, okay? What did you expect? Belmont?

And, well, naturally, she and I didn't know each other very well back then, either. Had a lot of learning to do. Sure. Likes and dislikes. Interests and disinterests. Yankees or Dodgers. Texas or New York City. Sunny side up or sunny side down. Toothpaste tube in the middle or at the end. You know, all that. I mean, I'd met her a few times and all, but you can't get to know each other very well over dinner at your parents' place or hers. Your parents tend to do most of the talking. "Bar's related to President Franklin Pierce, son." Bar Pierce, duh, of course she's going to be related to Franklin Pierce.

"We're related to all the American Presidents," I said, trying to reach my tongue around to dislodge a squiggle of roast beef that had gotten caught between my teeth. "Uncle Dogsbody told me so."

"Ahem." Dad gave me one of his looks. What? Wasn't it true? "That was, in fact, precisely my point. That you and Bar are distant relations. *Very* distant, I might add." Meaning we aren't kissing cousins or anything. Not insectuous. "But you both have the same royal blood coursing through your veins."

"It's not blue, though."

"No, son, it's not blue." Big insincere smile to my future in-laws. Dad always did know how to charm folks.

So, but no, you don't get to know your bride-to-be very well in that kind of slocumprinces. We had to ask each other stuff after we were married. And I could never come up with many questions to ask. Bar asked me a million things for every one I could think up. I can't remember a single thing she asked, though, now. Isn't that funny? Important stuff, though. It was all of the upmost importance; that was obvious.

Moms is still listing all the things she had to teach Bar to do. It's a long list. We're going to hire a live-in maid, of course, just as soon as we get a bigger place. Until then, though, it's been pretty nice having Moms here. She's kept Bar busy, too, so I could study. Well, not study so much as go to school. I never was much of a studier, I guess. Even at Andover, I preferred to be out with the boys than cracking the books, burning the midnight oil at the library. All that. Here at Yale I pledged Deke. That's DKE, Delta Kappa Epsilon. Don't go to their functions much, but I like to *belong*. That's me, a belonger. Not a beshorter, ha ha. I keep my grades up, though. I have to have a C average to graduate, and I always manage to get at least that. The tutoring sessions Dad's arranged with my professors really help. The night before a test, I just go have a chat with the professor, and we talk about the stuff that's going to be on the test, sort of go over the questions and answers in a comprehensive sort of way. I take notes, or else, if my hand is feeling sort of tired, the professor gives me a sheet of paper to study off of, you know, sometimes the actual test with the right answers marked on it. It's not cheating, though, because my dad's on the board. He's a trustee. You get special attention when your dad's a trustee, or you're a star quarterback or something. Dad's trying to get me into Phi Beta Kappa, too.

Also, Dad says I won't have to be here the whole four years. Two and a half years ought to be enough. They've got some sort of special accelerated program for GIs, or sons of trustees, or something.

"But Moms," I say now, "aren't you forgetting one big thing?"

"What's that," she says sort of flatly, turning an exasperated face toward me. I recognize the face. I see it a lot, in fact.

"Little George."

"Ah, yes," Moms says. "Little George." Sucks in air sigfinically. Raises her eyebrows.

"What, Mom?" Bar says.

"Nothing."

"Mom," Bar says a little more insiciently, "what is it?"

"Nothing you need to be concerned about."

"If it has anything to do with Little George," Bar says, "of course I need to be concerned about it!"

"Well, all right," Moms says, "maybe you do need to be concerned about it, but you don't need to hear it from me."

"Hear *what*, for God's sake?"

"Don't you go raising your voice to me, young lady, taking the Lord's name in vain."

"Mom, what *is* it?"

"What is what?"

"What is it that I don't need to hear from you? It's something about Little George, isn't it?"

"Never you mind," Moms says. "And please, the both of you, I've got packing to do."

"Mom," Bar says, taking her mother's wrist sort of forciply, to stop her from packing, "you're not packing or doing anything else, either, till you tell me."

Moms turns her glare down slowly from her daughter's eyes to the hand on her wrist. Looks at it in bemazement for a while. Then back up. Bar sort of quails before that look, like a quail, and lets go. Moms jiggles a pair of slacks in the air until the creases lie just right, then carefully folds it. We stand there watching in silence.

"Well, if you must know," she says finally, "I think the boy is a monster."

"A monster! Mom, what on Earth are you saying?"

"Maybe a monster is too strong. But there's *something* wrong with that child."

"Wrong? Whatever could be wrong?"

"Well, he's stupid, for one thing."

"Mom! This is my *son* you're talking about!"

"Not just yours," Moms says, cutting her eyes nastily over at me.

"No, George's too. But what do you mean, stupid? A stupid monster! Mom, you're scaring me!"

"Well, that baby boy scares me."

"Scares you! How could a tiny infant scare you? *Especially* you."

"What do you mean by that, young lady? Especially me."

"Well, Mom, admit it. You aren't scared of anything."

"Maybe I'm not. But I'm scared of that child. He looks at me funny."

"He's just a child, an infant, a baby! He doesn't know *how* he looks at people! His eyes just move around the room."

"No, they don't."

"What?"

"His eyes don't move around the room. They fix on a person. They feed off a person. He locks those eyes onto you as if he wants to suck the marrow out of you. Turn away from him for one instant, and it looks like his whole being is going to collapse."

"What *is* this nonsense, Mom? You're making Little George sound like he's, I don't know, *possessed* or something!"

"Possessed? No, I don't think he's possessed. Unless it's by a demon of stupid."

"Stop calling him that! He's three months old. You can't

possibly tell how smart he's going to be yet."

"Oh no? You'd be surprised what you can tell at three months. Take him to a doctor and see. Not that there's a doctor inside the borders of this great Texan bastion of enlightenment that would know anything about intelligence. But have him tested by a specialist. I'll give you a hundred to one odds the boy's retarded."

"Retarded! Mom!"

"Maybe just slightly retarded, I don't know, I'm not the expert. But I do know he's got that look, that unfocused cringe, that pleading puppy-dog look of the retarded child. And I know for certain that I can't stand being in the room with him one more day, or I'll shoot myself. That's what you Texans do out here, isn't it? Shoot yourselves, or somebody else, whenever things don't go right? I'll just march out onto the street, stop the first cowboy I meet, which shouldn't take long, you can't swing a cat in this town without knocking over three of them, stop the first one I meet and ask him nicely if I can borrow his six-shooter, or whatever the damn things are called. Then just point that thing at my temple and blast away. I swear to God, Barbara Pierce *Bush*, I'll do it. I'll do it for sure if I have to look at that boy's face one more *hour*."

Bar blinks twice, just sort of stares at Moms for a while. Then she nods.

"Okay," she says. "Okay, Mom. If that's how you feel, go. Come on, George. Mom needs to pack."

"But Bar—" I start to say.

"Never you mind," she says. "Come w—"

There is a knock on the front door. Bar and I exchange glasses. Sort of look at each other a little. In the eyes. We don't wear glasses, mostly.

"I'll go," I say.

I go downstairs and open the front door. There stand two men in white coats. Like doctors. Both of them have beetles on them. Like, live ones. Shiny green ones, crawling around on their doctor coats. Just five or six on each doctor. But still.

"Hello?" I say. "Can I help you, gentlemen?"

"We're here for the boy," one of them says.

"The, uh," I say, "the boy?"

"Your son," the same one says. "We're taking him in for adjustments."

"You're—what now?" I say. I can't quite take this out. In. Fathom it in.

"Taking him in for adjustments," the other guy says. "Don't worry, we'll have him back in a week or two."

"You'll have him *back*?" I say. "Bar?" I call up to her. "Can you come down here, please?" She comes down. "Bar," I say, trying to be decent about it, trying to be evle-headed, because hey, these men are just doing their job, "these gentlemen want to take Little George away for a week or two. For 'adjustments.'"

"What sort of adjustments?" Bar says.

"Sorry, ma'am," the first guy says, "that's classified."

"But he's *my son*!" Bar almost shrinks. I reach out an arm to calm her. She shunks my hand off angrily. I look at her mildly. She looks at me madly. Okay, okay. I get it.

"Be that as it may, ma'am," the guy says, "we've got our orders."

"Orders from whom?" Bar says.

"From a Prescott Bush," the guy says. He fishes in his coat pocket and pulls out a letter. Hands it to Bar. Bar starts reading it. I lean over to read it with her. She snatches the paper away, won't let me look. Okay, I don't need to look.

"Your *father* authorized this?" Bar demands, glaring up at me.

"I swear," I say, "I knew nothing about it!"

Moms appears at the top of the stairs with the baby and starts walking down.

"Here you are, boys," she says, handing Little George over to the second man. "Take the little tyke. And adjust him good. He's no good to anybody like this."

"Yes, ma'am," the first one says. "That's the general idea."

Bar is speechless, but somehow paralyzed. I don't know what to do. I just stand there and watch them take our baby away. As they close the door, the beetles are already crawling all over Little Georgie Porgie.

Documents

Notes Of Dr. Holt, Attending
(November 4, 1946)

The birth of Laura Lane Welch was concluded at 10:15 p.m. No complications except for the problems attendant upon flooding. First birth I ever had to wear hip waders. Who ever heard of a sink pipe discharging salt water and hundreds of wiggling sardines? In an operating room? And I did manage to sew up those odd pulsating flaps on the sides of Mrs. Welch's vulva. I still say that those are the result of that trauma she had before.

Lincoln "Sightings" Reported
Arabaptist Preacher Blamed
(Houston Chronicle, February 29, 1948)

A Weatherford man claims Abraham Lincoln lives at the bottom of a nearby lake and has appeared to dozens of local fishermen.

A Dripping Springs man insists that Abraham Lincoln lives at the bottom of his well and only comes out when it rains.

A Corpus Christi resident claims Abraham Lincoln lives out in the Gulf and can be seen riding the waves on a stormy night atop his "devil-water-cow" Bessie.

None of these rumors has the slightest basis in fact, Republic of Texas scientists say. They are what folklorists call "folk legends," which breed and spread throughout a population precisely because they are so outlandish.

"They appeal to the imagination," Rice Institute folklore professor Bruce Sofa explained. "They are a form of primitive narrative art. Like Homer's epics, they are about what *could* be, not about what really is."

The chief source of these rumors would appear to be the notorious Arabaptist preacher Mohammed Jesus bin Lennon of San Antonio, who claims that his grandfather C. L. Lennon uncovered Lincoln's "death scam" back in the late 1880s.

According to bin Lennon's grandfather, Lincoln faked his death at Ford's Theater in order to escape his wife and moved to Weatherford, Texas, where he lived in obscurity under the name Billy Bob Hamilton, working in a feed store, for another quarter century, till 1881.

Many Weatherfordians of his day noted the striking resemblance between him and the late President—especially as Billy Bob Hamilton had a wicked penchant for wearing a black beard, a black suit, and a tall black stovepipe hat, and liked to tell people that he was indeed Abraham Lincoln, or else his little brother, or first cousin, or best friend.

Sometimes, he claimed to be Lincoln's widow, Mary Todd Lincoln.

The Rev. bin Lennon claims his grandfather wrote a book about his "discovery" called *Lincoln: The True Story*. After the manuscript had been rejected by a dozen publishers, Lennon, a failed Southern Baptist preacher, decided to publish it himself, and held a series of revival meetings to raise money for the book's publication.

At those meetings, he repeatedly told the story of Lincoln's perfidy and government collusion in its coverup, urging listeners never to trust the Federal government again.

Despite many setbacks, he did finally raise enough money to cover production costs, and the book was printed.

Unfortunately, shortly before its release, a mysterious fire burned down the publishing house and purportedly not only destroyed every existing copy of the book but killed its author as well.

However, the Rev. bin Lennon says he has the only remaining copy in his safe and is now in the process of updating it.

According to the Rev. bin Lennon, the supposed death of Billy Bob Hamilton in 1881 was also a fake, and Lincoln, in fact, lived on in Texas under a succession of assumed identities but was always instantly recognizable from his tall, lanky body, his jet-black beard, and his signature stove-pipe hat.

The Rev. bin Lennon claims that Lincoln's current incarnation is as a traveling brush salesman possibly named Larry Minturge or Bosphor Pustile, but that he is, in actual fact, "some kind of immortal diving beetle from outer space or Lemuria or someplace" who is only cleverly disguised as a human.

The Rev. bin Lennon is convinced that there are others like him on our Earth, and that they have been interfering in human history at least since ancient Egypt, but that, after the Struggle for State's Rights, the entity known as Abraham Lincoln lost all interest in playing god and settled down to quiet, small-town Texas life.

Although the book sounds like the work of a lunatic, it contains many facts, as well, and cannot be dismissed too lightly. For example, Lennon correctly notes that the War of Northern Aggression was the result of a conspiracy between Negroes and Jews with the object of diluting racial purity, as our own University of Texas historians have recently confirmed.

The story of these "insect-like creatures" from Atlantis or some other planet, however, is clearly a children's fairy tale that defies rational belief.

In the aftermath of the Rev. bin Lennon's remarkable "revelation" late last week, there have been dozens of "Abraham Lincoln" sightings throughout the Republic of Texas. Not one has been substantiated by reliable witnesses.

"Sure, I seen Abe Lincoln," said Marshall Fungall of Rough Butte to a Houston reporter Sunday. "Just last week. He was sittin' on a stump just outside a town here, wearin' that tall hat a his, soakin' wet. Four or five dusty fish flappin' onna ground near him. Ever so often, he'd reach in the pocket of his drippin' wet long black coat and pull out a minnow or somethin' and slide it right down his gullet, yessir."

Fungall, a known lush, claims that, after some observation, he just had to confront the man. "Well, I goes up an' says, 'You Abraham Lincoln?' an' he says 'Yes, sir,' and so I says, 'I thought you was dead,' and he says 'No, sir' an' blim-blam, gits up an' sloshes off in them wet shoes a his, tall as can be."

Fungall claims that as "Lincoln" ran off, he was reciting the Gettysburg Address loudly to himself. "Only it was diffr'nt. 'Stead of sayin' the ' four score and seven' stuff, he was sayin' 'Reeaall soon' our forefathers are a-gonna, and then other stuff."

Fungall claims to have been sober at the time.

Other Lincoln sightings have occurred in Dallas and Brownsville.

A Fisherman's Story
(TBI Files, June 14, 1950)

AGENCY INFORMATION
AGENCY TBI
RECORD NUMBER 23-0769901-114003
RECORDS SERIES HQ
AGENCY FILE NUMBER 3-047-92011
DOCUMENT INFORMATION
ORIGINATOR TBI
FROM SAC, NO
TO DIRECTOR, TBI
TITLE [No Title]
DATE 06/14/50
PAGES 4
DOCUMENT TYPE AUDIOTAPE/TRANSCRIPTION
SUBJECT TOM CONKLE

CLASSIFICATION CLASSIFIED
RESTRICTIONS TOP SECRET
CURRENT STATUS CLOSED
COMMENTS TOP-LEVEL SECURITY CLEARANCE REQUIRED

Notes: Tape was made in Sheriff's office, Hutchinson County, Fritch, Texas, June 14, 1950, pursuant to Operation Wet Cowboy. Sheriff Fennel has no knowledge office is bugged. Fritch citizen Tom Conkle is known by his neighbors and coworkers as a serious, honest person who occasionally, as he likes to say, "gets into the bug juice"—has too much to drink. Body of water in question: Crawford's Pond, near Lake Meredith. Topographical maps suggest pond is insufficiently deep for creatures described to live under its surface. Local TBI office recommends cautious sonar probe.

Voices: SWF = Hutchinson County Sheriff William "Bill" Fennel; TC = Tom Conkle

(TC) Sorry, Sheriff, I can't stop shakin'. Drove over here like a bat outta hell.

(SWF) So, Tom, let's go over this one more time. You say you were just sitting on the pier, using a cane pole and chicken livers to catch catfish?

(TC) That's right, Sheriff. Drinkin' a coupla Lone Stars, munchin' a bagga pretzels.

(SWF) How many Lone Stars, Tom? Sure you didn't choke on a pretzel and pass out, imagine all this? The story you're telling is perty damn weird.

(TC) I swear, Bill, I only had maybe two. You know I can hold my beer. And I ain't choked on no pretzel.

(SWF) Were you catchin' anything before it happened?

(TC) I caught, like, four catfish. Kept two big ones. Threw the other two back.

(SWF) And this was before the—

(TC) Yeah. Before.

(SWF) These fish looked OK? Nothing weird about them?

(TC) Nah, jes' regular catfish. Big ones, though. Biggest ones I ever pulled outta Crawford's pond. Prolly twenty pounds each.

(SWF) God-damn, son. Those *are* big fish. And you got 'em up with a cane pole?

(TC) Well, now, that *is* a lil weird, now I think about it. I din't hafta pull. They just sorta *floated* up, real gentle-like. When I lifted 'em outta the water, they didn't fight er nothin'. Just sorta grinned at me. Din't even flinch when I pulled out the hook. An' then, they jes' layed there, all calm, like they was waitin' for somp'in.

(SWF) Huh. And then right after you caught the second big one, the—

(TC) Yeah. Goddam devil water cow, glowin' red eyes an' purple horns. Wearin' weird underpants. Floats up to the top of the pond.

(SWF) This is where it gets hard to believe, Tom. Weird underpants, like boxer shorts for cows, with moons and stars and planets on 'em. You said it had a nigger mermaid on its back, wearing a top hat?

(TC) I swear, Bill, it did. An' the nigger woman was wearin' a black coat, too.

(SWF) And all these big tall folks was under the water in that there tiny pond?

(TC) I liked to not believe it, my own self, Sheriff!

(SWF) Uh huh. And then this nigger Amazon told you to give it the fish?

(TC) Well, she told me to give the fish to the devil-water-cow. All talkin' like she's underwater an' it was hard to hear.

(SWF) So you did?

(TC) Hell yeah, I did! This woman looks *mean*, Bill. Coat's all covered in strips of weeds and with a big old spear with three points on it in one hand, an' a fish tail. So I held out the catfish, an' that critter jes' lipped 'em all gentle-like, took 'em from me an' dropped 'em back in the pond. Then, outta the devil-water-cow's mouth comes these tennigles, all snaky-like, and they shoot up into my nose—

(SWF) Did it hurt?

(TC) It was so *fast*, there wadden time to hurt, and then I guess it started talkin' to me through these tennigles, cause I could see an' hear all this shit, like a movie in my head.

(SWF) Like what kind of movie?

(TC) All about how use ta was these devil-water-cows lived on the moon. There was lots of 'em. An' they was happy. An', let's see, some praying mantis-type critters came and started killin 'em, and killed most of 'em, except some that got away to Earth on flyin' saucers that was druv by big ol' hairy ele-phants and lived in some kinda island in the South Pacific, name a Manuria or somp'in like 'at, and the mantises chased 'em, an' then some of 'em hid in ponds an' lakes an' some in other places, an' one of 'em met Abraham Lincoln, who prom-ised to help 'em, but then he got sorta sidetracked freein' the niggers, and so it's only now that he's started tryin' to help 'em, and meanwhile, the mantises an' these Texas scarab bee-tles are after 'em and are turning teenagers into flesh-eating zombies, and—

(SWF) I think you better see a doctor, Tom. Y'know, a head doctor. There ain't nothin' I can do about shit like this. This ain't a matter for the law.

(TC) But Bill, you know I ain't the only one what's seen these critters. You know that doctor saw stuff, too, and that big ol' mantis that Old Man Eggers said ate his prize steer! And Hal Welch done tole me a hunnerd times his little girl Laura wakes up every night with live fish in her bed. You knowed me thirty year, Bill—I ain't never lied to you! And look at my nose! See how it's all tore up around the edges from them ten-nigles? An' that movie, it was really, like, real ...

(SWF) Tom. Come with me. Let's go to the hospital.

(TC) I don't want to, Bill.

(SWF) Come on, Tom. You really need to go.

(TC) I'm all right, Bill, I really am. Just shook up. I mean, that nigger mermaid musta been eight foot long, with big ol' hooters like torpedoes spray-painted black, and them tennigles—ugh.

(SWF) Then let's at least go have a beer, calm down, forget this ever happened.

(TC) My cooler's still at Crawford's pond. You take me to get it, and I'll show you.

(SWF) OK, Tom. OK. If it'll make you feel better. Jes' calm down, f'chrissake.

Farmers Convicted of Capital Crime
(Crime Report, June 30, 1952)

Seven farmers along the Texas Gulf Coast have been arrested, tried, and sentenced to death for spraying their fields with illegal insecticide. Republic of Texas police are investigating the smuggling ring that is bringing the contraband into the country.

The convicted farmers will be executed by giant Japanese hornets in the famed hornet cages that are now a standard feature in Texas prisons. The two-to-three-inch hornets, imported specially for this purpose from Japan, carry a toxin that produces paralysis, kidney failure, and, eventually, a slow and painful death. Several thousand hornets swarm in each cage.

Family Man

(Poppy, November 22, 1953)

Baby Robin is dead. Died of leukemia last month. She was three. Almost four. Pauline Robinson Bush. We named her after Bar's mom, who died in a car crash a couple months before Robin was born on Christmas 1949. She was going around saying Little George was an idiot. Bar's mom, I mean. Not the baby. Somehow, that numbs me. Robin dying, I mean, not Bar's mom. I get sort of, I don't know, dreamy. You know, like, dreamy. Not quite there. Bar'll talk at me for several minutes, and I'll look right through her. Just look right through her there. Not listening. Or I'll go in and watch Little George taking a bath. Just sit there on the toilet and look at my little boy's wet, naked body. Not saying anything. Not really thinking anything. Just watching the wet skin shimmer. The perfect shoulders. The sweet ribcage. The narrow haunches rising up out of the water as he drowns plastic fish. His little bald dingle and the shrunken package beneath it, like a ... like a, I don't know what. I could look at his backside forever, seems like. Those soft round globes, round as ... well, as globes. Pink and hairless. As long as I'm looking at his backside, I don't have to look at the vacant, vague aggressionnessless in his face.

Jeb was an infant when Robin died. Little George was seven. We didn't tell him Robin was dead for a long time. Little George, I mean. Jeb wouldn't have understood even if we did tell him. He was an infant. Well, not an infant, maybe. Eight, nine months, along in there. John Ellis Bush. Get it? J.E.B. Jeb. Named after my sister Nancy's husband, John Ellis. Naming's important. Uncle Dogsbody taught me that.

"She's sleeping, George," we'd say. "We don't want to disturb her."

"Huh? Okay."

He always did seem to care less about things than our other kids, even before. After Robin died and we finally broke it to him, it's like he's boxed himself up and mailed himself to, I don't know where. Somewhere. Plasters a big grin on his face, gets angry at anybody who gets in his way, and that's that. That's his personality.

But, you know, Bar keeps insisting he's fine.

"So he's simple, big deal; what's so great about complex? You wanted a tortured artist for a son? You wanted Van Gogh? You're no Rhodes scholar yourself, you know." Or Einstein. Sometimes, she says I'm no Einstein. As if she was! Were. There's only one Einstein, and we're not him.

Or: "So he's a little one-dimensional," she says. "So what? It's easier to love him that way."

Though to me, it doesn't look that easy for her to love him either. They fight most of the time. Yelling at each other like a couple of bantams. Banshoes. Bushies. The two of them in the same pose, leaning forward at each other, their arms hard down by their sides, fists cinched. Clinched. Squinched. Like, squeezed tight. As in anger. Otha takes some of the pressure off, spends time with Little George so Bar can go do something else, like volunteer on her committees or, back when Robin was dying, visit her in the hospital. But a lot of the time, it's Bar. Ignorance Bar.

Otha's our maid. Otha Taylor. She's lazy as the day is long. Always wanting to go home early. Well, that once anyway. I came home at five, and Otha was nowhere to be seen. Bar said she'd sent her home early. Said she wanted to read to our boy herself for a change, Otha should go home. A very, very bad predecent to set, of course. My dad taught me that. Never send the help home early; they'll start expecting it. Once a month? Once a week? A special go-home-early day? Why not make every day a special go-home-early day? Why not just stay home and collect your pay without working?

So I explained to my wife, calmly, about how servants are, what they're like, how they think, how they aren't like us, and she ended up in tears. Just like a woman! Everything's so damn emotional with them. Didn't go out for days, had to cancel some of her luncheon encagements, big whoop de doo. Claimed the swelling in her cheek was too pronounced under her left eye, she couldn't cover it up with makeup. Whatever. Stay home, coddle the servants.

So, you know, I started spending more and more time away from home. Golfing, some. My dad comes up, and we play eighteen holes. You know, just to get out of the house, enjoy the sun on the grass. Or I go down there and we do the same. Dad's an avid golfer, and I can usually keep up with him, sort of. Fiercely competitive, Dad. President of the Republic of Texas since January this year, 1953, and the old man wants to beat me as bad as ever. And does. Beat me, I mean. Grambling's illegal in Texas, of course, but we make friendly bets, which he always wins. A buck a stroke. He flew up the day Robin died. We were out on the course the next morning, bright and early. Wanted to beat the heat of the day.

Been traveling more on business, too. Few years ago, went into business with John Overbey, a successful landman here in Midland. Our job was to figure out where the oil was and then convince the rancher or dirt farmer whose land it was under that the land was worthless and should be leased to us for practically nothing, then broker the lease to the big oil companies. It was pretty exciting work. We spent a lot of time in the restaurant of the Scharbauer Hotel, in Midland, here. They've got all the walls hung with maps of the oil fields. Some days, an oil lease would change hands three, four times.

John was strictly small potatoes. No capital. But he knew the business, so I teamed up with him. We flew to New York to raise capital: *my* way of doing business. Met with Uncle Herbie, my mom's brother George Herbert Walker Jr. Took John up to Kennebunkport for the weekend. He couldn't get over it. Poor boy from Texas going for a bracing dip in the Atlantic off Walker's Point, climbing up out of the cold water into a towel and a martini held out by a servant. New experience for him, I guess. We raised $300,000. $50,000 from Jimmy Gammell from Scotland over there. Jimmy's dad was Uncle Dogsbody's buddy in Moscow in 1945, head of the British military mission there, back when Uncle Dogsbody was U.S. ambassador to the Soviet Union. Now he's ambassador to Great Britain. Uncle Dogsbody is. Jimmy's some kind of big investor now. Maybe his dad is, too, I don't know. Eugene Meyer gave us another $50,000. Owner of the *Washington Post*. Dad once thought of pairing me up with Mr. Meyer's daughter Kathy, but Mr. Meyer said no. Dad chipped in $50,000. A bunch of smaller fry to fish. We put Uncle Herbie on the board of Bush-Overbey Oil. Flew back to Midland, moved into an office on the ground floor of the Petroleum Building.

We did okay, I guess, John and I. But I kept dreaming of bigger things. I wasn't getting filthy rich. I wasn't even getting mordantly rich. I was no closer to fulfilling Uncle Dogsbody's promise that I'd be President of Texas some day than I was the day he made it, out there in our field. Dad got his part; he's President now; I'm still a nobody. I'm indivisible. With liberty. I'm the President's son. Big deal. Not even his first son. And justice.

So, just this year, we threw in with the Liedtke boys. Hugh and Bill and John and I. Back in February, right around the time Jeb was born and Robin got sick. We kept saying enough of these royalty leases and land sale tax dodges, the big money's in drilling. We've got to go after the oil ourselves. So we did. Went back to Uncle Herbie. He's Managing Director of

G. H. Walker & Co. He underwrote the stock and converbial dentures that we offered the public. Uncle Herbie bought a lot of the stock himself. Jimmy Gammell came on board again. The Singer sewing machine people, too, the Clark family estate. Uncle Herbie was very creative at raising money. He got money managers to raid their pension funds and endowments. He ended up putting together about a half million for us. The Higsdon boys put together another half million on their side, through their backers in Tulsa, Ray Kravis, and them. We called the new company Zapata Petroleum. Hugh saw it on a movie marquee. *Viva Zapata!*, starring some guy with the impromisable name of Marlon Brandoil. Oil, get it? Hugh liked it because you didn't know whether Zapata was a good guy or a bad guy. A patriot or a bandit. That was us. Somewhere halfway in between. Very romantic. Very exciting.

Hugh had an idea. He had a hunch. He knew of this place out in Coke County called Jameson Field. There were already six wells there, but pretty spread out. All of them doing well. Had been for years. We buy up the leases to the ground in between those wells and drill the bejesus out of it. Hugh was sure the wells were connected. One big underground pool of oil. Only problem: the land leases would eat up our whole nest egg. Eight thousand acres. That's a dooky of a lot of land. $850,000 for the land, the rest for the equipment and labor. No oil down there, we lose everything. We go tummy up. Uncle Herbie had the jiggers. The skiggers. The skitters. He didn't like it one bit. I mean, he didn't like it *at all*.

But we insisted. And we were right! I mean, Hugh was right. But I was right to go along with him. Bill and John, too. We bought those leases and punched those wells, and whoosh. Gushers. Seventy wells so far this year, and every one a gusher. We're pulling over a thousand barrels of oil out of the ground every damn *day*. If we can keep that up, that's a million-plus dollars in revenues a year. Zapata stock started off at seven cents a share. It's up to $17.43 as of today. Uncle

Herbie's happy now. Can't argue with success. You just can't argue with it.

So, as soon as the money's flowing in, the next thing I want to do, of course, is move out of those ugly little tinker-box houses on Easter Egg Row. Hey, we're flushed! So we go house-hunting. Bar wants us to play it sort of safe, pick out a nice mid-sized house in a better neighborhood, but me, I want to go for broke. I tell her this, and she laughs, barks really, says we *could* go broke, Poppy, and then what? But I'm the man, and I decide, so we settle on a three-thousand-square-foot brick home at 2307 Sentinel. It's got a pool and a cabana. The lot backs up on Cowden Park, so it feels much bigger. It feels like the park belongs to us. Sort of like our big place outside of Houston when I was growing up. George would play Little League ball in Cowden Park, and we'd walk to his games. Then have all the other boys' families over for a cookout after the games. Not that Little George is any good at baseball, not like his dad. He can't hit, or catch, or throw very well. But still. You know. Maybe he'll learn. He's young.

I'm not much of a pool swimmer, but I go in and splash around every now and again, after the pool boy runs his check for alien lifeforms. Can't be too careful. My youngest brother, Bucky, moves into town, though, and he and his friend Fay Vincent live with us for a while, and they swim in the pool every day. Fay's a guy, imagine giving a boy a name like that, but there's nothing between them. It's all on the up and up. They change out in the cabana, and sometimes they leave the door open, and I watch from the upstairs window, through the Venetial blind there, and there's *nothing* between them. Bucky never so much as lays a hand on those fine American haunches Fay's got, with that muscular little holler on the side. I get Bucky and Fay jobs in the oil field, and they come home covered in greenish-blackish slime and go straight into the pool. You can see the oil slick on the water after they've gotten out and the ripples have died down. Bar complains, but it does no good. If they shower first, both the shower stall and the pool end up with oil slicks. She wants me to hose them down before they go in the pool, but I tell her that oil paid for the pool and the shower (talk about filthy lucre! you wanted to be filthy rich! ha! ha!), the slick is just a little reminder of where the money came from. But she won't have it. For her, it's just disgusting.

Thing is, she didn't grow up in Texas. It shows.

One day, I'm in there, watching Bucky and Fay change into their swim trunks in the cabana through the blinds, when the phone rings. It's my dad.

"George," he says. "Don't use the pool."

"Huh?" I say.

"Don't use the pool. It could be dangerous."

"I hardly ever use it," I say.

"Don't let *anybody* use it," he says. "There have been some reports."

"Reports?"

Just then, Bucky and Fay dive into the pool, and the fucker *explodes*. High sky. It's like raining fish. Three of them flap up against the window I'm peeking through, like they're trying to get in, moving their little lips. "Don't do it." That's not what they say. I'm just rerembering.

"Dad," I say, "I gotta go. My pool just blew up."

"Damn," he says. "Too late. Any of the grandkids hurt?"

"Don't know yet," I say. "Bucky and Fay were in it."

"Oh shit," he says. "Well, I'll send a team around. And Poppy?" he adds.

"Yes, Dad?"

"Don't use the bathtubs, either."

"Okay, Dad."

Don't use the bathtubs? How are we going to watch—uh, wash?

I go downstairs. Three panel trucks are just shrieking to a stop out front. I step out onto the front step to greet them.

"Man," I say, "you guys were *fast*."

"Please, Mr. Bush," one says, "I'll have to ask you to keep your family inside. We'll handle this. You could have live fish on the premises."

"Oh," I say, "right. Okay. You got it. Let me know what you find."

"Will do, sir."

So now Bucky's dead, too, it turns out. Blowed up. And that means just one thing: he and Fay will never change into their trucks out in the cabana. Ever again. The "team" Dad sent gets everything cleaned up in an hour or so. Stay away from water, they say. Don't swim in it, don't bathe in it, don't drink it. Drink beer or wine or fresh-squozen fruit juice. That's safe.

This is some kinda terraneist action by our enemies. Make no mistake, we will not rest until they're all dead and behind bars. Within days, thousands of fish and fish-lovers have been rounded up and thrown in cages and aquanariums in a special government facility in Port Aransas on the Coast. This is the first time I hear the name Skipjack LaTuna. He's one of the dangerous terraneists arrested and dumped in a big deep-sea aquaranium. But I guess he must get out or something pretty soon, because he keeps exciting finned inswimmections against us for years.

Probably some liberal lawyer gets him out. Or helps him excape. You can't put anything past a liberal. Even though we make 'em register with the government and carry cards. The ones that are still walking around free, I mean.

But then life gets back to normal. We learn to wash without water. The government comes up with some new technology that is better than water. Better living through chemistry. The pool extrusion is like a little wake-up call for me. A don't-be-so-dreamy call. No more giving Little George a bath, for one thing. So I sort of snap out of it a little.

Some days I take Little George out to the oil fields, when he's not in school. Good education for the boy. He'll be out here as a man some day, earning his way like his dad before him. He asks all manner of questions of the roughnecks that work for me. Boyish things:

"Why is your nose so allfire big and red?"

"What's that there big spot on your shirt?"

"How come you ain't got no hair on top of your head but lots of it comin' out your nose?"

Stuff like that. Not much about the oil business. He never does take much of an interest in that.

We eat with the men on their lunch break. Bar fixes us a sack lunch. We find a place to sit on the base of the derrick and eat with the guys. Little George always wolfs his down fast and goes off to play. Or has to pee and wants me to help him, so I do, and then he runs off to play. While he's over kicking a rock around, I go back and sit with the guys.

"So, Mr. Bush," one of them says. I forget his name. It's the strangest thing. I can remember names in a breeze when it's a business associate, or somebody in politics, or society. I remember their wives' and kids' names, too. But I can never remember my guys' names out here in the oil field. Not much of a psychoanalyzer, but I'm sure that means something. What, though, I just don't know. Guess I don't give it a lot of thought. It's just not that important to me.

"Call me Poppy," I say.

"So, Poppy," he starts again. "I think it's great, the way you help that little tyke. Must be tough on you and the missus, him bein' simple like that and all."

"Yeah, it's tough, sometimes," I admit. I think it helps build report between me and the men, for me to show a little weakness. Show them the boss is only human.

"I noticed you holdin' his little thingy there," he adds, "while he peed. Poor little fella can't find his own lizard when it needs drainin', huh?"

I sort of flash a little. Floss. Flosh. It's never occurred to me before, but I'm thinking now that maybe other dads don't hold their seven-year-old sons' weewees while they twinkle. I revolve to put a stop to *that* practice right away. It's a shame, though, because I do sort of like the feel of it. Sort of worm-like and rubbery. Sometimes, I imagine it swelling a little between my fingers. Kind of a nice image. Like a fish, almost. Like something from the bottom of the ocean. Swelling up from below, sort of a brimy smell to it. But obviously, I can't afford to let these guys think there's something wrong with me. Or anybody else. So that's it. That's the last time. From now on, Little George needs to pee, he's on his own.

"Yeah," I say and nod, a little sadly, "he does have some difficulty like that. I figure he'll learn one of these days."

"Bound to," the guy agrees. "Say, must be nice to have the kids' grandma around the house, though, huh? Take some of the pressure off the missus and you."

"Grandma?" No idea what he's talking about here.

"Sure. I saw them together in town the other day. Your ma and the boys. Little George there was pushing the baby in the stroller."

"My mother isn't in town," I say. "Must have been Otha, the maid." Otha's sixty-ish.

"No, no, I know Otha," the guy says. "Otha's my cousin, in fact."

"No shit! How about that."

"No, this looked like the kids' grandma. Figgered your ma must be in town."

Then, of course, I realize who it must have been. "Probably," I say carefully, "it was Bar." Keep my tone light. Don't want this big guy to think he's offended me or anything. "My *wife*."

"Your wife! No. This lady had gray hair. Almost white. Real nice-looking lady. But she couldn't have been your wife."

Bar's hair went gray while Robin was sick. So now, all of a sudden, she looks like my mother. I'm twenty-nine years old, and my wife looks like my mother. I pass it off casually. We move on to other subjects. But it sort of gets harder to swallow my lunch. It somehow seems to stick in my throat.

And now suddenly, strangely, disturbantly, my single-minded son George somehow comes to seem to me like my only consonation, coronation, my only hope, the only way I'm ever going to feel good again. I fight it. I tell myself not to be ridiculous. I tell myself grown men don't have thoughts like this. But over and over, I catch myself imagining Little George having to pee again.

Documents

Swimming Pools Closed Across the Nation
Department of Hygiene Officials Declare Bathtub Water
"Unsafe and Potentially Explosive"
Use of "Safe Snappies" Urged
(Houston Chronicle, November 25, 1953)

Following a rash of unexplained swimming pool and bath-tub explosions this week, TDH officials closed all public swimming pools across the Republic and urged those with private pools to exercise extreme caution in using them.

Added today to the danger list were bathtubs, since over a third of the explosions occurred in home or motel bathtubs.

"Better yet," said Dr. Teddy Heinrichslauten of the TDH, "we recommend staying out of the water completely, and this would include bathtubs. The department is urging consumers to purchase 'Safe Snappies,' that new brand of moistened towelette available in stores across the country, to use in their daily cleansing instead. It would be much safer and healthier, and better for the economy, too, at least until this crisis passes."

"Safe Snappies" are the brainchild of Houston entrepreneur Dolph Harkin, who developed the product while studying what to do with shark and dolphin hides discarded by the fishing industry. The light and pliable hides were found to make excellent moistened towelettes after being subjected to a special process in Harkin's Houston factory.

The process remains a closely guarded industry secret, but the product has been steadily growing in popularity, especially since a massive ad campaign featuring Dr. Heinrich von Lugen was launched last month.

The ads, by now familiar to all Texans, include the jingle sung by a group of mermaids surrounding Dr. von Lugen:

"Safe-safe-safe and snappy, too; they'll make your skin feel just like new!"

Certainly the recent spate of swimming pool and bathtub explosions will help sales of the product as jittery Texans begin to fear the water.

Over fifty Texans have died and another two hundred have been injured in incidents involving explosions in pools and tubs across the country since last Friday.

Yesterday, three Plano businessmen, all bath-and-shower accessory salesmen, were killed in separate incidents, along with one Mrs. Davery Dockton, a Plano housewife.

Osgood Crowell, owner of Crowell's Towels in Plano, was killed while demonstrating a bath mat for Mrs. Dockton, a regular customer.

"Well, Osgood and the missus went into the bathroom to see how it would fit," said Dockton's husband, Ed, between sobs. "It fit nice, but she wanted to make sure it was absorbent, too, so she put some water in the tub, stepped in it to get her feet wet, and stepped out onto the mat. Then, kaboom! Blew both of them to smithereens. If I hadn't been in the kitchen getting Osgood a glass of iced tea, I reckon I'd be dead, too. Damnedest thing. We never had a bit of trouble with that tub before, except for a few fish coming up through the drain hole."

Earlier in the day, the other two salesmen, whose names have not been released by the TBI, were killed while installing cabanas at the Plano Holiday Inn. Details are sketchy, but eyewitnesses report an explosion "big enough to send a few thousand gallons of water a hundred feet in the air."

"I saw the water shoot up, all mixed in with fire an' brimstone. Then it came down and rained all over the street with bits of concrete and wood and blood an' stuff. After that, there was a bunch of frogs all over the street, hopping around," one man reported.

TBI officials refuse to speculate on the source of these explosions, but deny that they have anything to do with recent experiments on South Padre Island involving the creation of "thick water" that resulted in violent explosions.

"It is true that, under the direction of the government," a TBI official said, "some experiments have been conducted regarding how to make 'thick water,' as described in the Books of the Maccabees. It was known to be an effective fire starter in ancient times, and the hope was to create a cheap and effective energy source that could be made out of water, since the oil and gas fields are drying up."

"However," he continued, "the project was abandoned after we discovered that the water was highly unstable in the presence of Gentiles or non-kosher fish. It tended to explode. The Republic of Texas has, as you all know, issued a strongly worded protest to the State of Israel for exporting dangerous product ideas. We think this is part of a larger Zionist conspiracy, frankly. Clearly, the Jews aim to control the world's water supply."

Pressed for more information, the unidentified agent would only say that he would "provide no further information other than to say that, obviously, the Republic of Texas does what is in the best interests of her citizens, and the thick water experiments are in no way linked with these explosions but only to Jews and maybe a few Vietnamese fishermen. Believe me when I say that Texas law enforcement agencies will not rest until the person or persons responsible for these explosions are brought to heel."

Meanwhile, TDH officials urge the public to remain calm. And, of course, to use Safe Snappies for washing up. "There's no need to be dirty," Dr. Heinrichslauten points out. "Cleanliness is, after all, next to godliness."

New Uses for Safe Snappies
(Texas Roundup Magazine, January 31, 1956)

Word of mouth has been driving up sales of Safe Snappies in the past few months.

"Me and the wife," says cotton farmer Clem Monger of Beeville, "started piling up the used Safe Snappies out in the yard maybe six months ago. It wasn't no brilliant plan or nothing; we just couldn't be bothered to put them Safe Snappies in the trash can and haul them to the dump. Then maybe three months ago, you know, just before the October harvest, we began noticing something. The locusts was swarming, but not over our crops. They was swarming around the pile of used Safe Snappies. We hit the panic button at first, a course. Locusts swarming on a Texas farm! Can't be good, right? 'Specially since they outlawed pesti—I mean, insecticides. But now it turns out, with Safe Snappies piled up in the yard, the locusts don't pay no attention to the cotton crop. They just love them used Safe Snappies."

"Safe Snappies are a wonder," agrees Cash Coltop, also of Beeville. "When ol' Clem started talking about the locusts on his farm swarming to the used Safe Snappies in his yard, the wife and me put our heads together and started coming up with new uses for them. We noticed that wiping ourselves down with Safe Snappies before we went out into the field kept the bugs off us. Didn't hurt 'em none; they just wasn't stinging or biting us. Mosquitoes would come around, dive-bomb our ears, like, but they wouldn't settle in to suck our blood. The hornets and the red-paper wasps would make passes around us too, but wouldn't sting. We think they like the fish smell but won't cut through it to our skin."

Safe Snappies developer and manufacturer Dolph Harkin has begun to market his product with such first-person accounts from Texas farmers. But the Republic of Texas Department of Insect Safety has also launched a research project aimed at making the active ingredient in Safe Snappies more widely available as insect-safe alternatives to the insecticides that were banned in the weeks of the founding of the new Republic.

Castro

(Poppy, November 22, 1960)

"Hey, don't worry," Ferrie says, those weird eyes of his twinkling like animal crackers, "the guys fuck up, we'll send Poppy in."

Big laughter. I laugh too, of course. Not really sure what we're laughing at, but entertrailing a tiny worm of fear that he really means it. I'm not even sure who "the guys" are, or what they might fuck up *at*. But I know I don't want to be trusted with anything major. What if *I* fuck up? Who would they send in *next*?

But I talk myself out of it. Tell myself that Ferrie's just joking. His sense of humor is as weird as his appliances. His arpenises. His looks. Whatever. He has some strange disease that doesn't let hair grow on his body, and he wears cheap red wigs cut out of real carpet and fake glue-on eyebrows to cover it up. Some coverup. Might as well wear tentacles and bug eyes. Sometimes I wonder if he wears fake pubic hair, too, so when the Cuban queens that are the only people he ever makes love to, they tell me, take his pants off, they won't die laughing at his baldness down there.

David Ferrie. He's my pilot. Well, my contact. Like that word, contact. I'm *in intelligence*. I'm *working undercover*. Bar and the boys know nothing about this. It's my own little secret life away from home. My handler, that's the word. My control. That's what Ferrie is. He picks me up, and we go. He Ferries me, get it? Like, carrots. Carries. Drives, or something. I wonder if it's his real name. Spies always have code names. He's always got a car. He drives, I ride in the passenger seat beside him. We drive to the Houston airport, and I rent a plane on the Zapata Offshore account. Usually a cargo plane, but sometimes it's a little Cessna or something. We fly somewhere else. Some landing strip or small-town air field. I go inside for a cup of coffee while they load the plane with something. I once tried to hang around and watch them load the plane, too, but Ferrie antlered me inside. I got the feeling he didn't want me watching. Frostable deliability, I guess. So they can lie about it. Like, cold. Frosty cold. The less I know, the better for me later. And the better for them. I can't give away state secrets. Another time, I stood up to stretch and wandered over to the window, looking out onto the tarmac. The guy behind the desk hellumphed. I got the message. Got it loud and clear. Stay away from the window. I stayed away from the window. I didn't want any trouble.

Then we get back in the plane and fly to another place. Sometimes, we pick up people. Cubans. Ferrie speaks Spanish fluently. I've got a few words but can't pick up what they're saying. It must be because they're Cubans. Ferrie tells me Cuban Spanish is the dirtiest Spanish in the world. And I'm not usually very good at understanding dirty talk.

Sometimes, our plane is met by another car and driver, and we go to a riverfront and get in a boat. A speedboat, usually. Boy, oh boy, do I love speedboats. I love to go fast, with the wind in my hair. My hair is kind of fine and wispy. It blows nicely in the wind. I sometimes feel a little sorry for people with hoarse hair. It can't be nearly as much fun for them to ride in a speedboat. Or, say, a conventible. And how does Ferrie's cheap wig stay on? He must have really strong glue. Or else, maybe he, I don't know what.

We go to New Orleans a lot. There's a place on Camp Street where Ferrie and some of his buddies have an office.

Ferrie's from New Orleans, I think he told me. New OR-lins. New OR-lins. Have a hard time with that. Always want to say New Or-*leens*. They've got all manner of listening appomadox in that office. Appalettuce. Allaradish. Listening devices. Guy Banister's usually there. But I meet him in the camps sometimes too.

The camps are where we usually go. Somewhere along the Gulf Coast. Usually in Florida somewhere, but all along the Coast, really. Into Texas and even Mexico. That's where we are now, in fact, at a camp in Florida. The camps are full of Cubans. Cuban refugees. They all hate Fidel Castro a lot. Fidel Castro took over Cuba on January 1 of last year. Like a new tax year. 1959, the year of Fidel Castro. Or Infidel Castro, as Ferrie likes to call him. Because Castro's a godless communist, and that's what infidelity means. These camps are like training pants or something. Training cramps. The Cubans who got away want to go back and take the country back away from him, make it safe for crampitalism again. I guess Ferrie and Banister and the rest of the white guys are just mainly helping them.

There are some scary-looking Italian guys here today, too. The one that looks like the boss of them is named Mr. Traffic. Mr. Traffic, something like that. Mr. Traffic Accident. But in Italian, of course. He has a bunch of bodyguards or assistants or slugs or something with black hair and bad skin and flat, ugly eyes. It's like something out of a gangster movie. Sometimes, there's an Italian guy in the Camp Street office in New Orleans, too, some guy named Johnny Roselli. He's got lots of bodyguards, too. New OR-lins.

I can't figure out who's in charge here. It seems to me like Mr. Traffic Accident might be. He's big and powerful and scary enough to be running things. But he's just sitting there quiet and letting the others talk. That's what I always do, too, but I'm not in charge. And I've never seen Mr. Traffic Accident here before. This is the first time. Ferrie talks all the time, and he's white, and seems to know a lot, but he doesn't seem to be the head cheese either. Head cheese, that's funny, considering what his head looks like. Then there are Cubans who seem to know a lot, too, which seems strange to me, given the low average interrogence of Hispanics. Can you really trust an operation of this size to people who speak Spanish?

Operation Zapata, they're calling it. I'm pretty pleased with that. Named after my company, Zapata Offshore. Of course Zapata is Spanish too. Mexican. It means boot. I don't know if I mentioned that already.

Felix Rodriguez, Luis Carriles, Chi Chi Quintero. The Martinez boys, Rolando and Eugenio. Those are some of the Cubans who seem to be briskling with power and knowledge around here. Also, Frank Sturgis, but that doesn't sound like a Cuban name to me. Once, I met a guy named Hunt, Howard Hunt. I figured he must be related to our ex-President H. L. Hunt, maybe President Hunt's son, but he said that was a different Hunt. I guess that must be true, because President Hunt was way fatter. Is way fatter. Was, when he was President, back in the '40s, and still is. I mean, fat, not President. My dad took over from him in 1952. He was the second President of Texas. My dad's the third. H. L. stands for Haroldson Lafayette. Howard Hunt's CIA. I guess if he was President Hunt's son, he'd be TIA. That would make the most sense. He talks about his bosses in the Miami office by their last names, Shackley and Clines. They call Shackley the blond ghost. I guess maybe he has blond hair. I've never met either one of them. Ghosts, maybe. Both of them. Boo.

I've never been to the Miami office. I guess they want to keep some distrence between me and the CIA in this. Bronzable deniability. Just good stagecraft. That's the word they use in intelligence work for doing your job right. Stagecraft. These guys do their job right, all right. They're good men. I feel fortunate to be working with them. Right alongside them, in the trenches. Fighting stenches. JM Wave. That's the Florida part of the operation. That's their name for it.

I guess you'll want to know how I got involved in all this. Uncle Dogsbody pulled me in, if you want to know the truth. Zapata Petroleum ran great for a year or two. You know, back in 1953 and 1954, when we created it and struck it big. But then we began to lose pressure in the Jameson Field. There was still plenty of oil there, but we'd pumped so much out of it so fast that we couldn't get it to the surface so easily any more. We started pumping water into the underground formulations there. We called that "enchanced recovery." Because that was our only chance, I guess.

And it worked. Sort of. But it was clear that that was a short-term renegade. Generade. Gennedy. Pasadena, whatever. Fix. We were going to have to divertify or head for the red. And we did divertify, and did head into the red. We started Zapata Offshore in 1954, and made a smart profit on that for a year or two, then it headed for the toilet, too. The red toilet. The bloody stool toilet. 1957, we lost $150,000 in Zapata Petroleum but made a tidy profit in Zapata Offshore. Profit sounds like prophet. As in Old Testament prophet. I wonder if that's significant. The next year, we lost big-time in both. About a tune of a million dollars, half a million in each. 1958. Did I tell you Zapata means boot in Spanish? Well, that boot got kicked in the ass. Or kicked us in the ass. But it didn't matter, in the end, because Uncle Dogsbody came to the rescue. In 1954, he told us the U.S. and Texan governments were about to oxen off the mineral rights to offshore areas. As in for drilling oil. Since we had friends in high places, he could guarantee us deferential treatment. As in him. He was our friend in high places. High place. Well, others, too. The whole network. The Bushes and the Walkers and all their friends. Uncle Dogsbody doesn't have any kind of official post in the Eisenhower administration there; those Americans have two different parties up there, Republicans and Democrats, and the people who really pull the strings have to honor that. The Bilderbergers. Sounds like fast food. A bilderburger with fries. A double McBild with cheese. 100,000 sold. Anyway, Eisenhower's a Republican, and Uncle Dogsbody's officially a Democrat, so he's out for now. Well, he's been an ambassador, a pretty important ambassador, Moscow and London, but still. He can't be Secretary of whatever, or director of the CIA or anything. That's Allen Dulles. Director of the CIA, I mean. Mr. Dulles is my dad's old legal counsel for Eastern Europe at Gowan Brothers Harriman. He was legal counsel for Gulf Oil, too. He's one of Uncle Dogsbody's main boys. His brother John Foster Dulles was Eisenhower's Secretary of State or something until he pissed Uncle Dogsbody off and had a heart attack or something. Probably from sheer fear. Not a hot idea to piss Uncle Dogsbody off.

So anyway, Uncle Dogsbody's outside the government for now. That doesn't stop him and his Bilderberger buddies from pulling strings, of course. I can't get over that name. Bilderberger. It sounds so funny! Bilge water. That's boat talk. Bilge, bilge. But so he promised to help us. We could get in on the ground floor. Or actually, the ocean floor, get it? Not much oil left under the Texas dirt; we'd need to go offshore. All along the Gulf Coast, not just the Texas Gulf Coast. Off Mexico, too, and the islands of the Caribbean.

"But Uncle Dogsbody," I protested, "that's a major shift in our operations. That's going to mean a whole new direction. Probably a whole new company. Massive influension of cash."

"I'm glad you mentioned that," he smiled. His smile was as clackery mandingulary as ever. We were talking in the Zapata offices in Houston. He'd arrived unannounced and knocked on my window. I opened it; he flew in, instantly beetles everywhere. Not my favorite part of his visits, I guess. "I think, in fact, I can help you out."

Turns out the intentigence commulities of our three great English-speaking nations, Texas, the United States, and Great Britain, were looking to exspend their operations too. Their culvert operations. That's the stuff that nobody's supposed to know about. Not even the legistatory bodies that were supposed to be the ones to inappropriate the operating budgets for integillence work. Oversight committees, and such. Meaning if there was an oversight, they would catch it. Only Uncle Dogsbody and his interrogence colleagues didn't want them to catch it. They wanted the oversight committees to go on sighting out over the uh, ulvert operations, overt ones, the official ones, like in CIA headquarters in Langley and TIA headquarters in Galveston, and sort of miss the other stuff, the real stuff that they weren't supposed to know about. Like overthrowing that fella in Guatemala there. Jacobo Arbenz. They'd just done that, that year Uncle Dogsbody came to me, 1954. They wanted to do more of that. Shape political realities in our part of the world a little more actively.

And to that end, they needed to divest in companies that would serve as "fronts" for culvert opertations. Storm drain stuff, I don't know. Wet work, they call it, because when it rains, it pours. That water really comes gushing through the culvert, and whoever's in it gets wet. They'd raise the money somehow, get some from the legistimators, izvest it in drugs, weapons, you know, high-risk high-profit items, turn it around, make a pile on the hind end, invent it again, and so on. And they'd sink that money into businesses that would front for them. So it would seem like everything was on the up and up. Then, it would be those companies carrying out the illegal activities. Well, not exactly illegal. Just stuff the actual intelligence agencies weren't supposed to be doing in the name of the Free World. World safe for crepitalism. The companies would launder drug money for them, for instance. That meant it was good if the companies lost money in their legitimant operations and needed more cash. The cash would come from big investitors, who would also not officially be on the payroll of the intelligence agencies. Money would flow. That was the main thing. I understood that. Money needs to flow.

"So," Dogsbody says, this is still back in 1954, now, "I

want you to form a new corporation. Call it Zapata Offshore. It'll officially offer its services to the Seven Sisters in drilling underwater wells. Buy up offshore royalty leases and broker them to other oil companies. Go public. You'll have no trouble selling shares; I'll see to that. Get Hugh and Bill involved in the actual oil side of things; I want you to stay out of all that."

"Okay, Uncle Dogsbody. What do you want me to do?"

"We'll have plenty of jobs for you, don't worry. In the meantime, you work on the financial and legal stuff with Herbie Walker. I've spoken with him about this. He's already onboard."

"Right."

So we did it. Got busy. Got everything set up and running. Bought a deep-sea drilling rig called the *Scorpion*. Cost us three and a half million. A pretty penny. A million and a half from the stock sale and another two million from bonds. The money came flowing in, just as Uncle Dogsbody promised. It was a thing of beauty, the Scorpion. Uncle Dogsbody told me to stay out of that end of things, but I couldn't help it, I had to go look for myself. They choppered me in. Love the sound of that: choppered me in. The first-ever three-legged self-elevating mobile drilling barge, built by some guy in Mississippi. The fucker was *big*. They lowered it into place with the legs refracted, then exstrended them to raise the platform above the waves. That's why they called it self-elevating. It was like an elevator. The British call it a lift. Because it *lifts* you up. They had some sort of electric motors on those legs, I guess. I don't know why they didn't get wet. The motors. They had to work under water. We got that baby up and running out in the Gulf off Galveston in 1956. Hit nothing, lost money. That was fine, though, because of my secret arrangement with Uncle Dogsbody that the others didn't know about. Uncle Dogsbody chose the name, too. The *Scorpion*. He said he liked the ring of it. The sting of it.

He chose the name of the next one, too, which we commissioned that same year, 1956. The *Vinegaroon*, another stinging insect, a native of West Texas, he said. More money from our investors. Magic, it was there. We stuck the *Vinegaroon* out in the water off Vermilion Parish, Louisiana, and he stuck his backside down there into the water and stung the doodoo out of those underwater oil fields. Blammo. A hit. Block 86. Combination gas and oil. Over a hundred barrels of distillant and three and a half million cubic feet of gas every damn day. We got half of the royalties off all that. Plus, we leased *Scorpion* to some kind of Gulf/Standard Oil conglomerate. Allen Dulles helped us set that deal up. Mr. Fulles never struck me as being particularly smart, but he's Uncle Dogsbody's boy, so he doesn't really need to be.

So, you know, for a while, we had money coming in. You'd've thought Hugh and Bill would've been happy about all that. They weren't. I don't know what their problem was. But they said they liked ground oil better than offshore. They just didn't cotton to it, they said. Strange way of putting it, because you know the old saying about cotton and oil. Plus, Hugh and Uncle Herbie just never could get along. Both strong personalities, very strong. That's why. I always get along with everybody; that's my way. More honey than vinegaroon. And flies. So we began to move toward a split. I would get Zapata Offshore; Hugh and Bill would get Zapata Oil. By 1958, we were losing money hand over shirt-tail in both, like I say. We'd expected lots of major oil companies to need our services. The Seven Sisters. They didn't. We would have folded without major investments channeled to us through my Uncle Herbie, who Hugh hated, and my Uncle Dogsbody, who he didn't really know about. Not that way.

So last year, we split. I needed $800,000 to buy out the Liedtkes' interest in Zapata Offshore. Again the money miraclically materinalized. Uncle Herbie said no problem, and it wasn't. Some industry observers were sort of surprised at that, at the time. We're losing money, the future seems bleak, we could go under, and we have no trouble at all rounding up close to a million bucks in new investments. How do you explain that? Well, all I've got to say is, what they don't know won't hurt 'em.

And that's when David Ferrie started showing up at my door. He said the magic word: "Mr. Harriman sent me." My double life began. My involvement in big historical event horizons.

So okay, back to the present, tonight, a hot night in early October, Walt Woodul set to become President of Texas next month, Eisenhower's Veep, Gordon Gray, set to become President of the U.S. Both men pledged to our cause. Official and unofficial funding in place. After a few hours of laughing and shirting the chute, a Cuban girl brings us some Cuban food for dinner, rice and beans, and we wolf it down. A lot of the guys play grab-ass with this girl, who's maybe 25. She just laughs, sits in one guy's lap for a second, then springs up. It's late when the food comes, maybe 9 or 10 p.m. When we're done eating, Ferrie pulls me aside and walks me to a dirty little cabin. It's got a bed in it and nothing else. It's the usual arrangement. It isn't luxurious, but that's the life of an intennisence asslet. You have to learn to rough it.

"You'll want to stay put," Ferrie says. "Don't go wandering around the camp. Some of these Cubans are fucking crazy. They see some strange white guy walking around, they'll shoot to kill."

"No problem," I say. "But one thing. Any chance you could get me a broom?"

"Broom? What, you want to do a little housecleaning in here?"

"Yeah," I say. "I want to sweep for bugs."

He laughs like I've made a joke. Short: Ha. Ha. "Don't worry," he says. "It's clean."

"You call this clean? This place is filthy. There's bugs everywhere."

"I tell you, it's clean," he says, with a kind of pained expression on his clown face. His fake eyebrows look horrible when he gets annoyed. "You can take my word for it. Nobody comes in here but our people."

"Well, it's clear that nobody comes in here to *sweep*," I say with some heat.

"Nobody *needs* to sweep, Poppy," he says. "It's *clean*. It's fucking clean as a whistle. Now, forget about bugs, okay? Just forget about them. Try to get some sleep."

"Get me a broom, and I'll be fine."

"You want a broom? Okay, I'll get you a broom. One broom, coming right up." And he stomps off, muttering. I think I hear him say something like "Fucking Dogsbody Harriman," which, it occurs to me, is not a good thing to be muttering.

He comes back in about fifteen minutes with a beat-up old broom. Practically throws it at me. I spend the next hour or so sweeping. The ceilings, especially. There are spider webs on top of spider webs. Stuff crawling on the walls. Under the bed. Once I satisfy myself that I've gotten all the bugs, I strip the bed, shake the sheets out the door, bang the bare mattress with the broom handle, and then put it all back together again. Okay, *now* I'm ready for bed.

About ten minutes after I blow out my candle, there comes a soft knock on my door. I get up to open it and find a young boy outside. Cuban boy, skin like dark honey. Maybe thirteen, fourteen, along in there. He looks frightened, like he's just woken up from a nightmare. He has a ratty blanket wrapped around him, like that's going to shelter him against a cruel world. Bare torso. Blue jeans. He gazes up at me pleadingly.

"*¿Que puedo dormir*," he says, "*en su cama e'ta noche?*"

Well, once again, I don't understand what he means. He must be Cuban. Maybe one of the freedom fighters here at the camp? Do they recruit them this young? Maybe the young son of some brave warrior? He looks so sweet and helpless my heart goes out to him. I want to clasp him in my arms and shield him against the hard, ugly people out there that would hurt him. But of course I don't. That wouldn't be right. People might talk.

Until, of course, he walks over to my bed and points to it. Mimes climbing in, with that same pleading look in his eyes. He—he wants to sleep in my bed tonight? Just for warmth and safety and a big, strong pair of arms?

So, of course, I agree. What am I going to do? Send this poor boy back out into the night? Into the valley of the darkness of the shadow of death? With just his ratty blanket and his tattered blue jeans between him and the source of all his fears?

So he slips off his pants in an innocent way, and we climb into bed together. We're pushed right up close to each other, the bed is so narrow. Where else are we going to go? I open my arms in an uncular sort of gesture, and he cuddles right up close. It's very nice. It reminds me of hugging my own big little boy at home. He's about this age, in fact. Thirteen, fourteen. But I can't sleep. I'm in a bit of a state, I guess. I'm sort of excited. My heart is pounding in my ears. I'm afraid he'll accidentally bump into me down between my legs and notice that my thoughts aren't purely, um, protectorate or unavunclish. And then it happens: his arm flops over and lands right on Little George! Who isn't all that little just now. He gives a little gasp. I think my goose is cooked for sure. But then he *grabs* onto it. Just grabs it hard. Squeezes it and looks up into my eyes. Then, turns over onto his tummy and spreads his sweet bare thighs a little. Motions for me to climb up on top of him.

I *cannot* believe what is happening here. I just cannot fathom it. It makes my head spin. This act is pressionable by death in Texas. Thirty-five years old, and I've only ever imagined it. I'm sure if I do what he and I both obviously want me to do here, I'll be corrupting this poor child and going to hell. But I can't get around the fact that he's *guiding* me to it. He *wants* it. It's somehow *important* to him that I do it. Somehow *comforting.*

So what would *you* do? I follow my instincts. I follow my desire. I possess the boy. We're not in Texas any more. He tells me his name is Rafael. I know I'll cherish that name forever.

When I wake in the morning, he's still sleeping. Softly, I crawl out of bed, letting my eyes linger on his supple, young, naked body in my bed. It's early, still sort of dark. I feel around for his jeans on the floor. When I find them, I go through his pockets. And am shocked to find a twenty-dollar bill in one of them.

Where would a poor Cuban boy get twenty dollars? Could he have stolen it from me? I check my own wallet. It's all there. Everything accounted for. 100% chickshake. And how could he have stolen it from me anyway? He didn't have a chance before we went to bed. During the night while I slept? Why would he only take twenty and leave the rest? And why would he hang around till morning? No, he must have *come* to my shack with the twenty-dollar bill in his pocket.

I know now. Suddenly, it comes to me. He's a spy. He's in the pay of Fidel Castro. He has infideltrated the camp to spy on the anti-Castro movement. He came to me hoping to find out when we attack. Luckily for our side, I told him nothing. Still, I have to find out what *he* knows, and who he might tell. What if he tells everyone what we did last night? What if he tells Bar? What if he tells my *dad*?

So in a fury of resolve, I grab the broom and press the handle down hard on his neck. He wakes up and stares up at me with terror. I'm not exactly strangling him, but the threat is there. It's right there under his nose. Under his chin. He talks or he dies.

Well, he's talking all right. But it's all in fast Cuban Spanish. I can't make heads or hairs out of it. I play it cool. I shift my weight a little and produce the twenty-dollar bill. Right before his frightened eyes.

"*¿Que?*" I say. It means "what." It's pretty easy to say. It sounds like "Kay." Sort of like the girl's name. Or, like "okay" when you're in a hurry and sort of leave off the "o." "*¿Que ... es ... esto?*" That means, "What is this?"

"*¡Lo me ha dado el Señor!*" he says. *Señor*, I get. It's "mister." He got the bill from mister somebody?

"¿Que Señor?" I'm starting to enjoy this. I'm interrogating a spy—*in Spanish!*

"¡El Señor Harriman! ¡El Señor Harriman!"

What? He pronounces it kind of funny, with no "h" and broad "ah" s and rolled "r"s, so it sounds like "ottoman," but it's clearly Harriman.

"¿Señor *Dogsbody* Harriman?" I ask incredulantly.

"¡Si, si, *Señor Dogsbody! Si! Señor Dogsbody me le envió!*"

Señor Dogsbody ... *sent* him? Is that what he's saying? Whatever it is, if he's got something to do with Uncle Dogsbody, he's okay in my book, and I let him up. Throw the broom away. He's still a little afraid of me, I guess, but instead of cringing or running away, he tries to placate me by reaching in my briefs. Turns on his tummy again. Sort of eagerly. Waves me on.

Well? Uncle Dogsbody sent him to me. A present. Uncle Dogsbody must ... uh, *know* about me. Knows that I have thoughts like this from time to time. And doesn't mind. Seems to be encouraging me to let go a little, have a little fun. Satisfy my desires. So do. I do. I satisfy the hell out of those desires.

About two minutes after we're all dressed again, there comes a discreant knock on my door. "Y'all ready in there?"

I open. It's Ferrie. He glances at Rafael, but his eyes don't show anything.

"We're all set," he says. "Let's roll."

We roll.

Documents

Padre Island Marine Institute Wiretap
(TBI files, June 19-20, 1961)

Source: TBI
Agent: Dirk Bransom
Date: June 19, 1961
Unedited selections of interest

Monday 0900 incoming:

PIMI, may I help you?

Yes, I'd like to speak with Blenny Scooter, please.

Mr. Scooter is in a meeting. Is there anyone else you can speak with, or shall I take a message?

Is Ms. Wrasse in?

Yes, one moment, please.

[click]

This is Faye Wrasse. May I help you?

This is Scopas Tang. I'm checking in. Blenny's in a meeting.

What've you got? Any news from the Gulf?

There are three boats out there now. All of them stuffed to the gunwales with dolphin hides.

Are you sure?

Yeah, I'm sure. We have an agent inside. You need to pass this on to the big tuna.

Any idea what they're planning?

Word is, they're gonna unload the hides and truck them to a factory near Waco to be turned into rucksacks and rain gear for the police and army.

No seals?

Word is the seals had been wised up to the operation and cleared out before the ships got to the island. Only a couple of sentinels left. A couple of interns clubbed and skinned them for practice.

Was the Professor there?

Of course. I hear he supervised.

He's back here now, at Baylor, trying to drum up support for splitting seal-clubbing off of whaling as a separate academic department.

Fucker. What about Laura?

Give her time. She's only fourteen.

Get the word to her. She needs to know.

Our agents are on it. Insecticide.

Good.

Well, I gotta go. Got a job up the Pedernales.

Watch for hooks and nets.

You too.

Monday 1034 outgoing

Jinny? Blenny Scooter here. I need to speak with Professor Ishmael.

Dr. Ishmael is unavailable at the moment, Blenny. He's in a meeting with the dean. Are you in Waco? Are you naked?

No, I'm still at PIMI, and never mind about spawning. Listen, you've gotta tell the professor that Tang is headed up there, I think.

Tang? He's in the Gulf, trying to find the hides.

He found them. Talked to Wrasse this morning, told her everything. Tried to feed her some line of shit about going up the Pedernales.

Will he try to hijack the trucks?

I wouldn't put anything past that slimy son of a bitch. He wants LaTuna to spread the story.

You think he works for LaTuna?

No. He still works for the Neptune Continuum. TIA's in

it, too. But TBI's still got our phones. I think you better tell the professor, when he hears that Wrasse has gone down, to watch his back.

The professor is personal friends with the Bushes—you know that they respect his theories about marine armageddon. He's safe.

Nobody's safe once the fish start talking. Even you, Jinny.

Tuesday 1200 incoming

PIMI, may I help you?

Faye Wrasse, please.

One moment.

[click]

This is Ms. Wrasse.

Bug spray.

What?

Dolphin channeling.

I'm sorry, I don't—

End of the world. Watch yourself.

[click]

Hello. Hello?

Tuesday 1215 outgoing

LaTuna? Is that you?

Wrasse? I can barely hear you.

They're after me ... [inaudible] to kill me.

Wrasse? What? Who?

I'm leaving you a message in the [inaudible] so if they get me, you can [inaudible].

[click]

Wrasse? Wrasse?

[click]

Two Feared Dead in "Anarchist Fracas" at Marine Institute
TBI Blames "Neptune Continuum"
Marine Institute Spokesperson Points Finger at TBI
(Brownsville Banner, June 23, 1961)

Assistant Program Director Faye Wrasse and Executive Director Blenny Scooter, both of the Padre Island Marine Institute, were missing and feared dead following a bizarre and destructive incident near the dolphin tanks here at this facility yesterday.

While details are still sketchy, what is known points to another attack by the anarchist group, the "Neptune Continuum."

"This seems to be the work of the NC, all right," said TBI field agent Mike Lasso. "It has all of their trademarks—talking fish, dolphins running amok, more end-of-the-world nonsense."

PIMI spokesperson Carroll Dottyback feels the TBI was responsible. "This Neptune Continuum thing is just too handy, if you ask me," he said. "The last ones I saw around here before the sh*t hit the fan were TBI agents. In fact, the damn place has been lousy with TBI all week, posing as tourists and getting in the way. It's ridiculous. I mean, I'm as big a patriot as anybody, but these guys are really beginning to get on my last nerve. Wrasse and Scooter are my friends, and if I find out that the TBI has anything to do with their disappearance, I'll … well, I'll be mighty disappointed."

What is known is that, around two o'clock on Tuesday, Wrasse and Scooter were called to two separate incidents on the PIMI campus. Wrasse was called to an incident where a tourist had been grabbed by a large dolphin and pulled into the tank.

"The friggin thing just snatched my dad," said an eyewitness to the event, Jimmy Gargen, son of Lance Gargen, the victim. "It snagged him by the shirt and pulled him right in the tank. Then it wrapped its flippers around his chest, and my dad started talking. Talking like a dolphin, you know, like the fish was making him talk. He was saying all kinds of weird stuff, like 'roach poison' and 'fishkill' and 'politics of destruction' and stuff."

Wrasse approached the tank and attempted to rescue Mr. Gargen, but the dolphin became very agitated and began squealing and hopping around.

"It just grabbed this woman, dropped my dad in the water, and dived down in the tank. These divers then came along and jumped in after her. They pulled my dad out, but now all he does is make squeaking noises and jerk his head around all weird."

The divers searched the large tank for several hours, but no trace of Wrasse has been found. It is feared that she is dead. The TBI has ordered all of the dolphins destroyed in order to see if she was somehow eaten by them, and the tank will be drained and dismantled to search for her remains.

The second incident, involving Mr. Scooter, was equally odd and deadly. He was called to the seashore exhibit, where a tourist had been observed talking to the horseshoe crabs in the children's area.

"My impression was that the tourist was becoming agitated by something the crab was saying," one eyewitness reported. "But you aren't supposed to talk to the fish anyway. I mean, there are signs all over telling you it's against the rules to talk to the fish. But this woman, I mean, she was chatting away at first. And then, instead of leaving like she should have, she starts, like, getting all upset and screaming like, 'That's a lie, you stinking lying crab!' and 'Shut up! Shut up! I don't care!' and things. Stupid woman."

Apparently, Mr. Scooter arrived just as the woman was grabbing a crab, holding it inches from her face and screaming, "You're a liar!" at it. Mr. Scooter convinced the woman to come with him, witnesses report, but she would not let go of the crab. They went into a nearby office along with a security guard. Some minutes later, the guard came out with the woman, but the crab and Mr. Scooter have not been seen since.

"We fear that the woman and the guard were agents of the Neptune Continuum and that they killed Mr. Scooter," said Agent Lasso of the TBI.

Carroll Dottyback disagrees. "All of these people were friggin TBI agents," he insists. "And it's high time for Mr. Nixon to take some action."

The Afterlife Diary of Robert E. Lee
(early sixties)

Dear Diary,

Saw Deios Arachios again today. He summoned me to His Clacking Glory again, something about my beard. (*Bugs don't have facial hair!* he screams, which is a lie, fucker's mostly hair Himself.) Anyway, after some of His polyarmed goons threatened me with the insecticide, I yielded, let them shave me, and during the shaving, He mentioned casually that they're naming that school in Midland after me. He says it's important that that faction on the school board that wants to name it Abraham Lincoln High get beat. Whatever. I got a hundred or more schools named after me. Lincoln's got more than that. He says that we gotta stay on top of things now since I went and lost that war. (*That* again.) Anyway, something about a girl with vaginal gills and egg sacs in that school and the Two Tommies, the general who'll run the Persian Gulf War for our side and the man in black who'll wipe the memories of people who see bugs from outer space, the school *matters*. The Bush clone goes there, too.

Me, I just wish that heaven had turned out like the chaplain said at Washington College that day they went to put me in the ground, and it rained so hard the whole countryside thereabouts was flooded, and bridges and canals and locks and so on were destroyed, and the fish came up out of the ground and mocked with rubbery lips and Bronx cheers the passing of the survivors of so many hard-fought battles, who had remained steadfast to the last, the scaly sons of bitches.

Booths

(Poppy, March 17, 1963)

Man, this place is dusty. Dust everywhere. Dust on the floors. Dust on the walls. Dust on the windows, even the busted ones. Dust on the bleachers. I don't know, it looks like nobody's been in here for years. Maybe since before Impedance. Impedendance. Maybe even longer. Why we couldn't meet someplace nicer, I don't know. I don't decide these things. I just go where I'm told. CEO Zapata Offshore, reporting for duty. Zapata impedanna. Zapata dinna danna.

I know some of these guys out here on the folding chairs. David Ferrie, of course, I know. E. Howard Hunt, I know. J. Edgar Hoover, of course, American FBI director, hi there, Edgar. Gyorgi DeMohrenschildt is the only one I've never met before, but I've heard about him. He's some kinda Polish or Russian count or something. Works for the KGB or the CIA or something, but he was a Nazi in the war. He's on our side, though, I think, now.

And, of course, I know Uncle Dogsbody, buzzing back and forth up by the ceiling like some kinda restless housefly. One end to the other and back again. Good thing this gymlasium has high ceilings. He's got room to fly.

Oh, maybe that's why Dad wanted us to meet here! Man, I'm so slow! Of course that's what it was. Musta been. High ceilings.

The guys I don't know are all sitting over on the bottom bleacher bench that's pulled out. They look somehow vermiliar. Maybe because they could be idectical quinpoot-lets. I mean, five of them, like twins. They look a lot alike. Like the same guy, practically. Clowns, maybe, like what that Dr. von Lugen did to me with Little George there. Though Little George and I don't look at all alike. Well, not that much. Not like this. Not like those five twins over there, in their costumes all the same.

Five of them over there, five of us over here. Well, not quite five of us. Five of us, not including me, so that makes four total. Or six. But there's one empty chair over here, so that makes a total of five.

Dad's late again. He's a busy man now that he isn't President any more. Now that this Lyndon Johnson cheated him out of the predecency. Abraham Lincoln's doing, Dad says. And Skipjack LaTuna and all those other fishy terrorists. Always conniving, those fishes. Always trying to umbernine us. Bunderwine. Dunglerdine. Whatever. Always the fish with their kissy lips and sinking ships. "Don't do it!" Democrats. Fishy democratic forces trying to sap our strength. Insecticide. End of the world. As we know it. Liberals, pfooey.

DeMohrenschildt is talking to Hoover. "No, it's true," he's saying, "look: no belly button!" He lifts up his shirt. Sure enough, no belly button. "Not of woman born!"

Hoover just looks at him and says nothing. He's got something in his left hand, a pair of women's pink panties, maybe. He raises them to his nose and takes a long, eyes-closed sniff.

Howard Hunt scoffles at DeMohrenschildt's belly.

"Hell," he says, "that operation can be done in a half hour by any Saigon doctor worth his mail-order diploma."

"But," DeMohrenschildt says, "can your Saigon doctor put human brain in gorilla's body? Obviously not, Mr. Hunt, if your speech any indication."

DeMohrenschildt talks funny. He's got some sort of accent. I guess he never really took to our Texan way of talking too good.

"Fuckin laugh a minute, ain'tcha, Gyorgi," Hunt says.

Then Ferrie cuts in, sort of rudely, but what can you expect from a guy like him: "What I want to know is, who the fuck are *those* guys?"

He trosses his head toward the twins over on the bleacher blench. I've been wondering the same thing myself. Who *are* those guys?

"Cubans," Hunt says.

"The fuck they are," Ferrie says. "They don't *look* like Cubans. Hey!" he calls out to the twins on the beachers, "say something in Cuban!"

"Ay ay ay ay!" one of them says.

"See?" Hunt says.

Then Dad walks in, carrying the Geronimo box. He used to keep that skull in the Skull and Bones Tomb at Texas Yale. But then he started carrying it around with him. I don't know why. He'll tell me one of these days.

"That don't mean nothin'," Ferrie says. "Anybody can say 'ay ay ay ay.' "

"Not with no Cuban accent, they can't," Hunt says.

"That ain't no Cuban accent," Ferrie says. "If that's a Cuban accent, this"—pointing to his head— "is my real hair."

Dad sits down in the empty chair and sets the box on the floor in front of him. He's always real careful where he sets that thing down. It's pretty important. I don't know why. He won't tell me. He keeps promising. And I know he'll keep his promise. He was our *President*, till this Johnson clown came along with his fishy tricks.

Clown? Did Dr. von Lugen make him, too? I wonder. He's probably too old for that, though. Dr. von Lugen didn't even come over here from Germany until Johnson was my age, and that's too old for clowning, really.

"If the rug fits," Hunt says snively.

Ferrie gets right in his face and is about to say something or do something. He's like a cannonball. Always ready to epscold.

"Howard, David," Dad says, "enough. Let's come to order, shall we?"

"Ferrie wants to know are those guys Cubans," Hunt says. He's looking at Dad, but his hand is doing something to Ferrie behind his back. "Tell him, Pres."

"Look, both of you," Dad says, "all of you—in this operation, it doesn't matter who anybody is or where they come from or what their name is. Okay? Or what their goddamn hair's made out of. Got that, Hunt?"

"Sure, boss," Hunt says.

"Got that, Ferrie?" dad says.

"Yeah, yeah," Ferrie says. "I just—"

"Enough!" Dad yells.

"Right," Ferrie says.

"Are you going to shut up?" Dad says.

"I'll shut up," Ferrie says.

"Good," Dad says. "Now. Let's get down to it, shall we? First order of business. Any luck finding Abraham Lincoln?"

All the guys out here in the chairs shake their heads. I shake mine, too.

"What are you doing shaking your fuckin head, Poppy," Ferrie says. "You ain't been lookin' for him."

I'm about to say something when Dad jumps in.

"I thought you were going to shut up, Ferrie," he says.

"Yeah, yeah," Ferrie says. "I'm shutting up. Go on."

"I mean it, now," Dad says, looking Ferrie right in the eye.

"Yeah, you mean it, I mean it, we all mean it," Ferrie says. "Go on. Really."

"You're not going to keep interrupting?" Dad says.

"Go on already!" Ferrie yells.

Dad stares at him for a little while longer, then turns over to the twins over on the breachers.

"You boys?"

"Ford," one of the twins says.

"Excuse me?" Dad says.

"Ford," another twin says.

"All right," Dad says.

"Ford," a third twin says.

"I get it already," Dad says.

"Ford," the first one says again.

Now, all of a sudden, Ferrie bursts out again.

"Them ain't no fuckin Cubans!" he yells. "Them's fuckin John Wilkes Booths! I knew there was something mighty fuckin fishy about them guys!"

John Wilkes Booths! No wonder they looked familiar! Well, I mean, not that I ever saw one before. But still. Ha!

"Ferrie," Hunt says, "shut your hole, or I'll stuff your fuckin rug in it."

"See what I have to put up with from this fuckin grand-ma-rapin freak?" Ferrie whines to Dad.

Hunt grabs Ferrie's rug off his head and tries to stuff it in his mouth. The rug comes off with a nasty *rrrrrip*! Ferrie is totally bald underneath. I've always wanted to see what he looks like under there. Now I know.

Hunt and Ferrie start fighting. They fall off their chairs. Ferrie's trying to gouge Hunt's eyes out. Hunt is slamming his fist into Ferrie's pudgy little belly from about three inches out. It looks like he's really hitting hard, too. He is one strong thud, Howie Hunt.

Dad just sits there like he always does, sort of long-suf-feragely.

Finally Edgar Hoover pulls two guns out of wherever he was keeping them and points one of them at Ferrie, the other at Hunt. The panties are still in his left hand.

"TBI, boys," he says. "Stop or I'll plug ya."

Hunt and Ferrie stop fighting, eyeing Hoover's guns.

"I hope to Christ that ain't your panty hand pointed at me, Edgar," Ferrie says.

Hunt and Ferrie climb back up and get in their seats.

"Shit for brains," Hunt mutters at Ferrie.

"Limp dick," Ferrie mutters at Hunt.

"Okay," Dad says finally, "are we through with junior high now? Can we get back to the unfortunate demise of President Johnson?"

"Uh," I say, puzzled, "unfornichate—you mean—he's dead already?" Because if he is, what are we *doing* here in this dusty place? I'm about to start sneezing.

"No, son," Dad says. "I'll explain it to you later."

"But I thought—" I start to say.

"Later, son," Dad says.

"Okay," I say. "I just thought I was supposed to make a phone call from Dallas, and—"

"You are," Dad says. "That's still on. You got your spiel memorized?"

"My what?" I say. "Oh, the thing I'm supposed to tell the TBI? Sure. James Parrakeet is going to kill the President."

"James *Parrott*!" Dad collects me stermly.

"That's what I said," I say, "James Parrott." But really, I think, what the hell difference does it make, because neither one of those guys *is* going to kill the President. We are. It's just a disfraction. A dismirection.

"Shmuck," Ferrie says.

"Hey!" Dad warns.

"Pres," Ferrie says, "I know he's your kid and all, but do you really think—"

"Yes, I do, David," Dad says, "and I'll thank you to stay out of my private family affairs."

"Look, Pres, I don't care who you fuck on your own time, but we could *all* get fucking fucked if your goddamn kid here forgets what to do."

"He won't forget," dad says. "Will you, George?"

" 'Will you, George?' " Ferrie says sort of sarcrastingly.

"Forget what, Dad?" I say.

"Never mind," dad says. "We'll go over this at home. DeMohrenschildt—"

"Yes, sir?"

"Oswald ready to go?"

"Absolutely," DeMohrenschildt says. "On orders from KGB."

"I thought you were a Nazi," Ferrie says.

"You Texans, with your narrow one-way loyalties."

"David," Dad says, "don't start again."

"I'm just *askin'*," Ferrie says. "Sheesh, have a fuckin conniption about it, why don'tcha?"

"If I have a fucking conniption, David," Dad says, "you'll know it. You'll be glued to the wall like one of Dogsbody's beetles with your little legs wriggling."

"God, you're a weird fuck, Pres," Ferrie says. "You mind if I—"

And without warning, Ferrie swoops up the Geronimo box, opens it, and pulls out the skull.

"I wouldn't," Dad says, "if—"

"Is this really Geronimo's skull?" Ferrie says.

In a flash, the five John Wilkes Booths surround Ferrie with guns to his head.

"Put the skull back in the box, David," Dad says evenly.

"Is it true you dug him up in the dead of the night at Fort Sill, Oklahoma?" Ferrie says.

"Back in the box, David," Dad says again in the same tone. "Now."

The five John Wilkes Booth clock their guns.

Ferrie looks around him at the guns and nods.

"Hey," he says. "Sure. No problem."

He slides the skull back in the box, puts the lid on, and hands it to Dad.

"Thank you," dad says.

Now, all of a sudden, Uncle Dogsbody swoops down and lands in front of Ferrie.

"David Ferrie?" he says.

"Yeah?" Ferrie says. "What's it to ya?"

"I love you," Uncle Dogsbody says, and kisses Ferrie full on the lips.

Ferrie wipes his mouth in disgust. "Hey!"

"Now shut up and play nice," Uncle Dogsbody says. "Or I will fucking kill you."

And he flies off again, back and forth, up and down the gym.

Ferrie gapes and gestures around for support. Everyone else avoids his eyes. You don't piss off Uncle Dogsbody, David. You just don't. That's the last thing you want to do, boy.

Documents

Hal Welch's Diary
(May-June 1963)

May 3, 1963

I guess I'll start keeping a "journal," as the doc calls it. He still says that the whole Lincoln thing ever since I was a kid is just a recurring bad dream, but he knows I know it's real. And Mr. High-n-mighty Joao M. Celestino *is too* the name of that damn old Portagee sea captain who keeps coming around claiming to be the one who made sure Edwin Stanton's little bug friends were hanged *after* they were shot with bug spray. He claims that I see Lincoln and Celestino because I feel guilty about masturbating. Well, for one thing, I never do. Did. I mean, coz I want to. And I definitely never think about that pretty mermaid-thing that came to the cabin that night, after me and Laura went fishing and saw, well ... and even if I did actually fertilize her egg sac, I didn't catch no coy mistress herpes virus from her. That doc at TDH says that's *impossible* and, anyway, wouldn't hurt my wife. Anyway. He says I can burn this whenever I want to and *nobody* will ever read it but me.

May 25, 1963

This journaling seems to be helping. I haven't had another attack of coy herpes or whatever since January. That one was bad, though. Those little gashes on my throat. Had to wear a scarf to work, good thing it was January. Guess I'll keep writing this stuff down. Maybe that fish girl will leave me alone in the bathtub, too. But she came back last week. Shot all those eggs out in the water and then made me, y'know, whack it, then sucked the eggs into her mouth. And who ever saw a fish with red eyes? And legs? Anyway, writing it down makes me feel better. Gotta burn this thing soon, though, before someone finds it and reads it.

But that goddam Portagee "Johnny Sky" Celestino says he'll "harpoon me" if I do. Hell with him. He's the one who made sure all those people got hanged back in 1865—he screws *me*, I'll screw *him*. I got proof in the shed. That sample of Secretary Stanton's DNA. The one Dr. Mullercider said was from a fucking *insect*. Thanks, fishgirl, even if you did make me sick.

June 8, 1963

Saturday. Took Laura fishing again as I said I would, even though the pastor told me that she was getting too old, and besides, she was a girl. I don't buy that. I mean, even if she is a girl, she has to know fishing like a boy, or how else is she gonna get a husband? And too old? What? He thinks I can't be trusted with my own *daughter*? He must be sick, talking about how she's a woman, just *look* at her, and all that, like he's been looking. I certainly haven't been looking. Anyway, it was a good trip. Except for me finding out she's seeing that Douglas boy. He's a fisherman. He'd know. And *nobody's* gonna know about that night. I can still hear the heavy breathing of that thing and its spiny flaps slapping on the sand as it came up out of the water. I may be a redneck, but I've seen pictures of those things—a coelacanth, extinct, they said. Yeah, well, one attacked my daughter!

Lincoln Memorial Defaced; Texas Agents Implicated
(Washington Post, June 14, 1963)

The head of former Former President Abraham Lincoln sitting on the throne in the Lincoln Memorial was removed from its body by assailants wielding a diamond saw sometime late Saturday night or Sunday morning.

"Lincoln's head was neatly removed with an especially sharp saw," said Sergeant Alf Daviselli of the Washington Metropolitan

Police. ALONG LIVES TEXAS! had been spray-painted on the floor, he added, noting that eyewitnesses saw several "long, lanky fellas in boots, chaps, and cowboy hats" running from the scene.

Left behind in the Memorial near the statue were seven green scarab beetles, of a type common in ancient Egypt but long thought extinct, until their appearance in the Republic of Texas a year or two before independence in 1931. Strict vector control has prevented the so-called Texas scarabs from spreading into the United States; this is the first appearance of the Texas beetles on the American side of the border.

Police speculate that there were many more beetles at the scene during the commission of the crime, but that these seven were inadvertently crushed under the bootheels of the perpetrators.

Another theory, currently being dismissed by official sources, is that the seven beetles were deliberately crushed and left behind by the culprits as a "message" to U.S. leaders.

"In Texas," explained Professor Peter Panting of Georgetown University's Department of Texas Studies, "Abraham Lincoln is widely associated with the 'progressive' policies of both Texas President Lyndon Baines Johnson and our American President John Fitzgerald Kennedy. The belief is that Lincoln is still alive and living somewhere underwater in Texas, where he is masterminding a campaign to undermine or even overthrow the Texas police state, possibly as early as the millennium."

Professor Panting added that the seven dead beetles may well be a warning of some sort. "Texan extremists may be planning some sort of attack on these two Presidents perceived as 'Lincoln's men,'" he said. "Perhaps seven progressive politicians will die. On the seventh day of the seventh month, perhaps, which would mean in just three weeks' time. We can't be certain what the seven stands for, but extra caution is advised."

Police are also investigating reports of a "panhandler" who

has been seen in the vicinity recently. He has been reported to be an "Abraham Lincoln lookalike."

Reports from persons who met him on the street, always near the Lincoln Memorial, indicate that he wore a long black frock coat and top hat and had a beard with a wart above it.

It is not known whether he is connected in any way to either the defacement of the Memorial, or to the recent disappearances of street people and alien/UFO buffs who used to frequent the memorial and capitol mall areas. Their bodies have not been found, although some body parts that cannot yet be linked to them have been found in the reflecting pond, including several feet of large intestine and a mandible (jawbone).

Park Rangers are not surprised at the defacement. "This memorial has been going to hell ever since that alien thing and big UFO rally a few years ago. Shame. Used to be nice. Now Lincoln ain't got no head," said one ranger who declined to be identified.

"I bet you anything it's them UFO nuts did this," he added.

Members of the intelligence community, however, have suggested that the defacement is the work of the Texas Intelligence Agency.

"Texans have long sought special souvenirs of value to their culture from the U.S.," said an unnamed source at an unnamed government agency. "And public monuments have been targets before. You recall the case of Grant's finger. This appears to be another case."

The government of Texas, in a terse statement, denies any involvement.

"As far as I'm aware," President Johnson told the press late last night, "Abraham Lincoln is dead and buried in Arlington Cemetery, up there in the U.S. Leastways, I personally ain't never seen him, and if you believe these nuts that say they have, well, you need to have your f—ing head examined. Texans ain't got no interest in Lincoln, lemme tell you that straight out. We got our own Presidents down here, and we like them a hell of a lot better than any y'all got to offer."

Investigation continues.

Teens Crash; One Dies
(Midland Reporter-Telegraph, November 23, 1963)

Two cars collided at the intersection of RR 7 and RR 13 yesterday evening. Three Robert E. Lee High School students were involved in the crash.

The two girls in one car, Laura Welch and Judy Dyke, were unharmed.

The boy in the other, Mike Douglas, was thrown clear of his Bowie convertible and broke his neck. He died instantly.

Police reconstructing the scene believe that young Welch, heading west on RR 7, ran the stop sign at the intersection and did not see the southbound convertible entering the intersection on RR 13. As a result, she plowed into the front left corner of Douglas' Bowie, with fatal consequences.

Three details stick out in the collision.

First, both country roads were absolutely empty at the time of the accident. It is never a busy intersection, and when the two cars collided, there was not another car in sight. It was, police officers were told by Judy Dyke, a warm, clear night, more like September than late November. She and her best friend Laura were chatting and laughing, and perhaps that distracted Laura for the brief moment required to run the stop sign and collide with the other vehicle.

"But we weren't drinking, I swear, we *never* do," Dyke assured reporters. "Or smoking. We were listening to the radio, though, and they had a thing about President Johnson being shot, and maybe Laura was upset about that or something."

Police say that there is no sign that Douglas slammed on

his brakes or made any other attempt to stop before the collision. He had no stop sign.

Second, the drivers of the two cars were boyfriend and girlfriend. Laura and Mike had been "going steady" for about six months at the time of the accident. Friends of the pair said that the couple had "crashed into each other" in the school hallway earlier that same day, and Laura's books and papers had gone flying. Eyewitnesses say that the angle of collision was uncannily similar to that of the crash that took young Douglas' life. Police are not ruling out the possibility of foul play at this time.

Third, when police arrived on the scene, both the body of Mike Douglas and his Bowie automobile were covered with live fish, still flapping about and gasping for air. There was no tackle box in the Bowie or other sign that young Mike had just come from fishing.

And fourth, when the two girls were bundled, weeping and screaming, into the ambulance, Judy Dyke moaned something odd about the fish on the road talking to Laura. The two EMTs in the ambulance later disagreed as to her exact words: one claimed she said the fish had "warned" Laura about giant praying mantises from ancient Atlantis, while the other claimed she said the fish had simply asked Laura for a small bite of cheese.

Laura Welch, who is still under heavy sedation at Midland Baptist Hospital, is the daughter of Harold and Jenna Welch of Midland. Harold Welch and his partner Lloyd Waynick own and run a successful construction company in town. The family was unavailable for comment.

Mike Douglas was the son of Jackson and Robin Douglas, also of Midland. They described their son as a "good boy, didn't drink or smoke or do drugs." After graduating from high school he was planning to go to the University of Texas and major in broadcast journalism, perhaps become a talk-show host. Mr. and Mrs. Douglas told reporters that they believed the accident was "nobody's fault" and said they would pray for Laura Welch and her family.

Funeral services for the Douglas boy will be held tomorrow at 2 p.m. at Sam Houston Lutheran Church.

Hit List

(Poppy, February 22, 1967)

The note just appears on my desk. I never do find out who put the damn thing here, how it got here. My gal, Mrs. Zwieckel, knows nothing about it, and she's about as trustable as they come. Trust-onable. Trustworthright. "I have no idea, Mr. Bush," she says. "Nobody went in there. I was right here all the time." I step out for a quick whiz, ten thirty in the morning, and when I come back, it's there on my desk:

Zoo. Elephants. Noon. Rafael.

Rafael! The name sends slivers up my spine. My knees bunkle; I can't stand up; I collapse into my chair. I haven't seen Rafael in over *three years*, since the week before the JFK/LBJ hit. The dangerous liberal tide stemmed in both countries. Mission accomplished. Big John Connally, our President, a strong, responsible leader with a vision for the future. A TIA asset himself, of course, and only too happy to pitch in on the assassination that put him in the driver's seat. Dick Nixon, too, Connally's new Veep and a good man. One of Uncle Dogsbody's favorites. There in Dallas on The Day. Doing what, I don't know. Nelson Rockefeller, JFK's successor up there in the United States while he's in a coma. Another good man. We're all back on track now.

LBJ and JFK. They deserved to die. You just can't trust

guys who go just by their initials. It just isn't natural. Big John Connally, now there's a name, a real Texan name. Those initial guys were in cahoots, LBJ over here, JFK over there. JFK beat out Gray in the closest erection in American history. We all suxpankted vote fraud; those Kennedys were way into dirty tricks like that, but Uncle Dogsbody's people couldn't prove it in time for a "democracy" like the United States. So JFK became President, and everything went to hell. Not just the Bay of Pigs; everything. And LBJ became our President. I don't know how he did it. I thought my dad had these things sawed up. Sawn up. Sooned up. Sewned up. He created this country, back in whenever. Back before I was born, practically. But that LBJ was a conniver. He connived. He knew how to do it. And he liked to do it. My dad told me that. Just before the election, one of his people took out Dad's Vice President, Walt Woodul, and somehow LBJ became the new Veep. Then edged Dad out, got his name on the ballot in place of Dad's. How? Nobody knows. None of our people know. Skipjack LaTuna knows. Evil, rich fish-lovers with their fingers in every aquarium and two cars in every garage. Two irons in every fire. He pulled apron strings. He worked behind my dad's back. He worked behind Uncle Dogsbody's back, too, I guess, because how could he be working for Uncle Dogsbody? And the only way he could get elected President of Texas without Uncle Dogsbody knowing about it was to do it behind his back. Or with Uncle Dogsbody's conniption. Connivtion. Connivance. Contrivance. Conviction. Conscription. And that's not Uncle Dogsbody. He would never go behind my dad's back. If LBJ went behind my dad's back, Uncle Dogsbody wasn't back there with him. Uncle Dogsbody was alone, probably up in front of my dad, where he could see him coming. It was some other uncle back there with LBJ. Had to have been. Who else could it be?

Maybe Uncle Sam. Uncle JFK.

They conspired; that's what they did. They connived. They

stole the presidency away from my dad, who deserved it more than anybody, maybe, because he was the backbone of this country, the spine, the spinal cord. The rip cord. This country got in trouble, they looked to my dad. For years. And then a grateful people made him President. And LBJ stole it right away from him. Right out from under his nose. One hand behind his back. So he could practically taste it. Just like that.

And then the first thing LBJ did when he got into office was to start conniving some more, conniving this time to undermine the moral fiber of our country. Ramming liberal legislation through. All sorts of "freedoms" and things. Freedom of speech, freedom of the press, freedom of religion. As if we didn't already have enough freedom as it is in this great country of ours! As if we weren't already the freest country in the world! Texas is a *cinnamon* of freedom! But LBJ thought we didn't have enough. Women should vote. They already could, through their husbands! Women should have equal rights with men. Uh huh! As if they could handle it. It's a rough world out there, too rough for the soft, delicate hands of women. And minorities! LBJ wanted to, what was his word, unpower minorities. Disunpower. Disempower them. Something. Give them power, is what it came down to. Dirty Mexicans and Indians and Negroes, basically, is what he meant. Lazy, dirty immigrants. Rapers and murderians. People without a piss to pot in, or do anything else in, either. People with nothing to do but rape and gape. Give them power. Power over me, and people like me, is what that means. People who have struggled for what we have, who've worked hard to get ahead. Give them power over us. Power, power, power. It's a harsh word, but it's the truth.

And LBJ didn't like the war in Vietnam any more than JFK did. They wanted out. They never wanted us to send ground troopers in. Storm troopers. Douglas MacArthur, that crafty old American traitor, told JFK that any President who tried to fight a ground war in Asia needed to have his head examined.

What about chemical warfare? What about napalm? Would you need to have your head examined to use Agent Orange? And what about all the jobs the war has created in the weapons industry? What about employment both in Texas and in the United States? Should we just pull out and cause mass unemployment and loss of revenants among arms manufacturers?

So but anyway, we all agreed to lie low for a few years, let the heat pass. Two Presidents taken out of commission in one motorcade! Bound to be heat. So no Rafael. No sweet, sweaty afternoons, stolen nights of mutual pleasure. But now, three years have passed, and here he is again, wanting to meet! Wanting to, well ... you know. All that.

The morning creeps by. I can't work, of course. No way. Finally, at a quarter after eleven, I tell Mrs. Zwieckel that I'm going out, slip into my jacket, catch the elevator down. I've decided to walk to the zoo. February's been a little chilly but sunny and nice this year. Low sixties, not much smog. I can see all the way across the street today. Easily. Right at the corner, there's a police squad breaking up an anti-Vietnam War demon-station. I'm so focused on my meeting with Rafael that I almost walk right into it. Like a demon. Narrowly miss getting sapped. Whap! Whap! Whap! Who *are* these people who keep begging the cops to beat them up over a war halfway around the world? The kids aren't fighting back; they've trained themselves somehow to just take it. Just lie back and enjoy it, like a rape. Like a Mexican. One cop lands a blow on a boy's glasses. They shatter, and blood spurts. Maybe he'll think twice about protesting his government's policies next time.

And then, a couple of blocks down, *another* demon-station, also in the process of being dispersed with truncheons and saps, the bloodied kids loaded into a waiting paddy wagon. The signs say something about human rights. Human rights! More LBJ hippochrissy! The man's dead, but these dangerous ideas just won't go away! Liberals care about human rights here in Texas but not in Vietnam. They'd gladly let a communist dictator run roughrider over the Vietnamese people, but just let a legally desecrated authority here at home so much as sternalize a bum or a Negro or a Mexican, and they're all up in arms.

No further unpleasantness on my walk. I get to the zoo about ten minutes early, pay the submission fee, stroll casually toward the elephants. It takes every ounch of mental energy I have to stroll *casually*. Grown men don't bolt. I picture Rafael in my mind, wonder whether his beard will have started to grow yet, finally. Whether he'll have more than a few wispy tufts of pubic hair this time. Three-plus years since we met last, three-plus years of clandustical meetings during the Bay of Pigs campaign and then the assassination stuff, that's six years or more since the first night he knocked on my door, late '60 to early '67, and in all those years we were meeting, he never grew a day older. I envy him his tamembolism. I'm 42 and showing it. My cheeks and belly starting to sag, heavy black bags under my eyes. Starting to look craggy, very craggy. But I'm guessing Rafael will not have aged a day since we last met.

You can walk all the way around the elephant pen. I do. No Rafael. Am I early? I tap my watch, hold it to my ear, looking back the way I just came. Give him a few minutes.

Then someone takes me by the arm from behind and says, "Walk with me." I whirl. It's David Ferrie. He's outdone himself with the hair and eyebrows this time. Looks like he's carefully cut out hair-and eyebrow-shaped swatches of some piss-strained old carpet and glued them to his bald head, but somehow, he's also managed to make himself look like my dad. It occurs to me that he thinks he's *in disguise*.

I plant my feet. "Where's Rafael?"

"Don't be fatuous," he says impatiently, yanking on my arm. I'm kind of indigniphant. I'm not fat. "There is no Rafael. Never was."

"What do you mean, *is* no Rafael, never was? Of course there was! He wrote me a note, asked me to meet him here."

"I wrote you that note, you big lunk."

"*You* wrote it!" There's a rushing in my ears. I can't think straight. "Then—"

"I signed it Rafael so you'd come. All right? I didn't know whose side you'd be on."

"Side?"

"In the war."

"War?"

"Hit or be hit," he says crimpically.

"I don't *understand*," I say. Was that a wail? Did I wail? I hope I didn't wail. Wailing isn't dignified.

"Come on, walk with me, and I'll explain it."

So I let him steer me along the path. My feet move. I try to adjust.

"Thing is," he says, "they're taking us out. Somebody is, I don't know who. Every one of us who had something to do with Dallas. You've—"

"Taking us out where?"

"Killing us, you moron."

"Oh. But that must be, what, hundreds of people!"

"Right. And hundreds are dying."

"Like who, for instance?"

"Bunch of people you probably don't know. People connected to Oswald. Landladies, employment officers, neighbors. Witnesses who came forward with stories about men on the grassy knoll. People who took, or watched, or bought copies of, or talked about a Super-8 movie of the shooting. Anybody who mentioned in public that they knew about the hit in advance. JFK's girlfriends. Incidentals. But also the primary people. They started taking out my guys back the very next summer. Hugh Ward and Guy Banister in consecutive months, May and June of 1964."

"How'd they die?"

"Hugh died in a plane crash in Mexico. Chep Morrison was in the plane, too. Morrison, you know, was Mayor of New Orleans. Pilot was a guy I used to work with named Jack Martin. Used to be called Suggs or Scroggs. He was minister of some weird religion. He'd been in jail in Texas for performing an abortion or something. He was a mean drunk. You always had to listen to him rave, or he'd call you up at three in the morning and threaten to kill you in all sorts of disgusting ways. Banister had a heart attack."

I shrug. "Planes crash. People have heart attacks."

"Then," he says, rolling over my feeble protest with an uh-huh look, "the summer after that, Maurice Gatlin fell off a sixth-floor balcony. Oops. Guess he just leaned over too far, huh? He's in Puerto Rico. Hotel in San Juan. Has a sudden heart attack and topples over the rail. Wheeeeeeee splat. That same summer, Alvin Beauboeuf and Melvin Coffey stepped into the path of an oncoming freight train outside of New Orleans. Splat splat. Charles Graham died in a single-car automobile accident. Got in an argument with a tree, and lost. No ice on the road, hey, it's summer, but maybe he was drinking? Catherine Wilkinson was shot in the head on a dark street in the French Quarter. Dangerous part of town after dark. Should have stayed on Bourbon Street, where it's light, Cathy! Christopher Maria was found hanging from a rafter dressed in women's clothing. Ruled accidental death. Autoerotic asphyxiation. Chuck Rolland tried to break up a gang fight out on the ice and got himself iced. Layton Martens was shot and thrown in a dumpster."

He pauses, looks down at his feet for a moment. Scuffs a little pattern in the yellow dust with his right foot.

"But that stuff is ancient history," he says, looking back up at me again. "What's got my panties in a twist now is that they've come after two more of my people just this month. Eladio del Valle and Mary Sherman. Eladio was shot *and* axed in the head. Mary died in a fire. Smoking in bed, maybe? But she also had a bullet in her body that got conveniently left out of the coroner's report."

"How'd you find out about it?"

"I have my sources. I'm still connected. And that's what worries me. Everybody who's connected is getting iced."

"Who else?"

"Anybody who ever had anything to do with Jack Ruby, for example. The man himself just died last month, of course—"

"Of cancer, I read."

"Lung cancer. Injected into him."

"Really? They can *do* that?"

"You'd be surprised at what they can do. There's been a rash of stripper and waitress murders, too. You didn't hear about that? Probably not, circles you move in. All of them danced on Ruby's stage or served his customers drinks. Betty MacDonald hanged herself in a Dallas jail. Teresa Norton got shot in the head. Little Lynn Carlin also got herself shot. Delilah Walle got shot by her husband one month after the wedding. Hey, chalk that one up to irreconcilable differences, huh? Hank Killam got married to one of Ruby's dancers, but they didn't ask him to wax his wife; he got his own throat slit. Jimmy Levens over in Fort Worth hired some of Ruby's strippers after Ruby got tossed in jail; he croaked, too. Ruby's first lawyer, Tom Howard, took two reporters to Ruby's apartment two days after the hit on the Presidents, the day after Ruby killed Oswald. Bill Hunter and Jim Koethe. All three of them are dead. Bill was accidentally shot by a cop. Another big oops. Tom had a heart attack. Jim got a fatal karate chop to the neck. Creative, huh? Just like the fucking movies. Lot of other reporters investigating the case got iced, too, including vice presidents of *Life* magazine and shit. Any other investigator who got too close to the truth, or knew from the start and hinted at his knowledge: dead. Any CIA agent who's suggested the Agency might have been behind the hit, like Gary Underhill, shot in the head. Ruled a suicide. Judge Joe Brown, who presided over the Ruby case. Heart attack. Clarence Oliver, Dallas DA's office private eye who was working on the Ruby case. Dead, but I couldn't find out how."

I'm starting to feel a little quillsy about all this. "Do you think," I say, swallowing hard, "maybe, that *my* life may be in danger too?"

He shrugs. "I don't know. You may be safe. You seem to be Dogsbody Harriman's boy. Still, you were involved. You know things. You did things."

"I hardly did anything!"

"You made that phone call to Dallas FBI the day of the hit."

"So? That was a perfectly innocent phone call."

"Telling the FBI someone was going to try and kill the President in *Houston*. Perfectly innocent, uh huh. Nobody on one of the real hit teams, of course; some freako Bircher from the University of Houston. James Parrott. How's that innocent? That was part of our misdirections. All those people set up to draw attention away from what was really going on, part of the smokescreen, like Oswald and the guys on the grassy knoll. You were part of it, Poppy. You did your bit."

"But a harmless part! I didn't kill anybody!"

"Neither did I. Neither did Guy, or Hugh, or Maurice. Neither did Eladio or Mary. They're all dead. Except me. So far." And here he crosses himself, which is strange, because I never knew Ferrie was sacreligious.

We're walking by some sort of African savannah. Ferrie spots a deer-like thing fucking another, and turns to watch. Some sort of gazelle or ibex or something. Mothers are shooing their kids away. Two little boys who don't seem to have mothers watch wide-eyed. They've got plastic ray guns tucked into the backs of their pants. One of them goes behind the other and starts mimicking the boy ibex or whatever it is on his friend. Holding him by the shoulders. Another wave of longing washes over me. Where is Rafael? What is he doing right now?

"And another thing," Ferrie says without turning, his heavy, sarcadontic, fake-eyebrowed eyes still on the fucking animals. "You made that phone call *from* Dallas."

"So? Where else was I going to make it from? I was there, naturally."

"So," he says, turning to me now, "they know you were there. They've got a record of the exact phone booth you called from. They might come after you. Anybody with links to Operation Zapata who can be shown to have been in Dallas the day of the assassination is under suspicion. Howard Hunt and Frank Sturgis were there, and they're in deep shit."

"But *me?*"

He shrugs, turns, and starts walking on. The savannah show is over. I tag along, thinking shit, shit, shit. What about me being President? What about that? I can't be President if I'm iced, waxed, or whacked!

We walk along in silence for a while. Ferrie steers us into the monkey house. The crazy things are jumping and swinging to beat the band. It's like a sillime for how I'm feeling right now. A similarimee. An anenome. One of the monkeys is holding another monkey's pee-pee. Just sort of quietly. Rafael!

"You know," Ferrie says finally, "there's also a memo from Hoover to the effect that Bill Forsyth briefed you and Captain Edwards on the assassination and its connection to the anti-Castro insurgency movement. Two days after the assassination."

"So? I was briefed, so what?"

"So he identifies you as 'George Bush of the Texas Intelligence Agency.' "

"What did he do that for! That faggot fuck!"

He grins up at me wolfishly. I sure wish he'd never seen me with Rafael.

"So," I ask manfully, mannishly, manlily, like a man with a deep, deep voice, hoping to find some kind of lid to put on my inner dreads, "who's surviving this? Who's still alive?"

"The big guys. Lansdale, Milteer, Hemming, Hunt, Bundy, Sturgis. The mob guys, like Johnny Roselli and Sam Giancana. Clay Shaw. George DeMoronshit, too. I'd'a thought that slimeball'd be dead by now, but I guess he's one of the big boys in all this."

"Who *is* he, anyway? I met him three or four times, and every time, he was somebody different. He's a Polish or a Russian count. He's a Polish officer or a Russian journalist. He's an oil engineer. He's Oswald's best friend. He's a Nazi and a KGB agent."

"Yeah, he's probably all those and more. He was Oswald's CIA control officer. One of Reinhard Gehlen's boys."

"Whose?"

"You don't know Reinhard Gehlen?"

"No."

"Damn. I thought for sure he'd be one of your drinking buddies. He's one of Dogsbody Harriman's best assets. Hitler's spymaster in charge of the Soviet Union, back in the late thirties and early forties. Defected to the US after the war with all his files, kept running his spy network inside the USSR from here, then from West Germany again. The BND. The Bundes-something. A legitimate intelligence agency. So much for war crime tribunals, huh? They were plotting some kind of new Russian revolution. Inside agitators rising up and overthrowing the communist dictators. Still are plotting it, for all I know. Allen Dulles cultivated him for Harriman as Nazi Germany was crumbling. Gave him two hundred million dollars of American taxpayer money and said 'Go play.' DeMohrenschildt's one of the guys he plays with. DeMoronshit doubles or triples for the KGB and the CIA. Personally, though, I don't think he's a Nazi. He just likes the game."

We're in the insect house now. A couple of boys are giggling over in the corner. It's kind of dark in here, but they look to me like the two boys from the savannah. It gradually becomes clear to me as Ferrie talks that they're giggling about him. Finally, one of them gets his courage up and calls out, "Hey, mister, your face is falling off!" Gills of gaggles again. Gales of giggles.

"Fuck off, kids," Ferrie says, as if batting at a pesky fly.

"Mister, are you a *alien* or something?" the other boy calls out now. "From a *space ship?*"

"I mean it, kids, fuck off," he says again, with only a little more heat in his voice.

"Death to aliens!" the boys cry in unison and pull out their ray guns, start firing madly at us. Ferrie snaps a gun from the back of his pants before I can even restiger what's going on, drops into a firing grouch. Slouch. Crouch. Seems pretty clear to me that he's really about to shoot these kids, but he catches himself in time. The boys freeze, drop their ray guns, and run like pellhell.

"Damn kids," Ferrie mutters. "Stalking us all across the zoo and then pulling plastic guns." He shakes his head at himself. "I'm losing it, Poppy. I'm fucking losing it. I'm jumpy as hell. Thing is, I wouldn't put it past the Agency to use a couple of snot-nosed eight-year-olds to take me out." He walks over and gives the ray guns a vicious stomp. Looks resentfully up at the bugs behind the glass. Raps the glass hard with his knuckle. "These things give me the creeps. Why would anybody pay *money* to come look at them?"

But instead of leading me out of there, he slides his gun back into his pants and leans against the railing. "And then, of course," he says grudgingly, as if there had been no interruption, "that fuck Jim Garrison is still walking around, who knows why."

"Who?"

"Jesus Christ, Poppy, don't you know *anything?*"

"I guess not."

"The New Orleans DA. Every time he gets close to a witness, the witness dies. But Garrison keeps breathing. One of life's little mysteries."

"So," I say, thinking I've got to get back to the office,

thinking I'd really rather not think about this hit list stuff *at all*, "what do you want from me, exactly?"

"I want to get on the survivors' list."

"Survivors' list?"

"Sure. The people marked to live."

"You sure there even is one? What if it's every man for himself?"

"There must be one. Everybody's getting whacked except a select few who are pulling the strings. I want to be one of the ones pulling the strings."

"I wouldn't have the foggiest idea how to put you on that list, if there is one."

"Don't play dumb with me, Poppy. All you've got to do is whisper a word in Dogsbody Harriman's ear, and I live. It's that simple."

"Really? Well, hey, it's worth a try, I guess."

"Are you *serious*?" Suddenly he's my best friend. "You'd *do* that for me?"

"Sure. You asked me, didn't you?"

"My God, Poppy, that's great. I don't care what the guys said about you, all those years; you're all right."

"What *did* they say about me?" My heart drops down into my throat. But Ferrie just waves me off. He doesn't care what they said. That's all in the past. That's water under the duck's back.

He takes both of my hands in both of his, presses them tight. Looks into my eyes. I feel sort of noxious for a second. Then, "Gotta run," he says, and takes off toward the insect house exit. Just as he reaches the exit area and is silhouetted in the bright sunlight there, a tall, thin shadow steps up out of nowhere and thwacks him a good one on the neck. A karate chop to the neck, just like whoever it was. The reporter guy. The arm that delivers the chop seems double-jointed. It bends back at a weird angle before coming down on Ferrie's neck. Ferrie slumps to the floor. The shadow disappears.

I rush over to his body. Feel his neck for a pulse. Nothing. He's dead. Too late for the survivors' list, I guess.

"Good job, George," a familiar voice says, pulling me up from behind. "But the cops will be here soon. We don't want them finding David Ferrie's assassin bending over his body."

"But, Uncle Dogsbody," I cry, "it wasn't me! It was somebody else! I saw it all!"

"You did? Who was it, then, if it wasn't you?"

"I don't know; some tall guy."

"You're a tall guy, George."

"But I swear, Uncle Dogsbody, it wasn't me!"

"Sure, sure," he says soothingly, "whatever. But let's get out of here, shall we?"

"Okay." I let him guide me out, away from Ferrie's body, across the zoo. He's taking such long strides that I have to run a little to keep up. I take a few short little hops and skips, too. How does he move so fast? I'm no slouch as a walker myself. Or as a bush—get it?

"Uncle Dogsbody," I say as we go, panting a little, sort of out of breath.

"Yes, George?"

"Uncle Dogsbody, please, please, oh *please* —"

"What is it, George?"

"Please, Uncle Dogsbody, please put me on the survivors' list! Please! I mean it!"

"You're on the survivors' list, George."

"Really? You put me on the survivors' list, Uncle Dogsbody?"

"You're on it, George. I put you there myself."

"Oh, Uncle Dogsbody, I'm so relieved! I'm on the survivors' list!"

"You're my boy, George. You always were. Nobody's going to hurt you."

We walk out of the zoo in silence. I'm feeling mostly exalted. I feel like skimping. But I'm feeling some other things, too. For example, an almost uncontrollable urge to ask him about Rafael. Never *was* one? But, you know. *Almost* uncontrollable. I control it. I'm a big boy now. I'm on the list.

Documents

Texas Beetles Beat the Beatles
(Billboard, February 6, 1969)

The Beatles played the Austin Municipal Auditorium in the Republic of Texas last night, in their only Texas date on their White Album tour. It was only the second concert ever held there, after Donovan played the venue last October. The word on the street was that allowing the openly "liberal" British invasion band to invade the Republic of Texas marks a slight but significant relaxing of the police state's fierce ideological vigilance over their population.

The band played some of their old hits but also a strong list off their new album, including "Back in the U.S.S.R.," "Ob-La-Di, Ob-La-Da," "While My Guitar Gently Weeps," "Blackbird," "Rocky Raccoon," "Why Don't We Do It In The Road," and "Helter Skelter."

The newsworthy moment in the concert, however, came when the band began to play "Revolution 1," and the stage and the four members of the band were swarmed with the famous Texas scarab beetles. At first, the band thought it was funny: the Beatles swarmed with beetles! But it quickly became clear that the beetles were determined to shut the song, and perhaps the entire concert, down. It was clearly a political protest against the sentiments voiced in the song—or perhaps just the title, since infamously, the Texan police state does not tolerate what it takes to be incitements to revolution.

Beatles fans in the front row began shouting at the beetles, protesting their protest, along the lines of "This isn't a revolutionary song; it's an anti-revolutionary song!" But of course shouting at beetles, especially Texas scarab beetles, has never proved particularly effective. They just don't listen.

The Texas Rangers acting as security for the concert did

listen, however. They rounded up the shouters and escorted them off to jail.

It's true, in fact, that while the song does back away from revolution, it is pointedly directed against "minds that hate." And it did seem that the swarming of John, Paul, George, and Ringo was a swarming of minds that hate. Hate strikes back.

Shut down by the beetles, the Beatles walked off stage and took a half-hour break. When they returned, they played "Happiness is a Warm Gun," which was received by the audience and the beetles alike with great enthusiasm. The beetles swarmed the stage again, but instead of running up onto the four bodies of the band, they seemed to be dancing along.

Anonymous commentators have since speculated that the beetles were taking the song's apparent celebration of firing guns literally, instead of as a veiled critique of gun violence—or, some say, as a veiled allusion to John Lennon's sexual relationship with Yoko Ono (the "trigger" that the song's speaker fingers apparently being Ono's clitoris).

In an interview with the band after the concert, the interviewer asked about the beetle swarm, and the band members took it lightly, calling the scarab beetles "unusually harsh music critics." The interviewer suggested that perhaps the band preferred the predaceous diving beetles of the Abraham Lincoln contingent; looking puzzled at the suggestion, the band said they felt a closer kinship with dung beetles.

TBI Interview of William Ryan, Jr.
(January 21, 1969)

By SA MONZA P. WALL and SA CHIP SHEAVER

WILLIAM "BILL" RYAN, JR., was interviewed in the office of DR. LUCID TONES, Director of Psychiatric Services at Humble General Hospital, where RYAN is currently his patient. Dr.

TONES was present for the interview.

RYAN advised he was born March 28, 1908, in Silverado, Nevada, the oldest son of WILLIAM RYAN (a miner) and KATE HALBERSTADT RYAN, both deceased. Mrs. RYAN was of German birth. Mr. RYAN was her second husband; her first died in a mining accident. RYAN informed that his siblings include THOMAS MICHAEL RYAN, born 1910, and THELMA CATHERINE RYAN, born 1912. One year after the birth of THELMA (nicknamed PATRICIA or PAT, due to her birth on St. Patrick's Day), Mrs. RYAN convinced her husband to give up mining and move to what was then the State of Texas. According to RYAN, they bought a small livestock farm outside of Humble.

RYAN stated that his mother, a heavy smoker, died in 1925 of emphysema. At that point, thirteen-year-old PAT took over the care of her father and brothers. In 1928, RYAN related, his father too, also a heavy smoker, took ill with emphysema and was bed-ridden for several years before dying in 1931.

RYAN said that late in 1929, his sister PAT became pregnant, and in August of 1930, his eighteen-year-old sister PAT gave birth. RYAN insisted that his sister was a very proper young woman and did not have a boyfriend and did not indulge in loose relations with boys. RYAN described his sister, in addition, as extremely busy with the care of the house and her father and two older brothers and, therefore, quite simply as lacking the necessary time to "go steady" or the like.

According to RYAN, PAT told him and their brother, TOM, at the time that she had no memory of sexual relations of any kind. RYAN further stated that PAT was extremely confused throughout her pregnancy and that care of the house and their father became erratic. After delivery of the baby in August 1930, she returned to normal, except that, according to RYAN, she never did regain memory of the events that led to her impregnation.

RYAN related that one evening around nightfall in December

1929, he and his brother, TOM, happened to be looking out their bedroom window on the second floor of their house when they spied a tall, thin man coming out of the barn. Then, RYAN said, he seemed to "sprout wings and fly off." RYAN indicated that he and his brother, TOM, believed then that this must have been some sort of optical illusion, perhaps a dust twister caught by a random ray of the setting sun, but that now he had grown convinced that it was, in fact, W. AVERELL HARRIMAN, who RYAN asserted is an evil bug from ancient Atlantis that has been manipulating human history for thousands of years and is the true father of his sister's child.

When he and his brother TOM rushed outside, RYAN reported, they found no trace of the man or any vehicle. Inside the barn, unconscious in the horses' feed trough, they found their sister, PAT, fully dressed. She was covered with what RYAN later discovered were Texas scarab beetles. According to RYAN, all his sister, PAT, could remember—then or later—was going into the barn to feed and water the livestock. She heard some sort of screeching sound, RYAN said PAT told them, but didn't even have a chance to turn around before something struck her and she blacked out.

RYAN reported that he and his brother, TOM, carried PAT to the car and drove her to Humble General Hospital, where she was checked for signs of sexual assault. None were found at the time, RYAN said: no signs of a struggle, no scratches or bruises. Nor were traces of semen found. RYAN stated that an ER doctor (identity unknown) told him that she only had a small bump on her head, and her maidenhead was intact. The official conclusion was that she had not been raped. However, RYAN recalled, six weeks later, she tested positive for pregnancy, and the examining physician, DR. GEORGE HOPEWELL (deceased), determined that conception had, in fact, occurred around the time of the incident in the barn.

RYAN asserted that when his sister, PAT, went into labor in August 1930, she began acting strangely, hopping about the house with her hands crooked in front of her like a praying mantis. She had to be taken forcibly to Humble General Hospital, RYAN recalled, and, in the car, kept trying to bite her brothers on the neck. RYAN stated that he and his brother, TOM, were told by DR. HOPEWELL that the baby was stillborn, and that he and his brother considered this a great blessing.

But according to RYAN, his sister, PAT, always insisted doggedly that the baby was born healthy, a full-grown eighteen-year-old BOY, and that she had given him up for adoption right there in the hospital. The woman in the bed next to her had miscarried, RYAN recalled PAT telling him, and was grieving over the death of her baby when PAT told her that she couldn't possibly keep her own baby, as people would talk if she kept a full-grown teenage son born out of wedlock. The woman, Mrs. HANNAH NIXON, wife of FRANCIS A. NIXON, the Quaker owners of a gas station and country store in Humble, decided on the spot to adopt the boy.

RYAN insisted that PAT told him Mrs. NIXON told her she and her husband FRANCIS were going to name the boy RICHARD MILHOUS after her father.

Conclusion 1: This bizarre story concerns the birth of our current PRESIDENT.

RYAN further asserted that his sister PAT took her Associate degree at Humble Junior College and then transferred to the University of Texas at Austin, where she was graduated *cum laude* in 1937 with a Bachelor of Science in merchandising. Later, she became a teacher of business education courses at Humble High School.

RYAN stated that RICHARD MILHOUS NIXON took his B.A. at Rice Institute and his J.D. degree at Rice Law and accepted his first job at Sterling, Sterling, and Sterling, the Humble law firm founded by two brothers of President Ross Sterling. RYAN remembered that the firm served as the city's legal advisors, and NIXON primarily worked as a police prosecutor, but also did corporate and tax law connected with the oil business.

RYAN recalled that his sister PAT assured him she absolutely did not "keep up" with her "son" RICHARD MILHOUS NIXON during their college years or the early years of their working life. According to RYAN, PAT told him that it was not until they were both given leading roles in a Humble Pie Theater production of the George Kaufman and Alexander Wolcott play *The Dark Tower* that they met again and fell in love.

RYAN related that he and his brother TOM were horrified at this development and opposed the relationship strongly, but that their sister PAT was stubborn and married Mr. NIXON in 1939. Since, according to official records, PAT's child had been stillborn, there was no legal impediment to the two marrying.

RYAN asserted further that his sister's husband RICHARD MILHOUS NIXON was never "quite right." According to RYAN, NIXON walked stiffly, like a praying mantis; his jaws clacked like insect mandibles when he talked; he had to shave in unlikely places; he ate bugs.

RYAN stated that NIXON drank grain alcohol heavily and would become quite tipsy, but never sloppy drunk, and would never lose consciousness. RYAN also related that NIXON today showed no adverse signs of three decades of excessive alcohol consumption, and that the PRESIDENT's paranoid ravings preceded his alcohol abuse.

RYAN reported that his brother-in-law RICHARD MILHOUS NIXON involved him in his drinking activities from the start, and that he RYAN had for some years considered himself a full-blown alcoholic. RYAN stated that he himself had not had a drink in 65 days, after what he described as a "religious experience."

According to Dr. TONES, it was RYAN's ecstatic descriptions of this "religious" experience that led to his committal to the closed psychiatric ward at Humble General Hospital. Dr. TONES reported that it involved an underwater Divine Comedy in the basement of the Scaly Shepherd Church in East Colburn, in which RYAN was led by ABRAHAM LINCOLN through the three underwater worlds of Slavery, Reconstruction, and Full Citizenship. RYAN confirmed that he had described this experience to his family and friends, and even to many credulous members of the general public who did not know that he was a notorious drunk, liar, and insurance salesman.

RYAN further asserted that it was on the urging of ABRAHAM LINCOLN that he came forward with the "true" story of the birth of President RICHARD MILHOUS NIXON.

Conclusion 2: WILLIAM RYAN, JR., should remain committed to the closed psychiatric ward for life, where he should be administered high doses of antipsychotic medications such as Thorazine or Haloperidol that will prevent him from spreading his ridiculous fantasies among the staff and patients in the ward.

Laura's Dream
(February 19, 1969)

Pres, Don't know what this means, but you'd better pass it on to the Big Guy. The good reverend who wrote it up and gave it to me has been sent to a reeducation camp for a couple of weeks.

—*Gyorgi deM.*

But, Pastor, it was so *real*!

Dreams often seem that way, Laura. Your dream does *not* mean, however, that you want to have sex with a fish.

But it felt—good ...

I'm sure it did. You're a grown woman, Laura. You're twenty-three years old. Some day, when you find a good Christian man who asks you to marry him, you will do those things with him, and they will feel good, I promise you. It is no sin to enjoy the pleasures of the flesh with the proper mate and God's blessing. The pleasure you felt in your dream was, I'm confident, merely an anticipation of that future blessed state.

But the way he put his mouth on me—down there ... I don't think any human man could do that, Pastor.

I—

And I woke up dripping *wet*.

You mean—

No! Pastor! Like, *water*. All over.

Oh.

And can men *talk* while they—you know—pleasure a woman with their mouths?

The fish talked?

He wouldn't shut up. And his words were like the hum of a great engine deep inside me.

What—did he say?

At first, it seemed he was chanting in some ancient language. I couldn't make anything out. It sounded sort of like *sea-drexl-brine*.

Sounds fishy, all right.

But that was just at first. Then it sounded like *sin-sex-in-pride*.

A good Christian warning against loose morals, for sure.

And then I thought I was hearing *in-tact-o-phide*.

Huh, no idea there. Did he say any actual words?

After a while, he started talking about Abraham Lincoln. About what a great man he is.

Was, you mean.

No, he talked as if Lincoln were still alive, and working to protect humans from the Evil Ones.

Evil One. The Devil, you mean.

Oh, it was all so confusing, Pastor!

Dreams are often like that, Laura.

Rubbers

(Poppy, May 1969)

"Rubbers!"

"Hey, Rubbers!"

"Rubbers, come quick! Dick wants you!"

"Pay no attention to Dick, Rubbers; he's just putting you on!"

"Dick's got a hardon for you, Rubbers!"

"Quit riding Dick so hard, Rubbers!"

"Get offa Dick's back, Rubbers!"

"Hey, Rubbers, don't go off like that!"

"Don't go off half-cocked, Rubbers!"

"Hey, Rubbers, wait a minute; I'm coming too!"

"No, you go on a head, Rubbers!"

"You go on in first, Rubbers; I'm coming right behind you."

"Don't strain yourself, Rubbers; you'll spring a leak!"

"Rubbers needs to take a leak so bad, looks like he's gonna burst!"

"Jizz a second, Rubbers!"

Oh ho ho. These boys are *so* funny. "Okay," I start to say, "you guys, what the hell, sure, I can take a ribbing—"

And they're off again.

"Rubbers can take a ribbing! Give me one of those ribbed rubbers, Rubbers!"

"Rubbers with ribbing!"

"Ribbers with rubbing!"

"Ribs for her pleasure; rubs for yours!"

"Ribbity-rubbity roo!"

"Looks like we got a rise out of him!"

"Rubbers rising!"

"Rising to the occasion, Rubbers!"

Every damn day in Congress is like this for me. I stand up to make some serious moltion, and I hear the whispering and the furtery giggling in the rows. Fursery. Furvily. The boys are red in the face from trying to title their stiffers. I mean, sniffle their snipers. Trifle their snappers. Well, sumpress their chorkles and gufflaws. Trying to hide their girth from the gallery, is what I mean. Mirth. Trying to hide their mirth from the mallory. Mallardy. Maggoty. The good folks up there voted these boys into office, and all they can do is make silly adolexic jokes. I've got something to say about our brave Texan soldiers defending our freedom over in Vietnam, there, or want to call for enhanced measures against our enemies over and underseas, or want to propose a Congressional revolution to commend Dick Nixon for the terrific job he's doing as President, and all they can do is make contraceptic jokes and try not to burst a blood vessel.

And, you know, it's all because I care about the population implosion. Because I care about Negroes and Mexicans and Indians making more babies than white people and want to do something about it. You'd think they'd be more respentful. This is Texas, after all. This isn't the United Cynical States of America. This isn't California, whoa, dude, hang ten. Do they really want to be overrun with people of low IQs, mondaloid parents knocking out eight, nine, ten babies when they could have slipped on a condom or gone down to their friendly neighborhood sterizilation center and taken care of it for good? Sure, maybe the problem hasn't reached empidemic propulsions here in Texas, because we've had the good sense to instiment reasonable eugenic programs, but what about the rest of the world? What about Uganda? What about Toga

Toga? What about Davy Jokes' lawner?

And why *is* it so hard for ordinary people to buy condoms in Texas? We want them to aim for Zero Population Growth, ZPG, like the sound of that, ZPG, *zzzzzippig*, but then we don't sell condoms in drug stores, grocery stores, or newspaper kiosks. There's a, I don't know, a something. A confrontation. A complex. A conflash. Conflict! There's a conflict between our money and our mouth. Between our policies and what we want people to do.

General Draper says it's a survivor, or something. A carrion. Carrillion. Carryhairy. A carryunder from olden times. We wanted people to be moral, right? Back in the whatever. Back when we were first creating this great country. Morality for everybody. No sex. Well, not no sex, just no illimit sex. No sex out of weblock. No sex outside of the marriage bed. And why would you need condoms outside of the marriage bed? I mean, why would you *not* need condoms outside of the marriage bed? In the marriage bed, you need sex, not condoms. Just pure sex. Pure noncondormist sex. For noncondormists. Because they thought morality meant not *touching* those parts down there. And you have to touch one of the parts to put a condom on it. I'm not saying which part; you get the idea. It's the part that there's only one of. Well, the woman has a part that there's only one of, too, but this is the part that the man has that there's only one of. Don't touch it. That was the idea. Don't touch it, and you're moral. Or touch it as little as possible. Touch it a little, maybe, when you go to the bathroom or when you wash yourself in the shower. But only then. Not other times. Or maybe only by accident. A light glancing blow on your way past. Going other places.

So but anyway, General Draper says that some really moral people believed that putting condoms on in the stores only encouraged immortality. I mean, putting condom racks on in the stores. In on the stores. Back then. You know, back in the olden days. You put a condom rack in the store, say a bridal store, and people will start to get ideas. They'll put one and two together. Aha, sex! Like, there *is* a thing called sex. They'll think about it more. They'll want it more. Put condom racks in up stores, and small children will start thinking about sex. Sex, sex, sex. That's all they'll be thinking about. Buying those condoms and using them for sex. Which seems a bit extreme to me, but maybe that's just me. I mean, I found some in my dad's drawer once when I was about sixteen, and I had no idea what they were for, let alone spent all my time thinking about sex, sex, sex. But that's what people thought then. That's what they thought other people thought. They were extreme. They were extremalists. They thought condoms would make people *think* about sex, and if they were thinking about it more, they'd be doing it more, too. And that would be immortal.

So they made condoms hard to buy. In fact, almost impossible, unless you had special permission to travel to the United States or Mexico, or your dad was in the government or something.

And General Draper and my dad and I think that's just plain wrong. Here we're spending all these millions of dollars sterilizing the undesirable parts of our great Texan populace, which itself was thanks to General Draper himself and my dad and some other visuairies back in the forties and fifties, but we're keeping condoms away from the very people who should be using them most, the stupid people with bad genes. Who cares if they have lots of sex, so long as they wear a condom while they do it?!

See, that's how modern people think. A new generation. It's our turn now. My dad and General Draper's generation had their chance; now it's ours. They said sterilize; we say condomize!

Well, General Draper's a big supporter of the condom movement, too. He's sort of behind it in a big way, in fact. When they asked me to run for Congress, he and my dad sat me down, explained it all to me.

"We're learning, son," General Draper said. "Slowly but surely, we're learning. You see, at first, we thought you could just legislate things. You don't want people to have sex? You make it illegal to have sex. That simple, right? Wrong! Turns out people will have sex no matter how illegal you make it."

"They will?" This has just never occlured to me. I mean, it's not true between Bar and me. If sex was illegal, we just wouldn't do it. Period. End of story. We hardly ever do it as it is. I mean, apart from everything else, she's kind of fat, and old, and looks like my mother. But even if she was younger, and skinnier, and had lovely short black hair, and olive skin, and just a tiny hint of a stubble on her chin, and a few straggly black hairs on her chest, and her voice cracked a little when she talked, we'd probably still hardly ever have sex, because it's just not right, it isn't. In fact, it's wrong. I mean, not between a husband and a wife, of course. But still.

"Turns out, yes," General Draper says—said, this was back whenever—"they will, son. Believe it or not. Sex is very important to the lower orders. They say it's the only thing they don't have to pay for, which, of course, is not true because what about prostitutes, eh, boy?"

I look at him sort of blankly. "Prostitutes? What about them?"

"Just a joke, son. I just meant you have to pay for prostitutes, is all."

"You do?"

"Of course. That's why they're called prostitutes, son. Prostitute, from the Latin for 'you gotta pay for it.' "

"Oh." I think about that a little while. "I guess I've never had a prostitute before, then."

"Of course you haven't, Poppy, my boy, of course you haven't!" He slathers a big, uneasy grin over his face, claps me too hard on the back. "I never meant to imply that you had! Just a little joke." He pauses. "So! Where was I?"

Frankly, I have no idea.

"Oh, right. Sex. The lower orders. Not having to pay for it. Right. The upshot of it was that we learned something, son. We learned that there are things that you can't legislate."

"Like what?"

"Like sex, boy!" He looks quickly over at my father. He still seems a little nervous. I've got no idea why.

"You can't legislate sex?"

"No, of course not! That's precisely what we've been talking about!"

"Not even requiring it? Like saying everybody *should* have sex?"

"Why," he says slowly, rolling his eyes a little over at my father, "why on Earth would you want to do that, son?"

"I don't know, you said you can't legistimate sex, and it just seems to me you can."

"Well, of course you *can*, but —"

"And it seems to me that if I'm going to be a legistater, I mean a Congressman, it's a pretty bad habit for me to get into, thinking that you can't levitate things. I mean, why even bother, then? Why get into the Congress if you can't congrationalize things?"

"Well, see, that's exactly my point, son," he says, pulling out his handkerchief and dabbing at his forehead a little. "That's exactly my point."

"I'm afraid you've lost me."

"The point is—what *is* the point, Pres? The point is," he says, "is that legislators do *other things too* than just legislate."

"They do?"

"Of course they do, son. They educate."

"Really?"

"Absolutely."

"Don't educators educate? Like teachers and them?"

"Yes, yes, of course they do. Educators educate, and legislators legislate. But sometimes legislators *act* like educators. Sometimes legislators educate, too!"

"And educators legislate?"

"Well, no. Let's not get carried away with this. But legislators educate. Yes. That's one of the most important things they do. That'll be one of your most important jobs, once you get into Congress, son. Educating people about condoms."

"Condoms?"

"Condoms."

"Educate them?"

"Exactly."

"Like, teach them how to use them?"

"No. Teach them that they *should* use them."

"Why?"

"Because they should!"

"Really?"

"Really. I wouldn't lie to you about a thing like this, Poppy."

Feeling a little confused, here. "Should I be using them too?" Thinking maybe this is a new thing I'm missing out on.

"No, no, of course not, son."

"But then — "

"Only people who don't want to be having more kids."

"But Bar and I don't want to have any more kids."

"But that's different."

"You've lost me, I'm afraid."

"You and Bar are past the age when you *could* be having kids. See? You don't need them any more."

"So we should have been using them back when we were first married? Is that the idea? Young people should use them?"

"Sure, son. Young people. Young people of a, well, a certain sort. Not you and Bar. The other sort."

"What other sort?"

"Poor folks. People with no money and no brains."

"Oh." The light's coming on now. Sort of a dimmer switch light. "I get it. We've got money, so we don't need to use condoms."

"That's right, son."

"And brains? We've got brains, too, right?"

"Absolutely." Another quick glance at Dad. "You Bushes are smart as whips."

"And that means no condoms."

"Right."

"If you've got money and you've got brains, you can just stick your willie in there any way you want. But if you're poor and stupid, you've got to cover it up."

"Well, uh ... right, son. In principle. We'll need to work on your technique a little, maybe."

"My technique?"

"Your presentation. The way you talk about it to the public."

"Oh. Okay."

But when I go home that night and tell Bar all about my new job and what it will entail, her eyes crinkle up with amusement.

"You, Poppy?"

"Me, Bar. Who else?"

"You're going to teach people about condoms?"

"What's a condom, Mommy?"

Little Dorothy walks by just then, of course.

We're standing by the railing upstairs, where the kids have to walk by us to get from their bedrooms to the bathroom. Not the best place to have this discussion.

"Nothing, sweetie. Grownup talk."

"You guys never tell me anything." Dorothy's nine. Sometimes, I can't believe the way she talks to us. I would never have dreamed of talking to my mother like that.

I sidestraddle Bar's question.

"I'm going to Congress, Bar. Like my father before me."

"Your father was never in Congress, Poppy."

"I mean, politics like my father before me. He was President. I'll be in Congress."

"Talking about condoms." Dorothy's gone.

"That's right. General Draper explained it all to me. My dad was there, too."

"Do you even know what a condom *looks* like, Poppy?"

My mind goes blank for a moment. What's she trying to get at, exactly, here?

"Sure. Sort of."

"Do you know what you *do* with one?"

"No, but General Draper is going to work with me on my technique."

"I'll just bet he is!" She presses two fingers hard to her lips. Her fingers go white with the effort. It looks like her eyes're going to burst wide open.

"Of course he is, Bar. If he promised to, he will."

"He'll take you in hand, will he?" She's sort of gasping now, with her shoulders hunched.

"He already has. He has me well in hand."

A weird, stifled giggle escapes. "You know, Poppy ... "

"What, Bar?"

"You know what they're going to call you in Congress?"

I wrack my brains for a minute.

"Uh ... no. Poppy?"

"Rubbers!" she cries. "They're going to call you *Rubbers*!"

And with that, it all comes pouring out. That breaks the camel's back, and she cascades into pails of laughter. Grails of laughter. Which, in retrospent, I don't find so funny, now. Because that's what they do call me. Rubbers. It's almost as if Bar went around to the Congressmen and told them to call me that. But of course, she didn't. Still, it rankers, a little. That she said that. It bothered me at the time a bit, too. And it bothers me even more now. Rubbers!

Documents

Texas Recognizes Mormon Independence
(Houston Chronicle, May 6, 1969)

Saying that the government approved of the high moral standards of the Church of Jesus Christ of Latter Day Saints, although not its doctrines, President Nixon today declared that he would recognize the new "Republic of Moronica," formerly the U.S. State of Utah.

"I don't believe in their specific doctrine, of course, but I do like their references to Jesus, and of course, we generally approve of nations founded on Christian religious principles," the President said. "And, naturally, it is in our interests to recognize American states that secede from the union, especially dry and fish-free states like Utah. We wish them well, and only hope that one day good old Southern Baptist doctrine will replace some of this foolishness they espouse."

Speaking from Salt Lake City, President Brigham Bob Smith thanked Texas for its support. "Even if they are heathen, we appreciate their strict sense of morality and justice."

Mormons from all over Texas and the U.S., and even foreign countries, have been moving to the new Moronican Republic in droves, looking for a better life and the legal right to marry as many pubescent girls as they want.

Skeeter Stubbins Sentence Commuted
(Crime Report, June 1, 1969)

The capital case of Skeeter Stubbins took a surprising turn yesterday when the controversial death sentence for the developmentally handicapped thirteen-year-old boy for possession of a can of insecticide and intent to slaughter insects was commuted to life in an institution.

With the help of his mother and two little friends, Skeeter managed to convey to authorities that the can didn't actually contain Raid. The judge in the case, the Honorable Rupert "Grin" N. Barrett, perhaps belatedly ordered a forensic examination, which showed that the substance sprayed by the can was actually not an insecticide at all but a deodorant. Apparently, Skeeter was using the can to *pretend* to kill insects, in a childish game that, the judge opined in his statement commuting the death sentence, boded ill for the boy's and his family's future.

Accordingly, by order of the court, Skeeter was removed from his family and remanded indefinitely to the Waco Hospital for the Criminally Insane. His parents were sentenced to six years at hard labor, and all of their assets were confiscated.

9

National Guard

(Dubya, June 13, 1969)

"You lucky *fuck*," Fly shoats, his eyes kind of like wide open.

"Hey," I say moderastly, "it ain't nothin'."

Heads turn all over the officers' club.

"What," Chubby says.

"What," Road says.

"What," Ding says.

"It's nothin', fellas," I say. "Go back to bidnis."

Bidnis is drinkin' beer and feedin' the jukebox and hittin' on the ladies. They bus these ladies in from all over the fucking country, seems like. Nice girls, most of 'em. Nobody you'd want to marry, natch. They're mostly just girls with tits. Some of the guys fuck 'em, but they always wear a raincoat, cuz the girls are pretty rainy. Somehow, I just never quite feel like it. It just don't seem worth it, to me. I don't know why.

These are all boys from good families. It's like a country club here. Fact, I know all these guys from the Houston and River Oaks country clubs. All the best families in Texas send their sons to this outfit. Sure beats getting your ass shot off in Vietnam, the guys always say. I don't say that. Fact, it makes me sorta uneasy when they say it, I don't know why. I ain't much on psychoanalyzizing myself, or nothin'. So. But.

Thing is, my dad practically got his ass shot off in Japan. And I could practically get mine shot off here in Galveston. I could. You know, like, what if. The Russians could attack

Texas through the Gulf of Texaco, and *then* we'd have a fucking mess on our hands, boy. Then it'd be up to us. Then it'd
be just the Fighter Wing of the Texas National Guard between
the good people of Texas and the total distraction of their
way of life. Then they wouldn't fucking be joking about the
Champagne Unit. Nobody would. No fucking way.

Junk says his dad got me in. Junk is John Adger. Junk and
I grew up together on the mean streets of Midland. Played on
the same Little League teams, swam in the same pools, and
belonged to the same clubs. The Adgers moved to Houston
around the same time we did. Junk says his dad, Mr. Adger,
called Speaker of the House Ben Barnes and asked him to put
me at the top of the wailing list. Five hunnerd guys were lined
up trying to get in here, and old man Barnes put me at the
top. So Junk says. I don't know, personably. I had to take a
really hard fucking test to get in. Pilot amplitude. I scored
pretty fucking good on that, too. Twenty-fifth percentile,
that's no mean fleet. I mean, that's nothing to fucking sleaze
at. They wouldn't of taken me if I hadn't of scored so high.
They wouldn't of given me an onomatic concussion of second
lieutenant and assumed me to flight school. I mean, it's usually only guys who were in ROTC in college that get that sort
of remisson. ROTC or else Air Force expedience. But because I
got that great grade on the altitude test, they shot me right in
ahead of the rest. They must of scored really low, those other
five hunnerd guys. Like, in the eightieth or ninetieth percentile, somewhere way down there. The hunnerd-and-twentieth,
or something. They do that badly, they probably deserve to
get their asses shot off in Vietnam.

"How's he a lucky fuck?" Ding says to Fly.

"Cuz he was born with a silver dick in his mouth," Road
says.

"Oh ho ho," I say, pretembling to sludge him hard in the
gut and then clotty chop him on the neck, "you fucker."

"Any a you flyboys wanna dance," some blonde babe says,

pushing herself into our little circle. Fly turns to her with a big smile, but Ding says no way, puts his arm around her tummy from behind, and won't let her go.

"Hold on, there, sweetheart," he says. "We got a little matter to settle here."

She don't seem to be too unhappy there in his arms. She puts her hands on his arms and smuddles up into his neck.

"He's got a date," Fly says.

"A date!" Chubby yells. "Even I can't get one of those!"

"A date?" Ding says, bending around to google at the girl sort of humorantly. "*That's* what this is all about? A fucking date? Where y'all goin', bowling?"

"Roller-skating?"

"Horse back riding?"

"The movies?"

"The symphony?"

"The opera?"

"Ballet?"

"Strip club?"

"Jazz club?"

"Chess club?"

"Girl Scout jamboree?"

"Friday night bingo?"

"Saturday night dinner at the old folks' home?"

"Sunday School picnic?"

"Monday Night Football?"

"Tuesday Welding?"

"What the fuck is Tuesday welding, you stupid fuck?"

"Oh, you don't get it, and *I'm* the stupid fuck."

"Damn right, you're the stupid fuck, you stupid fuck."

The girl in Ding's arms has been watching this with big eyes. I'm the guy leaning back against the bar, slurping his beer with a kind of zombastic smile. Like, *whatever, whatever, whatever*. This is how we spend most evenings, you wanna know the truth. Probably not all that different from how guys spend their evenings in Vietnam, what do you wanna bet. Standing around the officers' club shooting the shit.

"It's a date," Fly says, "in Houston."

"In Houston!" the guys yell.

"Well, that's different!"

"That's a whole nother story!"

"That's a horse of a different color!"

"Man, and here I thought it was just some date in *Galveston*. But no, it's in *Houston*!"

"You get back, you better tell us all about Houston," Ding says. "Boy, oh boy, the big city. The bright lights. You lucky fuck."

"I heard they got paved streets up in Houston," Chub says.

"Traffic lights," Road says.

"Skyscrapers," Fly says.

"Hookers," the girl puts in.

"Oh ho!" the guys yell, looking at her sorta in supplies. "Hookers!"

"Drug dealers!"

"Antiwar protesters!"

"Hippies!"

"Enemies of the state!"

"Exhibitionists!"

"Inhibitionists!"

"Prohibitionists!"

"The date," Fly tries to throw in, "the date," he says again, but nobody's listening, they're all way into this thing about Houston, "the fucking *date*," he yells, and finally they all stop and look at him, "is with fucking Tricia Nixon."

Sudden silence. The guys are expressed. Exprinted.

"Some girl, probably," Ding says slowly, "with the same name as the President's daughter."

"Some welder's daughter," Chubby says.

"Tuesday welder's daughter," Road says.

But they can't get a new head of spam up. They're really expressed.

"So, but," Ding says finally, "Bush," he says, "come on," he says, "fess up," he says: "you fuckin' her?"

"I, uh—"

"You givin' her the old hunnerd-percent-prime-Texas-beef injection?"

"You dicking Dick's daughter?"

"You stickin' little Bush up her bush?"

This don't work either, hardly. The guys can't joke about Tricia Nixon. I mean, she's the *President's daughter*. That's like practically holly.

"Guys, guys," I say finally, sorta laughing. "I'll tell ya all about it."

"Tell us!"

"Tell us all about it!"

"Tell us already, goddammit!"

"I've never met her."

"You what!"

"You lying fuck!"

"I've never once in my life crapped eyes on her."

"Get the fuck outta here."

"Get the fuck outta Dodge."

"Go peddle your sick lies to somebody who'll believe 'em."

"God's truth, boys," I say. "I've never met her. This is as big a surprise to you as it is to me."

"So you're trying to tell us," Ding says, "that President Nixon is sitting around one day in his office, and little Tricia comes running in in tears. 'Daddy, Daddy, I'm so *miserable!*' 'What's the problem, baby girl?' Dick says." Ding does a fair impressario of Dick Nixon. "'Daddy,' Tricia says, 'I don't have a *date!*' 'No date, huh,' Dick says. 'Well, I hear Congressman George Bush has a handsome, dashing son in the Fighter Wing of the Texas National Guard, down there in Galveston. Maybe I could get him to take you out.'"

"Something like that," I say, biting at a hangnail.

"Is it true what they say," Chub says, "that President Nixon calls your dad 'Rubbers'?"

"No," I say sorta hotly, "it's not true."

"Is it true, then," Ding says, "that you're not taking a rubber along on your date with the President's daughter?"

"What's true," I say, "is that you guys are full of shit."

"I heard there's something a little strange about her," Fly says.

"Who?"

"Tricia Nixon, you dim bulb."

"What?"

"That she's, like, I don't know, covered with hair or something."

"What, like a monkey?"

"No, like an insect."

"Cool. Bush here could be boning a bug."

"Forget the raincoat, Bush; take a can of Raid."

"That's a controlled semblance!" I yell. "Somulence!"

"Take her," Ding says, but he thinks he's so funny he can't get it all out at once, "take her, Bush," he says again, "to a roach motel."

"You guys are as funny as a clutch," I say, and drown my beer.

So, but, what, you probably want to know how the date went, right?

It wasn't much. The President sent a limousine for me. I wore a black tux. They took me right to the President's Mansion. I hadn't been there since Grandpa Pres was President. Back when I was about fourteen. Dad met the car and walked me in to see the president.

"So, George," he said.

"So, Mr. President," I said.

"Thanks for doing this for me," he said.

"No problem," I said. "Whatever I can do to search my country."

"Fucking chip off the old block," he said, turning to geeze up at Dad, "ain't he, Poppy?"

"Absotively, Mr. President," Dad said.

"Here's the deal, George," the President said. "You take her to the dance. You dance with her. You buy her a drink or two. You make polite chitchat with her. You bring her home. That's it. You got it?"

"I got it, Mr. President," I said, and snapped off a smark saluke.

"Good boy," he said. "Just remember," he added, with a kind of ho-ho snurk, "don't do anything I wouldn't do."

"I won't," I promised.

And he walked to the door to have somebody go get Tricia. While he was doing that, Dad leaned over and whispered in my ear.

"You know what he means by not doing anything he wouldn't do, right?"

"Uh, not exactly, Dad."

"He means sex."

I was sort of socked. Soxed. I mean, just plain soccoed. "He wants me to have sex with his *daughter*?" I gashed. I mean, wouldn't that be almost insectuous? I mean, if he'd do it too?

"No, no," Dad said, shooshing me. "He *doesn't* want you to have sex with her."

"Oh," I said. I was releafed. I mean, what if she did have bug hairs all over her?

But then she came in, and she looked pretty normal in a white lacey dress and a white purse. I took her to the dance. Well. You know. The limo driver took us. But I went with her. I walked across the floor to our table with her.

And the weird thing? There was fucking *fish* all over the floor by our table. Can you fleature that? Live fish. Just flapping around down there.

"What the fuck?" I said.

"What?" Tricia said.

"Well, Tricia McFisha," I said, "maybe you can tell me what all these fucking *fish* are doing all over the place in here, hmm?"

"I don't know what you're talking about," she said.

And here's another weird thing: I kicked at one of the fish, and it tried to jump up at me. Yes, it did. The fucker. Tried to nose right into my pocket. I batted the goddamn thing away, and it landed on somebody else's table. Prackly on their plate. They looked over at me all huffy, but I just looked back at them like, *hey, I didn't bring these fucking fish in here.* 'Cause I didn't. It's that simple.

Around then, a waiter noticed all the fish and called for a busboy, and pretty soon, they had 'em all rounded up and herded out. Busboy was some kinda haremist or something. I mean, like a academian, or a commiedemian. A mocker, or a mockic. A funny guy. You know, the guy who's always trying to make you laugh, and shit. 'Cause while he was taking the fish away in this big plastic dish bun, he ducked his head and made this tiny little fish voice, said, "Don't marry her, Dubya! Don't marry her! She's got bug hairs all over her!"

I whippled around when I heard *that*, obviously. But the guy was all, *hey, it wasn't me.* We both looked around for who it could of been, but it had to of been him, I'm telling you.

So but then, you know, after we sat down, I had to ask Tricia. "Hey, Trish, no offense, but you don't have hairs all over you, do you? You know, like a bug? I mean, the guys said you did, but I didn't believe them."

She algaed. I mean, she said I was right. No hairs, I mean. And then she sorta started looking away a lot, and not wanting to talk much. So maybe, I don't know, maybe the guys were really right? Or something? I mean, it was obviantly *some* sort of spore slot for her. And then she wanted to go home, so we went out and got in the car and went home. And that was my date with Tricia Nixon.

The guys, of course, won't let me forget about it for months after.

"Hey, Bush, how's Fish?"

"Hey, Bush, how's Dick's daughter?"

Or: "Hey, Bush, how's Bug Hair?"

They never do believe me when I said she was pretty much a normal girl, no bug hairs that I could see. They just can't give it a rest. I think there's something servicely wrong with those guys.

Documents

Memo to Richard Nixon re: Skipjack LaTuna
(June 13, 1970)

Dick,

Rumor's going around that Skipjack LaTuna has a human girlfriend. Apparently, he's got a room-sized tank that they swim around in buck-naked. We're checking on it, but all we've been able to dig up so far is that she's from Midland. Possibly connected to Poppy Bush? Maybe be careful what you say around him.

Seems to me there's a danger and an opportunity here. The girl may be a way the Lincolnites are trying to get to us, but she may just be a girl, in which case, we might could turn her, make her an asset for our side.

—Howard

New Police Gear Causing Skin Problems and Mental Disturbances
Officials at a Loss to Explain, but Recall All Gear Manufactured at Waco Plant
(Texas News Roundup, September 19, 1971)

Minutes after donning his brand-new raincoat slicker during a freak electrical storm in Houston, Officer Dale Throbin began having problems.

"It was like someone had poured a jar of fire ants on me," he told reporters. "And then I began to feel like I was drowning. I mean, like I was really underwater. And by the time they got me to the hospital, all I could do was repeat the text of the Emancipation Proclamation over and over. And I don't even *know* the text of the Emancipation Proclamation. Something by a U.S. President, they tell me."

Doctors are unable to explain the incident, but similar incidents in Dallas and Austin have caused them to point the finger at the new slickers and rucksacks given to police this week.

"We had seventy more incidents in Houston and eighty in Dallas," said Dr. Homekin Plant of the Texas Department of Hygiene, "and we're not sure how many in Austin. All much like the incident with Officer Throbin. All of the incidents occurred shortly after the officer used a new raincoat or stashed something in a new rucksack. And all of this gear was manufactured at the Waco Defense Gear Company plant."

Officials of the TDH have closed the plant while an investigation is underway, and all of the gear has been recalled.

In Dallas, two officers directing traffic around an accident during a thunderstorm had just put on their new slickers when they fell to the ground and began splashing in the puddles in the road, squeaking and squealing and clapping their hands. Subdued, sedated, and taken to the hospital, they were found to have developed gross thickening of the skin, along with a pronounced "slickness" to the derma.

In Austin, a D.A.R.E. officer had just filled his rucksack with JUST SAY NO pencils when he began breaking out in scales. "They looked just like scales on a fish, growing all up and down my arms," he said. "And all I could think of was herring. How good a nice raw herring would taste. I went to the market, and, ummm, I guess I made a fool of myself in the fresh fish section. I don't know what came over me."

"We aren't any closer to an explanation yet, but the gear does appear to be made of a highly unusual kind of leather," Dr. Plant told reporters. "When we find out what sort of hides these are, we may be able to offer some conclusions."

10

United Nations

(Poppy, December 7, 1971)

6:59 a.m. Eyes blink open. Glance over at the alarm clock. Ten seconds till it goes off. Count down: Ten, nine, eight, seven, six, five, four, three, two, one. Buzzzz. Old Mr. Regular. Slap the button and bounce up out of bed. I'm the Republic of Texas' Ambassador to the United Nations. I'm an important person. Important matters await my attention. No time to waste sleeping late. Bar is a huge lump under the covers, unmoving. Bar-Bar-Uh.

7:01 a.m. Check my reflection in the bathroom mirror. "Handsome and trim at forty-seven," the papers said when I got this job. Getting kind of craggy. Not a young man. Entstinguished. Statesmanlite. Statesmanrite. Statesrightsman. Smooth my hair down with my hands. Fine hair, very fine. Wispy. Windswept.

7:05 a.m. Move my bowels. Into the water. They still use water in their toilets up here in the United States. I drop a FishAway pellet into the water before I sit down, of course. Can't be too carefreeful. You just can't. Not where I'm sitting. Here in our beautiful luxury apartment on the forty-second floor of the Waldorf Towers. Our enemies would love nothing more than to snatch me right down the drain. The poops drop out of my white bum. Bum. The British say bum. Like the sound of that, bum. I'm not a bum, but I've got one. Wum. Got wum. That almost rhymes.

7:12 a.m. Change into my exercise togs. Sky blue. Fairy blue. Not very manly. Not a fairy, though. A real man. A man's man. He-man. Oilman.

7:15 a.m. Go into the exercise room. Turn on *Good Morning, America*. Climb up on my exercycle. Ride like the wind for the twelve minutes that the program lasts. Like the wind. The fan's cheating, maybe. No wind in here otherwise. Need it, though, to dry my perspication. Hair sticks to my head if I don't.

7:30 a.m. Shower. Close my eyes, imagine someone else's hand soaping me up down there, sproing, somebody's standing up today. December 1971, eight years now since Rafael. Tried to be good. Mostly tried. Tried to save appearances. Don't want any trouble. Bar's kind of big in front, all those babies, hardly feel anything down there. Never asked her about the back; wouldn't be right, wouldn't be legal. Give her wum in the bum. Wide, white, pasty bum. Crinkly stuff, celloplane, cellophane, celluphone. Getting soft now, thinking about Bar. Twenty-five years.

7:39 a.m. Dry off. Dress. Black socks, gartled. White long-sleeve shirt. Gray suit pants. Maroon tie. Yale tie-clip. Monogrammed cuff-links. B B. Bush Bush. Barbara Bush. Bilder Berg. Gray suit coat.

7:45 a.m. Greet Consuela in the dining room. She's Cuban. Her English ain't great, but there's a lot of it. Coffee, toast and jam, fried egg sunny side up, two slices of bacon. We found her through friends. You know how that goes. Somebody knows somebody who knows somebody who needs a job; cheap, reliable, will keep her mouth shut. In this case, Ted Shackley pouched for her personally. And he should know. Blond ghost. Boo.

7:53 a.m. Brush teeth. Kiss Bar on the warm, wrinkly forehead. "Mmm," she says, and goes right on sleeping. Not a morning person, Bar. Kids still asleep, too. Consuela and I are the only ones that get up in the morning.

7:56 a.m. Overcoat. Briefcase. Out the door. Elevator down to the lobby. Out the devolving doors to the street. Uniformed Negro, livery, very livery, liver makes your skin purple, smiles with big white teeth and says, "Your car is right over here, Mr. Bush." Lots more Negroes up here in the United States than back home in Texas. Parents didn't use rubbers. U.S. is way behind us in sterilization. World leaders. Keeping the world safe for despocracy.

8:00 a.m. Negro boy opens car door for me to slide in. Slip him a dollar bill. Nice boy. "How are you this morning, Mr. Bush?" My driver. What's his name. John, or Jim, or Jumbo, or something. "Just fine, thanks." At least he's white. At least he's always on time. Negroes don't believe in clocks. Just don't believe in them.

8:09 a.m. Stuck in traffic. Down the hill to Turtle Bay. Like that name, Turtle Bay. Never been to the bay, never saw any turtles. They're there, though; you can bet on that. West River. Something like that. Hobson's River. Liberals up here care more about turtles than the bottom line. Save the turtles! Bring the turtles back to Turtle Bay! Put the fish back in fish sticks! Bankrupt three hundred businesses!

8:13 a.m. Arrive at the U.N. Glass palace, they call it. Because it's mostly glass, and it looks like a palace. Stride in through the front doors. U.N. ambassador. Republic of Texas Ambassador to the United Nations. Up to the Texas mission.

"Morning, Mr. Bush. Here's your overnight cable traffic." "Thank you, Mrs. Smith. That's a particularly attractive dress you're wearing today." "Why thank you, Mr. Bush." Doesn't hurt to butter up the help a little. "Mr. Lais is waiting in your office." "Great. Traffic slowed me up this morning." "Isn't it awful?" "It certainly is." I bet nobody drives her to Turtle Bay every morning. She probably takes the bus.

8:18 a.m. Conference with Tom Lais, my executive assistant. We go through the day together. Dick's call at ten. Lunch with the ambassador of Burundi at noon. They're on board with us on Taiwan. Supposed to keep pushing for them, for Taiwan, even though Dick and Henry are still secretly pulling strings for Beijing. I'm their guy on the Taiwan thing. I'm part of the game plan. I fight to keep Taiwan in the Security Council so they can say we made a decent effort for the R.O.C. Didn't let our little slant-eyed friends down. Well, we did. Well, not yet. But we will. We're letting them down as we speak. But we want to make it look like we're doing our best to keep them in. I do whatever Dick and Henry tell me to do. Of course. Always. That's my job. Back in the spring, when I was first posted here, I made some comment to the press about the Sauds that hadn't been fed to me by Houston. Sods. Joe Sisco was on the horn to me an hour later. On the horn, love that phrase. Horn. Rhino horn. Horny rhino. Joseph Sisco, one of Henry's boys. Formerly of Kissinger Associates, now Assistant Secretary of State for Middle Eastern Affairs. Affairs, sounds like Joe's job is to stand around while Henry has affairs with Muslim women. Guides his dick in, calls out encouragement. "You don't speak for the Texas government on the Middle East," Joe yelled at me, "I speak for the Texas government on the Middle East, I'll do the talking, you got that? And if there's any leaking to be done, I'll do the leaking, too." I'm a cabinet officer, he's a fucking assistant secretary, and he tells me what to do. I do it, though. Of course I do. Joe moves his mouth, and Henry's voice comes out. Joe rolls up on one cheek, and Henry lets out a fart. Joe fucks the Middle East with Henry's Dick. It was something Uncle Dogsbody told me, that thing I blurkaed out about the Sauds, something about his colleagues over there, the bin Soddens. Ladens. Whole lada love. Whole lada bugs. From Atlantis, there. Tall, gray fuckers, clack clack. Beetles everywhere. Dad says I should be used to them by now. Henry wants to recognize Beijing. Dick's drunk most of the time; he does whatever Henry wants. Henry's pretty much running things in Houston. Henry was in Beijing secretly back in July and again unsecretly month before last. But Henry wants me to support Taipei. Two Chinas. "I don't think we have to go through the agony of whether the Republic of China will accept or whether Beijing will accept," I told reporters last month. "Let the United Nations, for a change, do something that really does face up to reality and then let that decision be made by the parties involved." Thought that came off nicely. Face up to reality for a change. Do something for a change that really does, for a change, face up to reality. The parties involved. I'm really starting to get the hang of this dipsomatic rhetoric. Taipei and Beijing don't want two Chinas. Dick and Henry don't want two Chinas. It's just dimplomacy.

9:00 a.m. Meeting with Chris and Tap. Deputy Ambassadors Christopher Phillips and W. Tapley Bennett of the State Department. We talk about Taiwan a little, but mostly Pakistan. Think I've got a handle on this crisis now. Yahya Kahn is our boy. He's Dick's personal friend, so that's that. Last year, outside agitators came in and started pushing for free fish. Free elections. Vote fish. Fin fish. It was all those damned fish-loving East Pakistanis' doing. Those Bengals. Bengal Tiger fish. Bengal Bengal. There's some kind of League over there, some kind of Guppy League or something. They want to break off. Break away. Nasty, nasty people. We don't like those people over there. Those Bengals. We like Islamabad. Islamabad, very bad. Well, actually very good. Islam is bad, but Islamabad is good. We like Yahya Kahn. Get your Yahyas out. That's what the Guppy League is saying. Sheik Mujibur Rahman. Funny names over there. Moojee Boor. Yah Yah. Look how much solider and seriouser our names are over here: Richard Nixon, Henry Kissinger, George Bush. Solid. So they had the election, and the Guppy League won lots of seats in the national assembly over there in the East. Most of them, I guess. Almost all of them. This was a very bad thing, I'm not exactly clear why, I guess because the Guppy League is bad and Yahya Kahn is good, and anything the Guppy League does that makes Yahya Kahn look bad is llasa apso bad. So Yahya Kahn decided to stamp out the Guppy Cup, or whatever it's called. The Guppy Club. Stamp it right out. Arrest the man with the silly name and stamp out his organization. I would have done the same thing. Anybody would. No reason why a leader who believes he's doing the right thing should tolerate that kind of uppityness, my dad always says. Yahya Kahn just did the Texan thing, the patriotic thing. He maintained order. He maintained respect for the proper authorities. And okay, maybe his army went a little overboard. Killed a few civilians, too. Maybe a million. Maybe three million. Somewhere in there. Ballpark figure. I have a cable this morning from somebody over there, some embassy guy, saying he saw West Pakistani soldiers setting fire to a women's dormitory at the University of Dacca and machine-gunning the guppies down as they came out. The girls, I mean. Rat-a-tat-a-tat. Students. Probably intellectual types, all agitating for the Guppy League. Probably shacking up with boy intellectual Guppy types and having babies and doing drugs. Growing gills. Swimming with dolphins. Good riddance. Ten million refugees swarming over into India. So what, they were probably the worst sort anyway. Rabble-rousers, connivers. Welfare moms and their out-of-control litters. They're all Negroes, of course, what did you expect. They've got way too many people over there, anyway. Not enough food. Survival of the fittest. They're starving in Bengalia. The refugees are starving in India. The Indians themselves are starving. Starve, starve, starve. Sacred fish. For a fish may be somebody's muhhhhh-ther. Gotta bring those numbers down somehow. No condoms, of course. No scarilization. Kill a few millions, maybe fewer will starve. And anyway, Dick wrote to me in person, in his own hand: "George: Don't squeeze Yahya at this time. RN." Cherish that note. And so what if Yahya Khan sent air raids into India four days ago, trying to wipe out the Indian Air Force on the ground? Isn't that his right as an autoshopthalamous leader? To wipe out the enemy wherever he finds it? Them? It? And does that justify Indian aggression against Pakistan? Trying to take Bengalia away from them? Blockading their ports? Infiltrating their aquariums? Bringing the Russians into it, Indira Gandhi's buxom buddies? So three days ago, I spoke up in the General Assembly against Indian aggression and called for a session of hostilities. Secession of hospitalities. India has no call to go internatting into Pakistan's infernal affairs. Butting in. Sticking their nose in. Internatting. Like, internationally. I made a revulsion. Revolzed that everybody should just go home and let Yahya Kahn do what he has to do to maintain order in his own damn country! They're voting on it this afternoon. Then, just yesterday: India "recognizes" the independent state of Banglafish! The nerve! How can you recognize something that doesn't exist? Desh, I mean, of course. Bandaidesh. Bungalodesh. I sense some immunity in Chris and Tap as we go over this. Immunition. Immutiny. They don't like Yahya Kahn. They don't like Pakis! That's it, isn't it! They're somehow opposed to Dick and Henry's position in all this. They want us to take a more moderate stand, or even, Tap hints, come out *against* Pakistan. What can you expect? They're State Department stooges. Moe and Curly. Boink! They answer to their boss, Bill Rogers, who's against Pakistan. William Rogers. The Secretary of State. Bill is Dick's friend too, but Dick answers to Henry, and Henry says support Pakistan, so that's that. Nominally, I guess I should be under the Secretary of State's authority, too, but of course, everybody knows Henry's the real boss. "It's all," Tap says bitterly, "because back in sixty-nine, Nixon asked Yahya to be his fish-free channel to the Chinese. And now he doesn't even *need* a fish-free channel to the Chinese! Kissinger fucking flies *over* there practically every month. And they'll be on the Security Council in a week or two. There's a Chinese U.N. delegate in New York right this instant, stashed away in a terrarium, waiting for the final decision to let them in. Henry could fly up here and sit down with that guy. Instead he has to go on futzing around with some cheap Paki butcher." "That's not the only reason," Chris corrects him with some kind of adirondack *look*, "and you know it. Indira Gandhi's in bed with the Russians, Yahya with the Red Chinese. We've got to support Yahya so Kissinger can send the right message to Zhou that we're on their side." "And that justifies *genocide*?" "I'm not *defending* it for Christ's sake," Chris snaps. "Of course it doesn't justify genocide. But Kissinger doesn't care. It's all just geopolitics to him. 'Vhy iss it our business how zey govern zemselfs?' he keeps saying." " 'Zey' being the Pakistanis." "Right." "He'd damn well *make* it our business if Yahya started spouting Marxist ideas." "Of course he would." "Okay, so he doesn't care about genocide. Does he care about nuclear war? Does he care about Soviet missiles pointed at Houston?" "What Soviet missiles? What nuclear war?" "You don't think he's pushing the Soviet Union to the brink over this?" "Come on, the Soviets aren't going to bomb us over stupid little Pakistan." "They just signed a twenty-year friendship agreement with India yesterday!" "So, what, we've got friendship agreements with scads of countries, that doesn't mean we're going to start bombing people right and left over them." "Boys, boys," I say, feeling very uncular. "Come on. Enough already. We're not here to *make* policy. We're the mouthpieces of the people who make policy. Settle down for crikey's sake." After they leave, I jot down some notes on their remarks to pass on to Henry. He should know what his people are saying about him.

9:46 a.m. Run down the hall for a quick B.M. Dick's calling me in 15 minutes, and I've got an angry snarl in my large intentions. The row of toilets in their stalls gleams fishily. And me without my FishAway. I have to risk it, though. I trop my drowsers and sit tremblingly. I'm all exposed down there. I push hard but fast and can only push out three nasty little pellets. Practically goat turds. I feel all hot and prickly and red in the face from pushing. I pull up my pants with a little shover and go back to the office with a red, inflamed asshole, like somebody dragged thirty feet of hot bob-wire through there.

10 a.m. Back in the office for Dick's call. Some TBC news crew is in his office this morning. "A Day with the President" or some such. He's decided to use it to help fight the good fight against slackers who don't like Pakistan in this crisis. Not many are. I mean, do. The Western media are all against us. Most Western politicians are against us. They all say Pakistan is the aggressor, not India. Pakistan did the genocide thing, Pakistan invaded India, India's just defending herself. So it's kind of an impopular opinion, saying that India's the bad guy. Girl. But it's Henry's policy, so it's Dick's opinion, so it has to be mine too. We've settled on ten o'clock, which is right now. My phone is going to ring, and I'm going to pick it up. Mrs. Smith isn't going to answer first. It better be Dick, is all I've got to say.

10:06 a.m. The phone rings. It's Dick. "George!" he cries out, in his burberry public voice. Burbly. Bustly. Blustery. In private he calls me Poppy. "How's it going up there in New York?" "Just fine, Mr. President." In private I call him Dick. But this is television. You've got to follow proctolocol. "Listen," he says, "I've got some people in the office, here, so I can't talk long, but I wanted to give you a little pep talk on the situation over there in India and Pakistan. You've got to do what you can, all right?" "Absolutely, Mr. President." "More important than anything else now is to get the facts out with regard to what we've done, that we've worked for a political settlement, what we've done for the refugees and so forth and so on. If you see that some here in the Senate and House, for whatever reason, get out and misrepresent our opinions, I want you to hit it frontally, strongly, and toughly; is that clear? Just take the gloves off and crack it, because you know exactly what we've done, okay?" "Okay, Mr. President. Will do."

10:26 a.m. Alone for the moment. Time for reflectionism. Time to think it all through one more time. General Assembly meeting at 2. *My* revolution. Relovution. Relosution. And Dick's call. He calls *me* on TV. I'm the one. He didn't want to give me this job. He didn't want to give me any job. My dad's spies told him all about it. Told Dad, I mean. And Dad told me. Dad was pushing and pushing on Dick to give me something, Secretary of the Treasury, some big gooey plum. Some Cabinet post. Dick promised and promised but then hemmed and hauled. Dick owes my dad big. And Uncle Dogsbody. Uncle Dogsbody once said to my dad "Dick's my boy" and had a kind of softness in his voice that he doesn't have when he says that to me, or even my dad. I was starting to get the feeling that Dick didn't like me. But then Barry Goldwater crapped up on him. Cropped up. Chopped up. Chopped out. He was going to give Barry the U.N. ambassadorship, but Barry made some indiscrinct remark to the press about China, big in favor of Chiang Kai-shek, and Dick nixed him. Get it? Nixon nixed him. And I got the job. "All right, all right, goddammit," he resportedly snapped to Haldeman, "I'll give Bush the fucking U.N. ambassadorship, get that fucking Prescott offa my back." You can bet that got back to my dad, too. A few more times like that and Dick is going to be out, let me tell you that much right now. Imperched, or worse.

11:35 a.m. Mrs. Smith calls on the intercom. "Mr. Bush, shall I ring down and have your car brought round? It's almost time for your luncheon appointment with the ambassador of Burundi." "Yes, thanks, Mrs. Smith, that will be fine." Burundi. Burundi. Like the sound of that country's name. Burundi. All those oohs. Boo Roo 'n Dee. Boo Boo 'n Yogi. Muruned in Burundi. Straighten up my desk a little. Put on my overcoat. Smile at Mrs. Smith on the way out. Toodle-oondi.

11:44 a.m. Out the glassy front doors and into my car. The driver holds the door open for me. That's his job. I do my job and he does his. We zoom out into traffic and up the hill.

12:05 p.m. Arrive at Raffaele's. Nice little Italian place on 43rd. Quiet, friendly astrosphere. Good fulsome food. I mean it really fills you up. Filsome. I just like the place, is all. It's my kind of place. My kind of people. "Good afternoon, Mr. Bush. Good to see you again. Your usual table, sir?" "Yes, thanks, Luigi. I'm expecting the ambassador of Burundi for lunch today." "Yes, of course, Mr. Bush, I'll see to him personally." He walks me back, lays a menu on the table in front of me. "Your usual to drink, Mr. Bush?" "Yes, thanks, Luigi."

12:08 p.m. The waiter brings my gin and tonic. I sip it patiently, pretend to look through the menu. I already know what I want. I always have the same thing. Raffaele's Speziale. It's some kind of ravioli thing. There's meat inside the little noodle pillows.

12:15 p.m. A middle-aged white man with slicked-back hair and widow speaks slides into the chair opposite me with a Bloody Mary in hand. I'm pretty sure this isn't the ambassador of Burundi. He's probably an African. The ambassador, I mean. Not this person, who's clearly white. "I'm sorry," I say, "I'm—" "Poppy," he says, "I'm hurt. You don't recognize me?"

"Damn," I say. "George DeMohrenschildt. What on earth?" This is a real blaster from the plaster. It's been seven, eight years since I last saw him. "I don't use that name any more," he says. "Call me Guppy." "Guppy?" I gulp. "Like the fish," he explains with a hearty smile. Fish! I'm instantly on my gourd. He's never looked less like a count. I mean he never looks more like a count. A Polish or a Russian count. Sort of sardontic and superior. But good-hearted about his superiality. Middle-aged playboy, probably still swoops the ladies off their feet. Sloops. Slooms. Spoons the ladies. "I'm sort of expecting someone, Guppy," I say awkwardly. "I know, I know," he says easily, "the ambassador of Burundi. He'll be a little late. He told me to beg your forgiveness for his tardiness, said you should go ahead and eat without him. He'll catch up with you for dessert." "How'd you know I was meeting the ambassador of Burundi?" I say, confaffled. Confroggled. Combobbled. "I'm still plugged in, Poppy," he says with a wink. "And, well. I decided I'd stop by and give you a message from your uncle." "Uncle?" I think he must mean Uncle Herbie. "You know," he says, "the hairy one." He twimples a little. I'm still sort of nom de plussed. Uncle Herbie isn't hairy. "Hairy?" I start running through my uncles' faces in my mind, looking for beards and mustaches. Or maybe long hair. Not having much luck. "The hairy *man*," he says. All my uncles are men, but none of them are hairy. Hairiness doesn't exactly run in my family. He sighs, looks at his watch. "Your Uncle Dogsbody," he says finally. "Oh, *that* uncle," I say, but still feel a little confabulated, because Uncle Dogsbody isn't hairy either. "How is Uncle Dogsbody?" "Fine, fine," DeMohrenschildt says, "just fine. Keeping busy." "That's Uncle Dogsbody, all right," I say. "Always busy." "He wanted to send you a message about Henry Kissinger," he says. "Oh?" I ask. "What about Henry?" "He's—" But just then the waiter comes up to take our orders, and DeMohrenschildt clams up. I order my usual. DeMohrenschildt gets a ham on rye and a side order of creamed corn. Apple pie for dessert. I've never seen any of this on the menu. Hey, it's an Italian restaurant in New York, not a Texas diner. But DeMohrenschildt orders it, and the waiter doesn't say boo. Boo Burundi. Love that name. So round, so roond. Roondy. "So," he picks up where he left off, "what Uncle Dogsbody wanted me to tell you is that Kissinger is KGB." I'm in the middle of sipping my gin and tonic and spotter it a little. Sputter. Spatter. KGB? Henry? Why then—DeMohrenschildt must have seen the panic in my face because he reassures me, "No, no, don't worry, it's not what you think. He may be KGB, but he's still Dogsbody's boy. So it's okay." "He's one of Uncle Dogsbody's people?" I ask. I've been working with Henry all year and this is the first I'm hearing of it. "Of course," he says. "He's worked for the Rockefellers since the war. Who do you think the Rockefellers work for?" I nod glumly. "They found him in Germany back in the late thirties. Kid was running his own intelligence service. Ratting out Jews to the Nazis, it seemed to our people then, though it's likely he was playing some more complicated game. Mind games, power games. Henry Kissinger Is God games. All that recommended him highly to Allen Dulles, of course, who loved the Nazis and loved complicated intelligence games. Unofficial word in intel circles back then was his real dad was Dogsbody himself." I raise an eyebrow. "What," he laughs, "you thought the old man never got his rocks off?" My head is swimming. Like some kind of fish, maybe. Or a fishstick. "They helped him and his mom and dad escape to London, then to New York, then on to Houston. Got him into military intelligence for Texas during the war. Sent him back into Germany as an 'interpreter.' He did interpret, of course, but his main job was army counterintelligence. He stayed on there after, too, with the occupation forces. Driving General Draper's car. That's when he was recruited by the KGB." "The KGB," I repeat, a little doubliously. "The one over there in Russia, you mean, right?" He smiles. "Do you know of any other? He was recruited to a special homosexual espionage cell called ODRA. His code name was Colonel Bor." "Mujibor?" I say jewiciously. Guppy blinks. "No, Poppy," he says. "Colonel Bor. Pay attention." I nod, trying not to brush. Frush. Turn all red in the face, I mean. "After the war," Guppy continues, "Dulles got him into the OPC, Office of Policy Coordination, whose whole purpose was to recruit ex-Nazi 'freedom fighters' for American intelligence against the Soviet Union. Perfect set-up for Kissinger, of course, who always loved to play both sides against the middle." I can't get over this. Homosexual? Affairs with Muslim boys? Doesn't KGB mean that Henry's the enery? Emery? Emeny? Henry has always talked like the Soviet Union's the number one bad guy in the world today. That's why we're supporting Pakistan against India, because Pakistan's on Red China's side and India's on the Russians' side. We've got to support Red China against the Soviet Union. The Red Chinese are bad but the Russians are worse. Balance of power. America and Texas and Western Europe and Red China against the Russians. Just like it was us and America and Western Europe and the Soviet Union against the Nazis and the Fascists, back in World War II. Balance of power. Guppy's been watching me sorting it all out. "Look," he says, "don't let it bother you. Really. Put it out of your mind. You're working at the top level now, Poppy. You have to stop thinking in petty little us vs. them terms. Communism vs. capitalism. Freedom vs. dictatorship. Bugs vs. fish. That's all for show. Really. All just part of the game." "The game?" "Sure. The Cold War. The Take Over The World game." "But," I say, "we're playing that game. Right, Guppy? We're trying to win that game. We're working with the U.S. and Western Europe to win that game." "Sure," he says airily. "Why not? Of course we're playing it. And playing it means playing to win. But the real action is *behind* the game." "Behind it?" "Absolutely. Think about it. Suppose the Soviet Union actually won the game. Or Red China. Suppose they won the game and there was no action going on behind the game. Then the big boys on our side would have nothing, right?" "Right," I say, slowly. "And," he says, "suppose we won. Where would the big boys on *their* side be?" "They'd be nobodies," I say. "They'd be poor, or in jail. Or dead." "Exactly. And nobody wants that." "They don't?" "Of course not. Well, at least the big boys that really run things don't. No matter what happens in the Cold War, they want to be in a position to keep running things from behind the scenes." "I see." "Just like at the end of World War II. The Nazi front faces went down, of course. The politicians. They had to. Politicians are part of the game. But the real powers survived, and got richer and more powerful. The financiers, the spymasters. That was Allen Dulles's job, making sure all the really important people got out and were able to resume their activities somewhere else. Same thing would happen if the Soviet Union went down. The top Communist leaders would be out on their ears, yesterday's news. The real movers and shakers would be primed to buy up major industries, services, and communication networks, and would become rich beyond their wildest dreams. They'd know it was coming and have all their ducks in a row. They'd have their Swiss bank accounts and their Western backers and would snap up the country in a month or two. So," he concludes sort of grandly, "we work together. Everybody does. The top people in every country that matters, including the Soviet Union and Red China. We've got top people working for them, they've got top people working for us. It has to be that way, or major changes would take the other players by surprise." "But," I say, feeling like maybe I'm protesting too much on this thing, but I can't help it, it still doesn't make sense to me, "isn't that sort of the fun of ruining a game? Doesn't that sort of ruin the fun, is what I mean? Not being surprised, not having to deal with surprise?" He laughs sort of contentiously. Contemptatiously. Contempestuously. Contretemptuously. "Put it this way, Poppy. Back when you were a kid playing games out in your yard, there outside of

Houston, what was the most important thing of all?" "Winning," I say promptly. "Exactly," he says in a praisy sort of voice, like he's the teacher and I'm his star pupus. "Winning. Not having fun, not dealing with surprises, not enjoying the outdoor air or the physical exercise, or any of that other stuff. Winning. Period. And that means not losing. Not losing, Poppy, no matter what. So," he shrugs, "you know. You do what you have to do to win." Our food comes. We dig in. I keep milling over what he's told me. "But," I say after a few forkfuls of the Speziale, "not losing no matter what means that you'd have to, I don't know, rig the game or something, right? If you're playing teams, you'd have to pay somebody on the other side to play badly, or something, so you'd be sure and win." "Now you're getting it, Poppy," he beams. "But isn't that *cheating*?" I say, feeling sort of a guess. Guest. Gassed. My mother was all for winning, but death on cheating. "In a way, sure," he agrees. "But think of it this way. You're playing two games at once. One for real, one for show. You're in a play, right? You're one of the actors. And there's a game in the play." "What kind of game?" "Say, a baseball game. Say it's some sort of big outdoor theater, and they have a whole baseball game as part of the play. You with me so far?" "Sure." I'm thinking, what a great play that would be. But I bet they couldn't find an outdoor theater big enough for it here in New York. Unless they held it at Yankee Stadium. Maybe then? "And you're only playing that baseball game as an actor. Right? So that, when the script says you have to cheat, you have to rig the game, it's not really you cheating, right? It's the character you're playing. It's Shoeless Joe, or somebody." "Who?" "Never mind. A character in the play." "Oh." "Your role requires your character to cheat. It's not you cheating. Follow me?" "I guess so." "Okay, now say you and the rest of the cast have a little side bet going. Whoever gets the most applause wins the pot. And that's the real game. That's the one you're really playing. The baseball game, that's just the play, the drama, the imaginary action. The one behind the scenes is reality. That's the one you don't cheat at." "I see," I say. And I think I do. It's starting to look a little clearer to me now. "But what if," I say, "what if there's a lot of money in that pot. You wouldn't want to lose *that*, would you? You'd want to make sure you did everything possible not to lose the pot, right?" DeMohrenschildt is grinning now. "Right," he says. "Go on." "Well, wouldn't it be worth your while to tell all your friends to go sit in the audience and applaud for you like mad? That way you'd win the pot." "Good thinking, Poppy," he says. It seems to me like I've just gone up in his estigration. "Except," he says, "what if all the other actors are doing the same thing?" "What, filling the audience with their friends?" "Right." "Well," I say, "then you'd need to make sure you knew in advance which members of the audience were friends of the other actors, and, well, make something happen to them." "Happen?" he asks, maybe a little disingeniously. "Sure," I say. "Like say they all sat in one part of the bleachers and that section were to collapse under them, and they all died. Or even just had to go to the hospital with broken legs and punctured lungs and stuff. Then your friends would cheer the most and you'd win." "But that's cheating, isn't it Poppy?" "I guess. Sure, why not. But if everybody else is cheating too?" "Exactly," he smiles. "So," he says then in a let-me-get-this-straight tone, "what you're saying is that there can be several different levels of play-acting, and several levels of game-playing, and therefore also several levels of cheating. Right?" *Is* that what I'm saying? "I guess so," I say a little lamely. "And you have to be very clever," he continues, "to keep playing all the different roles at once, and not get caught cheating at any of the various games you're playing, so as to keep giving the other players the impression that you're playing fair, and to keep signalling to your confederates that you're still on their side and guaranteeing that they'll win with you as long as they keep playing fair and guaranteeing that you'll win with them as long as you seem to be playing fair too." My head is swimming. But that sounds like a reasonable summary, so I nod and say "Right." "And," he says, wiping his mouth after his last bite of pie and folding his thick white cloth napkin beside his plate, "one of the things you might want to do if you wanted to send a private signal to one of your confederates would be to make sure that there *was* no ambassador of Burundi, say, so that no one would interrupt your little chat." "Was no—?" He's lost me again. These spies, whew! "Thanks for the lunch, Poppy," he says, standing with a smile. That famous county smile. Countly. Counchy. Crunchy. That smile that makes him look like a count. Shakes my hand. "Since we work for the same employer," he says, "I'm sure he won't mind you adding me to your lunch receipt. Gotta run, bye." And he's gone.

1:00 p.m. The ambassador of Burundi still hasn't shown. I need to get back to the office. The General Assembly is voting on my resolution at 2. Condemnifying Indian aggression. Cowboys and Indians. Circle the wagons. I tell Luigi to pass my regrets on to the ambassador if he comes and finds me gone. He promises, and accepts the creduity I slip him. I go outside and find my car double-parked in front of the restaurant, as usual. My driver, whatever his damn name is, sees me coming and hops out to open my door. We head on back down the hill.

Documents

Harry Bienstock's Letter of Resignation
(December 23, 1971)

Effective December 31, 1971, I hereby resign from the Texas Bureau of Investigation. Much as I love my job—or rather, have loved it for most of the 27 years I have been doing it, until very recently—I simply cannot continue to operate under the current climate of undermining and recrimination.

For the last twelve years, I have been assigned to the Anti-Ichthyological Unit (or the Anti-Itch, as we in the Unit call it colloquially), with special orders to infiltrate and provide intelligence on the Skipjack LaTuna organization. Given the fact that I am categorically *not* a fish, I believe I have performed exemplarily, and should have received commendations and promotions for my work. Instead, I have been vilified and calumniated as both incapable of impersonating a fish and as a fish-lover and even a fish myself. One particularly vicious rumor even suggested that I was a LaTunaist who had originally joined the TBI in order to spread disinformation and protect the organization's secrecy! As if I had not already been working for the Bureau for a full fourteen years when we got our first inkling that such an organization even existed! Had I been a "fish" of that nature, that would have been an extraordinarily long set-up, let me tell you!

Although reluctant to dignify such absurd accusations with a reply, all I can say to those who have made such allegations is that they are wrong, and to those who heard such allegations that they should carefully consider the source.

The fact of the matter is, it would have been next to impossible even for an actual fish (which I'm not) to infiltrate the LaTunaists. For one thing, you have to hold your breath underwater. How long can *you* hold *yours*, Mr. TBI Administrator?

Hm? For another, you have to live inside a fish suit for days on end, without bathing or exposure to fresh air. And you must have mastered four or five fish languages, and I mean *mastered*: the slightest linguistic slip, and you're floating belly up and your wife is collecting survivor benefits.

Not only that, Skipjack LaTuna is a master of disguise, of dissimulation. He is quite capable of appearing to be in four or five places at once. Disinterested and trustworthy eyewitnesses (*not* fish) have reliably placed him at different scenes around Texas, and even beyond our borders, at precisely the same instant. He can appear to be a human being, a loyal Texan, a trusted political leader, even a long-time intelligence agent, and only give himself away, if at all, by a mischievous twitch of a whisker—and then vanish, leaving only a trail of fish slime and his signature sardonic laughter behind him.

Well, from now on, they will have to do it all without me.

The most ludicrous allegation of all (this one really makes me laugh) has been that I am myself Skipjack LaTuna. This is the sort of absurd defamation that one expects from our enemies; it is just too much to take when it comes from one's own colleagues. If I were Skipjack LaTuna, would I have—oops, gotta go

Internal Memo
(May 14, 1972)

AS/HPQ: Texas ANG: FOR YOUR EYES ONLY
RE: Results of UA on GWB

UA 1: Sample procured by MO, GWB self-sample. Clean urine, but found not to be the urine of GWB. Analysis indicates this sample was from a pregnant woman.

No cover. MO reports GWB likely carried in a vial of urine. GHWB will procure next sample personally. Indicates importance of sample. Must not be open to suspicion, as black squads will have to dispatch outside investigators.

UA 2: Sample procured by MO. GWB escorted naked to lab, to be observed producing sample, by order of GHWB. GWB struggles with MO. Sample procured. Results: Cocaine positive. Marijuana positive. Methaquaalone positive. Methamphetamine positive. Opiates negative. Ivermectin positive.

Transcript Follows : Explanatory Prior To Loss of Urine Sample and Reported Events

TBI tape transcription #0001703133
5/14/72
Ellington Air Force Base, flight surgeon's office

Voices: GWB, Lt. George Walker Bush, Texas Air National Guard; MO, Medical Officer Cap. Jay Harwood

(GWB) It's not mine.
(MO) I saw you piss in the cup, son.
(GWB) It's not mine, though.
(MO) You realize your father ordered this test.
(GWB) But it's not mine. Tell him.
(MO) He has already been informed.
(GWB) You told him it wasn't mine.
(MO) Sir, I watched you deliver the specimen.
(GWB) But it wasn't mine, anyways. I can still fly, right?
(MO) I will recommend you be grounded.
(GWB) Awww, that sucks. I want to fly. That piss isn't mine. Help! Hey! Uncle Dogsbody, help!

LOSS OF AUDIO—screeching metallic sounds

Pursuant to your request, investigators found at the scene, following loss of audio and entry by military police:

- A large number of greenish beetles, some squashed

- MO, sitting upright in chair, reportedly "pithed"

- Medical records missing

- GWB missing

TBI tape transcription #0001703134
5/14/72
Ellington Air Force Base, outside flight surgeon's office

Voices: GWB, Lt. George Walker Bush, Texas Air National Guard;
WAH, W. Averell Harriman

(GWB) Awwww, man. That was wild! You blew that place apart!

(WAH) I can't let the future president be ruined by youth-ful indiscretions.

(GWB) Huh? I didn't take any skreshins.

(WAH) George, you have to understand something. Even when your implants aren't working, we are still watching over you. These drugs you're taking are starting to undo the good surgical work that has made you what you are today. You have to stop. Your brain could overload and melt. The Ivermectin is an insecticide and could be fatal in the Atlantean bloodline. You've had stiff muscles and pain in your joints.

(GWB) Yeah, so?

(WAH) Black, tarry stools. Chest pain. Chills and cold sweats. Dizziness. Eyelid irritation. Fast and irregular pulse. Painful urination.

(GWB) What are you, my doctor?

(WAH) You feel like you're constantly moving.

(GWB) I am constantly moving. I'm a happening kind of guy.

(WAH) But most times you can't tell whether you're mov-ing through your surroundings or your surroundings are mov-ing around you.

(GWB) Who cares? Don't they come to the same thing?

(WAH) I'm warning you, George. You have to stop.

(GWB) Man, I don't want to stop.

(WAH) You need to have a religious experience, George. A complete turnaround.

(GWB) Huh?

(WAH) When the time is right, you will start having questions.

(GWB) What questions? Not a test! I hate tests.

(WAH) Questions about life and death, heaven and hell. God.

(GWB) Huh? I don't get it. I thought you were worried about me messing up my implants, and the piss test, and me not being President.

(WAH) It's important for a President to have moral values, George. Spiritual beliefs.

(GWB) Uh—okay. So, can I still fly? Can I still get high?

Break-in

(Poppy, June 1, 1972)

6:59 a.m. Eyes blink open. Glance over at the alarm clock. Twelve seconds till it goes off. Count down: Twelve, eleven, ten, nine, eight, seven, six, five, four, three, two, one. Buzzzz. Old Mr. Regular. Slap the button and bounce up out of bed. Another lugrubidous day as the Republic of Texas Ambassador to the United Nations.

7:01 a.m. Check my reflection in the bathroom mirror. Is that a pimple? How can I be getting pimples at almost 48? (My birthday's next month.) I'm not a teenager. Doro's a teenager. She should be getting the pimples in this family. I don't eat candy bars or potato chips. I eat healthy. Just what Consuela cooks for us here at home, and the pandered food at the receptions we throw, and go to. And the receptional pandoras are professionals. They wouldn't make unhealthy food that would give ambassadors pimples. And my lunches at Raffaello's, of course. But that's Italian food. Italian food isn't greasy or pimply.

7:05 a.m. Go to the toilet. Drop in a FishAway pellet. Sit down and move my bowels. A little runny this morning. My tum-tum a little rrowly. Something I ate? Those yummy pasties last night? Maybe a little too pasty? Paste can't be good for the tum-tum.

7:13 a.m. Change into my exercise togs. Go into the exercise room. Turn on *Good Morning, America*. Climb up on my exercycle. Every morning it feels like the pedals get harder to push. Hard pedal-pushers. Worrisome news item this morning. I mean, I worry some, if that makes any sense. Some ruck-making American journalist named Jack Anderson says he has hard edipence that the same people who organized the Bay of Pigs invasion were behind the assassination of LBJ and critical wounding of JFK. Where could he have gotten elevence like that? Here I thought everybody who knew anything were dead. Well, he won't last out the week. Heart attack. Suicide. Accidental fall off a tall building. Anderson's calling the Warren Commission a whitewash. Doesn't he know that's dangerous talk? These Americans, I swell. Swelt. Smelt. Ain't they got the sense they was born with? Were born with? He wants the case reopened up again. The dangers of an out-of-control press. People get hurt.

7:30 a.m. Shower. The shower's like a, I don't know, spray of water or something, pounding my skin. Washing off the sweat and the grime. Grime, good word. Grime. Grimy. Like crime, only grimier.

7:39 a.m. Dry off. Dress. Black socks, gartled. White long-sleeve shirt. Gray suit pants. Maroon tie. Yale tie-clip. Monogrammed cuff-links. Bare Bottom. Big Brother. Bad Boy. Gray suit coat.

7:45 a.m. Greet Consuela. "Good morning, Mr. Bush." "Good morning, Consuela." "You sleep well, Mr. Bush?" "Yes, Consuela, I sleep well. And how are you this morning?" "I fine, Mr. Bush." Coffee, toast and jam, fried egg sunny side up, two slices of bacon.

7:53 a.m. Brush teeth. Kiss Bar on the warm wrinkly forehead. Push the white hair aside. "Mmm," she says, and goes right on sleeping. As usual. Not a morning person, Bar. Not a peep from the kids. They're all still out like a log.

7:56 a.m. Overcoat. Briefcase. Out the door. Elevator down to the lobby. Lobbyist. Bill Foyers. Out the resolving doors to the street. Uniformed Negro says "Your car is right over here, Mr. Bush," opens car door for me to slide in. Slip him a dollar bill. Nice boy. He's short enough I could rub his nappy head in a friendly fashion on the way down, but I don't. Somebody told me once that these American Negroes don't take kindly to having their naps rubbed. Don't like gestitures of friendship. "How are you this morning, Mr. Bush?" My driver. What's his name. Chip, or Chaz, or Chester, or something. "Just fine, thanks." He's got a name, I know he does. I just can't remember it.

8:09 a.m. Arrive at the U.N. Stride in through the front doors. U.N. ambassador. Republic of Texas Ambassador to the United Nations. Up to the Texas mission. "Good morning, Mrs. Smith." "Oh, Mr. Bush, good morning. I'm very much afraid you won't be able to use your office for a couple of hours this morning." "Oh? How's that?" This is highly irregular. I put on a frown. "No. Apparently you had some sort of infestation last night. When the cleaner went in to clean early this morning, there were fish in there." "Fish?" "Fish *everywhere*," she clearifies, her eyes wide. Clearophylls. Claraforms. "You mean, of course, silverfish, Mrs. Smith?" "No, no, Mr. Bush. Fish. With tails and scales and gills. They brought a fish-fumigator in. He's just left, but he said you shouldn't go in there before ten. It'll be toxic in there for two hours." "But I— But I— Fish? How on earth am I going to *work*? I have important *work* to do, Mrs. Smith!" I know I'm blabbing. But I can't help it. I'm a little discomputated. "Oh, I realize, Mr. Bush. It's terrible, isn't it?" I nod halflessly. "But we've made other arrangements. Mr. Lais will show you to your temporary office. Just till ten. All right? Mr. Lais?" I turn to follow her eyes and see Tom step up behind my right shoulder. "Right this way, Mr. Bush," he says.

8:17 a.m. I follow Tom down the hall. He opens a door on the left, holds it open for me. I step inside, and there behind the desk to my condrisible surprise sits *Dick Nixon*. Dick, here! The President of the Republic of Texas, in New York! Nothing in the media about his trip; no advance warming to me, his U.N. ambassador. I didn't even spot his Secret Service guys about. I can see Bob Haldeman slirking over in the corner, though. He doesn't say anything or give any inkidation that he's seen me. No ink at all. Not even a pen, I bet. Dick waves at Tom, a shoo-fry wave, go, go, and Tom pulls the door shut and leaves. "Dick!" I cry, with an uneasy glance over at Bob. "What on Earth are *you* doing here?" "Sit the fuck down, Poppy," he says in an incircere voice full of hominy, or well abominy, abdon-homie, pulling out a whiskey bottle and two cheap juice glasses. He fills them both practically to the brine and pushes one toward me, spilling some on the desk. Takes a long loud gupping drink from his. Like drinking beer on a hot day. Gup gup. "Have a drink, Poppy. Come on, drink up, dammit. We're in a shitload of trouble here." "Trouble, Dick?" "A shitload of it, Poppy. Siddown and lissen." I sit down, take a sip of whis-key. This isn't what I expected. I expected to be sitting there on the other side of the desk, and no whiskey. Now I'm like a visitor with booze in my hand, at not even eight-thirty in the morning. Bar would never improve. This was supposed to be *my* temporary office. But now it turns out it's Dick's. That's okay. Dick's the big boss. But still. "There's been," Dick says pertentiously, in his deep grambly voice, "a leak." "A leak?" Suddenly all I can think of is a man standing at the urinal and a hole popping open in his tummy. White liquid spurting out. Or yellow, I guess. Some color. "A leak, goddammit. And I'm *really* riled up about it, Poppy. I'm just about fit to be fucking *tied*." He slams his fist on the table, then rubs his puffy little hand a little where it hit the table. He downs the rest of his whiskey and refills his glass. His voice seems a little slurried. I guess this isn't his first glass of whiskey this morning. I jump a little when his little fist hits the table. I'm a little jumpy, I guess. A little spooky. "Fucking Jack Anderson. You see the news this morning?" I nod. "He says," I dissemarize, "he can link the Bay of Pigs with the hit on LBJ." "Exactly. The fucker. The dirty low-down fucker. Word on the street is there's a goddamned diary of some sort, a journal. Some stupid fuck who was involved with both operations kept a goddamned journal, of all the fucking stupid things to do, wrote down all the links between Miami station and the hit in Dallas. Exactly what we've been most afraid of, goddammit. This could be disastrous. Fucking disastrous." He takes a long pull on his whiskey and rolls his eyes around the room, like, I don't know, some kind of bull or something. A bull in a china shop, before the slaughter. A fly buzzes somewhere near his head, and he half-tips his head toward it. We both sit there for a few moments in silence, waiting. Then his hand suddenly slakes out and snags the fly. I'm impressed. I never knew Dick was this fast. Catch a fly! He sees me looking, and shrugs a little. "You have to sneak up on them from behind," he says sort of quietly. Even modestly. I've never heard Dick talk this way before. "So they don't see you coming." All the while he's say-ing this his chubby fist is working on the fly. It looks like a snake eating a rat. Or uneating it. Hunching and bunching. Finally he gets it up to the top, up by his thumb, to where it's just barely sticking its eyebally little head out and wiggling it around in acrony. Anglony. Argosy. He brings it up close to his face, tips his right eye down to glare at the little guy, then puts his fist to his mouth and carefully lips the fly out. Now I can see its little hind legs waving in the air just outside of his lips. Now a quick suck of air and it's gone. Gulp. He washes it down with another long pull of whiskey. "So, now," he goes on lithely, as if he had not just eaten a fly, "that fucking stupid useless dickless wonder of a journal has got stole. Far's we can tell late last night. And now our enemies are fixin to use it to bring us down. Bring—us—down. Bring us fucking down." He slavors the words, rolls them around on his tongue. "Wh—what enemies?" I stamber. "Who else?" he says, drinking deep and giving his jowls a quick shake. Yabbeda-yabbeda. "Who fucking else keeps pulling this kind of stunt? Fucking Abraham Lincoln and his fishy minions, of course." "Skipjack LaTuna?" "I'd bet my left nut on it." These people will stop at nothing to push Texas over the blink into social chaos. We've arrested them, desported them, executived them, depth-changed them, polluted the lakes and streams, but they never seem to go away. They're everywhere. They hide like, like, I don't know what, like tyrnamites, or something. Then they come out of the woodworks and the drinking fountains and steal diaries and journals and things, and wrack heavok. "So, okay, Poppy, lissen up." "Yes, Dick?" "I gotta ask you this." He drains his glass and fills it again. Smacks his lips a little. "Yes, Dick?" "Jew ever keep a journal of any kind, Poppy?" "No, absolutely not. Never did. No." "A diary?" "No, Dick. I swear." "Good. Very good. You're in the clear, then. We're gonna fucking find out who did, lemme tellya, and convince him never to do it again." I have a pretty good idea just how this person will be "convinced." "And also, of course," he continues, "we're gonna find this fucking journal and steal the fucker back." "Of course," I echo. "Do you have any idea where it could be?" "No. But the Bureau guys tell me LaTuna has this Anderson fucker stashed away in some fucking tank up there in Fort Worth. We'll start there. The, uh," he checks his papers, "the fucking *Gotta-Wait* Motel. Can you imagine? A motel called the Gotta-Wait? What fucking marketing genius came up with that one? Gotta-Wait. That's the last fucking thing you want when you check into a motel, having to fucking *wait* for Christ's sake. And the guys tell me it's one of these sleaze-bag rent-by-the-hour places, too. Fucking *waterbeds* in every room. Probably some kinda vibrating psychedelic light-show waterbeds with hippie chicks naked in them. Writhing in ecstasy." He gives a grotense intimation of writhing, his hands in the air, his drink sloshing brassily up in one hand. "This Anderson fuck probably has the fucking incriminating thing in his closet there in the motel, 'd be my guess." "But what if," I say, trying to sound calm about all this, comfitent, professional, "he makes photocopies? Surely he would erect himself by taking copies?" "Copies, my ass," Dick scoffs. "Copies can be discredited. Don't you worry none about copies. We need the original." "The original," I nod. "But, um, Dick," I say. "Yes, Poppy?" "Surely you aren't expecting *me* to go steal the journal?" His eyes go wide. Then he chortles a little. Then he bursts out laughing. "You!" He's holding his flabby belly now, laughing like a, I don't know. Like a dingo. "George Bush, stealing the journal! I can just see it! Oh ho ho ho! Ah ha ha ha!" I'm laughing too, of course. It's my policy. When the people around me laugh, I join in. I don't know what's so blamed funny here, though. I just asked a supple question. "No, no," he says finally, wiping his eyes, "not you, Poppy. We'll have a separate team for that. Some of our friends from ten years ago. Some of the people most directly impacted by this fucking mess." "Oh?" "Howard Hunt and his Cuban boys, you must remember them, right? Eugenio Martinez, Bernard Barker, Felipe de Diego, Frank Sturgis, Virgilio Gonzalez, Reinaldo Pico, those guys." "Of course," I say, thinking: these guys are all still *walking around*? "And a few others. Howard Osborne and Jim McCord, you don't know them, probably." "No." "TIA Office of Security. They oversee psyop stuff, all those scary mind-control operations like Bluebird, Artichoke, and MK-Ultra. Run the TIA sexops, too." "Sexops?" "Jesus, Poppy, where you been? Operation Rafael. Male and female prostitutes used to compromise public figures. Photographs taken, taped records kept. Very useful. Very good men." My heart stops on that name, of course. Rafael, my dearest. What could he be doing now? Does he ever think of me? Is he a grown man, with a wife and children? "Gordon Liddy. John Paisley. Some PI named Lou Russell. Best fucking men in the business. Henry's coordinating the whole thing. One of his guys, David Young, 'll be in charge. He's callin em the Plumbers, or something." "Uh, okay. And do you, um, want me to meet with them?" "No, no. What I want you to do, Poppy," he says, with a benelephant smile, "is to raise these guys some money." "Money?" "Yes, money. They're gonna need plenty of it. You're in tight with all those big oil boys, right? The Liedtke brothers, all those guys you came up with. And you've got all those banking connections up here in the States. Can you round up, say, a million dollars? With nobody hearing about it?" I think for a moment. "I suppose that might be possible. It might take me a while, though." "How long?" "A week. Two weeks." "A week'd be better'n two weeks, Poppy." "I'll see what I can do." "Good." And with that he suddenly larches to his feet, steadies his left leg with both hands, then grabs his glass like a cheap robot, spilling another big yellow spank of whiskey on the desk, and scumbles over to a far corner of the office. A panel opens in the wall and Dick steps into some sort of shiny metallic elevator. The doors snick shut and there's a whoosh and I'm alone in the room with Bob Haldeman. Bob pointilistically walks over to the desk and sits down in the chair Dick has just vacated. Gives me an insulin stare. "See ya, Poppy," he says, and starts mopping up Dick's mess.

9:13 a.m. I step out into the corridor, but realize that I don't have an office to go to. Not for another 45 minutes.

9:16 a.m. Stop in for a quick B.M. My tum-tum is all upset. I sit down on the toilet and spray brown water out my bum. My tummy hurts when I do it. It feels like somebody's popping champagne corks in there. On the wall just above my right shoulder somebody's written in black Magic Marker: "Don't change Dicks in the middle of a screw, vote for Nixon in 72."

I harmumph a little at that. Four months to the election. No, five. Who else are they going to vote for? A little lower down: "Don't do needle drugs, the only dope worth shooting is Richard Nixon," and, alongside it, "Where's Lee Harvey Oswald when we need him?" Could Dick *be* this unpopulous?

9:23 a.m. Two men come in, move to the far end of the restroom. They have a whispered conversation over there. I can't hear what they're saying, but I think I hear my name several times: Poppy. I can't leave while they're there, because they'll see me and think I heard them talking about me. My bum goes numb. That rhymes.

9:54 a.m. Finally escape the restroom, go back to Mrs. Smith's desk. "I wonder," I begin diddifently, dutifently, but Mrs. Smith waves me on past. "Oh, Mr. Bush," she says with a conspirotarial wink, "I'm sure no one will mind if you go in a few minutes early." I go in and close the door behind me. It still stinks in here a little. The fugtimator. I sit down at my desk and go to unlock the bottom drawer, where I keep my journal, but the key is gone. I search hide and hair for it. On the desk, on the floor, in my pockets. Nowhere. I shake and rattle the desk drawer. It won't budge. I pull the drawer above it out about halfway to look through it. It's full of all sorts of junk. I don't see the key, though. I slide it out a little more, so I can search through the back parts. Still nothing. I slide it out just an inch more, and it comes crashing down. Pens and paper clips and pencil sharpeners and Scotch tape and dead beetles and staples and airline booze bottles scatter across the floor. The door opens and Mrs. Smith sticks her head in. "Mr. Bush, are you all right? I heard a crash." "No problem, Mrs. Smith. My desk drawer just fell out. I'm fine." "Why don't you let me pick that all up for you, Mr. Bush," she says, walking toward me. "No, no, oh no, Mrs. Smith, heavens no," I protest. "I'll do it. Really. It's no problem." "Are you sure?" She stops, but looks like she's ready to override my protests if need be. "I'm sure." "All right. Call me if you need me." "I will, Mrs. Smith." She nods and leaves. Once she's gone I notice something. From where I'm sitting I can look right down into the locked bottom drawer. All I had to do was take the top drawer out. Which means, of course, that all a bugular had to do was take out the top drawer and presto: my journal. Which is, of course, missing. I go through everything in that cursed bottom drawer twice. It's gone. It's definitely missing. It's been stolen. Infestivation, my tushy. There's been a break-in. Our wicked, wicked enemies. That Skipjack LaTuna! I'll get him for this!

Documents

Texas Department of Hygiene Offices Destroyed in Explosion
Anarchists Blamed for Incident that Kills Famed Animal Hide
Researcher, Dr. Homekin Plant
(Houston Chronicle, May 5, 1973)

Famed researcher Dr. Homekin Plant, known for his work on the identification of animal hides and diseases resulting from handling animal hides, was killed in an explosion at his office last night.

"It was a terrific explosion," Houston police confirmed. "Everything was destroyed."

Dr. Plant, who, according to colleagues, was working on the mysterious "police raincoat syndrome" that has plagued Texan law enforcement officials for several years, was killed outright.

"Sadly, we may never know what caused these raincoats to be so hazardous," police spokesperson Patty Kolick confirmed. "And that may be why these offices were destroyed—so that we would be unable to trace the source of this infection back to them."

"The Neptune Continuum will stop at nothing to force its insane agenda on the people of Texas and, ultimately, of the world," she added. "All good Texans must oppose them."

When asked how she could be sure the nefarious Neptune Continuum was behind last night's explosion, Ms. Kolick declined to divulge details while investigations were under-way, but said that the police had received a reliable tip from a retired TBI agent implicating the NC.

Police Interrogation of Harry Bienstock (transcript)
(May 6, 1973)

Q. One more time, Special Agent Bienstock: how did you know Skipjack LaTuna was going to blow up Hygiene?

A. I told you, Detective. It just came to me.

Q. It came to you.

A. I got a hunch. Haven't you ever had a hunch before?

Q. I've had a hunch my wife was gonna be pissed when I came home drunk at 2 a.m.

A. See?

Q. Don't fuck with me, Bienstock.

A. Nobody's fucking with you.

Q. Are you trying to tell me Skipjack LaTuna talks to you over the ether or some shit?

A. I'm not trying to tell you anything.

Q. That you and he have long conversations on the astral plane?

A. You said that, Detective, not me.

Q. Come clean, Bienstock. You *are* LaTuna, aren't you?

A. Wanna look under my mask?

Q. Stop jerking my chain. X-rays showed a perfectly normal human skeleton under that flabby middle-aged skin.

A. So, who's jerking whose chain, Detective?

Q. I don't know how you're doing it, but I'm positive you're in disguise.

A. Maybe I'm disguised as someone in disguise, and under the disguise, I'm really Harry Bienstock.

Q. Who's LaTuna's human lover?

A. No idea.

Q. Where's his underwater lair?

A. No idea.

Q. What's he gonna try next?

A. No idea. Yet.

Q. Yet?

A. If I get a hunch, I'll call you.

Q. Day or night, motherfucker.

A. It'll be my great pleasure, Detective.

Private Dick

(Poppy, August 5, 1974)

I'm in bed next to Bar one night, back in Houston, now, I'm party chairman now, chairman of the Rotpat National Committee, Rotpat, that's Republic of Texas Patriot Party, still a Cabinet member but I think now a higher rank, higher and higher, that's the way to go, up and up, so anyway, I'm lying there in bed, asleep, I'm pretty sure, and I know Bar's asleep, I mean. I don't know it when I'm asleep, because I don't know much of anything when I'm asleep, or when she is, but the phone rings, and I wake up, and *then* Bar's asleep, at least. It's late, 1:15 a.m.

"Poppy?"

"Lou?"

It's Lou Russell, my P.I. Like saying that. My P.I. I've got my very own private dick. Well, he works for the Party. For the Committee. But I'm Committee Chairman. I'm the head cheese. He's the mouse. Of course he works for other people too. Has worked. He used to be Chief Investigator for the House Committee on Un-Texan Activities. Ferreting out closet columnists and homosexuals and other undesirables. Mouse for the House. Merit Ferret. He used to work for the Texas Bureau of Investigation. Special Agent Russell. Never met a TBI agent that wasn't special. He did some snooping for his lawyer, Bud Fensterwald, for Fensterwald's Committee to Investigate Assassinations. Looking into that LBJ assassination, I guess. Snooping, like the dog. Love that dog. Big, floopy ears. World

War I flying ace, just like me. Those boys were dead, I swear it. He worked for Jim McCord for a while in the TIA. He wasn't in the TIA himself, just worked for Jim. McCord Associates. Jim got him on with General Security Services, that company up there in Fort Worth that provided the guards that guarded the Gotta-Wait Motel. He was the inside man. He was the fish that got away. He was the sixth burglar, the one they didn't catch. When the heat got turned up on the break-in, he quit that job and started working for Allied Invalligators, Invalidators, Inventigators, something like that, and when we hired them, he came to work for me. My private dick. Like Dick Nixon, only all mine. In private. Get it?

"Yeah, Poppy," he says, "it's me."

"Lou," I say, rubbing my eyes and squinking at the clock again, "do you have any idea what *time* it is?"

"Never mind about that. We've got to meet."

"Okay, but it's going to have to be some time later this week. I'm really busy."

"No, it's going to have to be *now*."

"Now?" I hear my voice climbing. The famous Bush whine. I don't mean to do it. I don't want to do it. It just happens. "In the middle of the *night?*"

"Poppy," he says heavily, "put it this way. You want to live through this Gotta-Wait thing?"

"What, uh, what do you mean, Lou?"

"I'll tell you all about it when we meet. But believe me when I say *live*. Take me very seriously when I say *live*. As in, take me *literally*."

"What," I say, my voice catching a little, "live, as opposed to, uh, whatever, *not die?*"

"That's the general idea, Poppy."

"Did, uh, did somebody die, Lou? Did somebody get, um, whacked? Iced?"

"Yeah. Root."

"John Root?" His boss at Allied.

"Of course."

"How?"

"Heart attack. I just heard about it tonight."

"Could it have been, uh ... natural causes?"

"It's all natural causes, Poppy. Your heart stops beating. They put you in the ground. You turn into dirt. All natural. Just how natural do you want to get, here?"

I gulp. "Where do you want to meet?"

He gives me an address in the poshiest part of Houston. Embassy Row. We hang up. Bar turns over, groaning a little. She's got a lot to turn. "Who was that, dear?"

"Nobody. Never mind."

She doesn't even open her eyes as she says: "Are you having an affair, Poppy?"

"What! Bar!" I'm hortified. But then I hear her churkling sleepily.

"Just a little joke, dear."

Whew. "Go back to sleep, hon. It's some crisis or other. I'm the only guy that can handle it."

"Mm hm. I'm sure you are, dear." But she's still smiling, a little.

I get up and get dressed. Quickly and quiacally. Go through the kitchen into the garage and get into my shiny new black 1975 Austin. Early August, and the '75 models are already out. Over there in the U.S., they don't bring out next year's new cars till September. Here in Texas we're fast. We're effulgent. Our cars are bigger, too, and faster, and use lots more gas. Ever since the oil shortage I helped the Texas oilmen stage last year, American car manufacturers have been improving their cars' "fuel efficiency." Not here in Texas, though. We know we've got plenty of oil, oil to burn, oil to, I don't know, use up fast, and we like to flute it. Flooze it. We do everything in a big way here in Texas. Big jesters.

I glide through the nighttime streets with a swish. I mean, my car does. I don't mean it's a swishy car; my tires are the ones going swish swish; the streets are a little wet from the rain this afternoon. It came down in *thimbles*. I mean, the drops were like thimbles. Like as much water as would fit into a thimble. But not the kind of thimble that has all those little holes in it, like a stringer or something. Stranger. Calendar. You know the kind I mean.

I find the street, and the house. It's a big old Victrola. There are lights on in some of the windows, but the curtains are all pulled. I can hear dimpered sounds of music coming from the house. *This* is Lou's house? My entstignation of him goes up considerately.

There's no doorbell. While I'm looking for it, though, a man's voice comes over an intercom.

"May I help you?"

"Is, uh, Lou home?"

"Lou who?"

"Lou Russell. He asked me to meet him here."

"Who are you?"

"George Bush."

"Hold on a sec."

I stand there for much longer than a sec. Finally the door opens a crack, and Lou peeks out. "Poppy. Good. Come on in."

I follow him down a sentry hall. The place is sort of over-dectorated for Texas. Sort of over-fancy, if you know what I mean. Red velveeta everywhere. Galsy curtains. Dappered over lampshades. Overstuffed furniture. Biggo rental rugs. We go into a living room of some sort. To my upending surprise, there are four or five *practically undressed women* in here, stretched out on couches or sitting back with their legs up over the arms of easy chairs. I can actually see naked breasts in here. As in, bare boobs. What *is* this place?

"Hey, girls," Lou says. "Meet my friend John." For a moment, I think he means John Root, but he's dead, of course.

"Hi, John!" they all sing out. "Wanna be my john, John?"

"Call me Poppy," I say with a nervous laugh. I've never

talked to a woman whose boobs I could see plain as day before. Well, except Bar, and that was a pretty long time ago. And she's my wife, anyway, so that's different.

"No names here, John," Lou says sort of smilingly but insisternly. But isn't John a name?

Apparently, we're just passing through this room. We don't stop to talk to the girls, lovely as some of them are. Good, healthy Texan girls are the loveliest girls in the world, I always say. One of them is sort of dark and young and slight. She's leaning up against the wall in just a pair of jeans and an amptitude. She's got almost nothing up on top. I mean, her boobs are pretty small. Practically flat. Like a, I don't know, like a little hill or something, only you don't notice it's a hill when you're walking up it because it's so little and there's only this little nipple on top and it's only from the nipple that you can tell you're standing on a boob. I want to stop and chat with her a little, but Lou's bustling me on through. We go into the kitchen in the back of the house. It's sort of run-drum, not much like the front rooms. Old white paint flaking off, greasy floors, cheap dining room chairs with torn red plastic humpostery on rusted aluminimum tubing. Lou waves me into one of the chairs, pulls a bottle of whiskey out of a cupboard. Holds it up to me with raised eyebrows. He means: *you want some?* I measure off an inch with my right thumb and forefinger. That means: *a little.* He pours me some in a glass tumbler, sets it down in front of me.

"This your house, Lou?" I ask.

"Naw. They let me use a room in exchange for bouncer services."

"Nice place. But who are those naked girls out there, Lou?"

"Hookers, Poppy. They're hookers."

"Hookers?" I imagine all of them with their hands cut off and hooks in their place. Naked girls with Captain Hook hands.

"Whores. Prostitutes. This is a bordello, Poppy." I mouth

the word: *bordello*. Lou watches me closely. "A whorehouse," he says.

A light goes out in my head. "Oh!" I get it now. Men come here to have sex with those girls. "But," I say, a little puzzled, "isn't that sort of illegal in Texas?"

He laughs a little. "It's sort of illegal almost everywhere, Poppy."

"How do they get away with it, then?"

He shrugs. "Top government officials are in here every night."

"And, what, write up a report about it the next day?"

He claps me on the shoulder and laughs. "Good one." People are always doing that to me. I'll ask a question, and instead of answering it, they'll treat it like some kind of joke.

"Listen, Lou. That dark, sort of smoldery one—?"

"Who, Rafaela?" My heart skips a rope. "You like her, huh? We get through this, come on back, I'll set you up with her."

"Uh ... okay."

"She's popular with the Saudis, because she looks so much like a thirteen-year-old boy."

"Oh? I hadn't noticed."

"Yeah, those Arab bastards are in here every night fucking her up the ass. Saudi embassy is right next door. And those Saudis do love boys. D'ja hear the one about the Texan, the American, and the Saudi up in a plane? Engine dies, plane's plummeting down fast, and there's only two parachutes. The Texan grabs up both of 'em and tosses one to the Saudi. The Saudi shoots a thumb at the American guy and says, 'What about him?' The Texan says, 'Fuck him.' The Saudi guy looks at the American, then back at the Texan, and says, 'Do we have time?'"

I must not get it because it doesn't seem all that funny to me. But Lou doesn't seem to mind.

"You're right," he says, though I haven't said anything that could be wrong, "what am I thinking, telling jokes at a time like this. So. Root's dead. And frankly, I can't figure out why. He was following a dead end."

"A what?"

"A blind alley."

"Excuse me?"

"A red herring."

"I'm sorry?"

"A wild goose chase."

"I'm not—"

"Root thought the Gotta-Wait break-in was all about prostitution."

"Prostitution?"

"Tell me about it. A weird theory. He thought Jack Anderson was somehow involved with a prostitution ring or something."

"Proselytution ring?"

"Yeah. The Gotta-Wait Motel was a pretty sleazy joint. Why would he be staying there? Other than that, though, he had some pretty good ideas about the break-in. He figured out that it was a set-up, that someone had tipped off the cops. Pretty funny, him sitting there explaining his figuring on that one to me, not knowing that I was the one who tipped them off."

"*You* were?"

"Of course. You didn't know?"

"Huh. But weren't you— "

"One of the burglars? Sure."

"Then— "

"How'd I get away? Easy. When you're the one who tips off the cops, you get cut a certain amount of slack."

"Oh," I say knowingly, though frankly, I can't figure out what the hell he's trying to tell me. Slack?

"Why, though," he says, shaking his head in wonderment, "why the fuck would they kill him? That's what I can't figure out."

"He must have figured *something* out," I offer.

"Exactly. But what? He—"

Lou's interrupted here by an older woman. She's on the heavy side, but not nearly as motherly as my Bar. She waddles into the kitchen and sidles up to Lou. Whispers in his ear. Lou looks strackled, then grim.

"Come on, Poppy," he says. "Let's ride."

"What?"

"Don't fuck around now, Poppy. We gotta go. Now."

"Okay." I stand up, drain my drink. Man of action. I spring into action. Zoop! Zoop! I'm outta here.

"Where's your car?" he says.

"Out front."

"Okay, fuck it, we'll take mine. Come on."

I follow him down some stairs to the abasement. We blimp through it in the dark. He opens a door and we step out into the garden. The grass is wet around my shoes. We go through a rusky iron gate in the back, cross an alley, dunk behind somebody's garage. Lou steps up to some old cronker and unlocks the driver's side door, motions for me to go around. He unlocks my door from the inside and I slide in. The front seat is covered with fast food wrappers. He sweeps them onto the floor at my feet as I sit down. There's so many down there already that I can't see my shoes. He crankles the starter for about two minutes before the engine finally catches and clicks over. I mean, starts. It makes so much noise that it seems a little silly to me for him to *eeeeeeease* it out onto the road. As if whoever's after us couldn't hear us from five blocks away.

But we make it. Nobody seems to be following us. He keeps checking the near-view mirror and looking satisfied. After seven or eight blocks, his shudders relax a little. Shredders. Shodders. Whatever the word is. Those things at the tops of his arms.

"Okay," he says. "We did it. We're safe for the time being. I guess I shouldn't have asked you to meet me there. I forgot, that place is bugged."

"Bugged?" I'm thinking back to the dead beetles in my office. The fumerators. "I didn't see any bugs."

He looks at me a little funny. "You can't see 'em, Poppy. They're hidden."

"But sometimes they come crawling out, right? You can spot them down on the floor sometimes. In dark corners."

"Different kind of bug, Poppy. Microphones. Little tiny microphones. Listening devices."

"Oh!" I say. "I get you now." This must be private-dick talk. Bugged.

"Yeah." He looks over at me again, blows air out through his nose, chunkles a little. "Thing is, so many diplomats and government officials patronize the place it makes sense. You never know when you might need a tape of His Excellency Such-and-Such fucking a whore. As you reminded me, prostitution's illegal in Texas."

"A capital crime," I add.

"Let's not forget about that."

"So how'd you know it was, um, *bugged*?"

"I did it myself. Can you believe that? Did it myself and still forgot."

"*You* did? For who, Allied?"

"One of Allied's clients," he says vaguely. Wisely, I don't press. "So. Where to next? I guess I'll take you to this bar I know. Should be safe there."

"You think my life is in danger too?"

"Not really. You're too big."

"Then— "

"Then why did I call you out in the middle of the night?"

"Well, yes."

"Because I'm hoping you'll protect me. Because of this." He reaches into his inside jacket pocket and pulls out a beat-up manila envelope. It looks like somebody drove a car over it on a muddy road.

"This is for me?" I hold it sort of disgustfully.

"Open it."

I bend back the flap and slide the blue ring blinder out. To my surprise, it's my old journal. I haven't seen it in two years, since it was stolen from my desk.

"How did you— "

"I told you, when you tip off the cops, they cut you some slack."

"Oh. Well, uh ... thanks."

He shrugs. "Just doing my job."

"Did you read it?"

"Yeah. Interesting stuff."

"Is that why they're trying to kill you now, then? Because you read my journal?"

He flushes me a quick, panicky look. "You think?" He gulps. "Could that be why?"

"How long have you had it?"

"The whole time."

"Two years?"

"Yeah, why?"

"Why didn't you give it back earlier?"

"They told me to wait till the end."

"The end?"

"Yeah. The end of Nixon."

"They're going to kill Nixon too?"

"I don't know. But he's going down somehow. They don't like the way he's handling this international monetary crisis or something. I don't understand it. He's fucking with their money. They're losing money big-time because of him. Everything he does just makes it worse. Fucking world economy's bankrupt, I heard. Texas economy's in the toilet. Inflation out of control. The big boys can hardly invest their money in anything. Currencies are worthless. Commodities market's in an uproar. And they blame Nixon. So, he's out."

"But—how?"

"Gotta-Wait, of course."

"But that—but that's our enemies at work!"

"Enemies are where you find them, Poppy."

"Yes, but—"

"But nothing. Who do you think's behind this whole Gotta-Wait scandal?"

"Abraham Lincoln. Skipjack LaTuna."

"Oh, you think so, huh? Well, chew on this. The two guys that are turning up all the dirt on Nixon and his boys, publishing it in the *Post*? Woodward and Bernstein? Guess where they went to school."

"University of Texas?"

"Texas Yale. Skull and Bones, 1965." Three years ahead of my Little George. Wonder if he knew them? "They're spies, Poppy. These days. Naval Intelligence. They're big in the intelligence community. And *that's* who's running this thing. *That's* who's exposing the Gotta-Wait burglary."

"*Spies*?" This is too weird.

"The intelligence community and big money." He looks at me funny. "Somehow, I thought you'd know all about this, Poppy."

"Why?" Why do people keep assuming this about me?

"Because you come from big money. Because you've worked for the Agency. Because your dad was President. Because you're one of Dick Nixon's boys."

"Oh." Those all sound like good reasons. Why *don't* I know more about this, then?

"One night," he says ruminantly, leaning back in his seat a little, rubbing his eyes with his left hand, "I tailed Woodward. Just for the hell of it. Followed him to the bottom level of a downtown parking garage. I figured, a-ha, Deep Throat. Now I'm going to find out who it is. Had my camera ready to go. Just when the mystery man appeared, though, I had to leave. Freakiest thing."

"What?"

"All of a sudden, my car was overrun with big green beetles."

"What, on the inside?"

"Everywhere. Inside, outside. I panicked. Hit the ignition, started the car, and magic: the bugs disappeared."

"Literally, disappeared?"

"No. Fled. I don't know where they went. It was like in the movies. You know, just before the storm hits, or the fire breaks out, or whatever, all the bugs flee. I fled, too. I got out of there."

"Did you see Deep Throat?"

"Just a glimpse. He stepped out halfway from behind a pillar."

"Could you tell who he was?"

"Nah. Just that he was really tall. He towered over Woodward."

"Damn. Wonder who it could be?"

"Really. Well, here we are."

He pulls into a dark, sordy parking lot. His car fits right in with the others in the lot. There are weeds growing up through the clacks in the blacktop. We lock the doors and go inside. It's a dive. I mean, it really is a dump. Everybody in there is old, tired, working class, half-dead. Lou leads me to the bar, tells the bartender to give us a couple of whiskeys. He calls the bartender Mike. We've hardly taken two sips of our drinks when the phone rings, and Mike picks up. He turns around.

"Is there a George Bush in here?" he calls out.

"I'm George Bush," I say, sort of shellacked. He holds up the phone. I take the five or six steps over to it and put it to my ear. "Hello?"

"Poppy?"

"Dick?" I look over at Lou. He mouths: *Dick Nixon?* I nod. He rolls his eyes. "How on Earth did you find me here? I just walked in the door!"

"Never mind that, Poppy," he says. "Lissen up. We're in big fuckin trouble."

"We?"

"You and me, Poppy. We're in trouble, yes. Big, big fuckin trouble."

"What are you talking about, Dick?"

"You remember a conversation we had a couple of years ago, Poppy? Over in New York? I popped in for a little chat. You remember, right? Course you do. You ain't that fuckin' stupid."

"Uh, yes, sure, Dick. I remember."

"Well. Poppy. Funny thing is, I taped that conversation."

"You taped it?"

"I taped everything. I figured I'd use the tapes for my memoirs."

"But tell me you destroyed the tapes when this Gotta-Wait thing started going sore, Dick."

"Destroy the tapes? Jesus Christ, what are you, nuts? What about my fucking memoirs?" It sounds like he's pleading with me. To understand. To sympathize. To give him abolition. To ablutionize him.

"What about your fucking *presidency*, Dick?"

"Well, I—well—" I've never heard Dick so pathetic. He's about to cry.

"And so, uh, what about this one patricular tape, Dick? This one with me on it? You've got it there?"

"Yes, Poppy. I've got it right here in my hand."

"So, destroy it."

"I can't, Poppy."

"What are you talking about, Dick? Of course you can. Burn it. Put it in a wastebasket and light it on fire."

"I can't do that, Poppy. They've subpoenaed it. I'm supposed to turn it over tomorrow morning."

"You're supposed to. Dick, what in God's name are you talking about? Supposed to? What the fuck is that supposed to mean? You're going to go down in flames and take me with you, because you're *supposed* to do something? When did you ever do something you were *supposed* to do? Are you fucking *crazy*? Are you *that* far gone, you … you *savage*?"

I can hardly breathe. I take a few deep breaths, try to calm down. While I'm doing that, I look over at Lou. Some friend of his has come up and is talking to him. They're looking very conspirational. Leaning in close and whispering.

"Look, Dick," I say, clammier. "Just quit, okay? Just resign. Go in tomorrow morning and say, 'I quit.' Then nobody can make you hand over that tape. Cut a deal with Lloyd. He'll pardon you. He'll pardon the hell out of you. Just get out of office, and they'll leave you alone."

"But Poppy, quit the presidency? How can I? I've worked my whole life to get here! Just walk away?"

"Better to walk away with some dicknity, Dig."

"And not take you down with me, is that it?"

"That's about the size of it, Dick."

"You're so fucking selfish."

"Me, selfish!"

"Not just you. All of you Bushes. All of you rich fucks that run this country. I can't believe you're fucking hanging me out to dry on this. As if I did it! As if any of this was my doing! I was just doing what I was told! Stealing that journal, as if I gave a fuck! It wasn't my journal. It was somebody else's. Whose was it, Poppy? You know, don't you? I'd bet you anything it was somebody big. Your dad's, or somebody. Or yours. Huh, Poppy? Was it yours? It was, wasn't it?"

"Forget all about that, Dick. That's water under the dick's buck. The Doug's big. The main thing is to savalve some tremblance of dignity. Quit. Resign. And don't turn over that tape."

"Poppy, you fucker. You unbelievable, stupid, selfish fucker."

"Thanks, Dick. Feeling's mutual."

He hangs up. I walk back over to Lou. He gives me a stricken look.

"Lou, what?"

"I—I don't know," he says. "I feel like shit. I feel like—" He grabs at his chest and sort of dropples over onto the bar, then slides down to the floor. I bend down, feel for a pulse. It's very weak. I stand up.

"Mike," I yell, "call an ambulance. Lou's having a heart attack."

Mike nods and makes the call. I bend back down to Lou, wondering what you're supposed to do when somebody has a heart attack. Put their feet up? Loosen their clothing? Give them mouth-to-mouth? Yech. Lou hasn't shaved in about four days. He's got beetles crawling all over him. He looks really disgusting. Let the ambulance guys do it, if anybody has to.

Then I hear a fierce whisper from somewhere nearby. Somebody calling my name: *Poppy*. I look around and see Uncle Dogsbody poking his head out from the back room. He crooks a finger at me: *come on!*

I get up and go to him. He hurries me out the back door and into a waiting limousine. It's out in the street with its engine running. As soon as we're inside, it takes off.

"Uncle Dogsbody, I'm so glad to see you!" I cry. He looks exactly the same as he did forty years ago, when I first met him. He must be well over eighty by now.

"I'm happy to see you too, Georgie."

"Uncle Dogsbody, there's a tape!"

"I know, Georgie. Don't worry."

"But Dick just called. He's supposed to turn it in tomorrow morning."

"I know all about it, Georgie. I told you: don't worry."

"But I'm *on* that tape, Uncle Dogsbody! It could ruin me!"

"It won't ruin you, Georgie," he says tenderly. "I won't let it." I feel a wave of warmth sweep through me. If Uncle Dogsbody's on my side, nothing can go wrong. As long as Uncle Dogsbody's here, calling me Georgie, I'll be okay.

Documents

Sentenced
(Crime Report, May 30, 1975)

Rev. William Sloane Coffin, 42, college chaplain at Yale University of Texas, arrested for disorderly conduct, disturbance of the peace, inciting a riot, the corruption of youth, resisting arrest, public profanity, behavior unbecoming of a man of the cloth, betraying secrets of a secret society, moral turpitude, making a left turn without a proper signal, treason, hooliganism, public urination, possession of a controlled substance (baggie of Ivermectin), public questioning of duly appointed authority, giving aid and comfort to the enemy, consorting with undesirables, sending inflammatory materials through the mail, liberalism, conspiracy, unrestrained laughter in church, public mockery of government and university officials, tax fraud, and parking in a fire zone. Sentenced to death.

Louise Rose, 20, and Susanna Dickinson, 21, students at Yale University of Texas, for four (4) counts of unwomanly behavior, including coarse language, improper attire (lack of required undergarments), inflammatory gestures (raised middle finger, egregious pointing at own pudenda), and public displays of same-sex affection (lewd touching of breasts and buttocks); and seven (7) counts of overt disrespect for male authority, including shouted sexual ridicule of university officials and the shouting of absurd slogans such as "A woman needs a man like a fish needs a bicycle," "Marital sex is r*pe," and "All wives are wh*res." Sentenced to sterilization and ten years at hard labor.

Skipjack LaTuna, 55, for unspecified subversive activities involving fish. Sentenced in absentia to filleting, breading, and pan-frying.

13

Intelligence

(Poppy, September 21, 1976)

Ted sticks his head in. "Busy?"

"Not too," I say. "Come in."

He comes in. Tom follows behind him. They're like Curly and Moe. I mean, not that Ted's got curly hair, or anything, or that they're stooges. But that they're always together. Ted Shackley and Tom Clines. Ted's my associate deputy director for covert operations, under Bill Wells. Tom is, well, with Ted. Ted and Tom go way back together. Ted was head of JM Wave back in the late fifties and early sixties. The blond ghost, they called him. Tom was his second in command. Over there in Florida. CIA. Then he was head of the CIA station in Vienna, you know, the one over in Laos, and then in Saigon. Did damn good work over there, Weevil Operations and Rural Dementment Support, WORDS, or something. Operation Penix, they called it. He headed that up. Killing VC, is what it meant. Killing demented weevils and rurals. Extermigating those terrorists over there. Like golliwogs. Like, 100,000 of them. Somehow, he and his boys could always tell when a seemingly innocent civilian was really a weevil. They had a kind of instinct for it, I'm told. A gut feeling. Good men. I was happy when I appointed Bill Wells deputy director for covert ops and he wanted to bring Ted and Tom in. Absolutely. Positively. All those overexposures of the CIA over there in the United States made things a little too hot for Ted and Tom, so they jumped to Texas Intelligence. We're always happy to have a good man on board, down here.

"This is basically just a courtesy call," Ted says.

"Oh?"

"Yeah. Vis-à-vis the ongoing damage control on the LBJ/JFK hit, now that there's talk of reopening the case. We've got a list of people who shouldn't testify, either here or in the United States, and we're working together with the CIA, the FBI, and the TBI to plug any possible leaks. Sort of an inter-agency collaborative effort."

"Oh," I say. "Sounds like a very good thing."

"It is," Tom says. "Very good."

"So?" I say.

"So we just wanted you to eyeball the list real quick, make sure there isn't anybody on there that you'd want to single out for, um, gentler treatment."

"Gentler?"

"You know, as in, well, not be terminated."

"Oh. I see." Wow. This is what happens when you're Director of Texas Intelligence: you get to see the actual hit list! I'm really on the inside now! I'm one of the boys!

Ted hands over the list. I glance down it. It's got names and short delections of what they do, or why they're important. Next to each name, there's a bullet. That doesn't mean they're planning to shoot these people with bullets. Some of them will have heart attacks, or get pushed out of windows, or get clotty-chopped on the neck, I bet.

- George DeMohrenschildt. Oswald's CIA control. Has fish in high places.

- Carlos Prio Soccaras. Former Cuban President. Money man for anti-Castro Cubans.

- Lou Staples. Dallas radio talk-show host. Told friends he would break assassination case.

- Louis Nichols. Former No. 3 man in TBI. Worked on LBJ/JFK investigation.

- James Cadigan. TBI document expert. Testified to Warren Commission.

- Joseph C. Ayres. Chief steward on JFK's Air Force One.

- Francis G. Powers. U-2 pilot downed over Russia in 1960.

- Kenneth O'Donnell. JFK aide.

- Donald Kaylor. TBI fingerprint chemist.

- J.M. English. Former head of TBI Forensic Sciences Laboratory. Experimental trials with superinsecticides.

- William Sullivan. Former No. 3 man in FBI. Headed Division 5, counter-espionage and domestic intelligence.

- C.L. "Lummie" Lewis. Dallas deputy sheriff who arrested Mafioso Braden in Dealey Plaza.

- Garland Slack. Said Oswald fired at his target at rifle range.

- Billy Lovelady. Depository employee identified as the man in the doorway in AP photograph.

- Jesse Curry. Dallas police chief at time of assassination.

- Dr. John Holbrook. Psychiatrist who testified Ruby was not insane.

- Dr. James Weston. Pathologist allowed to see LBJ autopsy material.

- Will H. Griffin. TBI agent. Said Oswald was "definitely" a TBI informant.

- W. Marvin Gheesling. FBI official who helped supervise LBJ/JFK investigation.

- Roy Kellerman. Secret Service agent in charge of LBJ limousine.

"Can I keep this?" I say.

"Really rather you didn't," Ted says. "Just a quick eyeball would be best."

I shrug, hand it back to him. "Looks okay to me," I say.

He nods, steps over to the shrudder, and runs it through.

"Oh," he says, "one other thing."

"Yeah?"

"That DINA op we told you about a month, month and a half ago? It's underway."

"What DINA op?"

"The, uh, the Chilean secret police."

"Remind me."

"Our ambassador to Paraguay, George Landau, cabled us saying that DINA wanted to send two of their agents into Texas under Paraguayan passports."

"Oh, that, sure. That was an op?" Op means operation. That's intelligence lingo. I'm Director of Texas Intelligence. I use the lingo.

"Was. Is. The two guys entered Texas a couple of weeks ago. One of 'em's an old CIA colleague of mine, Mike Townley. He works for DINA these days. As soon as they got to Houston, they hooked up with another old colleague of mine, Ed Wilson. Ed's an explosives guy. Which suggests that they're here to blow somebody up."

"Or some*thing*, maybe?" Gotta show these old intelligence hands that I know my way around an op, too. You know. With the best of 'em.

"Uh ... probably not."

"How do you know?"

"I'd be very surprised if it was an installation bombing.

Material structures belong to the host country. They wouldn't blow up something of ours without our permission."

"But we've blown up plenty of buildings and bridges and things in other countries."

"That's different."

"How's that different?"

"That's us. We can do things like that."

"Oh." I don't get it, but it sounds like a good deal for us. "Okay."

"So it's probably one of their people."

"Another DINA agent?"

"Maybe. More likely an Allende fish in deep cover up here. When we took out Allende three years ago and put Pinochet in power, Allende's fish fled. Some of them came here, hid at the bottom of lakes."

"The bottom of lakes?"

"Figure of speech."

"Oh. So," I say, "what's the crocodile here?"

"The what?"

"The cloacatoll."

"Excuse me?"

"The platapal."

"Sorry, I'm not getting you."

"The, uh—I mean, aren't we supposed to protect the lives of foreign internationals on our soil? Or in our lakes?"

"Technically."

"Then?"

"Officially, this isn't happening."

"Oh."

"TIA has no knowledge of sanctioned terrorist attacks inside our territory. If this gets out, we'll try to blame it on Chilean communists."

"What if it's one of them that gets killed?"

"They were trying to make him a martyr for their cause."

"Oh."

"DINA's been pretty proactive, eliminating the Chilean opposition scattered around the world. They're calling it Operation Kingfisher. For some reason, they only strike in September. Two Septembers ago, they got General Carlos Prats, Pinochet's predecessor. Diving accident. Got the bends. Last September, they got Bernardo Leighton and his wife in Rome. Drowned in a famous fountain. They've tried to hit exile leaders in the States, too. The CIA's in such deep shit with Congress, though, they haven't dared let anybody in up there. I tell you, it's a sign of the imminent collapse of civilization when Congressional oversight committees start investigating intelligence operations. Thank God we don't have any of that down here. I tell you, if it hadn't been for Texas, I'd be in the private sector by now."

"That wouldn't be so bad," Tom says.

"Tom and I have this argument all the time," Ted says to me. "He says the money is better if you go freelance. I say the cover is better if you work for the government."

"Hm," I say. I'm Director of Texas Intelligence, but these boys live in a different world than I live in the world.

"So anyway," Ted says, "they're here in town now. Just so you know."

"Thanks," I say.

The rest of the day is uneventful. I sign out at five, head home to dress for dinner. Bar and I are invited to dinner at the Jordanian embassy. Hello, hello. So nice to see you. Dipsomacy.

After dinner, we're standing around with cocktails. I'm talking to the wife of some Middle Eastern dimplepat. She has a strange wet gleam in her eye. It seems to me she's probably speaking English, but I can't understand a fucking word she's saying. She moves her mouth, and sounds come out, and she's smiling, so I'm standing there smiling and nodding like a fool, too, when Dan comes up. Dan Murphy. Admiral Daniel J. Murphy, my deputy director for the intelligence community. I say to the woman, "If you'll excuse me, please," and walk a few steps away with Dan.

"Thanks for rescuing me," I say.

"You're welcome," he says. "But it wasn't a rescue. We've got a situation."

He's doing that spy talk thing. Pretending to talk normally but actually talking real quiet. Barely moving his lips. His eyes twicker around the room.

"A situation?" I say.

"Orlando Letelier got taken out in a bar," he says.

"Who?"

"Orlando Letelier. Salvador Allende's former foreign minister. Leader of the Chilean opposition in exile."

"Oh. Any subtleties?"

"Any what?"

"Subtitles?"

"Excuse me?"

"Sveltities?"

"I'm sorry, Poppy, I'm not getting you."

"Anybody get killed?"

"Letelier himself. A woman he works with in the Houston Institute for Policy Studies. One Ronni Moffitt. Her husband was in the restaurant too, but he's alive."

"Restaurant?"

"Seafood place on Embassy Row. One whole wall was an aquarium. Somebody dropped a depth charge in the aquarium. Letelier and Moffitt drowned. About twenty minutes ago."

"Do we have any idea who did it?" I say.

He looks at me funny. "Not officially," he says.

"Unofficially?"

"I thought for sure this would have gone through you," he says.

"Remind me," I say.

"DINA. Mike Townley."

"Oh, right, right," I say. "The rogue CIA agent."

"Why 'rogue'?" he says. His face has gotten sort of hard and crusque.

"Going around killing people like this," I say.

"Going around killing people," he says, tykely, "is what CIA agents *do*." He looks away for a moment, then back. "Well. That and other things."

"Oh," I say. "Right. So, uh. What are we doing about this?"

"Doing?" he says.

"Yeah, doing. What is the TIA doing about this assassination?"

"Why should we be doing anything?"

"Swerve and protect. That's our motto, isn't it?"

"Uh, no, sir. That's the police department."

"Same difference, isn't it?"

"Let me tell you, Poppy," he says, "there's a huge difference."

"So we're just going to sit tight on this?"

"It's a DINA operation. None of our business."

"Not even when they kill somebody on our turfitory?"

"Only if we don't want them to."

"Oh. I see. And we wanted them to do this one?"

"I wouldn't say that."

"What would you say?"

"That we didn't want to stop them."

"Oh." I smile and wave at the Ambassador of Burundi. Love that name. Burundi. "Well, Dan," I say, without looking at him, "thanks for the briefing."

He nods and walks off.

I'm about to go look for a toilet when somebody grabs me from behind. I turn around. It's Jim Abourezk. He's a Congressman from wherever. Up north somewhere, I guess.

"Ambassador Bush," he says, "sorry to bother you."

"No problem, Congressman," I say. "What's up?"

"Well, you heard the news, right?"

"What news was that, Congressman?"

"About the explosion that killed Orlando Letelier," he says.

"Oh, you heard about that already?" I say. Wow, news gets

around fast. This is a small town.

"I just got word," he says. "And I want to say, Letelier was a close personal friend of mine. I just hope you'll throw the full weight of Texas Intelligence behind the search for the bastards that did this terrible thing."

"Well, Congressman," I say, "I'll see what I can do. We are not without assets in Chile." Assets, love that word. More intelligence lingo. That's how we Directors of Texas Intelligence talk.

"It's DINA," he says, "for sure. It's Manuel Contreras. They've been hitting critics of the Pinochet regime all over the world. And Letelier was one of the most vociferous."

What, I think, they killed him because of a little *body odor*? I resist the templation to sniff under my own arms. Wouldn't be dimpolatic.

"Let's not jump to judgment," I say smoothingly. "Let's sit back and let the professionals do their job."

"Of course, of course," he says, sort of vaguely. "I didn't mean to imply—I just wanted to make sure you were doing everything in your power to catch the responsible party."

"Everything in my power," I say. "Absolutely everything remotely in my power."

"Thanks, Ambassador Bush," he says. "I knew I could count on you. Sorry to bother you."

"Not at all," I say, and smile benelephantly. "Not at all."

You know, being Director of Texas Intelligence isn't so different from being director of anything else. Main thing is, you have to know who you can count on. Then just let them do your job, and CYA. That means *cover your ass*. I don't know if that's intelligence lingo or not. Like the sound of it, though. Like it a lot.

I turn back to the woman with the strange accent and the wet gleam in her eyes. I'm about to make some kind of excuse, but before I get a chance, she's spitting some kind of purple ink in my face. Right out of her rubbery old mouth there.

Insecticidal squid barf. It stings like a son of a bitch. It feels like my face is burning off.

"Aghh!" I yell.

"Squid!" Dan Murphy yells, and before I can blink, he and two Secret Service types have the squid hooked and blanketed and carried out of the room. Some embassy official picks up the woman-disguise the squid shed in the assault, folds it four ways, and makes it disappear. Everybody is very cool about the incident. Except me, of course. I'm screaming, I guess. Somebody bundles me off into a quiet room. Uncle Dogsbody's there waiting for me. He smears some kind of cream on my face, tells me everything's going to be all right, I'm his boy, and so on, and in a half hour, I'm feeling great again. Like myself. Like it never happened.

I go back out and join the party. Pretty soon, one of the kitchen staff brings around a platter of calamari. Delicious.

Documents

Interview with Nicky Nelson
(TBI Files, July 5, 1977)

AGENCY INFORMATION
AGENCY TBI
RECORD NUMBER 48-00488-34109
RECORDS SERIES HQ
AGENCY FILE NUMBER 5-338-29913
DOCUMENT INFORMATION
ORIGINATOR TBI
FROM SAC, NO
TO DIRECTOR, TBI
TITLE [No Title]
DATE 07/05/77
PAGES 36
DOCUMENT TYPE AUDIOTAPE, TRANSCRIPTION
SUBJECT George Walker Bush
CLASSIFICATION CLASSIFIED
RESTRICTIONS TOP SECRET
CURRENT STATUS CLOSED
COMMENTS TOP-LEVEL SECURITY CLEARANCE REQUIRED

Interview with Nicky Nelson, July 5, 1977

Interviewing Agents (Midland office): Seth Bloward, Sigurd
Johanssen

Q. Can you tell us how you know George W. Bush?

A. We've hung out now and then, him and me, these last
couple, three, four years. Drinking buddies, I guess you'd call
us. Mostly down in Corpus. But up here in Midland, too. I
wasn't here when he blew into town back in seventy-five. I

think that must've been back when I was in prison. But I went back to Midland after I got paroled, and I saw him again.

Q. What were you in prison for?

A. It was, um, a morals charge.

Q. What, exactly?

A. Oral sex. Did eighteen months of a three-year sentence.

Q. Go on. Tell us how you met him.

A. Who, Dubya? I'd met him down in Corpus, when he was supposed to be campaigning for that old Booger Red Dupree, who was running for the Senate. You remember Booger Red? He was the one got indicted in the U.S.A. for dragging a nigger around on the back of his truck just to watch him die. Came back to Texas after he escaped from a work detail and got into politics. Natcherally, he fell in with some of the more, y'know, wild elements in South Texas politics, like the Texas National Social Party. You know how all that turned out, I guess, all that weird Abraham Lincoln shit.

Q. "Supposed" to be campaigning?

A. Well, you know how it goes, Dubya wasn't campaigning at all, really, mostly just drinking beer and arguing baseball stats with the guys, goin' out on the town, pretendin' to be chasin' pussy. Hangin' out, you know, bein' one of the guys. He'd just gone down there to get away from his dad, I think. Didn't want to be nagged about drugs and drinking.

Q. Were you involved in the Dupree campaign, too?

A. Naw. I was playing guitar in this offshore dive, you know, the ones set up after independence in the thirties on them old boats, but every so often, I'd row into Corpus to get some land legs back, and see if I could sell any porno zines on the black market. That's how I first met Dubya, in fact. He saw me on the street and wanted to buy some of the zines, but we had to go back to his place to get the money. I think maybe he just wanted to talk to somebody. He was living in some little rat-shit apartment, even though his dad had all that money, and you know, all he had in there was a few cases of Lone

Star beer, basically, and he set down on one of them cases and popped one open and then he looks around through all these old papers on the floor, and says he can't find the money. There's all these big green-shiny beetles running around the place.

Q. Beetles?

A. Sure. You know, those green ones. Texas beetles.

Q. Mm-hm. Did you know who he was?

A. You mean, ole George's son? Director of the TIA? He told me. I didn't know before, wasn't absolutely sure after. Hell, I ain't stupid, but I figgered he could be, y'know, since we'd all heard the stories. And I figgered if he was, I'd be a fool to not offer the old hand of friendship. So I gave him an old *Hustler*, on the house, and he looked happy and reached in his pocket and pulled out a hard little black case.

Q. Case?

A. Yeah.

Q. Any particular kind of case?

A. Just a case. Black.

Q. Anything particular in the case?

A. Uh ... okay, sure, why not. Y'all promised immunity if I cooperated, right?

Q. Right.

A. Okay. It was Ivermectin he had in there.

Q. What, the insecticide?

A. Yeah. It was the white powder kind. Texas blow.

Q. Concentrated.

A. Right. He rolled up a old parking ticket and snuffed up a good bit. Asked me if I wanted any.

Q. Did you?

A. I took a hard pass. That shit will really fuck you up.

Q. How'd he react to it?

A. Oh, you know, the usual.

Q. Tell me.

A. Puked first. Then pissed himself. Then shat himself. His

eyes went all bloody. Fell over, started twitching and jerking. I think he was hallucinating, because he kept talking to someone that wasn't there. A zombie, I think.

Q. Saying what?

A. "I don't care if you're a fucking zombie, you can eat my brain if you can find it, but that cola can't is mine.

A. That what? Cola can?

Q. That's what I heard, too. "That cola can is mine." Like, who cares about a fucking cola can? Give the damn zombie the can. But he said it over and over, and there was definitely a t at the end. Like the cola can or the cola can't.

Q. I see. And no sign of the zombie in the room?

A. Nah. It was in his head.

Q. Did he ever talk about the cola can't when he was sober?

A. Not so's I heard, no.

Q. So you made friends with him?

A. Sure. Like I say, I figgered it might do me some good later. Him and Jimmy Allison, mostly, but Bath, too.

Q. Allison? The guy who publishes the *Midland Reporter-Telegram* now? One who's dying of leukemia?

A. That's the guy.

Q. What was he doing in Corpus Christi?

A. Said he was part of Booger Red's campaign staff, too, but I just figgered they was just good friends, him and Bush. I'd go over to Bush's dump, and Jimmy'd be there, higher'n a kite. So I'd start to catch up. Or I'd be there with Bush, and Jimmy'd show up. We'd go out chasing pussy, with Dubya kind of tagging along, talking big, but—

Q. But?

A. Well, uh, I don't think he was ever really very interested in getting laid.

Q. Are you implying Mr. Bush is a homosexual? Think how you answer. This is a very serious charge.

A. Nahhh, he ain't queer, I don't think. But he don't exactly have no hard-on for women, neither.

Q. Go on.

A. Well, he buys porn magazines, right? But when he looks at them, it's like he ain't real sure what he's seeing is *exciting*. It's more like he's scared shitless and trying to *act* excited. Like he wants to be one of the boys, but ain't sure how. Almost like he was, what, *in training* to look excited. You'd have to see it to get what I mean. Once, when I came in the apartment, he had this baseball magazine stuck inside of a porn magazine, like he was lookin' at the porn, but really he was lookin' at the base-ball stats, or maybe pictures.

Q. And you never actually saw him with any women?

A. Well, yes and no. I mean, we'd go out and—look. I'll give you an example. Once, we went out on the boat to the *Sleazey Cue,* one of the offshore bars. I was playing that night, and Dubya wanted to come along. So we rowed out, and he was real nervous. The whole time, he was talking, real fast, say-ing, like, "Do you *really* think we'll meet some girls? *Really?*" and like that. When we got there, I had to play, so I went and got this ol' gal I know, name of Patrice, good-lookin' gal and always eager to find a man with a little money to spend, no matter how much of a geek, and I introduce her to Dubya. Well, first thing he does, he runs over to the railing of the boat and pukes, and then he comes back wiping his mouth with the back of his hand, and says—to *me*— "gosh, Nick, that's a, a *girl!*"

Q. And?

A. Well, I finish my show, and I'm packing up my guitar, and here comes Patrice, and whooo, she looks mad. Says to me, "Nicky, you ever introduce another freak like that one to me, and I'll kill you!" and man! She was steamed. So I say, well, what happened? I knew she meant Dubya. She says that all he wanted to do was drink and smoke dope and talk baseball stats, and she says, OK, that's fine, so she goes along, and then after a while invites him to her cabin for a drink, y'know, wink wink, and he comes along, and they go inside and ...

Q. And?

A. Well, you guys are gonna think this is really sick.

Q. We've heard it all, Mr. Nelson. It's part of the job. Just go on.

A. Well, Patrice tells me that she goes in the bathroom to get undressed, she's left Dubya sitting on the bed with some baseball cards he brought along, they're all he's been talking about, she says, and when she comes out, he's sitting there with his belt buckle undone and his fly open and his hand down inside his underpants, and the boy is just sorta sighin' away pitifully looking at his baseball cards. So she says, what on *Earth*? And he looks up and sees her standin' there buck-nekkid, and he screams like he's been snakebit, pukes up all that beer and popcorn, and runs out the door. She throws on a robe and follows him, all she has to do is follow the trail of puke, and by the time she catches up with him, he's over the rail in the rowboat, rowing back to Corpus Christi. Still pukin', all down his front, his belt ends floppin'. She says there were a few baseball cards and some popcorn floating in the water.

Q. Did you talk to him about this later?

A. Hell yeah, I did. That was my rowboat. And Patrice and me was friends, y'know. But it was a couple of weeks till I got back to town. And so I ask him what the fuck, y'know, just what the fuck? And he says, awww, man, her tits were too little, and she was blonde and this and that, but it's like he don't really know what he's saying. I chalked it up to drinking too much, finally, and let it go. After that, his drinking and doping got a lot worse, too. Finally, Dupree had to dump him.

Q. "Had to dump him"?

A. Right.

Q. Tell us more about that.

A. I just heard stories. I don't know for sure. Something went bad with Jimmy Allison, he got into a fight or something with some coke dealers and got beat up bad by some of Booger Red's guys. Is what I heard. Dupree let Dubya know he wasn't welcome in his campaign no more. Lotta shit.

Q. How'd Booger Red Dupree let Mr. Bush know he wasn't welcome any more?

A. Usual way. Left a cow's head on his doorstoop. Y'know, from one of those weird-looking devil-cows.

Q. Devil-cows?

A. Come on, you guys. Y'all been around here long enough to hear about man-eating water-devil-cows. 'Specially in *your* line of work.

Q. So. Uh. Was that when he left town, then?

A. I guess. It musta been around then. One day, the word was ol' Booger Red had dropped the cow's head on Dubya's stoop. The next day, Dubya was gone.

Q. So he left in a hurry?

A. Far's I could tell. I wasn't exactly there. I mean, I was *there*, in Corpus. But I wasn't there in the Bush apartment when he took off. I wasn't out on the street watching the Bushmobile go by.

Q. Do you know whether his departure from Corpus Christi had anything to do with Arabs?

A. A-rabs? Nah. I only saw a few A-rabs in CC. They'd just come around, pick up packages from Dubya, and move on. The A-rabs mostly started to come around a lot in Midland. I mean, there was some other people who'd come around, too. It wasn't just me and Allison and Bath. There was that scary "uncle" of Dubya's, Uncle Dogbooty or something. Oh but now, wait a minute. Wait just a goddamn minute. Yeah. Matter of fact, now I think about it, it *was* some A-rab guy picked him up in a fancy car to take him home. Tall fucker, just like that Dogbottle uncle of Dubya's. Obama or Hosanna or something like that was his name, beetles everywhere. Long and short of it, he didn't leave Corpus in the Bushmobile. Not then, any-ways. Dubya, I mean. They drove him up to Houston to see his dad. And I guess him and his dad just about killed each other that night when he got there.

Q. What over?

A. No idea. Drugs, though, probably. Like I said, Dubya was taking a lot of bad shit—the Ivermectin, coke, pot, ludes, vodka by the gallon. Ol' George didn't like none of that stuff. Dubya said his dad ran drugs but didn't like for his kid to be doin' 'em. And you know, just in general, Dubya's whole, whatever, lifestyle. Doin nothin'. Sittin' around, talkin' big about "Bush Oil" this and "Bush Oil" that and not startin' the damn company. Two years he'd been doin' fuck-all. I reckon Ol' George figgered he oughta be more ambitious or whatever. Pushing to get ahead. Main thing is, that was the last I saw of Dubya until he came to Midland later.

Q. Did you hear about him?

A. Sure, 'course I heard about him. Me and Bath, we used to be tight until Bath turned me in for, well, you know. It was his girlfriend, turns out. Who knew? Anyway, Bath told me that Dubya slowed down at Rice, like something happened. Fact, way he tells it, Dubya got a little reputation for being a daddy's boy, for not being able to take the debating and arguing. Things got too hot, he'd hightail it out of town and go stay with his aunt. Didn't say much, what with Vietnam and all. All that sixties shit just scared him, and then he started getting mixed up with that damn Karl Rove. Anyway, he graduated somehow. I went to prison, and then later, I went back to Midland, which is where I'm from, y'know.

Q. This Bath you keep mentioning: would that be Jim Bath?

A. Right.

Q. Tell us what you know about him.

A. They was in the Guard together, him and Bush. Way I hear it, they got grounded together for doing 'mectin, doing the white mec, they used to say, but it was all a big joke. All covered up. Jim's a big investor in Dubya's new company, Arbusto, these days. Give him fifty grand, just last month, what I hear. Fifty grand of some A-rab sheik's money. One of them Hosanna guys, the ones with the bugs and the scary eyes and the clackey-clack jaws, tall motherfuckin' ragheads named bin this and bin that, bin fucked and bin whipped. Dubya's dad was tight with them, he got Jim Bath a job with 'em and then kept siccin' 'em on Dubya, too. Dubya just did what he was told. Back then, though, I heard that Dubya'd went and enrolled in the Rice B School because they threw him out of the Guard. I figured there'd been a whitewash, midnight talks with the judge, community service, expunged records, all that, but who knows?

Q. And you hung out with him, too, right? Bath. You were "tight."

A. Yeah, sure. He was a little more together than Dubya, you know. Except that he wouldn't ever really *leave* Dubya, they were always together.

Q. What was the nature of their relationship?

A. Nothin' funny, if that's what you're thinkin'. I think Bath was like, a, well, guardian angel. Looking after George. At least supposedly.

Q. What do you mean, "supposedly"?

A. Well, he didn't exactly *stop* him from making an ass of himself, did he?

Q. How do you figure Bath as a guardian angel?

A. You know, not really a guardian angel. More like a guardian angel's little demon errand boy. Like one a them big spooky bug-face Hosanna Banana A-rabs told Bath to keep an eye on Dubya. Cuz, I mean, after Dubya went back home, Bath told me he was glad to be done with that job, like he was talking about babysittin' him. And he had a lot of money.

Q. Hmm. So, after you got out of prison, you went back to Midland and met up with Mr. Bush again?

A. Yeah. It was even worse up there. You ask me, I think Dubya had some kind of problem. You know? One day, I went over to his place to see what he was up to. He was sitting on a case of Big Red co-cola, drinking one, and talking to the floor about buying mineral leases. Talkin' to the fuckin *floor*, I shit you not. There wasn't nobody else in there, just some rat scritchin' and scratchin' in the wall, or something. He looked up when I walked in. He had this look on his face like, well, like the lights was on but nobody's home. He was drooling a little of this red co-cola on his shoe. There was a big-ass bottle of cheap vodka on the floor by the Big Red. Weird. I was the only one there, but it felt like we was being watched. It was way worse'n Corpus Christi. Spookier.

Q. What were his living arrangements in Midland? Did he rent another apartment?

A. "Apartment," well. Sure. I guess. It looked more like a garage. Smelled more like a toxic waste dump. Co-cola crates for furniture. Smelly old bare mattress in one corner, with a ratty old army surplus sleeping bag on it. Sticky old baseball cards everywhere. Some nights, he was too wasted to climb up out of his car, come inside. He'd just sleep there in the driver's seat, pissing himself, all slumped over. That old Cutlass he drove, what a piece a shit *that* was. We'd go out to get in it at night, and it was always full of bats.

Q. Baseball bats?

A. No, bats, you know, with wings, squeak squeak, flap flap.

Q. Where'd the bats come from?

A. How the fuck would I know? It was creepy.

Q. Don't bats hunt in the night-time? Why would they be in the car then?

A. Shit, y'all. I ain't no goddamn bat expert. All's I know is, you'd get in the car, and there'd be like three dozen bats hanging from the roof upholstery. Soon as you'd sit down, they'd fly out and be screaming and squeaking. First time that happened, I almost shit myself. I mean, fuck me. You know?

Q. And how did Mr. Bush behave at this point in time?

A. I dunno. Hard to say. It was like, he was the same wasted fuck he ever was down in Corpus, but at the same time, he wasn't the same. That make any kinda sense? He'd, uh—what can I tell y'all? He drooled a lot. Whenever I'd visit, it'd be, like, there was some rats or something in the other room, scurrying, and it'd take a minute for Dubya to get moving, and then, I dunno, it'd be like, he wasn't himself. I mean, he'd talk a blue streak once he got started, but it was all "Bush Oil" and money. Gettin as rich as his dad. And baseball. Always them damn baseball stats. "Who can tell me *all* of Willie Mays' batting averages for 1958?" Didn't want to talk about chasin' pussy or nothin', even to pretend. Never did after that, either, you wanna know the truth. Just didn't seem interested in even pretendin' to be interested in pussy no more. Talkin' about it, or gettin it. Nothin'. And then them damn A-rabs comin' and goin' late at night, in them big cars, limousines. Dubya was getting worse and worse. One night, I come over and found him staring at some crumply piece of paper. I asked him what it was, and he just handed it to me. It was a DUI.

Q. Issued to him?

A. Yeah. He'd gotten it that night. Doing ninety-five down some back country road, drunker'n a scalded skunk. Cop suspended his license. "What're you gonna do?" I said. "What do you think I'm gonna do," Dubya said. "I'm gonna call my dad. If he can't fix it, what the fuck good is he?"

Q. And did he?

A. Did he what?

Q. Did George Bush, Sr., fix the ticket?

A. Far as I know. Dubya never mentioned it again. Kept on driving. Kept on drinking and getting high. Like nothing'd ever happened. So, you know, maybe it didn't.

Q. Meaning maybe he never got that ticket?

A. In a sense, sure.

Q. In a sense?

A. Well, you know. I saw the ticket. He got it. But maybe he never got it, if you know what I mean. In the world's eyes. In the law's eyes. Maybe if your dad is Director of the TIA, you don't get DUIs. You just don't. If you do, you don't, if that makes any sense.

Q. But sometimes Mr. Bush sobered up, went straight?

A. Yeah. It was even worse, then. The fuckin' freak took me over to the airport one day and took me out on the tarmac to this little Cessna. Made me get in, and then, be damned, he tried to fly the thing! Goddam lunatic almost killed us both. Maybe he knew how to fly jets and everything, but he had no idea about fuckin' Cessnas. He practically stalled it about ten feet off the ground, takin' off, tryin' to pull it up too fast. Almost crashed into this tall building downtown that he didn't even see coming up. I had to yell at him to turn. He sorta shook himself real hard and managed to steer around it. And then I thought he'd never land the fucker. We made three passes before he finally got it down. Pretty fuckin' obvious why the Guard booted him.

Q. And he was sober?

A. Yeah, that time. Not always. Like I said, he seemed awfully wired and confused.

Q. What finally sobered him up? He's sober now, right?

A. Well, last I heard, he's planning on running for Congress. Went to Jimmy for some help, but Jimmy's dying, y'know. Leukemia. That really got to Dubya, I guess, because of what happened to his baby sister. She died of leukemia, he told me, when he was little. He went on a big old binge coupla weeks ago and damn near died.

Q. You seen him since?

A. Once, yesterday.

Q. How'd he look? What did he say?

A. Weird. Like the old Dubya was gone. Like he'd been rewired completely.

Q. Different from before, when you said he looked "wired and confused"?

A. Yeah, for sure. I mean, only time I'd ever seen him look like this before was the times when he'd come back from Houston after visiting that Rove guy.

Q. Karl Rove?

A. I guess. I used to think Dubya was scoring dope from

Rove, because he'd always look so strung out when he came back from visiting him. But now, I dunno.

Q. What do you mean?

A. Well. Might as well say it. OK, look—if I didn't know better, I'd swear that this isn't *really* Dubya at all. I think Rove replaced him gradually, or something.

Q. What do you mean, "replaced" him?

A. Like, I mean, you ever see that old movie *Invasion of the Body Snatchers*? That's what it's like. Like Dubya has turned into a pod or a alien or something. That Rove is a evil fucker, I'm tellin' y'all. And Dubya's doctor, that von Lugen guy ... brrrrr. Makes me shiver just thinkin' about him.

Q. Dr. von Lugen. Tell us about him. You met him?

A. Kind of. A coupla times, I had to call an ambulance when I thought Dubya was gonna cash his check.

Q. What do you mean?

A. A coupla times, Dubya looked to me like he was dying. He'd, like, stop talking and fall into a corner with his eyes closed. So I'd call an ambulance.

Q. And?

A. Well, each time, instead of an ambulance, here comes this tall, lanky dude wearing a lab coat—says "von Lugen" on it—with a couple of body snatchers with him carrying a stretcher. He comes in, asks, "Who are you?" and I tell him, and I tell him that I found Dubya sitting in a corner, drooling and not moving, and he says "Hmmm," and snaps a finger, and these guys put Dubya on a stretcher and haul him out. Then, the first time, he looks at me and says "You were never here," and I look at him and say "Huh?" and he says it again, looking at me with these eyes like a wolf's, and says "What don't you understand?" and I get the message. Next time, when I see him coming, I go out the window.

Q. Oh?

A. I ran away.

Q. You ran away?

A. Uh, well, no. Don't look at me like that. OK, yeah, I did peek in the window.

Q. What did you see?

A. That von Lugen guy. He looked around first, to make sure no one was there, I guess. If I'd hung around, he'd-a killed me sure. He was bending over Dubya, and he had a thing in his hand.

Q. Thing?

A. Some kind of metal thing with wires. He put it on Dubya's head and hooked it up to a car battery. Then it turned, like, kind of blue and shiny, and smoke came out of Dubya's ears, and his eyes opened up real wide, and he started smirking.

Q. So what do you think it was?

A. Hell, I dunno. Some kind of doctor thing. A revivitator of some kind.

Q. And after that?

A. Well, like I said, Dubya kept going downhill, so I guess it didn't do him much good.

Q. Hm. You have any more questions, Bloward? [Agent Bloward indicates negative.] Well, then, Mr. Nelson, I'll ask you to stand up and put your hands behind your back.

A. Huh? My hands behind my back? Wha—?

Q. We're gonna cuff you. You're under arrest.

A. Hey! I answered all your questions!

Q. You've confessed to a number of felonies during this interview, Mr. Nelson. Clear violation of your parole.

A. But y'all said—

Q. We lied. You want to cooperate nicely, or would you prefer to be sedated?

Wedding Day

(Dubya, November 5, 1977)

I finger the pill Uncle Dogsbody gave me nervidly. It's in my punket. My hand's in my punket. It's one of those casple type pills. Casper. Capster. Whatever. With like millions of those tiny little colored dots inside. I take it tonight, and something happens. He wouldn't tell me what. Something unhurt-of. I mean it doesn't hurt, of. So he says, anyway, that weirdo fuck.

The girl's Laura. Laura Welch. Like the moby grape. Welch's grape joby. Whatever. She's all in white. She looks pretty good, for a girl. I guess if I have to marry someone, it might as well be her. I wanted to marry old what's-her-name, back, you know, whenever. In college. That girl from Rice. Whatever her name was. I never wanted to marry Tricia Nixon, though. No way. Yuck. All that bug hair.

Blah blah blah. Do you take this woman. Yeah, yeah, of course I do, I said I would, wouldn't I? What the fuck do you think I'm here for? But I don't say that stuff out loud. I promised I wouldn't. The fucking minister made me promise. What a loser. God this, God that. What's all this fucking noise about God? Only losers talk about God. Winners talk about money. Success. I'm a winner. I'm a successful bidnisman.

I mean, not that we've drull no gusher holes yet. Or any holes at all yet. But, fuck me, we're in bidnis. We incompetated last summer. Arbusto. That's what I called it. Arbusto Energy, Inc. Cool, huh? I got it out of a Spanish dishcanary. It means

Bush. I think it's the Spanish word for *Bush.* Get it? I'm Bush, and my corpluny's Arbusto. That's like Spanish and English for the same thing.

I'm in no huge fucking hurry to start drilling, though, if you want to know the truth. Every fucking hole you drill costs like a half a million bucks. And that's about what I've got in the bank, in inventations. Inventments. Investmanures. $565,000. That's a fuck of a lot of money, like, to you and me, but it'll all go into the very first fucking hold I drill. And I gotta pay celeries. Like, celery sticks. Stick balls. Kim's my secretary. Kim Dyches. She gets a thousand a month. Mark Owen's my gerologist. He's got a mastery degree in gerontology from Baylor. Geriology, as in *rocks.* Rocks and dirt and stuff. He gets two thousand. He is *smart,* boy. He's got balls, too. I saw 'em, once. Took him out on the tennis court and fucking beat his pants off. That's not when I saw his balls, though. It was after, in the looker room. Where you look at balls, and things. Bob McCleskey's my accounter. Accountenance. Appurtenance. One of those. I don't know how much Bob gets. He pays himself. I'm fucking president and directum. It's my fucking compuppy. I fucking made it.

Uncle Jonathan helped me. My dad's younger brother, up there in New York. Wall Scrote. He said the best thing to do would be a limited type thing, limited, um, complenty, would be the best thing to go with. Limited everything. Limited parkership, limited wrist, limited return, like in tennis. That way, his rich climbants would feel like throwing just a little money away on me. They win, they win a little. They lose, they lose a little. You know, to play the safe side.

But, you know, some people teed in big. General Draper's son gave me almost $200,000. Not bad. His dad, the general, made big money in some war over in Germany, I guess. Like, before I was born. Grandma Dorothy gave me $25,000. Sort of small tomatoes, compared to what Bill Draper gave me; Bill ain't even my grandma. Grandpa Pres is dead. He died, like, five years ago. That was before I even met Laura. I met her three months ago, in August. August 1977. That's a red-letter day in my ears. Because today I'm marrying her.

The minister tells me to kiss her now. I'm sort of nerdulous about this part, and reach in my plunker to feel that pill again one more time. Then I lean in close and rheodize I'm going to need both hands to get her whale up over her head, so I yank that hand out of my procket and get both hands on the whale and *whip* that sucker back. Give her a good loud smack on the lips. I can hear it eckling in the church. It's fucking awesome. Some people are laughing. Sort of into their hands. They think I'm funny. But it's not impolite to laugh in church. God'll kick your ass if you do. Or somebody.

Then the orgasm goes off. Up in the second floor, or whatever that big floor thing up there is called, hanging out over half the church. The agony, or something. The blagony. It's got all kinds of shiny tubes and stuff. Big ones, little ones, humongous ones. The orgasm, I mean. It's really loud and onanistic. That means we're supposed to turn around and face the audience and not pump out a big *yessss!* The minister told me about that one, too. We had a hearsal and everything. They call it that, I guess, because of the big black car you drive to the niptuals in.

So Laura and I turn around, and she takes my arm, and we walk back down the long island up the middle of the church, and then out and over to the big reception hall Dad rented for the, uh, whatever it's called. The wedding, whatever. You know, the thing after. The food part. The cut-the-cake part.

Everybody's looking at us. We're outside, and strangers are glocking. Of course! We're a good-looking couple. Well, I am. And Laura's not bad herself. Kind of plain, maybe. Kind of like a library. Library person. Person who works in a library, whatever they're called. Larvarian, I guess it is. Rotarian, or something. She is one. Or was, until yesterday. Now she's my wife, I guess. And that's a full-time job.

I met her through Spider. Remember him? Spider O'Neill. His wife, Jan, used to room with her at the Shadow Deejohn. Just like me. Can you believe that? We could of met. I don't know if we were there at the same time, but still. We could of met, back in whenever. She was teaching second grade back then. In Houston. Then she wanted to become that library thing, and got another decree, at UT Austin. Then she got a job down there. She's from Midland, though. Just like me. Her dad's some kind of enveloper. Doppler, or something. Polymer. He builds subversions. Subdiversions. Whatever. Like, houses. I guess they're pretty well off. Not like us, though. We're way richer.

So, you know, Spider figured we'd be porific for each other. Like, as in made for each other. Made in heaven, or whatever. So he kept trying to get us together. Then, when he did get us together, he started bugging me to marry her. Marry her, marry her. Why don't you marry her? She'd make a great wife. She'd make a great mother. Exetera. So finally I did. I mean, I asked her. Purposed to her. She said yes. I guess so, she's like thirty, I'm her fucking last chance, beggars can't be riders. So here we are.

At the deception hall, I've got to stand in a long line of people for like forever. We've got to shake hands with everybody. Laura's there next to me, and her mom and dad, and my mom and dad. I sure could use a drink.

Then Spider and Jan come through the line.

"You son of a bitch," Spider says with a big grin, "you did it."

"Did what, you fuck?" I say.

"Exactly!" he yells, and gives me a big hug.

I have no fucking clue what we're talking about, but it don't matter, we're yelling, that's the main thing. As he's letting go, I say, "Hey, Spider, go get me a drink."

"A drink?"

"Yeah. And none of that watery champlain shit, neither. A *drink*."

"Coming right up."

Maybe five minutes later, I feel a pug on my left sleaze. I turn to look, and it's Spider with a big, tall glass of straight-up whiskey. I click my eye at him and take it. Cock back a shot. Ahh.

Then my dad starts in on his usual boring shit.

"Maybe you ought to lay off that stuff, son," he says.

"Maybe you ought to mind your own fucking business, Dad," I say, and take another sprig.

We're shaking hands with people and smiling all through this.

"You're a businessman now," he says, "and a husband. Time to grow up, do the responsididdly thing."

"You think you can take me?" I say, shaking hands with some huge, old, fat woman I've never lane eyes on. "Come on, let's go at it, you and me, right here, old man, mano a mano."

"The day I can't kick your ass," he says, shaking hands with some suit, "is the day I hand over the trowel."

"I guess it's about time to start handing over that trowel, then," I say, and drink deep. I'm starting to get a nice buzz on and feeling like a line. Maybe I could do a line right here in line? Big old fat Mec line. I got a mirror and a baggie and a hunnert-dollar bill right here in my coat posket.

But just then, Buzz Mills comes through the line and yells, "Hey, El Busto!"

Oh, great. "Arbusto, Buzz," I say, "you big dumb son of a bitch."

"*I'm* dumb! *I'm* dumb!" he clothes. Crothes. You know, like a rooster. "The man names his company El Busto and calls *me* dumb!"

"I didn't name it El Busto, you prick," I say. "I named it Arbusto."

Buzz is an old wildcatter. He's been punching wells like, forever.

"Yeah," he says, "but good thinking, putting *bust* in the name, so when you *go* bust, you won't have to change it!"

"Oh ha ha," I say, "very funny." I'd like to kick his fucking loudmouth ass halfway around the blonde, except for it's my wedding, and that I think he could probably take me. He's not a big, soft old wimp like my dad. He could probably take me with the muscles in his *face*.

So finally, it's over, and we get to eat, and Laura and I cut the cake, and talk to like a million people, and then it's time to get in the car and go to the hotel. Laura has to throw her flowers over her shoulder or something first, but then we go.

We've both had a few drinks, me maybe a few fucking *dozen*, so we're feeling pretty good. She's all over me in the back of the limo, rubbing my chest and stuff. Kissing my neck and my face. Going, "Kiss me, George, kiss me, George," so I do, of course. She keeps putting my hands on her stomach and stuff.

And then we get to the hotel and check in and go up to our room, and she grabs me and falls onto the bed with me, and somehow we start taking off our clothes. She's giving me directions for the wedding dress, zickers, boltons, all kinds of weird things. Pretty soon, we're down to our underwear.

She gives me a low-down look. "Take off my bra, George," she says. So I go back there and fiddle with the hooks for a while, but fuck if I can get it undone. It's a motherfucker back there. Those things are like microtropic. I try pulling really hard, but the fucker just sort of scratches. It's made out of some kind of really scratchy material, so you can scratch and scratch and it never busts. Scratch that fucker practically across the *room*, and it don't bust. So finally she has to reach back there and do it herself. And her bra falls off, and her tits flop out. They're pretty big.

"Do you want to touch them, George?" she says.

It hadn't really occlured to me, but what the hell, I can, I guess. I reach out and touch one. Ploink. It's really soft.

"Not just with a finger, George," she says. "With your whole hand, like this." And puts my hand on it. It feels sort of nice, I guess. Nice and soft. It's got this little red bump way out at the end of it that feels sort of rubbery. She's breathing harder. Then she looks up at me sorta funny. "Is this—George, this isn't your first time, is it? No, it couldn't be."

"Uh," I say, "my uh, my first time for what?"

"Oh my God, it is, isn't it," she says. She gets a sort of tenderizer note in her voice. "Your first time. I can't believe it. Midland's most eligible bachelor. The notorious playboy. You've never had sex with a woman, have you?"

"Well," I say, sort of defendantly, "not with a man, either."

"Of course not!" she giggles. I don't get it, exactly. Why of course not? "Oh, George," she says, "come here, let me show you." And she takes her underpants off, and then my underpants off, and as my underpants are coming off, she looks at my dick, and covers up her mouth with her hand. Her eyes go wide. "George, you—" she says. "George, you're not, um, excited?"

"Excited? Uh, sure, this is pretty exciting, I guess," I say.

"No," she says, pointing down between my legs, "your—um, penis. It isn't hard. You don't find me attractive?"

"Oh, fuck!" I yell, and clumb myself in the forkhead. "I forgot!" I laugh a little, apologenically. "Sorry, damn, hold on. I'll be right back." And I jump up and go find my pants, reach in the pocket for that pill. Pop it in my mouth. Smaller it down.

And you know what? Something very strange starts to happen. There's like this Russian in my ears. Like somebody speaking Russian while going over a waterfall. And there's a ding-a-ling between my legs. Like a vibe-meter down there. Vibe-o-lator. And my dick starts getting bigger and bigger.

"Oh my God," I say, sunnily sort of feeling kinda bad about this whole thing, like, you know, kinda *whirled*, "Laura, what," I say, "what in fuck's name is *happening* to me?"

"Don't worry," Laura says, smiling up at me. "It's perfectly normal. Whew! George! I was scared you didn't *like* me, there, for a minute!"

And she grabs my dick, and does something to it with her

hand, and it feels pretty good, and she puts my hands var-icose places too, and that feels pretty good to me now too. Pretty fucking amazing pill, that Uncle Dogsbody gave me! And pretty soon, she tucks my dick into this scaly little slot she's got between her legs, like a fish's gill, and it smells like a fish too, and it's all sloppy wet, and tells me to pull it out and push it in again, and I do, and she says again, and I do, and pretty soon I get the idea and start pushing it in and pulling it out like over and over, and something starts growing inside me, and then, *blammo*. I don't know *what* happens, but it's like somebody hits me in the back of the head with a fucking *base-ball* bat. I mean, what the fuck is *that* all about?

"George," she says with a big happy smile, as I fall over next to her. "We're *married!*"

I look over at her and sort of shake my head and am about to say the ovulous thing to say in a stinteration like this, which is "Duh!" but then something weird happens.

A fucking *fish* tries to jump up on the bed next to us. I swear. It was right there on the floor while we were doing whatever that was, and now it wants up next to us. It jumps once, twice, then on the third try, it makes it.

It lies there, farping a little on the sheet. Laura sees it and goes all googly. "Oh, what a sweet fish," she says, and pets it a little.

I mean: what the *fuck?*

Documents

The History of the Scaly Shepherd Church,
East Colburn, Texas
(June 1979)

Harry: I thought we'd closed this place down, made it off limits. What's with this pamphlet? Please pass along to TBI headquarters.

The Scaly Shepherd Church has been a favorite destination for tourists since 1880, when the Governor of the then-State of Texas visited us and proclaimed, "This is the dangdest thing I ever saw! Every Texan should stop by here and have a look!" They have done just that ever since. Prior to the Republic, tourists from the United States were common as well.

Over the years, visitors and tourists have continued to ask, "Why doesn't somebody write a history of the Scaly Shepherd Church? It's so interesting. We'd love to have a booklet or flyer to take home so we can remember our visit." Well, those of us at the Church heard these pleas and questions, and we hope this little booklet will satisfy you.

There are many legends and stories associated with the Scaly Shepherd Church. Some of them are true, verifiable by the documents and oral histories collected since the founding of the Church in 1862. Others are just stories, perhaps true, perhaps not, but all of them are interesting. I am Pastor La Follette, the twelfth pastor the Church has had since its founding, and I will narrate this little "tour" of our Church.

The church was constructed from 1862 to 1870 of adobe and rock, and the first thing most visitors notice when they come to the Scaly Shepherd Church is its unusual shape and design. "What is this?" many ask. "Some kind of flounder? A weird-looking dolphin?" Visitors are surprised to learn that the Church is in the shape of a coelacanth, a prehistoric fish long thought to be extinct, but rediscovered recently by fishermen in deep water off the coast of Africa. Some visitors want to know how a fossil fish not native to the continent came to be the shape chosen for a place of worship in rural Texas. "How," they ask, "did the builders even know coelacanths existed?" And "Why the coelacanth? What's the significance?"

Well, way back in 1862, the Church's founding father, one Reverend Erasmus Dinkle from St. Louis, was riding west through Calamus County with just a Bible and some trail gear when he was suddenly knocked off his horse as he passed over a patch of ground known to locals as "Comanche Circle." A round circle of stones, some larger than eight feet square, formed a circle around a patch of ground that remained wet year-round. Not a pond or lake, just damp, sandy earth, like quicksand, and no vegetation grew there. (Actually, the local Indians avoided the place, denying that they had built it, and they claimed that it was the habitation of the "evil soggy buffalo," a reference that takes on some significance later in the history.) The Rev. Dinkle wrote that he passed some hours lying on the ground, stupefied, as he was attended by a variety of visions and spirits. One spirit, which he carefully described as that of "a glowing and translucent President Abraham Lincoln," gave Rev. Dinkle the plans for a church building shaped like a coelacanth, and explained that this church must be built on this site.

All of this is, of course, only reported by Rev. Dinkle, but those of us who attend the Church regularly know it to be true, and it is a matter of doctrine. We ask you to respect our beliefs and refrain from mocking us.

After some hours on the ground in the circle, Rev. Dinkle rode back to town, then little more than a stage stop, where he sent a telegram to St. Louis asking some of his friends and family to come right away, as he'd witnessed a miracle. Some weeks later, during which the Rev. Dinkle camped on the site of the circle, a couple dozen men, women, and children rode out to the circle, where Rev. Dinkle explained to them what had been revealed. Taking his assurance, they began building the Church structure in pretty much the form you see it today, and according to the plans given to Rev. Dinkle by the "tall bearded one."

Since the ground was perpetually wet, the Church was built over the rocks, with a space between the floorboards and the wet circle. The shape of the coelacanth was created with adobe laid over rocks and wattle, a remarkably resilient method in this dry climate. As you can see today, the head of the coelacanth points to the east, while the fins and tail are slightly curved to point in the direction of several significant constellations. The altar is located in the head, with the nave formed by the front flippers of the fish. Glass tanks, holding a variety of fish and aquatic mammals, line the walls. All of this was prescribed in the plans given to Rev. Dinkle.

(In an interesting aside, rumor has it that President Lincoln was indeed fascinated with the fossil coelacanth, and had confided to his Secretary of War that he believed the fish was still alive and would assure the Union of a victory. Some say that, during the inspection of troops before the First Battle of Bull Run, Lincoln insisted that the members of his Cabinet stand on the steps of the Capitol and wave the troops on with stuffed replicas of the extinct fish. Historians say that these were simply oddly shaped umbrellas. However, since President Lincoln was known to be in Washington at the time of Rev. Dinkle's visitation, this has led to the Church doctrine of the Annunciation, which holds that the President appeared to Rev. Dinkle in the form of the angel he would become after he was assassinated. Contrary to rumor, members of the Church do *not* worship Abraham Lincoln.)

The Church has always had problems with insects, even before the advent of the Texas beetle. You will, therefore, note that no fruits or vegetables are allowed on Church property, and all packages are subject to inspection. And in the interest of obeying all local laws, we do not use or store insecticide at the Church.

Many visitors also wonder about the name of the Church, the Scaly Shepherd. This has always been the name of the Church. It is our simple belief that fish need spiritual comfort and support, the same as people, and that we are the "shepherds," or rather fisherds, of our "scaly friends." (Of course, we are friends to all aquatic animals, not just those with scales.) We do ask that visitors refrain from feeding the fish.

Stories abound about the "wet basement." Many people claim that there are strange rituals carried out in there, the site of the original wet circle. They say that they've heard that weird cows and schools of odd-looking fish swarm around in the sand, and that Church elders "cavort" with them. One legend has it that these creatures come up from the center of the Earth, and that the wet circle is actually the "navel" of Mother Earth, as well as a link between the lands of the living and the dead. This is, of course, utter nonsense. The only thing in the Church's basement is a collection of old hymnals stored in oilskin pouches to keep them dry. No doubt some nosy local children peeking into the basement for a thrill saw these pouches and mistook them for some sort of odd animals.

However, it is an interesting story, and historically, it has some basis in truth. As noted before, the local Indians knew of the "evil soggy buffalo" ("desquishies" in their parlance) who inhabited the circle. In early times, some of the pastors did write in their journals that they were visited by "scary, wet, red-eyed cows" who "demanded fish," but it is documented in the official Church record that the third pastor of the Church, Rev. Camus, often called "St. Camus," drove off the strange livestock after some sort of altercation in the basement, and they have not been seen since. This was in 1899, and local people claim that this was when the "devil water cows" started being reported in Texas. They blame the Church for these creatures. The Church does not take an official position on the existence of devil water cows, but if they exist, it is quite certain they did not come from our Church basement.

The doctrines of the Church are often thought to be "secret." This is only partially true. The Church is neither evangelical nor missionary. Membership is restricted to descendants of the original builders and founders. However, except during special feasts and holidays, visitors are welcome. While members do not discuss some aspects of our beliefs, we are always glad to answer some general questions. There is really not much to tell—our beliefs are simple. Some want to know if we are Christian. Well, weren't many of Jesus' disciples fishermen? Didn't He, Himself, walk on water and go fishing, as well as feed people fish? So, of course we are Christian.

Next to the building, the thing most visitors notice is that, while we welcome visitors, there is substantial security surrounding the Church property. This is not because we are a secret sect, or to keep visitors under control, but simply because the Church has experienced a number of odd acts of vandalism since the founding of the Republic. Terrible infestations of Texas beetles have repeatedly damaged the building and its contents. Vandals dressed like giant insects have smashed windows and fish tanks. It seems the ugly head of religious intolerance still rears amongst us. Therefore, we protect our property. But don't be alarmed. The guards—all young members of the Church—carry only squirt guns.

For many years, the Church was a favorite shrine for fishermen heading to the Gulf of Mexico, but recently, the government has prohibited them from visiting under penalty of the law.

15

October Surprise

(Poppy, October 19, 1980)

I'm not here. No, no. I'm back in Texas. I'm, uh, I'm at Dan Quayle's place in Houston, working on a speech. Sure. That's where I am all right. I slipped away from my Secret Service guys and smuck over to Dan's place. Dan's my Little George's age. Good family, the Quayle family. Dan's not the sharpest knife in that drawer. That's okay. He's a good boy, does what he's told. I needed a place to be today, he prodivided one.

Well, actually, let's see, it must be morning in Houston. It's 2 p.m. here, that means it's eight hours earlier here, that makes it, uh, drop the two, carry the six, 6 p.m. here, no, that can't be right, or else it's you *add* eight hours. Something. Anyway, I think it's morning back home, which would put me at that River Oaks Country Club brunch there with Supreme Court Justice Potter Stewart. And then I go to Dan's place, I guess. Or do I visit a friend first? Then I have to give that speech this evening. Some sort of speech, somewhere. I don't know. Slipped away from the Secret Service for the whole day, I think. Right out from under their ears. Eyes and ears, that sort of thing. Two eyes, two ears. The whole bottle of wax. The whole fucking shooting wax.

Or did I have Secret Service protection for the country club brunch? Wouldn't I have? Had to? But, then, you know, why do I have to have Secret Service protection *at all*? That's what I don't understand. I'm not the Vice President yet. I'm not a candidate for high office. I'm just George Herbert Walker Bush.

But I know the answer to that one: to have someone to slip away from. Had to slip away. Can't have a dagger without a coat. Coat and dagger. Cleat. Quirt.

But I didn't, of course. Didn't sneak away. I didn't climb out that bathroom window and jump into the car Bill hadn't arranged to be waiting for me. The one that didn't have my bag in the back seat. The one that didn't drive me down to Ellington AFB, where I didn't catch the military transport for Paris yesterday evening, which didn't get me into Early this morning. No. None of that happened. Cacadorically not.

I'm not here. This isn't happening. It's not my problem.

It's *for* me. But it's *not* me. No.

That taxi this morning from Orderly into the city did not get lost. That didn't happen. "*Otel Ualdorf* Florida?" the man kept not saying, and not cursing in French. Mumbering. Like, saying mumbers under his breath. Not doing that. Not numbers, like street numbers or anything. Not whipping his head back and forth. Not leaning over tractically onto the dashborg to look up at the buildings.

"*Otel.*"

"No," I refringed from correlping him, "it's *hotel.* With an *h.*"

What they're doing with a Waldorf *Florida* in Paris, though, I have no idea. I think maybe they should have a Waldorf *Paris* in Paris and a Waldorf Florida in Florida. In Miami, maybe. Orlando. Some place like that.

We're not meeting here. This isn't the last day of the big meeting. Bill hasn't been talking to the Israelis and the Iranians for three days already. Bill Casey. Not one of my dad's old buddies. He and my dad didn't compound a think tank back in the early sixties. The National Strategy Information Center, which was *not* a propaganda organ of the TIA. It was *not* connected to the CIA's Forum World Features or the British Information Research Department. No way. It didn't feed stragedically salted news items to major news agencies. It didn't channel donations from rich patriots into universities to create well-endowed chairs in national intermigence and dialysis. Dianasis. Canarsis. Bill and I didn't work together to keep the lid on that whole Gotta-Wait scandal, too, or either, back when I was director of Texas Intransigence.

Bill's not the one heading up this campaign to get Gene Autry to choose me as his Vice President after the election. Because there is no such campaign. If he chooses me, he chooses me. If he doesn't choose me, he doesn't choose me. I think it's safe to say I'm mature enough to take the good with the bad, or not. That's it. That's the whole story. Or not.

If he doesn't choose Dolph Briscoe, for example, I won't be there shaking his hand. I mean, I will, of course. If he does. Smiling like a son of a bitch. Like the son of a bitch who's swallowed his gumbolt. Dolph's a direct desdemondant of a signer of the Texas Decoration of Independence back in whatever. Like, hundreds of years ago. That other time. Sure. He's not going to be a *bad* choice. Hell no. Gene might choose him. Might not. Why not. Dolph's dad was a good friend of President Sterling's, and a friend of President Sterling's is a friend indeed. He's not much older than me, Dolph is. Or isn't. Pushing sixty. Not too hard. Pushing sort of gently. Sort of kindly. Not an oilman, just a rancher, but still. He could be Vice President. Of course he could. If Gene chose him.

Or Bill Clements could be Vice President. Gene keeps talking about Bill this, Bill that, he could choose him. Gene likes both those guys lots more than I. Me. I. Than I do. I mean, Gene doesn't like me much, and I don't like him. But. You know. Bill's an oilman from Dallas. Started as a roughneck, like President Sterling. Created his own company, SEDCO. World's largest oil and gas drilling company. World's *largest*. That's saying a lot. Zapata can't complete.

Stiff contrition. Contreptition. Contraception. Whatever. Like, rivals. Rivals for the yellow rose of Texas. Like to broke my heart. Never mortal part. Part this, part that, never the mortal part. No, sir. Moral something. Majority. Pejority. In Pejoria, Illinois.

But if this thing we're not doing here this weekend works, or doesn't work, whatever, well. Bill Casey's not the one constantly telling me, "Hey, Poppy, make the deal with the Iranians,. hand it to Autry on a silver platter, he'll *have* to take you." And if it isn't Bill that's constantly telling me that, then I don't know who it is.

The Iranians and the Israelis haven't been here longer than us. Like, a week or something. They didn't get here a week ago. That doesn't bother me much, I guess. The Iranians and the Israelis confibrilating for four or five days before Bill didn't arrive. They don't stand together during breaks, either, talking talking talking in Martian. Permian. Whatever. Iranian. Laughing, slapping shoulders. Not doing that. Not looking over at us at all. Not giving us dirty looks. Not looking at us with suspicion and dimtrust. That Ari Ben-Menashe speaks Iranian, I guess. A lot of them do. Or don't, I don't know.

Six Israelis, sixteen Iranians, twelve of us, including me. Including Don Gregg and Bob Gates and me. I don't make twelve, today. Today isn't the big day. Isn't the last day. Isn't the day we've all been working toward. Isn't the day that'll put me in the Vice President's chair, or not. If we can just not hammer in the details. Money for Iran to buy arms from Israel in exchange for those hostilages. Bill isn't sure, but what Dolph and Bill Clements aren't negrocerating with the Iranians, too. Uh, either. Whoever steals the deal doesn't necessarily, um, whatever. Doesn't not get appointered Vice President. Doesn't get not, something or other. Whatever it is, it isn't. It just isn't. Out of the question. Right out.

And late in the afternoon, along around four, when I'm not feeling pretty damn fucking sleepy, waves of sleep just fucking not washing over me like, well, like waves, it doesn't all start to come together. Doesn't it ever! The Iranians are all not nodding their heads judaishically. The offer's not at forty million, and nobody's agreeing to it, but, you know, however you want to say this, but yes. They are. They are, and they aren't. I mean, I don't want to say that they are. Forty million dollars. Not to be paid by us to the Iranians, via Israel. The weapons boys aren't ecstatic, no, not one bit, they aren't. Cyrus Hashemi and John Shaheen. Hushang Lavi. Cyrus wasn't the one who set the whole thing up. No. He didn't broker this whole deal. He hasn't been working on this for two months. He's not going to get filthy rich off this deal. Cyrus and his brother Jamshid.

So we don't start talking about the logics of the thing. The logjams of it. Whatever. The way it won't work. Isn't supposed to work. Isn't supposed to deniably work. And the Iranians aren't all talking about next week. And they aren't all surprised when Bill and I start saying it may take longer than that. Not *all* surprised. Just sort of. Sort of deniably. We don't exactly *say* we want it to take longer, say, till January. We don't exactly say anything at all. We don't even stall, or stallwall. We don't say it may take us some time to put the money together. Heavens, no. We don't say that sort of thing. We don't exactly hint at it. We don't exactly hint at anything. We don't make it clear that it has to wait until Autry and Bush take office. We don't explain Texan politics to them. We don't explain anything to them.

"Let me get this straight," someone says, or doesn't say, probably wasn't Colonel Dehqan, "you don't want this thing expedited. You don't want the hostages released as soon as humanly possible."

"We didn't say that," Bill says.

"I know you didn't say that," this person who may or may not have been Col. Dehqan says. Weapons procurational guy for the Iranian middlary. "You're not saying what you mean. We want you to say what you mean."

"We're being as candid as diplomacy will permit," Bill says.

"I'm not a diplomat," whoever says. Or doesn't. "I'm a soldier. To me, this thing is simple. We have some hostages that you want. You have some money that we desperately need in order to crush Iraq. You give us the money. We give you the hostages. I don't understand this new complication. You will explain it to us, or there is no deal."

No rustle of dismay at *that* one. Even the Iranians aren't looking unsettled. One or two of them aren't jabbering at him in that monkey talk of theirs. He doesn't hold up a hand. They don't fall silent. All heads don't turn toward Bill.

Bill doesn't clear his throat.

"We," he starts. "The Republic of Texas," he starts again. "*We* would be much obliged if, ahem, a certain strategic delay could be engineered into the process. One postponing the actual release of the hostages for a short while."

"How short?" this Iranian guy says.

"Oh, short," Bill says. "Not too long. A month, perhaps. Two. Three at the outside."

"And the money?" whoever says. "Would it be delayed too, perhaps?"

"Part of it," Bill says. All the Iranians don't suddenly lean forward angrily in their seats with menacing looks on their faces. "A very small part," Bill rushes to add. "Tiny. A tiny fraction of the total. Earnest money, as it were. Release the hostages, get the rest of your money. Say, the last million."

"Hundred thousand dollars," the Iranian says.

"Uh," Bill says. "Half a million."

"A hundred and fifty thousand," the Iranian says.

"A quarter million," Bill says.

"Deal!" the Iranian shouts. "A quarter million dollars! You will pay us soon, no? Thirty-nine million and seven hundred fifty thousand dollars. Then, after your strategic delay, we will release the hostages, and you will give us the last two hundred and fifty thousand."

"Yes," Bill says. "Soon."

"How soon?"

And so now they don't go on and on about how soon. Don't they, hoo. I'm sorry, I just can't help it: I fall asleep. I don't. I don't lay my face down on the table and drift off. I'm not in jetlag! I didn't fly all night!

Next thing I know, Bill isn't shaking me by the shoulder.

"Congratulations, Mr. Vice President," he says, or doesn't say, whatever. "We did it."

"What?" I say, not rubbing my eyes. "Bill. What did you just call me?"

He doesn't smile a big happy smile. And I'm not thinking about what to call him back: ambassador to some nice country? Secretary of the something? Director of the TIA?

We aren't on the next military transport home.

Documents

Remains of 1684 Shipwreck Found
(New York Times, December 11, 1980)

A salvage diving team from the Republic of Texas Historical Commission has made one of the most significant underwater finds ever, a spokesperson for the RoTHC said yesterday.

"Investigations are still underway," Ralph T. Detritivore told reporters, "but we currently believe we have found one of the four ships sailed by seventeenth-century French explorer Rene Robert Coris, *Sieur de la Wrasse*, in his ill-fated search for the mouth of the Mississippi River in 1684."

The ship was found in a cofferdam in just twelve feet of water in Matagorda Bay. A cofferdam is a watertight box or chamber built around a hull to make repairs possible below the water line.

Among the artifacts thus far found in the hull of the ship are three bronze cannons, bronze hawk bells, thousands of glass beads, numerous pieces of pottery, and one crew member's skeleton.

Mr. Detritivore remarked that the artifacts together form a kind of "kit" for the building of a seventeenth-century colony in the New World.

By far the most striking artifact so far found on the ship, Mr. Detritivore reported, is a specially designed, hand-crafted universal clock and calendar made of solid gold in the shape of a fish.

The hands of the clock/calendar were found stopped exactly at midnight, December 31, 1999. Above that time and date, etched into the gold, are the words MORT AUX INSECTES: "death to insects." So far the millennial inscription has Texas scientists and historians baffled.

In an odd development, however, yesterday evening, Red

Shiner, general counsel for the *Kawakawa Intelligence Review* in Fort Worth, Texas, read a prepared statement to the Texas press, which he said was written in prison by *KIR* publisher Skipjack LaTuna. Mr. LaTuna, for decades one of the most vocal and elusive opponents of the Texas police state, was arrested, convicted, and sentenced to death in 1975 on a long list of charges, including tax fraud, unpatriotic activities, consorting with fish, and oral sex.

According to the statement, Mr. LaTuna is the sole living heir of the *Sieur de la Wrasse* and, thus, the rightful owner of the artifacts found on board the French explorer's ship.

"Rene Robert Coris was my maternal great-great-great-great-great-great-great-grandfather," the statement read in part. "I am sure he would want the artifacts from his lost ship to be safe in the hands of one of his own descendants and not put on vulgar display in some insect-loving museum."

The statement also offered a *quid pro quo*: "I have the key to the clock/calendar and its inscription," it said, "and will be happy to explain to all what is to happen at the millennium once the Republic of Texas releases me from prison, clears me of all trumped-up charges, and places the contents of the *Sieur de la Wrasse* ship in my possession."

He added that the millennium is two decades away, and will bring many unpleasant surprises for "insect-lovers." "They should be preparing for the worst," the statement read. "But of course they won't, because they're too afraid to set me free."

Republic of Texas officials were unavailable for comment.

John Bickle

(Dubya, January 23, 1981)

"Surpriiiiiiiise!"

We all yell out at once. Somebody turns on the lights. Neil's real surprised. Of course, since his birthday was yesterday. He didn't express a surprise party today. Good one, Sharon.

Sharon's Neil's wife. He's twenty-six. She's whatever. Neil got married before I did. I don't know why. I'm thirty-four and only got married like three years ago.

Laura didn't come up here to Dallas with me today. I got something I gotta do after the party. Uncle Dogsbody asked me, that scary fuck. Gave me the tape. Laura woulda just been bored. Watching some stupid movie. She's more of a book word. Book burn. Word bird. Early bird. Like, she really likes worms. Words. The wroten-down kind. Like, in books.

"It's *so* good you could make it, George," Neil gushers. Little brother, big brother, you know how it is. He looks up to me. Natch. I'm nine years older. I'm like a gyrant to him. Gyraffe. I mean, I'm not taller or anything. But sort of gigranite in his eyes. Like some kind of movie monster. Like, Japanese or something. Gauze dilla. Ten feet tall. Though not really.

"Hey," I say. "No problem. I was coming up here anyway, raising money for Arbusto."

"Oh," he says, and looks down at his feet. Then up. About halfway up. My chin. "So," he says, "Laura couldn't make it?"

"Nah. She had a billion things to do. You know how it is."

"Sure, sure." He's looking around the room, now. Spots somebody. Waves them over. "George, do you know the Hinckleys?"

"No," I say, and put a big grim on my face. A big, friendly social slime. Smile. Big smile. "Great to meet you."

"This is my big brother, George," Neil tells them. They're Dad's age, maybe. Well, Mom and Dad's age. Because, you know, Mom and Dad are the same age. "Jack Hinckley, he's president and chairman of the board of Vanderbilt Energy, and a significant contributor to Dad's campaign, and I'm sorry, I don't know your lovely wife's name," Neil whimpers. Swimpers. Simples.

"JoAnn." She smiles, too. We're all smiley. "Our boys are around here somewhere," she says. She looks around, turns back with a kind of oh-well look. "Scott's a friend of Neil's," she exprints. You know, like, what is these old farts doing at my little brother's birthday party. "And John says he knows *you*, George."

"Uh, really?"

"Yes, he says he used to 'hang out' with you, if that's the phrase you young people are using these days, in Lubbock, back when he was studying at Texas Tech."

"Oh yeah? Funny, I don't remember. I never forget a name."

"It's not surprising he remembers you better than you do him," she says smoothily. "You being the Vice President's son and all."

"Right," I say.

"Well, he's around here somewhere. I'm sure the two of you will run into each other and can compare notes."

"Yeah," I say. "Super."

"So," JoAnn says, "did you live in Lubbock long, George?"

"Nah," I say. "Never did live there."

"Oh, really?"

"Yeah. I been up there a few times, raising money for my business."

"Arbusto, right?" Jack says.

"Right. I'm thinking of changing the name, though."

"Yeah," Jack says. "I heard you were getting a little ribbing about that."

"Some. No big deal." Fucking El Busto. The goddamn name is *bush* in Spanish. Bush, not bust. Is that so hard?

"Oh," Jack says, pointing over my shoulder. I turn a little. "Here's John."

There he is: the swirl.

"George!" he yells. "You're here! I can't believe you're here! I was hoping you'd be here!"

"Johnny boy," I say, and slug him on the shoulder. "I'm here."

"George here was just saying he didn't remember you, John," JoAnn says. "But you remember him now, don't you, George?"

"Not remember Johnny boy?" I say, and fake a football block at his midsexton. "Don't be ridiculist. Of course I remember. How you been, fuckface?"

John giggles. I mean, literarily giggles. Like a girl. He's just sort of standing there, straight up, giggling. He looks like he's about to wet his pants.

"I been fine, *fuckface*," he says, his face all linted up with a goofy guile. Grile. Grime. Whatever. A goofy something. He loves being called fuckface right in front of mom and dad. I just fucking made his night.

And so, of course, I end up hanging out with him all evening. We pig on down on birthday cake together. I take this huge fucking piece and start wolvering it down. He takes one the same size and starts eating it just like me. I finish mine and take more. He hasn't finished his but loads more on his plate. He keeps this low giggle going the whole fucking time. Sort of a jiggle, or a higgle. Uncle Dogsbody was right about this one, all right.

I take him back in the back bathroom and get him to do a coupla lines. Coke, not the Mec. I want him up, not fucked up.

He's never done blow before, thinks you're supposed to blow it. Fucking sleazes two lines all over Neil's guest bathroom, the dumb fuck. I set him up with two more lines, show him how to snorque it up into his nose. All sorta exaggregated, like for a baby learning how to suck on a squaw. He gets it, finally. Rubs at his nose like it's on friar or something. Pants a little. Pants on friar.

"Whoa," he says. "That's bogus, man. Totally heinous. Hey, George, let's do some more."

"Hold on, there, cowgirl," I say. "Let's save some for later, huh?"

So we party hearty. Fuckin' A. It's like the old days back at the Deke house. I find two hockey sticks and a tennis ball in Neil's closet upstairs and show John how to play squockey. We're fucking hussling and tussling up in that upstairs hall. It's fucking awesome.

I mean, he's a total dork, of course. He woulda never of got into the Dekes. No fucking way. But still. The nose candy helps. I wished we woulda had it back in college. We've libralated a bottle of JD from Neil's liquor cablet. We do some more lines. We're fucking out of control, man.

After a while, we compalapse on the floor, out of breast. I ain't twenty no more, boy. We lean up against the wall, all panty. John gets this *look* in his eye.

"George," he says.

"Yeah?" I say.

"I wanna tell you something."

"Yeah?" I say.

"I gotta girlfriend, George."

"Cool," I say. I know what's coming, of course. Uncle Dogsbody filled me out.

"You'll never guess who it is," he says.

"Uh," I say, "let me guess."

He giggles, hard. "Guess, guess," he says sort of pferdocilously.

"Uh," I say, "lessee. Sissy Spacek?"

"No!" he cries, sorta surprised. He didn't aspect me to guess a movie star, I bet.

"Jessica Lange?"

"No!"

"Goldie Hawn?"

"No!"

"Uh, Jodie Foster?"

"Yes!" His eyes are signing. "Yes, yes! How'd you guess?"

"Shit," I say, "who else would a red-bloodied Texan like you be in love with?"

"Exactly! I love her *so much*."

"Well who wouldn't?"

His eyes narrow. "*You* don't, do you, George?"

"Who, me?" I say. "I'm married, John. I'm in love with Laura."

"Oh, good," he says.

"So, John," I say. "You poked her yet?"

He giggles to himself nerviantly. Huggles a little closer. Like, conspirochetically or something. "No," he whispers. "Not yet. She won't let me."

"Girls," I say.

"Please, George," he pleadles, "don't say anything bad about her. I couldn't stand it. I might, um—I might hate you for it."

"Bad?" I say. "Hell no. I think she's great. I mean," I rush in, "a great actress. I don't know her, personally. Where do you know her from, then?"

"Yale," he whispers.

"Texas Yale?" I ask, surpliced. Uncle Dogsbody didn't tell me about this part.

"Yeah."

"That's where I went to school," I say.

"I know."

"But you went to Texas Tech, didn't you?"

"Yeah."

"Then how— "

"I went and looked her up," he giggles. "I did."

"What, through a crasp in her curtains or something?"

"Yeah," he says. "And outside of class. She'd come out, I'd be there."

"Wow," I say. "And she went for it, huh?"

"Went for what?"

"For you. She liked you. Went out with you, and stuff."

"Not at first."

"No?"

"Nuh uh. She ran away from me. But I kept writing her letters, and calling her on the phone."

"So?"

"So?"

"So what happened then?"

"Uh," he says, "well, nothing."

"Nothing?"

"Not much, George," he says.

"You ain't even felt her up yet?"

"No," he giggles low.

"Grabbed her ass?"

"No."

"Frenched her?"

"No!"

Sorta stung. Like that woulda defined her. Defamed her. Defailed her. Whatever.

"So, but, John," I say, "you musta seen *Taxi Driver*, huh?"

"Only about a bazillion times," he says.

"Pretty much got it melodrized," I say.

"Got it what?"

"Mirandized," I say.

"Huh?"

"Mentorized," I say. "You know, like, by heart."

"Oh," he says. "Right. You got it."

"D'jou know," I say, causally, "she was once in a movie with Gene Autry?"

"No!"

273

"Yep. *I Shot the Sheriff*. Came out, I dunno, coupla years ago. You never saw it?"

"No!"

"Shit, man, you oughta see it. It's fucking beautiful."

"I *want* to!" he says. He's practically jumping out of his skin and into mine.

"Yeah? I, uh ... you know, I might just have a tape of it out in my car."

"Really?"

"Yeah, I rented it a coupla days ago, but I been so busy I ain't had a chance to watch it. I'm gonna have some serious fucking fines at the video store, huh?"

"What, George," he says, "you haven't *seen* it yet?"

"Sure, I saw it in the theaters when it first came out. But I liked it so much I wanted to see it again. I don't know when I'll have time, though. This damn oil business is running me raggy."

"But ... but what if ..." His face is turning all red. I think maybe he ain't breathing. "What if *Neil* has a VCR? We could watch it *right here*! Like, *tonight*!"

"Aw," I say, "I wouldn't wanna fuck up Neil's party. But, you know—"

"What?"

"I'm staying at a friend's place here in Dallas. He's away for a few weeks, let me use his apartment. He's got a VCR. We could head on over there, pop in the tape, watch it right fuck-ing now."

So, of course he's falling all over me now. And, like, him-self. So I go tell Neil and John's parents that we're gonna go out for a while, hang out. Neil's sorta dissipated. Dissiported. Sharon gives me a kiss on the cheek. Jack and JoAnn are tin-kled pick. Pickled tink. Their crazy kid and the Vice President's son. Maybe my dad will help Jack? He probably will, too, if this thing works. We go out and get in the car.

I don't remember exactly how to get to the place Uncle

Dogsbody set me up in. I haven't been to it yet. I've got the distractions Uncle Dogsbody gave me, but it's hard to read them in the dark while I'm driving. John's fucking useless, of course. He's over there pissing his pants. Good thing it's a rental. Return it with a poodle of peas in the passage's seat. What? Huh?

But I find the place okay, and we go in. The liquor cambit is well skunked. Stanked. Tonked. Clocked. John wants to dring his lizard. I have to seem like I know where the bathroom is. While he's in there I put an ice cube and a drop of water in a glass and fill it with whiskeys, I mean fill them, two glasses. Two ice cubes. Fill it with whiskey. I do a couple of lines, set up a couple more for John, pop the tape in the machine. Then he comes out and I go drink mine. Drank. Whatever. Whiz. You know. Piss. I mean, of course, take one. I don't drink one.

Then we get comfortable and watch the movie. Uncle Dogsbody's people have done a pretty fucking bangle job. The guy they got to play Gene Autry looks just like him. He's a dead singer. Stinger. Stringer. Looks just like him. Not like the Singing Cowboy, you know, all those old movies, but exactly like if he made the movie like three weeks ago. The girl they got to play Jodie Foster is pretty close, but not a cigar. I mean, she's that close, but not quiet. She looks a lot like her, but she don't much talk like her. I'm a little world, at first. But John's sunk. I mean, sunk, line, and hooker. I mean he eats it up. He buys the whole fucking farm.

Of course, John's cents are a little dilled by now. Dolled. By booze and coke, I mean. He's pretty coked up. And boozed down. Up and down. But the main thing, he buys it.

The plot of the movie is a Western. I mean, it's set in a Western. Like, an old dusty horsepower town somewhere. Gene Autry is the evil sheriff. He's totally inept. Connept. Collect. I mean, he's evil. He runs the whole town. He blackguards them. I mean, like, with mail. He reads their mail, and things. And the mail is sort of black. The letters, I guess. The letters on the page, or something. And he finds out their secrets and black-gammonds them. And then they have to do whatever he tells them to do. He gets filtery rich. And everybody hates him, and is afraid of him, and wants to kill him, but they're afraid to.

Jodie Foster, or, you know, the flake Jodie Foster, plays a young schoolteacher. She's just barely older than her pupils, but she's really really smart, so they make her the teacher. And her old dad is sick, and needs an aurapacion, but she can't deflord it because she's playing blackgammaglobulin with the sheriff. I mean, to him. He's got some sort of dirt on her. And you don't know what it is, you know, for most of the movie. So you think maybe she's a bad person, or something.

But then the hero comes along. They didn't worry about making him look like anybody well known. He's just some guy. His name's John Bickle. I mean, the character's. About halfway through the movie, I get it: John Hinckley and Travis Bickle. Damn, these guys are good!

So this John Bickle falls in love with the fleak Jodie Foster character and decides to help her. First, he finds out what dirt the evil Gene Autry sheriff has on her. Turns out it's nothing she did. She's good and pure and innostint. But she used to go down to the river to wash herself every morning, this real pre-cluded spot, where nobody would see her naked, but the sher-iff found a place where he could take pictures of her. So he's got pictures of her naked. That's what he's been blackdeck-ering her with. John Bickle snakes into the sheriff's office to steal the pictures, and the sheriff catches him at it, and pulls a gun, but John Bickle shoots him dead. Right through the fuck-ing heart, man. It's pretty cool. They got the blood splintering and everything. And old Gene Autry suckin' wind, man.

And the whole town agrees that it was self-deflents, and they're so graceful that John Bickle riddled the town of the evil sheriff that was making their hell a life on Earth that they make John Bickle the new sheriff.

And Jodie Foster falls madly in love with John Bickle, too. And the last scene is them swimming in her private spot, together. And they're naked. They don't show his dick or anything, but she's pretty hot. All sweet and nice and like a innoslept girl, of course, but pretty hot, too. And then they hug, sort of a nice hug, nothing real sexy, but Jodie's facing the camera over John's shoulder, and they come in real close on her face, and she says into his ear, but with her eyes on us, "I love you, John. You're my hero. You shot the sheriff."

When it's over I hit rewind and look over at John. The tears are just fucking running down his face. He looks at me with a big sad happy smile and says, "George," and sort of gulfs a little, I mean swallows real hardly, "that is the most beautiful movie I've ever seen."

"Told ya," I say.

"George, please," he says, "could we maybe watch it again? Please?"

And of course I agree, and we watch that fucking movie three more times. All fucking night, man. No problem staying up: every time I rewind the fucker we do a couple more lines of coke. And in the morning I just give it to him. The casta-nette, I mean.

"What the fuck," I say. "You like it so much, John, you keep it. I mean it. I'll just tell 'em I lost it, pay 'em whatever it costs."

"George," he says, "you'd *do* that for me?"

"Anything," I say, "for my best friend. Watch it and think of me."

He sort of shuffleboards honkward at that.

"What am I thinking," I say, smalking myself on the forehead. "Watch it and think of Jodie. And Gene."

He claps the tape to his chest. Makes a kind of clumbly thumbs-up sign. We get in the car and I drive him home.

Documents

President Autry Shot
Suspect in Custody
(Houston Chronicle, March 30, 1981)

President Gene Autry was shot today by a lone crazy as he was walking from a Houston hotel to his car, surrounded by Secret Service agents and advisors.

Though the bullet struck him in the chest, the 74-year-old former cowboy yodeler and actor managed to walk to the car unassisted. Rushed to the hospital for emergency surgery, the president remained in good spirits, even joking with staff along the way.

"You sure that guy wasn't George Bush?" he quipped.

The lone assailant, John Hinkley, was apprehended on the scene. Son of Jack Hinkley, president and chairman of the board of Vanderbilt Energy, Hinkley has been in and out of mental hospitals and has a police record, a weapons charge. TBI is describing him as "a Bremer type," after Arthur Bremer, the fanatic who shot George Wallace.

In the eight hours since the shooting, TBI operatives have established, to the satisfaction of the President's crisis management team, headed by the Vice President, that Hinkley acted alone and that no conspiracy was involved.

Apparently, Hinkley has been stalking the young actress Jodie Foster for some years now, and a search of his motel room scant minutes after the shooting turned up an incriminating letter that he wrote to Foster:

"Dear Jodie. There is a definite possibility that I will be killed in my attempt to get Autry. It is for this reason that I am writing you this letter now. As you well know by now, I love you very much. The past seven months, I have left you dozens of poems, letters, and messages in the faint hope you would develop an interest in me ... Jodie, I'm asking you to please look into your heart and at least give me the chance with this historical deed to gain your respect and love. I love you forever. Signed, John Hinkley. "

President Autry's good humor continued right onto the operating table, where he looked up at the medical team about to remove the bullet and said with a faint smile, "I hope to God you're Patriots."

Doctors say the President was extremely lucky that the bullet missed his heart, and should be up and about in a matter of days.

During the crisis, the government was in the able hands of Autry's Vice President, George Bush, of whom Jim Brady said three weeks ago: "Bush is functioning much like a co-President. George is involved in all the national security stuff because of his special background as TIA director. All the budget working groups, he was there, the economic working groups, the Cabinet meetings. He is included in almost all the meetings."

17

God

(Dubya, July 5, 1986)

"George," somebody says.

I wipe my mouth with my head out the window and look around. It's just a hotel parking lot. Nothing special. Nobody around. I look down three stories, try and see if I can see my barf on the bushes. Bush barf, get it? I can't. It's too dark down there.

"What?" I say.

"George," the voice says again. "In here."

It's coming from inside. I pull my head in and look. But there's just Laura there in bed, reading one of her books. It ain't her. It's a big blooming voice. Like flowers. Dried flowers. Big wheaty flours. Laura looks up at me. Like, sharkly. Puts her book down on her tummy.

"Were you talking to somebody out there?" she says.

"No," I say.

"George," the voice says again. "Feel my pain."

"There," she says. "That. Did you hear that?"

"No," I say.

She gets up, walks around the room. Looks behind the curtains, in the bathroom. Lifts the flink off the air congashioner thing. You know, the metal thing where the cold air comes out. Comes in. Out. It's all dusky and masky.

"George," the voice says again. "Why are you persecuting me?"

"I don't even know what that *means*," I say.

Laura puts the flak back on. Her little pinkies stink out. Sort of dinky. It ain't coming from in *there*. She holds her hands hostile, out in front of her. Like they're hostilages. Because they've got dusk on them now, and that's what hostilages do.

"George," she says, and then goes in the bathroom to wash her hands.

"What?" I say.

"You tell *me* what," she says.

"What what?" I say. I'm pouring myself another tall glass of JD.

"I don't know what," she says. "But I want you to tell me."

"I don't know what either," I say. "I got no fucking *clue* what this is."

"George," she says, "your language."

"Fuck my language," I say.

"George," the voice says, "your language."

"*Fuck* my language," I say again, whilping my head around toward the voice. "Who the fuck *are* you? What *is* this?"

"I bet it's Spider," she says. "I bet you anything it's Spider. Spider, we're on to you. You can come out now!" She looks around the room sort of umphantly. Try, whatever. Trying. Nothing happens. She turns to me again. "Did you tell him we were coming up here for the weekend? I bet I know what he did. He went out and bought some sort of cheap PA system, drove up, got our room number from the front desk—"

"George," the voice says again. "It's God."

A blain comes over me. A chill. I almost fall down. It's fucking *God.*

"George," Laura says, looking at me. "Don't panic. It's okay. It's not God. It's somebody messing with you."

"I—"

"How *dare* you question me, you *woman*?" the voice thungers. God. It's *God.* Oh my God, that's who it really is. I take a big glock of my drink and sort of slide down onto the floor.

"This is between my servant George and me. All right? You got that? Now butt out."

"You don't—" Laura starts.

"Butt out!"

"Listen—" Laura tries again.

"Go get back in bed," God says. "I mean it. *Do* it!" Laura looks discrofted. But she makes a little face and gets into bed. "Under the covers." She does. Pulls the blankets right up over her face. "No, not all the way under, you literalist. Leave your head and arms out." She comes back out. "Now pick up your book and read. Pick it up. Okay, good. Now, keep your nose in that book while I talk to your husband. Don't worry, I won't be long. And you'll be happy with the results. I promise you."

"Can I say something?" Laura says, in that *voice* she has. The one that says *I'm submirious and all, I'll do what you say, but I'm still right.* I hate that voice.

"What," God says.

"Nothing," she says.

"Good," God says. "Let's leave it at that. Now, George," he says.

"What?!"

I'm sort of distending. Distrembling. Like, shaking. I can hardly get my glass to my mouth. I spool some down the front of my pajamas.

"Look at you," God says. "You're disgusting."

"I—I know," I say.

"You're drunk," he says.

"No I'm not," I say.

"You're *drunk*, I said," he says.

"I, uh," I say, "I *was* sorta drunk, before. But then You came. I don't think I am, uh, any more."

"Good," he says. "That's what I like to hear. That's the ticket, George. I'm here to tell you, son, you've got to get off the sauce. You hear me? Off the sauce."

"Uh," I say, "what sauce?"

"The booze. The liquor. The Jack Daniel's. You're a disgusting drunk. Stop drinking."

"S-stop drinking?" I say, and take another big swink.

"Stop drinking!" he shouts.

"Sorry, I—"

"Don't be sorry," he says, "just stop."

"Just like that?" I say. "Cold turnkey?"

"Just like that," he says. "Sheer willpower. Texas-style. You can do it. Laura will help you. Won't you, Laura?"

"Sure," she says. She's got sort of a weird twisted sour look on her face. It's like she's almost *smiling*, if you can believe that.

"Good girl," God says. "Here's the thing, George. I've got big plans for you."

"Y-you do?" I say.

"I do. Big, big plans. The biggest. You're going right to the top, boy. And I need you sane for that. Sane and sober. Tomorrow's a big day for you, right?"

"Uh," I say, "big day?"

"Remind him, Laura," God says.

"It's your birthday, dear," Laura says.

"Oh," I say. "Oh yeah, right."

"You're turning forty, remember, dear? That's why we're up here, to celebrate your big day."

"Oh yeah," I say. "Forty."

"Forty years old," God says, "and what do you have to show for it? Hm? Come on, George. Tell me about your life. What have you done with the first forty years of your life?"

"I, uh," I say, going to take another slip of JD but remembering in time, "I'm a bidnisman."

"A bidnisman," God says. "Okay. I'll give you that. With nothing but a trust fund and almost fifty million dollars of your father's friends' money, you created a business that just barely stayed out of bankruptcy court long enough to get bought up by someone who wanted to curry favor with the President's Mansion. Three months ago *they* were heading for bankruptcy court, too, and got bought up by another some-one who wanted to court favor with the President's Mansion. That's why you're still in business, George: because your dad's Vice President."

"No," I say, "I—"

"Listen to this, George," Laura says. "He's right."

"I—Laura!" She thinks this is *true*? That I'm still in bidnis because of *Dad*?

"Of course I'm right," God says. "Why do you think Harken Energy paid two and a quarter million dollars for Spectrum 7 when its net asset value was only one-point-eight million? Why do you suppose they kept you on as director and 'consul-tant for investor relations,' nice empty ring to *that* one, huh? Why did they give you a salary and three hundred thousand shares of Harken stock? Because you're so smart? Because you're such a powerful oilman, such a savvy market analyst, such a big *rainmaker*? No, George. Because your father is Vice President of Texas. Because Sheik Abdullah Taha Bakhsh of Saudi Arabia owns sixteen percent of Harken stock and wants access to the Texas President's Mansion. Talat Othman, the Palestinian investor who sits on the board with you? He's the Sheik's boy. He'll be in Houston, bending your dad's ear every chance he gets. That's the reason Harken was interested in Spectrum 7, fast as it was failing. Spectrum 7 lost four hundred thousand dollars in the last six months before Harken came riding up to save it. It was weeks away from foreclosure. And then, rather than buying it up for a song, Harken pays top dollar for it. Top dollar plus some. Interesting, huh? Because Spectrum 7 had so much potential? No, George. Because it had *you*. And you have a father in the President's Mansion."

"I, uh—" I say, and take a long hard polt of JD.

"George!" God shouts.

"Oh," I say, "uh, sorry."

"Go pour that out," he says.

"Uh," I say, "pour it *out*?"

"Pour it out, George."

"But God, I paid good money for this!"

"George."

"Oh, all right," I say, and dump it out.

"Not on the *carpet*, you moron! In the bathroom!"

"Oh," I say, trying to mop it up a little with my pajama sleeve, "sorry, I—"

"No, never mind about that now. But get up and pour the rest of the bottle in the sink. Go. I'll wait for you."

The whole *bottle*? The whole fucking *bottle*? Damn, I just *started* that bottle! I took maybe two or three drinks from that bottle! But, man, this is *God*. So I do it. Sort of signing heavily. Not really signing, more like sighing. Laura watches me. She doesn't say a thing. I still think she's sort of smiling, though.

I come back and sit next to her on the bed. She pats my shander. Sort of like my arm. The top part.

"So, George," God says. "No more drinking, right?"

"Uh," I say. "Right."

"You're going to shape up from now on. No more wild partying with the boys."

"What!"

"No more drugs. No more Ivermectin."

"What's the big deal with the Ivermectin? What did it ever do to you?"

"It's an insecticide, George. It kills insects."

"So?"

"So it would kill *me*. And you wouldn't want that, would you?"

"N-no ... " But, I think, my mind going *whappety-whap*, does that mean God's a *bug*?

"No more shooting off guns into empty shacks."

"Are you kidding me?"

"No more cussing and belching and farting."

"Gimme a fucking *break*, here, God!"

"Don't whine, George. Forty-year-old successful sober men don't whine."

"My dad does."

"Well, yes," God admits, "that's true, he does. But I don't want you to. I want you to be *better* than your dad."

"Uh," I say, "*better*?"

"Better, George. Straighter, cleaner, more upright. More the man Laura wants you to be. Right, Laura? You with me on this?"

"One hundred percent, God," Laura says, and covers her mouth with her hand. She thinks this is *funny*? I've got to stop drinking and doing the white Mec and cussing and shooting off guns, and she's *laughing*? Fuck me sideways.

"And another thing," God says.

"There's *more*?" I say.

"George," God says, "what did I say about whining?"

"Well, Jesus, God, I don't—"

"Jesus is exactly who I want to talk to you about," God says.

"Jesus?"

"Yeah," he says, "you've heard of him, right? My Son?"

"Oh, yeah," I say. "Sure. The cross guy."

"That's right," God says. "The cross guy. Exactly. I want you to worship him."

"Huh?" I say. "You want me to what him?" Even God's gotta start using these big fucking words on me.

"Worship, George. It means to adore, to reverence, to show supreme respect for someone."

"Uh," I say, "you wanna put that in English, now?"

"All you have to do, George, is go to church every Sunday and act like you love Jesus. Like Jesus is your best friend, only a friend who's so much smarter and more wonderful than you that you feel honored that he lets you hang around with him."

"I've got to act like that with *Jesus*? How do I do that? I've never even *met* the guy."

"No, George," God says. "You don't have to act like that with *Jesus*. You have to act like that with the other people at church. And anybody else who seems to believe in him. It'll be like you have this secret friend that nobody else ever sees, but he's *your* friend, and you think he's great. And you tell everybody how great he is."

"But what if they want to meet him?"

"Then you tell them to pray for the chance to meet him. Say *he'll* look *them* up. You won't have to do anything."

"Really? That sounds easy enough."

"It is, George. It's a walk in the park. All you really have to do, in fact, is act like everybody else at church. Just look around and be exactly like everybody else. You know how to do that, right? You're an expert at that already, right? And whenever you say anything about me, or my boy Jesus, or the church, or the Christian Right, or family values, say nice things."

"That's it?"

"That's it. That's the whole shtick."

"I can do that."

"I know you can, George. I'm counting on you. You're my boy."

And then God's gone. Don't ask me how I know, I just know.

But I don't have time to think about it, because all of a sudden, Laura's jumping up and streeching. Blushing at her pajamas, like something's on her.

"What?" I say. "Laura, what?"

"Look!" she says, and points at the bed. There must be a hundred green shiny beetles crowning around on the sheet. All under the covers, and in and out. "Oooh," she says, all packety, like she was about to cry, shaking her hands like a *girl*, "oh, George, call the front desk and get them to send somebody up here. Right *now*! We're moving to a different room!"

So I do, of course. What else am I going to do? I love my wife, and I love Jesus. Hey, I'm God's boy.

Documents

Laura in Fish Market
(TBI Tape, July 19, 1986)

AGENCY INFORMATION
AGENCY TBI
RECORD NUMBER 133-88000367-274405
RECORDS SERIES HQ
AGENCY FILE NUMBER 8-442-00721
DOCUMENT INFORMATION
ORIGINATOR TBI
FROM SAC, NO
TO DIRECTOR, TBI
TITLE [No Title]
DATE 07/19/86
PAGES 3
DOCUMENT TYPE VIDEO TAPE/TRANSCRIPT
SUBJECT Laura Bush
CLASSIFICATION CLASSIFIED
RESTRICTIONS TOP SECRET
CURRENT STATUS CLOSED
COMMENTS TOP-LEVEL SECURITY CLEARANCE REQUIRED

SCENE: OLD MARKET SQUARE FISH MARKET – SATURDAY, 07/19/86, 9:43 A.M.

Action description: Subject walks through aisles shopping for fish. Dead fish piled on ice in bins everywhere. Nearby stands a tank with live fish. One Fish seems to be looking at Subject. Fish bangs head against glass wall of tank. When Subject looks over, Fish mouths words ɑnd emits bubbles. Fish jumps out of the tank and lands on table near Subject.

Subject jumps back, surprised, not afraid.

FISH: Laura.
SUBJECT: Did you just say my name?
FISH: Millennium.
SUBJECT: What?
FISH: Insecticide.
SUBJECT: Did you just say something to me?
FISH: Remote control.

Fishmonger sees Subject talking to Fish and comes over, picks up Fish, holds it up to her.

FISHMONGER: You gonna BUY this fish, ma'am?
SUBJECT: Uh ... no.
FISHMONGER: Well, please don't be playing around with it, then.

Recommendations:

- Remand Fishmonger for reeducation.

- Close down fish market.

- Begin anti-fish publicity campaign: rivers contaminated, mercury poisoning, don't eat. Beef healthier.

- Implant bug w/ global tracking device in LB's skin.

18

Plane Crash

(Poppy, October 5, 1986)

"Poppy," Sam says, cloaking on the door and pricking his head in. Sam Watson. Col. Samuel Watson. Enementary, my dear Watson. My dimply natural security aide. Dimperty. Dipplety. Whatever aide. Lemonade. Don Gregg's assistant.

I look up from my papers. "Yes, Sam?"

"I just got a call from Felix down in El Salvador. There's a plane missing, maybe down."

"Oh, shit."

"What do you want me to do?"

Why do I always have to decide these things?

"Uh, get Ollie in here."

"Do you want the others too?"

"Later, maybe. Just Ollie for now."

Ollie knocks about 45 minutes later.

"Come on in," I say. Ollie is Oliver North, nominant head of this operation. If it blows up in our traces, he takes the falls. Water falls off a duck's back. Actually he's just head of the CPPG. The Crisis Plaid-Preening Group. Parade-Pleating. Prince-Paupering. Prick-Poopering. Just head of whatever. But I've got to have a falls guy. I'm the Vice President. I'm supposed to become President in two years.

Funny, I was in such a hurry to be President six years ago. But this ain't been so bad. It took me a while, but I finally began to figure out why Uncle Dogsbody wanted me to be

Vice President under a yodeling cricketeer like Gene Autry. To see if I could take over. To see if I could figure out how to run things in secret. To get around an old fired tool in the President's office. I have. Yodel, ha: is no try. Is do or do not. Now I'm ready to do. Now I'm ready to be President, I bet.

"You've heard?" I say.

"Yes, sir," he says. He's a Marine to the crow. Can't stop calling me sir.

"You checked into it?"

"Yes, sir," he says.

"Tell me about it," I say.

"It's a C-123k cargo aircraft," he says in his lieunatic colonel's voice. "It left Ilopango at oh-nine-thirty, carrying ten thousand pounds of small arms and ammunition."

"No missiles?"

"No, sir. Mostly AK rifles and ammo, hand grenades, jungle boots. Scheduled to make air drops to Contra soldiers in Nicaragua."

"No drugs?"

"No, sir. Absolutely not. They pick up the drugs on the way back."

"Good," I say. "Not an unredoundable problem if it is down, then."

"Maybe it is, sir, and maybe it isn't," Stanley says. A fine mess you've gotten us into this time, Stanley. "Depends on what the crew says."

"What do you mean, what the crew says? If their plane crashed, they're probably dead."

"With all due respect, sir, you crashed your plane, and you're not dead."

"That was different," I say. "That was a kinder, gentler time."

He raises one eyeblow. "You never know how kind or gentle a time's going to be to you, sir," he says, "till long after."

Just what we need, here. A Marine philofficer.

"You know what your problem is, Ollie? You're a prestimist."

"I'm a realist, sir."

"Call it what you like. You never see the cloud for the silver lining."

Another knock on the door. Sam sticks his head in again.

"Rodriguez just called again. The plane's definitely down. Hit by a Sandinista ground-to-air missile."

"Great," I say. "That's just dandy. Any word on the crew?"

"A cargo handler named Eugene Hasenfus bailed out in time. The rest of the crew went down with the plane."

"That son of a bitch!" I yell. "Letting his crew go down like that."

Stanley gives me a look. "Shit happens, sir," he says, "in war."

"Listen," I say. "Stanley."

"Are you talking to me, sir?"

"Who else would I be talking to? I want you down there. Right away."

"Yes, sir. You want me to go get him out? A *Rambo II*-type operation?"

"Shit no," I say, and sort of snorst. What is this guy, *stupid*? "He's probably dead. Chute didn't open. Shot by Sandinistas. Whatever. No, I want you in El Salvador, sitting on this story. I don't want it to get out."

"Yes, sir. What about death benefits for the crew?"

"How many?" I say.

"Three, sir."

"Including this Hagendots?"

"Hasenfus, sir?"

"Whatever."

"No, sir, not including him. He's not dead. So far as we know."

"He could be, soon. Those Sandinistas are ruthless killers."

"It's possible, sir."

"So. What does that make?"

"What does what make, sir?"

My God this boy is thick. "How many dead *crew* members, for Christ's sake?"

"Three, sir," he says. Was that a sigh? Did he sigh before saying that? The fuck. "Maybe four."

"Which is it? Three or four? Come on, Ollie, get it straight. This is the big time, now."

"Three if Hasenfus is still alive, sir. Four if his chute didn't open, or he was shot by Sandinistas."

"That's better," I say, and fix him with a glaleful bear.

"So, sir?" He's still waiting for something, the big galoof.

"So what, Ollie? Spit it out."

"So, did you want me to arrange death benefits for the crew, sir?"

"Sure," I say. "What the hell. Make it happen."

"Yes, sir," he says. "Any thoughts on the spin we should put on this?"

"I don't know," I say. "You expect me to think of everything?"

"I was thinking, sir. How about we say it was a Contra plane?"

"Good idea, Ollie. Do it."

"Yes, sir. I'll talk to Calero, get him to have Matamoros claim the plane was theirs." Adolfo Calero, FDN political director. FDN stands for federal something something. They're the Contras. Bosco Matamoros is the FDN man in Houston.

"Whatever. Just do whatever has to be done. Godspeed."

"Thanks, sir. I'll be in the air in an hour."

"And remember," I say as he strides toward the door. "I know nothing about any of this."

"Right, sir," he says. Did he roll his eggs at that? Was that an egg-roll I saw? Leg-roll? Lie-roll?

"So," Sam says after Ollie's gone, "you want the others now?"

"Yeah," I say. "Call them all. Have them find out everything they can and come to the Situation Room."

"You got it," he says.

But a minute later, he stilts his head in again.

"By 'call them all,' I take it you don't mean literally *everybody*."

"Who were you thinking of not calling?"

"Meese. Schultz. Regan. The President."

"Good thinking. We'll bring them in later, if need be. For now let's splick with the OSG." The Operations Sub-Group. It used to be the Taskerism Tear Gas. Termigasm Gorse Bush. Terrarium Tusk Floss. Whatever. But we did everything we promised to do against flosserism, so we changed the name. Floozyism. Something. Bad guys. The bad guys we were supposed to be contabulating.

Don Gregg comes into the outer office as I'm getting ready to go. He's my natural serlickity aide. Don used to be TIA, maybe still is. Worked with Ted Shackley, Ollie North, Felix Rodriguez, Dick Secord, and John Singlaub in Vietnam. Drugs and assmassiblations. Astermasturblutions. Vasdeferintions. Anyway, killings. That's the core team for this whole Iran-Contra operation, that Vietnam MAG-SOG group from the seventies. Operation Penix. Based on JM Wave from the early sixties, which, you know, I sort of worked with, too. Ted's in charge of Iran, Felix of the Contras. The others fit in best they can. Plenty to do. Plenty to coregulate. Corrodinate. Condomindinate. Weapons to Israel, to sell to Iran. Buy drugs with the weapons money, plow the profits into more weapons for the Contras. Aid to Honduras, to be passed on to the Contras. Fucking Boland. No aid to Contras. Gotta be sneaky. No aid to termigants. We hate Iran, very bad people over there, evil tremorists, bad guys, strike tremors into the hearts of all good-fearing citizens everywhere, but we helped the CIA overthrow the Shah and put Chowmeiny in power, so, you know. Training those Contras. Untrainable. Put our people in there. Recruiting Latino Texans to send down there, pretending they're Nicaraguan freedom fighters. Lot to calornicate.

Don and I walk over to the Situation Room together.

"This fucking thing is spinning way out of control," Don says. "Felix is talking."

"That son of a bitch!" I see red for a moment. I mean, lyrically. I see so much red I can't see where I'm going and I have to stop walking, brash up against the wall. This is happening to me more and more. I don't know why.

Don watches me out of the corner of his eye. And his eye's got a lot of corners, boy. The first time it happened, he got all societous: You all right? You all right? I yelled at him for it. Now, he just watches me.

I let go of the wall, start walking again. Don starts talking again.

"He's so proud of his 'VP connection.' "

"What," I say, still a little disornamented, "uh, *me*?"

"Of course. Ollie's been warning us forever that he's got a big mouth. 'George Bush and I are like *this*,' he's always saying. 'Whenever I'm in Houston, I go knock on George Bush's door and tell him everything.' "

"Ollie? Whenever he's in *Houston*?" Huh?

"No. Felix."

"Oh." Malt on that for a while. "I hope to God," I say, "he isn't still bragging about all that *now*."

"He is. One of our people down there just called me. He's telling everybody that he's head of this secret air supply operation that lost a cargo plane to Nicaraguan missile fire, and that he reports to Vice President Bush."

"Oh, isn't that just great. Tomorrow or the day after tomorrow, the international press is going to be asking me about this operation I'm running in Central America."

"Yeah. And you're going to need an answer."

"What answer is there? Not, of course. Got nothing to do with it."

"Needs to be better than that. It just isn't plausible that Felix is making all this up."

"Um, how about he's crazy? Boinkers? Off the fucking diving board?" I draw a little circle around my ear with my pounder finger.

"No."

"A closet lush?"

"I don't think so."

"Demonic possession?"

"No."

"What do you suggest, then?"

"Well, how about: you know what he's doing down there, and strongly support it, as does the President of El Salvador, Mr. Napoleon Duarte, and as does the chief of the armed forces in El Salvador, because this man, an expert in counter-insurgency, is down there helping them put down a communist-led revolution."

"What communist-fed resolution?"

"In El Salvador."

"Huh. Interesting. Is there one?"

"Hey, why not? Isn't there one everywhere? I mean, there's always somebody plotting to overthrow the government, right?"

"Like it." Nod a little. Nod in agredient. Frown thinkfully. "Like it a lot. But."

"What?"

"Isn't there just, I don't know, some way to shut him up?"

"You mean, permanently?"

"Or for the next, say, five or six years."

"I'm sure somebody can come up with a way."

"Good."

"It didn't come from you, though, right?"

"What didn't?"

"The suggestion."

"What suggestion?"

"Oh, right. I get it."

I don't. Talking to Don sometimes feels like talking to, I don't know, somebody I don't understand.

"But there's another problem," he says. "We got another Rodriguez with a big mouth, too."

"Oh shit."

"Ramon Medina."

"Who's *he* talking to? He's in fucking *jail*, for Christ's sake!"

"The American press, who else?"

"Who let *them* in to see him?"

"I don't know."

"Find out. I want his job."

"You want to be a prison guard?"

"No, you fool. I want you to get him fired."

"Oh. Okay."

"So who is this journalist? Any idea?"

"Some lady journalist. 'Investigative' journalist. They've got those up there. Out *investigating* things instead of raising a family. Martha Honey. Can you believe a name like that? Like flies to honey."

"So, what, it's just some sort of fucking *coindigence* that a plane goes down and before the world even knows about it, we've got a Martha Honey interviewing flies in jail?"

"I don't know. I agree, though, there's something mighty fucking fishy about it."

"So what'd he tell this Martha Honey?"

"That he gave Felix ten million dollars of Medellin money for the Contras because Felix told him he was such good friends with George Bush."

"That fuck! I'll kill him myself."

"Felix promised Ramon he could guarantee 'good will' for the Medellin cartel by talking to his bosom buddy George Bush. 'This isn't something that's going to go through twenty-seven bureaucratic hands. It's straight to the top. I give George Bush a call, he puts a word in the right ears.' "

"And he told this to a fucking *juggernist*?"

"No, to Ramon."

"No, I mean *Ray* told it to a jigglemist. Jigglenaut. Whatever."

"A journalist, yeah," Don nods. Ray Milian moved something like a billion and a half dollars for those Medallion people. Some kind of superaccountant. Superfly. Then he got arbusted. Picked up, flying to Panama on a private jet with five million dollars in cash. Then, he wanted help from his good friend Felix Rodriguez. And Felix's good friend George Bush.

Somehow, it's starting to seem to me like we're in the doo-doo this time.

We get to the Situation Room. Charlie, Terry, Jim, Craig, Noel, and John are already there. Charlie is Charles E. Allen. He's TIA. Terry Arnold is some kind of gesundhant. Gestaltant. Constaffant. Whatever. You ask him questions, and he answers them, that's about the sides of it. Jim is my executing assistant. Cardinal James L. Holloway III. Not Cardinal, Ardimal. Armoral. Armor hotdogs. Oh I'm glad I'm not an Oscar Meyer wiener. Craig Coy's his aide. Noel Koch is Dick Armitage's dapplety. Dick is Assistant Secretary of Defense. But Dick's not in the OSG. So he's not here. John is Vice Aldiral John Poindexter. He's bald. He's the senior NSC reprehensative on the OSG. That is what I'd never want to be.

Cuz if I was an Oscar Meyer wiener. I used to love that commercial. Back when my boys were little.

"Gentlemen," I say.

"Mr. Vice President," they say.

I love that. I walk into a room and say, "Gentlemen," and they all say, "Mr. Vice President."

"I wanna hear from Charlie first," I say.

"They already know a lot," Charlie says blondly. Blundly. Blandly. Like, sharply.

"Who's they?" I say.

He shrugs. "What difference does it make? *They*. The public. Our enemies."

"The public isn't our enemies," Jim says, sort of spuffily.

"What planet are *you* from," Charlie asks Jim sarcraptically.

"What planet are *you* from," Jim says back.

"Stop saying whatever I say, you fuck," Charlie says.

"Stop saying whatever I say, you fuck," Jim says.

Charlie reaches over and messes up Jim's papers.

Jim reaches over and messes up Charlie's papers.

Each tries to stop the other, and pretty soon, they're frailing at each other.

"Boys, boys," I say. "Enough. Charlie, what exactamently do they know?"

"They know about your trip to Honduras in March," he says, glorrowing a little at Jim. Charlie's got a very weird head. It looks like the top and bottom of two different heads, held together by his glasses.

"So? How does that hurt us?"

"They know you and Felix Rodriguez were there together. They know that you met with President Suazo, who Felix's partner was spending ten million trying to kill when he got busted. They know that you promised Suazo a hundred and ten million dollars in economic and military aid, in return for them letting us transfer Contra military supplies through their air bases. They know about the quid pro quo."

"They *know* this, or they suspect it?"

"They know it. Don't ask me how. We suspect a fish. We haven't been able to find him."

"Anything else?"

"They know we hit all those Sandinista leaders," Charlie says. "Miguel d'Escoto, the nine comandantes. And, um, let's see, they know about Luis Posada Carriles."

"Who?"

"Ramon Medina," he says.

"I don't get it," I say.

"Luis Posada Carriles is one of our JM Wave Cubans who later joined the DISIP and, in 1976, blew up a Cubana airliner and killed seventy-three people. DISIP is the Venezuelan intelligence agency. They busted him and threw him in jail. He was in jail for nine years. In August of 1985, somebody helped him break out of prison and put him in charge of the Ilopango air base."

"The whole base?"

"No, just our part of it. Our traffic. Loading and unloading. Safe-houses for TIA flight crews. Maids, whores, food, transportation and drivers, fuel for the planes."

"Oh," I say. "Of course. Ray. Ray Medina."

"Right," Charlie says. "He changed his name, for obvious reasons."

"So," I say, "does this mean we got him out of jail?"

"In a manner of speaking," Charlie says. "Felix did it. For us. He and Felix were JM Wave buddies. Back in the late fifties, early sixties."

"Does Luis know he's exposed?" Don asks.

"I sent word," Charlie says.

"That it, Charlie?" I ask.

"For now."

"Jim?"

He shoots Charlie a quick dirty look first. Then: "Michael Tolliver's talking to the press."

Loud groans around the room. This Michael Tolliver is one of our new pilots. Felix recruited him last year.

"The Texas press," Don says, "or the international press?"

"Texas press," Jim says. Huge sighs of relief. "So far."

"What'd he say?" Don asks.

"Described his cargo," Jim says. "Fourteen tons of military supplies from Galveston to Argucate air base in Honduras. Twelve-point-six tons of marijuana from Honduras to Galveston. Missiles from Galveston to Honduras, coke from Honduras to Galveston. And so on. Dates. Details. How much of this, how much of that. How much he got paid, and by whom."

"Names?"

"Felix Rodriguez. Chi Chi Quintero. Seventy-five grand a trip."

"Fucking cocksucking traitor," John mumbers. "Oughta fucking cut his nuts off."

"That it?" I ask Jim.

"Yeah."

"John?"

But just then, the door opens and Bob Oakley comes in. He's director of the State Deployment Countra-terrorism Office. He's all out of bread. He's planting hard. Pranting. Prancing. His hair's messed up. He's sweaty. He's a mess.

"They've got Iran," he blurns out, prumping himself in a chair. "They've got everything. Sorry," he says, looking around, "I interrupted something, didn't I."

"No, no," I say. "Go ahead."

"They've got Bernard Veillot and Cyrus Hashemi," he says.

"Hashemi's dead," I say.

"I didn't mean they've got the actual *guys*," he says. "They've got the stories. How we sold Iran two billion dollars' worth of weapons. How Hashemi and Veillot brokered the deal. How Vice President Bush and General Kelley approved it. How Veillot got indicted and went underground. How Hashemi, ahem, tragically died of leukemia."

"They *know* we hit Hashemi?" Charlie says. This is the first I'm hearing of it myself. It never creases to surmaze me how many people we kill.

"I told you," Bob says, "they know everything. How Cap Weinberger and Colin Powell made the actual arms transfer. How Poppy here met with Amiram Nir in Jerusalem this past July."

"I—uh, I—" I'm sort of splintering, here. "Not even the *President* knows about that trip," I say. "How did our enemies find out about it?"

"I tell you," Clark says, "there's a fish."

Just then, the door opens again and Buck Revell comes in. His mouth is gun set.

"Buck," I say. "Glad you could make it." Oliver's his real

name. But he goes by Buck. Pass the buck. Pass the butter. Pass the salt. He's Assistant Director of the TBI. Our Bureau guy.

"Sorry I'm late, gentlemen," he says. "But I found out who's doing this to us."

Nobody says anything. All eyes are on him.

"Well," he says, looking around the room, "who do you think? Who else? That fishy bastard Skipjack LaTuna."

"I *knew* it," I say too loudly. I can hear it as soon as I say it. It was too loud. I modgerate my voice a little. Like, downwards. "That son of a bitch. I hate his fucking fishy guts."

"I thought he was dead," Terry says. "Pan-fried."

"He got away," Charlie says. "He was always the one that got away."

"We finally caught him spying on us," Buck says. "He's been following every damn move we make and trying to thwart it."

"How do we know this?" I say.

"We've been spying on him, too," Buck says, "naturally."

"But *how*?" John says.

"You know, the usual: wire taps, tails, photographs."

"No," John says, "how are they spying on *us*? We've trebled security. We spy on ourselves. There's no way they could be getting this stuff from us."

"Well," Craig pipes up. It's the first time he's opened his mouth. He usually doesn't say much. He's just an aide. "We *have* had all those fish infestations. I just never did believe they were acts of nature."

"But we've exterminated them," Buck says, "every time. Ruthlessly."

"I don't know," Craig says. "Maybe it's the exterminator."

"Can't be," Buck says. "We send three guys in there with him, in their exterminator suits. Each time a different three guys. Each time, we tail him after he leaves here. Three teams, each from a different branch."

"But two, sometimes three infestations a *week*," Craig insips. "I tell you, it just isn't natural."

"There's a nest somewhere," Noel Koch puts in. "They gotta find the nest. You don't find the nest, you're going to have more infestations. Simple as that."

"That's cockroaches," Craig says. "I never heard that about fish."

"It's ants, too," Terry says. "Once, we had ants for six months before we found that fucking nest."

"Yeah, you're right," Craig says. "But ants ain't fish."

"I never said ants were fish," Terry says.

"No, I know you didn't," Craig says. "I just meant it's ants, too, but it's not fish."

"Oh, okay," Terry says. "I guess I can go along with that."

"Could be *silverfish*," Craig says.

"Boys, boys," I say. "Enough about infestations. We've got a problem here, and it's not an infest. It's a man. And his name is Skipjack LaTuna."

"Right, right," they say, and then shut up.

"And he's got a punishing company that's been a thorn in our neck forever," I say. "What's it called again?"

"Kawakawa Intelligence Review," Buck says.

"That's it," I agree. "And if that's integillence, running dirt down on your government, I don't know what is. And Commaconga, what's that, Japanese, or something?"

"Kawakawa," Brock says. "It's a kind of tuna."

"Oh," I say. "Well, that fucking figures, don't it." I look around the table for effent. Everybody looks back. "So but anyway," I go on, "all this dirt he's got on us, so-called, he's probably got slashed away up there in his pillbushing offices, up there in Fort Worth. Right?"

"Most likely," Buck says.

"So," I say, "let's go get it."

"What," Buck says, "tonight?"

"No time like the president," I say.

"It'll take me a few hours to get enough men together," Buck says, "and warrants. Let's hold it for the morning. I want at least four hundred agents on this raid."

"Okay," I say. "I don't care what you find there. I want his ass in jail."

"Shouldn't be a problem," Buck says.

"Still," I say, "this is all zipping up the cow after the barn door got out." That came out sounding sort of funny, but I can't stop now to figure it out. "What I mean to say is, the cow is already pretty much out of the bag, am I right?" Nods all around. "We're exhosed on this thing. We're going to need to cover it up, and cover it up good." More nods. "And that means, forest and firmost, keeping the President and me out of it. Out of it. *Completely*. Are we clear on that?" Nods, nods. "It goes without saying that whoever keeps me out of it gets a Cabinet position or some other plump job when I'm President. I go down, no rewards program."

"We gotcha, Poppy," Don says.

"Ollie takes the clap. The crap. The whatever. The, uh, the hate. The hate mail. That's the plan. He did all of it. It was all his idea. Right?" Nods. "He goes on trial, gives the court a bronzable backlight, backwash, lightwash, whatever, then gets a suspelted sentence. We look after him. We portrait him. Protrait him. Whatever the word is."

I gloam around the table. Nobody offers me the word. I guess that means they agree, don't they?

They better agree. Their asses are on-line. Mine more than theirs, improbably. I go down, they go down, we all go down. Plop goes the weasel.

Then, there would be nothing left of me.

Documents

Skipjack LaTuna Greets His Captors
(October 8, 1986)

Skipjack LaTuna squished back comfortably in his chair, the slick, wet coolness of it caressing his feverish body. His desk was raised slightly to allow him to see the tanks around the room, all now happily filled with his friends and operatives. And from here, he also had an unobstructed view of the street below. Well, almost unobstructed. There was a Republic of Texas flag hanging down to the left of the window, and every so often, the wind caught it and fluttered it across his line of vision. The fact that he had to keep one eye on the street and another on the door was no problem—his big saucer-shaped eyes set cleanly on either side of his hatchet-shaped face solved that dilemma.

He knew they would come tonight. That last issue of the *Kawakawa Intelligence Review* had no doubt pushed them over the edge, sent them into a frenzy of rage, and set them determined to finish him and the rest of his operations. LaTuna chuckled as he thought of the looks on their faces when they'd read the front page:

The world knows that the Bushes made a mint trading with the enemy and off of slave labor and tax fraud, but the world doesn't know they also made—and continue to make—a pile of money in the tuna fishing business. The pictures below, taken from a video by one of our operatives known only as "Sorry Charlie" (now deceased, killed by a TIA operative), show clearly the Bushes visiting one of their tuna factory ships, the Bashibimbo, flying an R.O.T. flag but registered in Korea. The Bushes have made untold millions illegally fishing in restricted waters and taking far more than their limit, but what will really shock you, Mr.

and Mrs. Public, is that they aren't in it for the money alone. No, as these pictures show, their visit to the Bashibimbo was a visit to the battlefront, as they clearly express unbridled pleasure at the sight of hundreds of drowned dolphins hanging from the side of the ship. The elder Bush is seen with a cocktail glass in his hand, laughing and pointing, while the younger Bush is throwing up over the side of the boat. Several operatives lurk nearby, and Dogsbody Harriman is hovering at the scene. The captain of the ship is beaming with pride as he gestures at the bodies of these gentle sea mammals, cruelly murdered in the "dirty little war" the Bushes are waging. Why, you may ask, do the Bushes hate these sea creatures so? Well ...

The text alone would have sent them into a snarling rage, he suspected. But the addition of the still pictures from the video, *that* was the kicker. The shot of Bush, Sr., holding aloft a copy of *So Long and Thanks for All the Fish*, and laughing as he set it on fire with a golden Zippo. The picture of Douglas "Banded Goby" Adams on the back, crumpled in the licking flames for all to see. Now, of course, they'd be after him, with only one thought: to gut and pan-fry every fish in the country. But especially, they wanted *one* fish, one named Skipjack LaTuna. No doubt, even now, they dreamed of crushing his corpse into some Miracle Whip and sweet relish and spreading it on Texas toast.

Well, let them dream. Hell, let them come. He nodded to a couple of burly, well-muscled tiger sharks by the door. They nodded back. Their stony faces told a tale or two—stories of TIA and TBI agents who "went diving for treasure" and never returned. LaTuna knew he could trust them with his life.

But there was far more to this than just a last stand against the Bushes and their minions. LaTuna could, of course, escape. But he chose to wait, to meet whatever was coming. Because, even now, as he slapped a cigar in between his huge wet lips and ignited it with a match, he chortled a bit in his chest as he looked at the loveseat across the room, by the door.

"Comfy?" he asked, blowing a cloud of azure smoke into the air.

Laura Bush nodded vigorously, her eyes wide and frightened above the diving belt that was wrapped tightly around her lower face. Her body was bound in a large piece of fishnet, the cork bobber still attached, lead weights underneath.

"Good," he nodded back. "Mr. Lincoln will be happy to get you anything you need," he soothed, "provided, of course, that it doesn't involve removing your gag." He looked with his other eye to the street.

A tall, bearded man, somewhat rumpled and wearing a top hat and black frock coat, sat by Laura Bush. He didn't move or blink. His hands were in his lap. In one hand was a Bible. In the other was a can of fish food.

LaTuna smoked and looked—one eye on the street, the other on the door. They would come. He'd really hated to do this to Laura; he felt, somewhere deep in his entrails, that she was different from the others—compassionate, a believer in freedom and the power of the people to change things. But she was also dangerous, and one of them, and clearly, not yet ready to embrace LaTuna's view of things. Anyway, she was just a pawn—Sun Moon had done something to her brain.

And Lincoln. Such a mystery. How he'd just appeared unexpectedly at the office with Laura in tow, wrapped in netting and gagged with a diving belt. He'd carried her in his long, bony arms, shuffling a little as he bent to get through the cabin door. He seemed sad, deeply burdened, and when he'd plopped Laura down on the loveseat and sat next to her, pulling out a can of fish food and a Holy Bible, well ... LaTuna had known then he couldn't run. *This* one he'd play out.

Suddenly, Lincoln spoke. His voice was deep and rang like a bell even though his lips didn't move very much. "Few will remember the sacrifice ..." he began, licking his thin Lemurian lips a little, "and when they recall what was done, few will honor or cherish the acts of heroism that these brave souls wrought on these hallowed waters that flow below the waters and below the lands of the Earth, *but*" — Lincoln emphasized this with a bony finger around the can of fish food —"they *will* remember that, as long as there was oxygen, there was a flicker of resistance, a flash of tailfin, as we trailed away into glory ..." And he fell back into glum silence.

Laura was shaking now, whether with the cold that comes with sitting in the damp of LaTuna's office, or with fear, or both, he couldn't tell. The lights were very dim in the office, to allow better vision.

A scuffling sound came from the decks outside the door. Low at first, then louder, and then there was silence. The tiger sharks stiffened at the ready, their gills pumping vigorously through the water tanks they wore around their bull-sized necks.

LaTuna held a fin to his lips. From outside the door, some more shuffling and shushing sounds, and then a voice, a very familiar voice.

"Goddammit," it whispered, "somebody, give me a light, here, on this drawer!"

Another voice urged, "Quiet, stupid." A light glowed through the opaque porthole in the door.

"Yeah, this is it. Now you be quiet. We don't know the layout of this place, so the explosives have to be just right. I wish you'd stayed at home. Stop scratching your balls. There may be someone inside."

LaTuna grinned a fishy grin, motioning to the tiger sharks.

Get Noriega

(Poppy, New Year's Eve, 1989)

"Who am I? Hm? Who am I, here? Can somebody tell me? Am I Joe Blow? Am I Alfred E. Neuman? Hm? Is that who I am? Somebody, please tell me, who am I?"

My aides look around diseasily. Nobody's all that happy to be asking this, I guess. Asking beetle this. Being asking this. Whatever.

"You're, uh, George Bush, Mr. President," Dan says. J. Danforth Quayle, dumbest man to be Vice President of Texas since, uh, I don't know who.

"What was that again?" I say. Everybody flitches with every word. Am I yelling? Is that what I'm doing, here? "Was that George Bush, Mr. Burger Flipper? George Bush, Mr. Burger Builder? George Bush, Mr., um, Nobody In Particular? Or what?"

"George Bush, President of the Republic of Texas," Dan says.

"Now that's what I thought, too," I say. "You know? Somehow, I had this idea that I was the President of this fairy public. I had this distilled memory of being elected to the pre-decency. Was I wrong? Was I wrong?"

"Of course not, Mr. President," Dan says again.

"Then why," I say, "somebody, tell me why," I say, "I cannot fucking get Manuel Fucking Noriega's head on a fucking silver platter around here!"

"We're trying, Mr. President," Brent says.

"Trying is for failures, General," I say. "Trying is for losers. I didn't hire you to try. I hired you to do. Get in there and do. Out there. Now. Before I lose my patience."

"But, Mr. President," Jennifer says, "what is there to do?"

"Did I ask you for your opinion? Did I ask you for your advice? If I want your advice, Jennifer, I'll give it to you."

"Right, Mr. President," she says. Sarclaptically?

"With all due respect, Mr. President," Brent says, "this isn't a military problem any more."

"It's not what?" I say.

"It isn't—"

"I fucking well heard you, goddammit it!" I say.

"I just—"

"How dare you tell me what's a military problem, Brent? Who do you think you are, telling me what's a military problem?"

"Retired Air Force General Brent Scowcroft, sir!" he says, snapping off a smart salute.

"Are you giving me shit, Brent?" I say. "Is that what this is, Brent? Are you giving me shit? First, you can't get me one stupid fucking puny little worm of a Panamanian drug dealer when I ask you nicely for one, and now you're giving me shit?"

"No, sir. I'm not giving you shit, sir. But I do think I'm qualified to distinguish between a military problem and a political problem. Sir."

"Mr. President, sir," I say.

"Right," he says.

"So, Brent," I say. "You think this is a political problem. Not a military problem."

"Yes, Mr. President, sir," he says. "I do."

Shit. Brent's been National Security Council Director forever. I mean, he was back in the late seventies under Bentsen, and I made him that again. And he's a general. Shit, shit, shit.

"Why don't you tell us all, then," I say, "if you can, why this is a political problem and not a military problem?"

"Well," he says.

"We invaded Panama," I say.

"Yes, sir," he says.

"That was a military operation," I say.

"Yes, sir," he says. "It was."

"We bombed the fuck out of Panama City," I say. "We counted four hundred and nineteen bomb bursts in the first fourteen hours of bombing alone," I say. "That was pretty fucking military," I say.

"Yes, sir," Brent says. "It was very military."

"Killed thousands and thousands of civilians," I say. "Very, very military."

"Excuse me, Mr. President," Jim says. Jim Baker. He's my Secretary of State these days.

"Yes, Jim?" I say heavily.

"We agreed to say there were only two hundred civilian casualties. Sir."

"Do you mind, Jim? I'm making a fucking point, here."

"Oh, right, Mr. President. Sorry."

"So, Brent," I say. "We fucking leveled whole parts of Panama City. Right to the ground. And we took ten thousand didicents prisoner, put them in concentration camps."

"Detainment camps," Jim corrects me again.

"Jim!"

"Sorry, Mr. President."

"We tossed the old government out on its ass," I say, "and put Guillermo Endara in as the new President. That's all pretty fucking military, wouldn't you say, Brent?"

"Yes, sir. Absolutely, sir."

"And in this whole fucking military operation," I say, "the whole fucking incompetent motherfucking Texas military could not capture and kill one stupid fucking Manuel Noriega. That, too, was a military problem, wouldn't you say, Brent?"

"Yes, sir. I couldn't agree more, sir."

"That fucker just waltzed out of town, right through our military lines. Like Santa Claus, or something."

"Yes, sir."

"And now he's holed up in the fucking Papal Dunciature, and our troops are outside playing their satanic rock music full blast, and the papals won't fucking give him up," I say.

"Nunciature," Carla says. "Sir." Carla Hills. She's trade, or something. I have no fucking idea what she's doing here. Do we trade with Panama? Maybe it's that whole canal thing? Who yankled her chain?

"What?"

"You said Dunciature, Mr. President," she says, sort of aponomatogetically. "It's Nunciature."

"Who fucking died and made you king of the English language?" I shout.

"Nobody, Mr. President. Sorry, Mr. President."

"If I fucking want somebody to correct my English, I'll correct it for them!" I shout. This really gets my groat, people correcting my English. "If my English is good enough for Queen Elizabeth," I add, "it's good enough for a bunch of redneck Texans like you all!"

"Yes, sir," Carla says, retempant.

"Where the fuck were we," I say.

"Outside the Papal Nunciature in Panama City," Boy says. Boy Gray. C. Boyden Gray, my main political adviser. Here's the guy who should know what's a political problem and what isn't! Not fucking Brent Scowcroft!

"Right, Boy. That's right. Outside the fucking Papal Whatever-the-fuck-it-is in Panama City. Those fucking no-rubbers Catholics, let's have as many babies as we fucking well can, hmm, I know, let's go out there to the Third World and tell the stupid and the poor to keep their wives barefoot and pregnant and overrunning the free world with their stupid poor babies, that's what we should do all right, that's what we will do, because we fucking well can because we're the fucking pope. No contras, no ceptions, no stereozations, no sirree, Bob! And now," I say, "and now," I say again, "they won't fucking give me my Manuel Noriega, no matter how much I demand him with my armed troops and play satanic rock music at them. And now," I say, "I want you to explain, Brent, finally," I say, "you miserable fuck, how this is not a fucking military problem!"

"We can storm the Nunciature, Mr. President," Brent says, all in a rush. "You just give the order and we'll storm it. No problem. It's not exactly a fortress. I think Bill will back me up on this." He gentures over toward Bill Crowe. The Chairman of the Joint Chiefs of Staff. Bill nods. "I repeat, sir, there is absolutely no military problem here. The military side is easy. It's the political fallout that you have to worry about here. Killing Catholic priests is a piece of cake, militarily. They ain't exactly Rambo. Politically, though—"

"All right, all right, already," I say. "Jesus Christ Almighty, how thick do you think I am? I got it the first time, for fuck's sake!"

"I wonder if I can try out an idea," Larry says. Lawrence Eagleburger. Jim's undersecretary of state.

"It just better be good," I say, "uh, Larry."

"It's just an idea," he says. "And a pretty simple one. But you know, sometimes the best ideas are simple. So simple you overlook them, at first. But then, once you think about them a little—"

"Enough with the philosophy already," Jim says. "Spit it out."

"Right," Larry says. "Why don't we just leave Noriega alone?"

All heads turn and stare at him.

"What?"

"What?"

"What?"

"What?"

Everybody's saying *what* at him. Like, disbereaving.

"Wait," he says. His fat cheeks like a, I don't know, some kind of fat animal. "I know it's a radical idea. But hear me out, please!"

"This I gotta hear," I say.

"Well," he says, "we're all agreed that we can't just storm the Nunciature. We can't just go in there after him. As Brent says, the political fallout would be massive. And he's not going to come out of there on his own, give himself up. He requested political asylum from the fucking Vatican, for Christ's sake."

"Tell us something we don't already know," Jim says.

"So what do we do?" he says. "We pull back. We give up. We seize the moral high ground. We're bigger than they are. We could smash them. But we don't. Because we're so moral. Because we're so democratic. Because we care."

"What the fuck have you been smoking?" Dick says. Dick Thornburgh, my Attorney-General.

"No, wait," Boy says. "This has potential."

Well, if Boy says it has potential, I'm going to listen. You bet I am. Boy looks like a boy, but he's really smart. Larry smiles at Boy and goes on.

"The thing is," he says, "Noriega isn't really a drug dealer. Endara is, not Noriega. Well, Endara's a drug money launderer, but that comes to the same thing. That whole thing about Noriega and drugs and corruption was just our official reason for going after him, back in 1985, under Autry. Right? Remember? We made that up. His real crime was not going to war against the Sandinistas. And that's sort of old news these days anyway."

"Not going to war against the Sandinistas and freezing Carlos Eleta's assets," Dick says. Dick Thornburgh, not Dick Cheney. Dick Cheney's not saying much. Dick's my Secretary of Defense. Dick Cheney, not Dick Thornburgh.

"Yeah?" Larry says.

"Yeah. Don't you remember? We got him involved in our efforts to stop the drug lords from laundering their money in Panama banks, and he got a little carried away. Started going after our guys, too."

"Really?"

"Sure. In February of 1987. That's when we went after him."

"Well, still," Larry says, "that doesn't change the fact that Noriega isn't the bad guy we've made him out to be. The world doesn't exactly descend into anarchy if we just let him go on living his life. Noriega on the loose doesn't increase the total quantity of evil in the world. He's out of power already. We've already put our guy in. We can afford to be magnanimous at this point. We can just walk away. Tell the Papal Nuncio, 'Hey, you want him, you can have him. We're too big to worry about one minor Central American ex-dictator.' "

He's done, I guess. Everybody's sort of looking around again, wondering what to say. Who's going to talk first.

It's me. I'm the one. I'm the President.

"Have you," I say slowly, "Larry," and another little pause, "fucking lost your mind?"

"What? Sir?" Larry gulps.

"Have you taken leave of your sensors?" I say.

"I, uh—"

"What Manuel Noriega is," I say, "or isn't, isn't reverent here," I say. "That's neither here nor now. The point isn't the evil we'd be leashing on the world if we let him go, you dumb fuck." I look straight at him. He quails a little. Dan's next to him on the couch. He quails a little too. Get it? Quayles? "The point is how we would look. We'd look big, you say. We'd look moral, and high ground, you say. No, I say. No, no, no. That's a big, big no to that. No. Absolutely not. Not, not, not."

"With all due respect, Mr. President," Larry says, "I just don't see it."

"You don't see it!" I crowd. Cloud. Whatever. "You don't see it! Well, I guess that's why you're doing whatever the fuck it is you're doing around here and I'm President! Huh? Could that be it? That I'm President because I see it and you don't? Did that ever occur to you, Mr. Cheeseburger?"

"Eagleburger, sir," he mumbles.

"Eagleburger! Eagleburger! What is an Eagleburger, anyway?

Is that a burger made out of an eagle? A bald eagle, maybe? Is that some sort of American fast food, Mr. Eagleburger? You get those fat cheeks from American eagleburgers, Larry? Is that where you got them? Well, let me tell you something, son. Down here in Texas, we don't eat eagles, and we certainly damn well don't make eagleburgers out of them! Armadilloburger, now there's a good Texas name!"

"Yes, sir," he says miserably.

"Here's the thing on Noriega," I say. "Here's the deal. Here's the dope. Here's the 'straight skinny.' Listen up. We've been going after him for two and a half, three years, now. It doesn't matter one fucking iota why. We've been going after him, period. Got it? Not one iota. We've been delousing him in the press. Drouncing him. Drenching him. Whatever. We've been calling him every fucking name in the book. Dictator, drug dealer, you name it. Corrupt government. We've spent tens of millions of dollars that we didn't have trying to oust him, kill him, throw the election against him. We've stuffed ballot boxes, stolen ballot boxes, trying to prove how corrupt he is. Nothing's worked against him, except one fucking thing: convincing the world that he is the bad guy we say he is. Now everybody believes it. You got that, Mr. Armadilloburger? Mr. Moral Ground Round? Everybody fucking believes it. They think he's a monster. They think he's evil. They think he's got really horrible skin. We've invaded his country, bombed his city, bombed his Comandancia and three whole neighborhoods around it flat, thrown him out of office, put our guy in his place, because he's evil. Because we've convinced people he's evil. Not because he is. Because everybody thinks he is. You got that? We pull out now, we're not just saying we don't care about evil; we're saying we don't care how much money we wasted going after him before. We cannot, cannot, must not back down now. It is absolutely essensorial that we stand strong now. That we follow this thing through to the bickle end. Right to the end, boy. We have to have his ass on a fucking blender. We have to. Or else we were wrong all along. Or else we're wrong now. Either way. We have to."

Silence.

Then: "The President's right, people," Boy says. "There's no politically acceptable way out of this thing now. We're stuck. We have to follow through."

I nod grumly at Boy. Turn to glorel a little at Larry.

"Can I make a suggestion?"

All heads turn back the other way. It's Bill Webster. Director of Texas Intelligence. Used to be my job. Bill was TBI director under Autry. I moved him over to Intelligence when I got elected.

"By all means, Bill," I say. "If you can come up with something, we'll all be, uh ..." Whatever.

"I was just thinking," Bill says. "We need to attack the Nunciature, obviously, right? But we're afraid of the political fallout."

Nods.

"Well," he says, "why don't we just get, um, somebody else to attack it? Sort of, you know, spontaneously?" We all look at him. My God. It's brilliant. It's perfect. It's the answer. "Some sort of, I don't know, spontaneous Panamanian people's uprising. Ordinary folks, fed up with the excesses of Noriega's dictatorship. Ordinary Joes who've waited too long for justice to be done." No wonder I applauded this man Director of Texas Intelligence! No fucking wonder! "I don't know how we'd want to do it, maybe keep it simple, have them storm the Nunciature, kill the priests and whatnot. Maybe accidentally on purpose put a bullet in Noriega's head. Maybe, who knows, get fancy, get these Panamanian citizens to hijack a plane or something, crash that fucker into the Nunciature, something big, not a Piper Cub, something big and full of fuel so it'll blow that fucker sky high. Or, what, get them a Volkswagen Bug, have them light it on fire, and lob it at the Nunciature with a catapult. Kaboom. Presto changeo: problem solved. And we didn't do it. Right? We can just stand back and tsk our tongues at the lamentable use of violence. 'Surely,' we say, 'surely a peaceful solution could have been found. ' "

"Bill," I say, "you are a fucking surfatriable genius. You hear this, Brent? You hear this, Larry? This is the mind of a genius at work, on a problem, to solve it. This is what it looks like."

Nods and consalgutations all around. Now we can go home, celebrate 1990. And we all go home. Happy New Year!

Documents

Ivermectin and River Blindness
(Houston Chronicle, February 20, 1990)

A muted and mostly unreported conflict has been brewing between Republic of Texas health officials and local Texan family doctors.

The local doctors have been putting pressure on the central government to relax the ban on insecticides in the country, or at least to legislate an exemption for low-dose Ivermectin, which has been banned since the founding of the Republic because it is often used as an insecticide.

Republic of Texas health officials have also long insisted, with ample clinical evidence, that Ivermectin can be quite dangerous to humans, leading in many cases to liver failure, seizures, and coma.

Infamously, when fish-loving physicians in Australia and Latin America began to prescribe and promote high-dose Ivermectin as a cure-all for viral infections in humans, tens of thousands of severe side effects were recorded among poorly educated segments of the population who blindly trusted fish and their ideological mouthpieces more than real Republican doctors and scientists.

It has been the standard use of low-dose Ivermectin world wide—and, of course, in pre-Republican Texas—to deworm cows and horses. And while technically worms are not insects, a typical parasitic "worm" in the gastrointestinal system or skin of a cow or a horse is the larva of a botfly (*Oedstrida*), which is a "worm" that *becomes* an insect. Using Ivermectin to "deworm" a horse or a cow, therefore, is to use it as an insecticide; hence its ban in the insect-friendly Republic of Texas.

Texan family doctors, however, have begun to challenge this ruling on the basis that elsewhere—including in the

United States—Ivermectin is approved for use in humans to treat river blindness (onchocerciasis), caused by blackfly bites. Bites of the blackfly (*Simulium*) introduce the parasitic worm *Onchocerca volvulus* into the human GI tract. Because *Onchocerca volvulus* is a nematode—a worm, not an insect larva—family doctors have been arguing that using Ivermectin to kill a non-insect should be permitted. Ivermectin at the low doses used for deworming cows and horses does not kill or otherwise harm the blackflies whose bites cause the blindness—the second most common cause of infectious blindness.

Republic of Texas health officials, for their part, have insisted that river blindness is an insect-*related* disease, and therefore should be protected from the destructive effects of Ivermectin.

"This stubborn adherence to an ideological dogma in the face of scientific evidence that controverts it," remarks Dr. Sally Froth of Waco, "is a whole other kind of river blindness—and no less devastating."

Who Is the Neptune Continuum?
(flier, fall 1990)

Poppy— These flyers are ending up on cars all over Corpus Christi and Galveston. I can't make hide nor hair of their agenda, weird shit, but they sure do seem to hate you Bushes. What do you want us to do about it? Joe

WHO IS THE NEPTUNE CONTINUUM? Awaken, Texas!

It seems that the Bushes, not content to hunt down our members and slaughter us like sheep, are now spreading lies about us in the press and encouraging Texans to turn us in wherever they find us.

Maybe, Texas, it's time you knew us. KNOW THAT WE STAND FOR:

Genuine democracy
Equitable distribution of wealth
Humans with gills
Dolphin channeling
No taxes

Who are we? We are your neighbors, your friends, the fish you see in your ponds, lakes, streams, and rivers. We used to be the fish you saw in your **goldfish bowls**, before the **Bushes outlawed goldfish** in private homes. We are gentle and kind, and mean no harm to anyone. We know that the END is COMING SOON. But unlike the Arabaptists, we welcome it.

It is time for a NEW WORLD ORDER. And that ORDER is all power to the PEOPLE! And the FISH! And the SEA MAMMALS!

We consign to the trash heap of history the following:

Scarab beetle infestations
Skull and Bones stuff
Money
Red Studebakers and fossil fuels
Bushes, Walkers, and Harrimans

We URGE you all to JOIN us! Our Hallowed Leader, **Neptune deTrident**, WELCOMES you all to JOIN US, in fond memory of our Martyred Leader **Skipjack LaTuna**, gill-netted, gaffed, gutted, and filleted by the Bush-Walker-Harriman conspiracy that TO THIS DAY most cruelly persecutes our finny friends in waters everywhere but SHALL NOT PREVAIL!

How do I join? you may ask...

It's as EASY as falling off a log, as long as you fall into the WATER. Just go to your nearest pond, lake, or similar fishy area, dive in, and ask the FIRST FISH you see HOW TO JOIN—don't worry about the REST ! WE'LL TAKE IT FROM THERE! **See you soon!**

Stadium

(Dubya, January 4, 1991)

"No," I say, "it's not!"

"How isn't it?" the guy says. "Explain this to me so I'll understand. Please!"

"It just isn't," I say, "that's all."

"That isn't a good enough answer," the guy says. He's standing there sort of defiantly. Like a fly. Ready to fly in my face. He's got his hands on his lips. I mean tips. The tips of his legs. You know, the tips that poke out at the tops of your pants. The hard little bumps there. He's got his hands on those.

"Well I'm sorry like hell," I say, "but that's the only answer there is."

"Well I'm sorry like hell, too," he says, "but if that's the only answer y'all can come up with, I'm going to have to assume that y'all just don't care enough to even *pretend* not to be cheating the taxpayers on this one."

"Someone else?" I say.

"What's the point, if you aren't going to answer our questions?" some voice yells out from the audience.

"Who said that?" I say.

"I did," the guy says, and stands up.

"Of course we're going to answer y'all's questions," I say. "That's what we're here for."

"Then answer the big one: how is this *not* corporate welfare? How is this not a government-subsidized real estate venture designed to enrich a group of private investors?"

"I'll tell you the same thing I told the other guy," I say. "It just isn't."

"We pay more taxes so you and your buddies get richer," the guy says. "That sounds exactly like corporate welfare to me. It sounds like the government interfering in business. It sounds like unfair taxation. It sounds like the opposite of free enterprise. It sounds like everything your dad is always fulminating against. But maybe you disagree with your dad?"

"No, of course not."

"Then?"

"Then what?"

"Then how can you defend the government taxing the people to enrich entrepreneurs? How is that *free* enterprise?"

"I can defend it," I say, "because we're going to build the greatest baseball felicity and complex ever built as a result of a partnership, a joint venture between some honchopanures who think big, who aren't afraid to risk, and the cenizens of a city that isn't going to pand stat."

And you know what? That's the honest-to-God truth. I swear it. My resortium and me, that's what we're doing. Dessicunt. Sediment. My sin something. My guys. The guys that put up most of the money to buy the Rangers. $86 million. And that's *Texas* dollars, mind, not them flimsy American ones. They only wanted half a million from me 'cause, you know, I ain't got that much. Had to sell my Harken stock to raise even that much. Harken was about to go bellyflop anyway. Had to sell them stocks before the CEO announced how bad we was doing. Wait till he announces it, and my stocks ain't worth the shit I wiped 'em with. I mean, woulda been wiping 'em with. If. You know.

Still, they made me the big boss. The front guy. Damaging general parkler. Hear that? *General.* That's like in the war or something. That's the most important job of all. I talk to the public. 'Cause I got a nice face. And my dad's the President. You know. Can't hurt.

Plus, we get this stadium built and get the government to pay for it, and I get a big bonus. Like a billion shares. Or something. A lot. Like fifteen million dollars or something.

"So we've got a joint venture going here now?" the guy says.

"That's exactly what we've got," I say.

"A joint venture where we spend all the money against our will and y'all garner the profits. That doesn't sound like a very good deal to me."

"Y'all aren't spending all the money. We're doing our part too. It's a *joint* venture."

"The owners spend thirty million dollars. The taxpayers pay a hundred and sixty million. Nice work if you can get it."

"The taxplayers aren't paying a hundred and sixty million," I say. "The city's selling bonds worth that much, and retiring them over seventeen years through a dollar slurcharge on tickets at the park *and* a tiny sales tax infleece. Mostly tickets at the park."

"Right, so if we love baseball enough to want to keep the ballpark in Arlington, we pay more taxes *and* more for tickets."

"Look," I say, "maybe it's time to give Nolan Ryan a word. Nolan?"

Nolan stands up. He's a good guy. Hell of a pitcher. He sorta sketches his long legs and stiffies it over to the dopium.

"Thanks, George," he says. Everybody's quiet now. This fucker's a hero. I couldn't believe it when he agreed to come out tonight. "Hey, folks. I hear ya. I understand y'all's position. Hell, I'm a big fan too. And I'm a taxpayer just like all of y'all. But ya know, I know from a fan's standpoint, and a ballpark standpoint, and the ballplayers' standpoint, we're in need of a new stadium. We just are. The one we're playing in is too small, too old. It was built for a minor-league franchise. We have to have us a new stadium. How are we going to get it? We have to finance it. But how? That's a good question, and it's a problem. Any time you have any kind of bond issue that pertains to taxes, you're going to have people opposed to it. But I'm a believer in progress, and I don't care what kind of progress you get, you have to pay for it, and it has to be funded somehow. Taxes? It's going to cost taxpayers a dollar a month. A dollar a month, folks! Isn't that worth it? Isn't it worth a dollar a month not to have to drive into Dallas or Fort Worth to watch a Rangers game? Isn't it worth a dollar a month to have a ball club and the prestige that it brings?"

They sit there quiet for a minute. Nolan is golden, man. He is fucking golden.

Then a guy with his hair in a long dirty ponytail stands up. Hippie type. Ripped blue jeans.

"Yes?"

"I'd like to ask Nolan Ryan a question."

"Yes?" Nolan says, leaning into the mic. There's a big beadfact squeelk and everybody jumps back and covers their ears. "Sorry," Nolan says.

"You say you don't care what kind of progress you get?" the hippie says. "Uh, Nolan?"

"That's right."

"Well, what if you get progress towards communism? Is that a good thing?"

"No, I didn't mean—"

"But you said you didn't care what kind you got. Right? *Any* progress is good. You're a believer in it. I guess that makes you a *progressive*, huh? Progressives believe in progress. But progressives, hey, ain't that just another name for *liberals*? Huh? Nolan, man? Ain't it? And ain't liberals just another word for *communists*? Government handouts, that's all this is. Like the man said, this is fucking *welfare*, man. That's what it is. Y'all're just a buncha welfare abusers. Crack mothers, is what y'all are. Crack babies on the government tit, suckin' it dry, man. Face it, that's—"

"Someone else?" I cut in.

But just then something happens. The back doors to the hall open. Something goes clop clop. All heads turn.

Somebody's riding in on something. I can't see who, exactly. Or on what. The sun is settling right behind whoever, whoever. He's sort of stilettoed. Situettoed. Statuettoed. Something. Like, his body's all dark. You know what I mean? Sun all around.

Then he's inside the hall, and the doors bang slut. Stut. Like a stutterer, you know, ba-ba-bang bang. And it looks like Abraham Lincoln riding a cow. Dripping wet. Dripping all over the gym floor. All around him on the floor, flappy fish. Flappety flappety flap. *All* around. Somebody dressed up like Abraham Lincoln. On a cow! Or a steer. A Texas longhorn? Are those long horns, or are they just regular horns?

And hasn't my dad and Uncle Dogsbody been looking for this guy, like, for fucking ever?

What should I do?

I don't do nothing. I just watch, like everybody else.

The Lincoln guy is just riding along up the aisle toward the front table where I'm sitting. Not looking to the sides, not saying howdy to folks. The cow, or bull, or steer, or whatever, is looking to the sides and saying howdy. I mean, not really. But sort of. In a cow sort of way. The fish flap flap flap along with them.

There's something about them fish that reminds me. I don't know what.

They looks like they just walked up out of some lake. Or, I don't know, swimming pool. Like one of those kiddie pools they got nowadays. Put it in your backyard, let the kiddies smash around in it on a hot summer day. With fish. And when the kiddies get up out of it, they're soaking wet. That's how these two look. Like a coupla bare naked little kids all covered with water. Except Lincoln's got this black suit on, and everything, and the cow's all hairy, like a cow are. And fish.

The Lincoln guy don't seem to be steering. The cow just

knows where she's going. She goes right up to the podium and turns around to face the crowd. Lincoln picks up the mic. Stays up there on his cow.

"My fellow Texans," he says. He sounds just like you'd aspect Lincoln to sound. The crowd is flushed. I mean, they're real quiet. "I want to say that in all the seven score and four years that Bessie and I have been living underwater with the fishes in this great state, and now country, Texas, I mean, bubbledy bubble, I have never, and when I say *never*, I mean *not ever*, seen a more honorable, a more honest and intelligent, a more civic-minded or fair-spirited man than this man right here before y'all today, George W. Bush. Let's have a little round of applause for George W. Bush, folks. Come on."

He looks over at me. It looks like he's about to cry. Sort of in a good way. People start clasping a little. Not very excusiastically.

"Now, ladies and gentlemen," the Lincoln guy says after a while, "as a former President of those United States up north, it is my deep abiding personal belief that this man, this *very* man, should be President of our fine country some day real soon. And it seems to me, quite frankly, folks, that if he says the Arlington Stadium is a project that will benefit the Arlington community, why, then it is. If he says it's a project that is in the best interests of the Dallas-Fort Worth metroplex, then it is. If he says that the entire Republic of Texas in all its grandeur and glory, heralded by the angels above and the water-cows below, cries out for the stadium, then by all that is good and decent in the world and beyond, we owe it to ourselves to give it to him. And he's got a great wife named Laura Bush, too. Thank you."

And he sets the mic back down on the podium, and the cow starts walking back up the aisle. He hasn't taken more than four or five steps, though, when somebody starts clasping. Clasping and unclasping their hands. You know, so it makes that loud clasping noise. Like a pause. Or a shnozz.

Then another starts doing it too. Sort of loud. Pow, pow, pow. Pretty soon they're all joining in. And standing up. Women are crying. Men are fridaying back tears. Parents are holding their small children up to shake Lincoln's hand. The fish are jumping all up and down. Into folks' pockets and purses. Talkin: "Dubya Bush is the greatest! Dubya Bush is the best!" I can hear 'em all the way up here.

The Lincoln guy don't pay no attention to none of this. He don't bend down to pick up none of the babies that's being passed up to him. He just rides on up the aisle, out the doors, dripping wet, fish flapping, into the settling sun.

Uncle Dogsbody? Should I have called the cops here, or something? Or the Bureau? Hell, this guy just got us the stadium, probably. And he said I've got a great wife named Laura. Though, you know, maybe she'll be, which, you know, I'm not. Whatever. But Abraham Lincoln! And his fish really like me. Is that a call-the-cops-on kind of guy?

Documents

Interview With Vicki Hartman After Past-Life Regression in TBI Flotation Tank
(TBI Files, August 7, 1991)

AGENCY INFORMATION
AGENCY TBI
RECORD NUMBER 267-32054-36749
RECORDS SERIES HQ
AGENCY FILE NUMBER 76-20486-7

DOCUMENT INFORMATION
ORIGINATOR TBI
FROM SAC, NO
TO DIRECTOR, TBI
TITLE [No Title]
DATE 08/07/91
PAGES 16
DOCUMENT TYPE AUDIO TAPE/TRANSCRIPTION
SUBJECT VICKI HARTMAN
CLASSIFICATION UNCLASSIFIED
RESTRICTIONS OPEN IN FULL
CURRENT STATUS OPEN
COMMENTS INCLUDES LHM

pp 3-7

Q. So then you began seeing visions?

A. Yes.

Q. Can you remember what music was playing at the time?

A. I believe it was Martha and the Vandellas singing "Walk Like a Man."

Q. You're sure about that?

A. I think so, yes. It was right after Roy Orbison's "Only You." That one had no effect on me at all.

Q. Did you in fact regress to a past life?

A. I did, yes.

Q. Who were you?

A. I was Ramses II, pharaoh of Egypt.

Q. A man.

A. Yes.

Q. Is this possible?

A. How do you mean?

Q. Well. You're a woman.

A. Men can be reborn as women. Women as men. That's how it works.

Q. All right. Proceed.

A. I was standing on the portico of the palace, looking out at Abu Simbel.

Q. What is Abu Simbel?

A. A great temple cut into the rock. Gigantic tombs and statues. Some people believe that the statue of Ramses II in the Shelley poem was there.

Q. Shelley poem?

A. "Ozymandias." Percy Bysshe Shelley. English Romantic poet.

Q. Oh. Never read it. Go on.

A. I was reflecting on who I was, where I had come from. I thought: *I am Ramses II. I am the son of Seti I, and the grandson of Ramses I. I have waged war against our enemies, the Hittites, those heathen, and lost. But when the people of Egypt rose up against me as a result of the loss, I quelled them with an iron fist. I shall be known as the greatest of the Egyptian kings. From my loins will spring kings, queens, and presidents.*

Q. Presidents?

A. He thought "presidents." Or that's how it came to me. Maybe it was a different word in Egyptian, but it appeared in my mind as "presidents."

Q. Go on.

A. He had some sort of foreknowledge of the future. This wasn't just some formulaic boast, my descendants shall be as the sands on the shore. He *knew.*

Q. Was it clear how he knew?

A. The "winged ones" had told him.

Q. The "winged ones"?

A. The Atlanteans.

Q. The Atlanteans?

A. You know, from Atlantis.

Q. Yes, I've heard of Atlantis. But people who lived there had wings?

A. They weren't people. They were aliens.

Q. Oh?

A. Yes. They came to Earth between sixty and seventy thousand years ago. They were very tall, between seven and twelve feet tall, and normally looked more or less human. But some say they were actually insects.

Q. Uh huh.

A. They probably originated from the Lyrian star system.

Q. Sure they did.

A. Do you want to hear this or not?

Q. No, no, go on.

A. You probably didn't know that over a dozen skeletons have been excavated that were over ten feet tall.

Q. Okay.

A. There is reference in the Old Testament to a race of giants. Genesis 6:1-2. The Spanish conquistadors left diaries describing men eight to twelve feet tall running around in the Andes, during the conquest of the Incas.

Q. Fine. Go on.

A. The Atlanteans worked with other groups to develop the smaller human being by genetic manipulation, originally for use as workers. Humans were originally automata, called Adamu. They were used in mining, food production, construction, and so on. There was such a great demand for them that they couldn't build enough of them. Then they were given the power to reproduce on their own, and they began to proliferate rapidly.

Q. Other groups?

A. You thought the Atlanteans were the only aliens on the planet? No, there were the Thuleans, the Hyperboreans, the Lemurians, and others as well, of course.

Q. Are these groups still around?

A. Most of them were destroyed long ago. A few are still around. They are extraordinarily long-lived. Some say Abraham Lincoln was a Lemurian.

Q. How were they destroyed?

A. They began to focus on material things and to ignore their true spiritual nature. Thus they brought upon themselves three terrible cataclysms, culminating in the one mentioned by Plato, around 10,500 B.C. Their major power source was a huge crystal that converted sunlight into energy, which was then transferred via pyramids to other parts of the continent. But they became greedy and tuned the crystal too high. It activated volcanoes and melted mountains, and finally caused the submergence of Atlantis.

Q. So, but, uh—some survived?

A. Yes. But even before that final cataclysm, many Atlanteans migrated to Egypt and were absorbed into its culture. Some interbred with the pharaoh's family and created a new super-human race. Others remained aloof from humans and were worshipped as gods. As a result, Egypt became the first great human civilization, responsible for the invention of writing, medical science, irrigation, and many other scientific innovations.

Q. So this "winged one" that Ramses mentions was, what, one of the aloof ones? One of the ones worshipped as a god?

A. Right.

Q. Did you see the "winged one"?

A. Yes.

Q. Describe him.

A. Very tall, very thin. Gray hair. Gray, raspy voice. He was wearing a business suit and carrying a briefcase.

Q. Ha!

A. I'm not kidding.

Q. Oh please.

A. I know it sounds ridiculous, but it's true!

Q. You're going to insist on this?

A. No, I'm just telling you, that's what I saw.

Q. This is going to hurt your credibility with the Bureau. Bad.

A. I don't care. I didn't ask for this job.

Q. A *modern* business suit.

A. Well, a bit old-fashioned, maybe. Out of style. Like from the twenties.

Q. But the *nineteen*-twenties.

A. Yes.

Q. God damn it. God damn it to hell. When I took the exam to get into the Bureau, if anyone had told me I'd be talking to psychics about bugs from ancient Atlantis wearing business suits, I'da fucking laughed in their face.

A. Do you want to stop?

Q. No, no. Let's get all of it.

A. The winged one was called Lord Daq-Bati. He appeared behind me.

Q. You?

A. I was Ramses II, remember?

Q. Oh yeah.

A. I could feel him come with a draft of cold air. He asked me why I looked troubled, and I said I was saddened. "The pharaoh of all Egypt is sad?" he said. "Why?" "I wish that I could see the future," I said. "My children's children and their children, ruling all the corners of the Earth." "You wish to see the future? " he said. "Come over here to the pool, I'll show you the future." And I looked into the pool, and saw swirling there many visions, some familiar to me from the history books, most not.

Q. What were some of the familiar ones?

A. Alexander the Great. Cleopatra and Marc Antony. Charlemagne. Marie Antoinette. King Ferdinand and Queen Isabella. Franklin Delano Roosevelt.

Q. You recognized all these faces in the pool?

A. Yes.

Q. And these were who, exactly?

A. I don't follow.

Q. Who exactly did this Lord Whosit say he was showing you?

A. My descendants. Ramses' descendants.

Q. So Roosevelt is descended from Ramses II.

A. According to this vision, yes.

Q. Did you recognize anything else?

A. Yes. The current President.

Q. Of Texas?

A. Yes.

Q. George Bush?

A. Yes. He appeared in the pool as well. Sitting at his desk in the President's Mansion. In fact, I recognized him as Ramses, too.

Q. What, say that again?

A. I said, as Ramses: "Wait! Look! That's me! That's me in the water!"

Q. Meaning what?

A. Meaning Ramses II looked very much like President Bush, I guess.

Q. Oh come on.

A. I don't know, I didn't see Ramses, I was inside him. All I know is what he said.

Q. Did this Lord Winged Guy say anything?

A. What, about George Bush?

Q. Yes.

A. Yeah, he said: "No, Ramses. It is one of your descendants. One very like you in many ways, true, but only a descendant with all of your special blood, as I told you. He is very much like you."

Q. President Bush is very much like Ramses II?

A. Yes. And I said, "He is strong, decisive, intelligent?" "No," Lord Daq-Bati said. "Weak and petulant. Not particularly bright, but eager to please."

Q. This is what some seven-foot alien bug said about *our President*?

A. Yes. I understood that the winged ones saw all humans that way. But Lord Daq-Bati expected Ramses to be better, and he wasn't. He was like all the others.

Q. So, was that it?

A. No. I asked him whether this descendant of mine also had a hundred children. He said, "No, his children are few, and not exceptional. But they will suffice. Here is his oldest son." An image appeared on the water. I didn't recognize the face, but I assume it was the son with the same name. Isn't that their oldest? George Bush, Jr.? And I said, "His eyes are like the eyes of one who eats the lotus."

Q. *You* said that?

A. Ramses did.

Q. Oh. Right.

A. And Lord Daq-Bati said: "It is as well. He will be the last of the line in this office." "The last?" I said. "But— " "Enough!" Lord Daq-Bati commanded. And now the image in the pool began to change; in the place of the oldest son of President Bush, there were suddenly millions of the sacred beetles that the winged ones brought when they came. They were swarming, milling, flying in clouds, and the water in the pool began to boil, and then the scarab beetles came out, flying in a swarm around Lord Daq-Bati. I turned around. I could not watch. I felt the cool wind on the nape of my neck. I knew when I turned, Lord Daq-Bati would be gone.

21

Unreelected

(Poppy, November 5, 1991)

Well, it doesn't look good. The off-year election results, I mean. Dick Thornburgh ran for Provincial Governor up in Dallas, and got five votes. Five! Hundreds of thousands of people voted, Dick's name was the only one on the ballot for Governor, so of course he got elected, but it's some kind of message, I guess, that the people are sending me. Sending us. That only five voted for him. That's what Jim says. Jim Baker. A message to me: we don't like what you're doing. Dick's a good man, but he's too closely associated with me, with my Cabinet. Dick was my Attorney-General. Then he wanted to be Governor. I campaigned hard for him, too. Covered his ass. Covered mine. Had Ross Perot whacked. He threatened to go public with my role in the assassination of LBJ, so I had him whacked. Love that word, whacked. Ross was already whacked! So my having him whacked was redundant. Not the first time I've been accused of being redundant. I've been called redundant before, so this won't be the first time. Still, people sent me a message.

What I can't understand is, what really turns my crank, is what people could possibly be upset about. I'm a strong President, very strong. Not a wimp. And, okay, we've had a bit of an economic downturn, sort of a slowdown, not really a recession, not at all. Not a depression! That's pretty ridiculous, calling it that. My enemies call it that. Compare what's going on right now to the Great Depression, back when Texas was created. But it's not, of course. It's totally different. This is more like a, I don't know, a downturn. A dip. A blip. Something you can hardly even see in the radarscope. Bleep. Bleeped out.

I told Jim that I thought he was wrong, wrong, wrong. And I do think that. I'm a nice guy. I'm quite lovable, once you get to know me a little. Get under my skin. Under my thumb. Bar says I'm great. My kids love me. Great dad. Gave me a little statue last Father's Day. World's Greatest Dad. And I think they meant it, too. Like, liberally. Like there's no greater dad in all the world than theirs. And I'm like a dad to the Texans, too. First Dad. Why can't they just love me like my wife and kids do? Why are they so angry? How could they be sending me a message about being angry?

But Jim said some people are hurting. The little guy. Like, the middle-class guy. The guy with two cards in his garage, two chickens in his pot. They don't have any money. So why don't they just work harder? Work smarter? And, you know, make more money? Get rich, like me? Or at least, you know, richer?

What worries me, though, is that the rich people don't seem to be real happy with me either. All those tax breaks! What more could I give them? Bailed out those S&Ls there. Half a trillion dollars to bankers who goofed a little, through no fault of their own. And they look at me like some kind of sausage or something. I throw these thousand-dollar-a-plate fund-raising dinners, and lots of people come, and we raise lots of money, but the people just sit there and look at me. They don't laugh at my jokes. They don't clap when I say patriotic things. When I get going on something I really care about, like not pandering to the poor, they look almost scared. Like they're scared of me. Me! Like, physically scared. Like they're afraid I'm going to lose control, climb up on the tables, start kicking their plates in their fat, self-satisfied faces, screaming.

So Jim says I need to make a statement about the election results. Say something to rally the people together. Keep it positive. Keep it upbeat. Don't go crazy. Don't start ranting and raving, the way I usually do, he says. Me, rant and rave! A quiet, restrained, friendly guy like me! Crazy people rant and rave. I just, well, sometimes get impassionate. Like, sort of worked up, over something that really matters. I need to project calm. A calm leader. Statesmanlike. The kind of guy who needs to be President for another four years. A year from today, this should be me, reelected. Re-e-leck-ted. Not Ted. Me. Get it?

So they set up a press conference. I congratulate Dick on his election to the Governorship of Dallas Province. I talk about the country and the economy. I say I know some people are hurting, and my heart goes out to them. I say I feel their pain, and that I think Dick Thornburgh is going to be a pain reliever. I look over at Jim. He's smiling. Good going, Poppy. Knock 'em dead.

And it's right around now that the protuskers start coming in. They don't say anything. They're just wearing T-shirts. All the same T-shirts. I can't read them at first. They're at the back of the room. Two, three, four, five. Pretty soon, there's ten of them, fifteen. And there isn't enough room for them back there, so they start filing up along the outside toward the front. They're being very polite. Everybody's smiling at them. Then, looking closer at their t-shirts, and looking sharply at me. Uh oh. Finally a few of them come close enough for me to read their shirts. They say, "The George Bush Anywhere-But-Texas Tour." Underneath is a list of the countries I've visited this year. There's a few. Maybe 25, 30. Has it really been that many?

And something starts rising up inside me. I don't know what it is, but it's pretty wild. Like a wild animal. Like some really wild one, like a tiger, or a dingle, or a shark, or something. A wild hair. Like an animal hair. A shark hair, not that they have a lot of hairs, or whatever. And I start, well, venting a little. I guess I go a little ballistic. I don't remember everything I said. I remember calling my critics some pretty strong names. "Tawdry," I guess. "Phony." "Second-guessers." "I'm not going to apologize for one minute," I say, "that I devote to advancing our economic principles abroad or working for world peace." The people in the front rows are shrieking away from me. It's just like at the fund-raisers. They're afraid of me. I'm a scary guy.

And then it comes to me. I won't go to Asia, goddammit. That'll get 'em off my back. I'm heading off to Rome in a couple of days, then a few days after I get back from that on a ten-day trip to Japan, South Korea, Singapore, and Australia. Supposed to. Won't go. Just plain won't go. That'll show 'em. I travel too much? I go anywhere but Texas? I won't go. I won't go, goddammit! That good enough for you?

So I announce it. Right here and now. Trip cancelled. Gotta stay in Houston till the end of November and work on getting my domestic legistative package through Congress. Ha! Drumpfed those fuckers! Got 'em where they live!

But after the press conference is over Jim is kind of tight. Lips are very tight.

"What," he says, "the fuck," he says, "was that? Mr. President."

"What?"

"That cancellation of your trip."

"What about it?"

"What was it? Why'd you do it?"

"Because I wanted to. That's all you need to know."

"I'm your Secretary of State. I need to know more than that."

"No you don't."

"Yes I do."

"No, Jim, you don't."

"Mr. President, I'm going to have to spin this. You're going to have to give me something to go on."

"What is there to spin? I cancelled the trip. Period. End of story. I told them why. I don't need to explain anything more than that."

"You told them that you need to stay in Houston to get your domestic legislative package through Congress."

"Right."

"What domestic legislative package?"

"My domestic whatever. Package."

"You don't have a domestic legislative package."

"Of course I do."

"No. Sorry. You don't. I'd know if you did. You don't."

"Well, something."

"Something isn't good enough, Mr. President. I need more than that. Especially when the Japanese, Korean, Singaporean, and Australian ambassadors start expressing their outrage."

"What outrage? Why should they be upset about this?"

"Because they're going to hear about it on the news. That ain't kosher. We're supposed to notify them directly, then go public with it."

I wave my hand dismindively. "Fuck 'em."

"You're President of the Republic of Texas. You can't fuck 'em."

"I won't. You will."

And so on. He goes on and on about this, but I blow him off. Fuck them, and fuck him. Fuck everybody if they can't take a joke.

By this time it's getting kind of late, and I'm thinking of going to bed, but at the last minute I think of some papers I need to get from my office. Prepare for Rome. NATO summit day after tomorrow. I walk into the office, and there's somebody in there. Somebody in my chair, facing away from me, swiveling it back and forth.

"Um," I say, "excuse me," I say, "but —"

The chair swivels around. It's Uncle Dogsbody.

"Uncle Dogsbody! What a—pleasant surprise!"

And then, of course, the beetles are all over me. I should be used to them by now. But.

"Hello, George," he says. "Sorry to barge in here so late.

But I had some urgent news to give you."

"News, Uncle Dogsbody?"

"Yes, George. Sorry. I'm taking you off the ticket."

"You're, uh—what?"

"Taking you off the ticket. The presidential election ballot next November. You're off."

"I, uh—I'm off?"

"This will be your last year in office, George."

"But, Uncle Dogsbody! What! How can you do this to me? What did I do?"

"You're out of control, George."

"I—I'm not!"

"You are, George. Sorry. I've nursed you through a lot, over the years. Over half a century, now. You've been my boy. I wanted you to be a great President. But you can't do it. You're weak. You're a coward. You're a bully. And now you've got this Basedow's disease, and it's fucking with your head."

"What disease?"

"Basedow's."

"No, Uncle Dogsbody. I've got Graves' disease."

"No. That's what your doctors said, to take the edge off. But it's Basedow's."

"What does that mean?"

I'm reeling, here. Not going to be P resident? I just get one term?

"Graves' makes you a little jittery. Basedow's leads to full-blown mental illness."

"Mental illness! Uncle Dogsbody!"

"And it's already here. You're already half-crazy, George. This thing tonight is just the last in a long line of precipitous and disastrous decisions you've made. It's all Basedow's."

"What thing?"

"Canceling the trip to Asia. It's pretty obvious to everybody what happened: you saw those T-shirts and overreacted. The Lincolnites wanted to get under your skin, and they succeeded. I need a cooler head in this chair."

"I've got a cool head, Uncle Dogsbody!"

"No, George. Sorry. The thing about Basedow's is that it's emotionally triggered. Any emotional upheaval can set it off. Any psychic shock. Any mental trauma. You've had thousands of them in this job, and each one pushes you over the edge. Each time a little farther. This thing could kill you, George. I'm taking you out."

"Kill me?! Uncle Dogsbody, the doctors said it was easily treatable!"

"They lied to you, George. The only treatment is total rest. A completely stress-free environment. Radioactive iodine can control the symptoms, slightly. But nothing can prevent the thyroid storm when a crisis hits. The pituitary gland overproduces its hormone, which provokes overactivity of the thyroid, which speeds up overall metabolism and exacerbates the emotional crisis, which further stimulates the pituitary gland, and so on. Around and around. The only way to keep you safe from your own thyroid gland is to take you out of the presidency. Put you out to pasture."

"Pasture!"

"It's a metaphor, George."

"That means you don't really mean it, right?"

"I mean the part about taking you out of the presidency. But not the part about the pasture. Your pasture will be Barbara. She'll take care of you. She'll feed you the foods that will help you get better. One of them, by the way, is broccoli."

"I hate broccoli! I won't eat any more broccoli!"

"I know, George. Everybody knows about you and broccoli. I suppose I should have told you, back then. I didn't think you'd react the way you did."

"That was you?"

"Of course. I've known about the Basedow's all along. Broccoli is one of a group of foods called goitrogens that help reduce and control the thyroid storm. I was hoping we could control it without the word on the Basedow's getting out. But you wouldn't eat it. So."

"But—but—"

"But what, George?"

"Surely you're not going to make Dan President?"

He chucklers a little. "No. I'm not going to make Dan President. There was another hyperthyroid brainstorm of yours. Dan Quayle as Vice President. Remember how everybody said no, no, no, but you just had to have him? Remember the fits you pitched, until they all gave in?"

"He comes from a good family!"

"It's not enough, George. As we've discovered with you, too, it turns out."

"So who's going to be President?"

"Clayton Williams."

"Clayton Williams! That savage!"

"He'll do the job just fine, George. He can't do it worse than you. Sorry if I'm blunt."

"I—I—"

I can feel the rage rising inside me. But I can't let it out with Uncle Dogsbody. I'm sort of afraid towards him. Always have been. Don't know why, exactly. He's always been wonderful to me. Still, can't help it. He scares me. I push the rage back down. I start trembling. I'm shaking pretty hard, I guess.

"Yes, George?"

"I just—one thing—"

"Yes?"

"You remember, back when I was a little tyke, out in our baseball field, you said I'd be President."

"Yes, of course I remember."

"And you said my son would be President, too."

"I remember that too."

"Which son?"

"One of them, George."

"Jeb? Neil? Marvin?"

"One of them, George. Leave it at that."

"But one of them will be President, right? Despite Jeb's connections with the Colombians, and Neil's Silverado scandal?"

"And Marvin's regional enteritis?"

"His what?"

"You didn't know? Everybody in your family has some sort of autoimmune disorder, George. Everybody. Because of you."

"Because of me? Uncle Dogsbody! How?"

"They're emotionally triggered, George. The strain of living with you triggers it in all of them. You got it from your mother."

"The strain of living with me! What do you mean?! What strain? They don't even live with me!"

"They did, George. They lived with you for twenty years each. That set the pattern in each one of them."

"But—but one of them will be President?"

"One of them will be President, George. I promise."

Okay. Okay then. Okay. That's that then. I'm out. One of my boys is in. Some day. But which one?

Documents

Baptist Preacher M. J. Bin Lennon Found Dead
T.B.I. Investigating "Suspicious Circumstances"
(New York Times, April 27, 1995)

The body of elderly Texas firebrand the Rev. Mohammed Jesus bin Lennon was found late yesterday near the back steps of the Weatherford Public Library by a neighborhood watch officer on routine patrol, the Texas Associated Press reports. The body, which has been taken to Fort Worth for examination, was oddly mutilated and covered with the ubiquitous "Texas scarab" beetle, witnesses report.

"The bottom part of his face was gone," recounts Meriwether "Hank" Simperfell, the neighborhood watch officer. "His, uh, whatchacallit, jawbone, was ripped out, looked to me. His chest was ripped open, and it looked like his guts was gone. And he was covered with them damn beetles. Later on I found this little Egypt-like box in the park behind the library, and when I looked in it, damn, there was all these guts! I reckon they was his."

The "damn beetles" Simperfell refers to are the "Texas scarab" beetles, unknown in Texas prior to 1929 but now reaching epidemic proportions in some parts of the country. These beetles, which, according to Texas scientists, are harmless, are protected under Texas law and are unknown in the United States or Mexico.

The Rev. bin Lennon is best known in Texas and the southern parts of the United States as a somewhat eccentric and bellicose Arabaptist preacher who has been calling for holy war against the American Deep South for three decades, and speaking frequently in his public ministries about conspiracies involving Abraham Lincoln, ancient insect wars between Atlantis and Lemuria, space ships, and the city of Mecca.

He is perhaps better known around the world, however, as the father of the late John Lennon, founder of the sixties British-Invasion band The Beatles. Born in 1912 under the name Alfred Maximilian "Freddie" Lennon, he changed his name legally to Mohammed Jesus bin Lennon upon his conversion to the Arabaptist faith in 1930. He first gained international notoriety in 1931, when he went public with his claim that U.S. President Abraham Lincoln had faked his death in 1865 and moved to Texas under an assumed name, and that, in fact, he was an aquatic space alien from a legendary submerged island in the South Pacific, then still living. He continued to insist on Lincoln's incredible longevity throughout the next sixty years, and would pull out "incontrovertible evidence" that Lincoln was still alive and living at the bottom of this or that lake at the slightest sign of skepticism in his audience.

The Rev. bin Lennon founded his Arabaptist ministry in 1934, but in 1938 left his ministry in order to marry the English beauty Julia Stanley, with whom he lived in Liverpool until 1943. His son John Lennon was born on October 9, 1940, during one of the heaviest German bombing raids the city had yet experienced. In 1943, God called the Rev. bin Lennon back to the Republic of Texas to resume his ministry. He returned to Liverpool for his son in 1946, but young John decided to stay with his mother, who however shortly thereafter left him in the care of her sister, Mimi Smith, in order to run off with a new boyfriend.

Ironically, the Rev. bin Lennon's son John was slain in New York thirteen years ago, and found in a state uncannily similar to that of his father: apparently mutilated by his attacker, he was missing a mandible, and his body was covered with rare (but not Texas) beetles. At the time it was simply thought that this was some sort of sick reference to the band's name. Now police aren't so sure.

"We will be looking into this," said Sgt. Detective Pete

Ambrustocelli of the NYPD, announcing that the unsolved Beatle murder case would not be reopened. "There have been no reports of these beetles in the U.S.A., and we want to make sure there never are."

In the late 1950s, John Lennon's band was successively named The Quarry Men, Johnnie and the Moondogs, and the Silver Beatles before settling into the name that became world-famous: simply The Beatles. Police, carrying photographs of the Texas scarab—which is actually not silver but an iridescent green—are now questioning former Beatles and friends about the origin of this name. Paul McCartney, who joined the band in 1957, and George Harrison, who joined a year later in 1958, both during the "Quarry Men" era, have declined to comment, claiming "it was a long time ago and none of that matters now that John's dead." The drummer, Richard Starkey, better known as Ringo Starr, is on record as insisting that the Beatles don't take sides between the scarab beetles led by W. Averell Harriman and the predaceous diving beetle that is Abraham Lincoln but the dung beetle, which rocks and rolls its feces in little balls.

The Rev. bin Lennon is also distantly related to Mary Todd Lincoln, whose family supported his publishing efforts for more than fifty years, including his 1955 annotated edition of *The Prophecies of Michel de Nostre al Mohammed*, a series of apocalyptic prophecies dating from the 1920s and generally unknown outside of Texas, except in Egypt and Saudi Arabia, where they have garnered considerable public interest.

Investigations continue into the Rev. bin Lennon's death. The Arabaptist sect has come under intense scrutiny in the U.S., where its calls for holy war have gained national attention. It is unclear whether bin Lennon's death is related to these events.

The Rev. bin Lennon was 83 at his death.

22

Ballot

(Dubya, November 5, 1996)

I can hardly fucking contrain myself. Laura gives my hand a squeeze, my fesh a smile. The girls are at school. I'm pretty slicked up. I mean, I'm expiated as hell. Sicked up, sunked up, punked up, whatever the fucking word is. Is this a time for words? Or is it a time for dids? Well, I already did, didn't I? It. What had to be done. What I wanted to do. Fuckin'-A, I wanted to! Just about worse than anything. Anything I ever did before.

It was Fido's idea, actually. Karl Rove. That's what I call him, Fido. Get it? Rove, Rover, Fido? Because Rover's a dog's name? Anyway, he's my bud. He's got great fucking ideas, I mean it. Like, all the time. If it's not one thing, it's Christmas, and the snow ain't falling. Hey, this is Texas.

So one day like two months ago, back in August, he says to me, "Dubya?" We're in his car, in downtown Houston. He's driving.

And I say, "What?"

And he says, "How does a guy become President of the Republic of Texas?"

And I say, "Fuck if I know." Because I don't. It's the truth. I really don't. I have no fucking clue. Well, I've got a clue now. But I don't then. Didn't now. Whatever.

"Way I figure it," he says, pushing his glasses up on his nose, "you get elected President of the Republic of Texas by getting your name on the ballot."

"Uh," I say. "Okay." Whatever you say, dude. I mean, it sounds about right to me. Whatever the fuck a ballot is, but I mean. You know. Fido knows about this shit. He knows a lot. Sure ain't much to look at, though. Big, fat, bald, pink head, like some sort of, I don't know, big, fat, pink thing. Like a balloon. Like a pink balloon with glasses on.

"One-party system," he says. "Right? One candidate for President. Whoever's name is on the ballot, that's who gets elected."

"Okay," I say. Then I get this great idea. "Hey," I say, "you wanna go down to Donnelly's, get fucking wasted?"

"Maybe later," he says. "Listen."

So I listen. I'm sort of impenishment at first. I mean, I don't pay much affection. It's kind of boring. Then I latch on, and I'm all, whoa, cool idea.

"Here's the thing," he says. "The name on the ballot for President this year's supposed to be Clayton Williams again. Another four years of timid, tiresome bidnis as usual. But what if, I'm thinking, what if sort of, you know, accidentally, that name got, whatever, changed?"

"Changed?"

"What if, when Texans went to their polling places in November, they opened up their ballots and the name on the line for President wasn't Clayton Williams but George Bush?"

"Cool," I say, staring sorta aisledly out the window. Houston sledding by. "But my dad's already been President. You think they'd let him do it again?"

"George W. Bush," he says.

"No," I say, "that's me. My dad's George H. W. Bush."

"That's what I mean, Dubya," he says. "It'd be your name on the ballot."

"Huh?" I say. "Mine?" I can't figure out what he's getting at, here. "But then—"

"Yes," he says. "Exactly."

"Then," I say, "uh, then I'd be President."

"You got it."

"But I—I—Fido! Could I?"

"Course you could," he says. "Why not? Your grandpa was. Your dad was. Why not you?"

"Wow," I say. "Damn. That's true."

"In fact," he says, and eases past an old lady in a white Town Car, "didn't you once tell me your dad's Uncle Dogsbody promised him that he and one of his sons would be President one day?"

"Yeah," I say, "but—"

"But?"

"Well," I say, "one of his sons. It could be one of the others."

"It could be," he says. "Or it could be you."

"Damn," I say. "You're right."

"Of course I'm right," he says. "And another thing."

He looks over at me and pushes his glasses up again on that sweaty pink nose of his. He's always sweaty. Always fucking pushing those glasses up. He's wearing those flappy cheapo plastic pinch-on sunglasses over his regular glasses. When he goes into a tunnel or something, he flaps them up. What a dork. He's real smart, though. He's like this polickitle genius. Like a fat, dorky Lee Atwater. He's got a real vegious mind. Ovedient. Deviant, whatever.

"What?"

"Well, I've been mulling this idea over in my head for a few months, now. Wondering whether it would work. And I was thinking I'd start making discreet inquiries into just where and how the ballots get printed. Just sort of out of a casual interest, you know. I asked two or three people who work in government printing, and nobody knew. Then last night I'm out walking my dog, when who do I run into? You'll never guess."

I shed my spotters. Spud my shellers. Whatever. Make my arms go up. Just the top parts. "Uh," I say, "I don't know. Nolan Ryan?"

"Nah. Dogsbody Harriman. Out for a late-night stroll. Just like that. He just happens to be in my neighborhood stretching his legs at the precise exact moment I'm out walking my dog."

"That's a, whaddya call it, a crinoline."

"A dress?"

"No, a rent-a-dent."

"A car?"

"No, one of those, you know—"

"A coincidence?"

"Yeah. One of those."

"No," he says.

"No?" I say.

"No," he says. "Listen. You haven't heard the best part yet. I say to him, 'Aren't you Averell Harriman?' And he says, 'Aren't you Karl Rove?' We both agree that those are in fact our names. And then he says, 'So, I hear you're interested in government printing. You thinking about a career change, maybe?' Get it? He's heard about my inquiries. He knows what's afoot."

"Big deal," I say, looking down at mine. "Everybody knows what a foot is."

Fido looks over at me again. "Uh huh," he says. "So," he says, "anyway, I say maybe I am."

"Maybe you're what?" There's an enormous, fucking tub-of-lard, fat lady in the car next to us. We're stopped at a light. She practically fills up the whole fucking front seat of her Cadillac. Like, two-thirds of it. Her bald stick of a husband is driving. She's over across from him like a, I don't know, huge, whatever, tub of lard. The car's all lunched over to her side. Like it's eating her for lunch.

"Thinking about a career change," Fido says.

"What?" I say. He's what? What are we talking about?

"Nothing," he says. "I'm just going along with him."

"What who?"

"Dogsbody Harriman."

"Oh," I say. "Right."

"Anyway, he says, 'Maybe I could help out a little.' "

"Help out with what?" We're moving now. The woman lifts her arm up onto the back of the seat, and the flab hangs down on both fucking sides.

"Well," he says, "that's what I said. And he says 'If you were interested in, say, printing out some presidential ballots, maybe I could steer you in the right direction.' 'Yeah?' I say. 'And what direction would that be?' And he hands me a piece of paper." Fido goes into his shirt pocket and pulls something out. "This. Hands it to me." And Fido hands it on to me. "Says 'good luck,' and he's gone. Poof. Like a pile of leaves sucked up by some really powerful shopvac or something."

I nod. "That sounds like Uncle Dogsbody, all right," I say. "He's a weird fuck."

So I look down at the paper. It makes no fucking sense to me at all. It says:

13 Republic Way, rm. 305a
Oct. 30, 11:35 pm
PW 1b9ll9tpr6nt

"Huh?" I say. "I don't get it."

Fido doesn't say anything. Just pulls over, stops. Points up out of my window.

"This is the place," he says. "Thirteen Republic Way. Look at the sign."

I look out. "GOVERNMENT PRINTING OFFICE," I read.

"So?" he says. "Get it now?"

"Uh," I say. "No."

"It's where the November ballots are going to be printed," he says. "I'm thinking your Uncle Dogsbody's trying to help us get your name on the ballot."

"Yeah?" Here's where I start getting interested.

"Yeah. Who knows? But I got a hunch. If we sneak in there at eleven thirty-five p.m., October thirtieth, into room three-oh-five-a, I bet we'll find the place completely empty. Why else give us a specific time?"

"Uh," I say, "you got me."

"And this number at the end must be the password for the computer program that prints the ballots. See? PW? Password. And the number itself looks like 'ballot print nineteen ninety-six,' scrambled."

I look again. He could be right. I give a low whistle. Really low. Almost no whistle at all. Cause I don't really know how to whistle. But Fido can see I'm imprinted.

"So we go in there," he says, "change Clayton Williams to George W. Bush, and hit print. They print out all night. Next morning, the office workers come in and box 'em up, send 'em out to the polling places. November fifth, people go to vote, and they vote for you. Hocus pocus, abracadabra, you're the eleventh President of the Republic of Texas."

"Wow," I say. "Cool." I don't know what to say. "Let's do it, dude."

So, we do. And it works. It works like a fucking pizza box. This morning, I voted, and there was my name on the ballot. Right there on the President line. Now we're in the living room watching TV, Laura and Fido and me, waiting for the returns to start coming in. And, man, am I primped up. I can hardly sit still. I'm all over the place, bouncing off the fucking walls, height as a kite. Had a few quick nips when nobody was looking, to calm me down. Calm, somber JD. Whoo!

But, damn—when the returns start coming in there's a blitch. A stitch. Whatever. A problem. Turns out some people voted for my fucking brother Jeb! A lot of them, in fact. Like, half. Fido's up barking at the TV screen. Yelling, waving his hands. I'm yelling and grizzling whiskey. The TV commutators are puzzled too. They're saying it's the first two-candidate presidential election in the history of the Republic of

Texas—and the rivals are brothers—and neither candidate was even salted to be on the ballot.

Fido's pulling his hair out. Laura's handing her rings. Well, fingering them. Like, twisting them around. Her hands, I mean. Around and around. Sketching the skin, making it go all winkly. Or unwinkly.

Then the phone rings. It's Jeb.

"George!" he yells, "you son of a bitch, what the fuck did you do?"

"What did I do?" I yell back. "You son of a bitch, what the fuck did you do?"

"I did what Uncle Dogsbody told me to do, you retard! I snuck in and changed the ballots so they had my name on them. But how did your name get on half of them?"

"I did the same fucking thing, numbnucks," I yell back. "I snuck in too. Exactly what Uncle Dogsbody told me to do!"

"That fucker!" he yells. "He's fucking with us!"

"That fucker!" I yell too. "He *is* fucking with us!"

"But wait," he says. "Where'd you go?"

"Huh?"

"Where exactly did you go to change the ballots?"

"The Goverment Printing Office," I say. "Where else?"

"What address, though?" he says.

"I don't know. Lemme ask Karl." He tells me the address. I tell Jeb.

He lets out a low whistle. That fucker can really whistle. Little brother, my ass.

"It's a different place," he says.

"What is?" I say.

"It's a different government printing office. There must be two. He sent me to one and you to another."

"So—" I say.

"So that's why half the ballots are for me and half are for you."

I get it now. "That fucker!" I yell. "Damn him!"

"I can't believe he did this to us," Jeb says.

"I never did trust that old hairbag," I say.

"Me neither," Jeb says.

"Well," I say, "there's only one thing to do."

"There is?" he says.

"Sure," I say. "You've got to, whatever."

"What?"

"I don't know the goddamn word," I say. Why does everybody always fucking inspect me to know the words? Why can't somebody else know the words for once?

"Gimme a hint," he says.

"What?"

"Gimme a clue."

"It's like, you know, give up."

"Give up?"

"Like you go on TV and say you're not the President, I am."

"You're not the President, I am?"

"No, I'm not the President, you are."

"That's what I said, dumbball."

"No, asschurn, you got it backwards."

"So, what," he says, "you're saying I should concede?"

"Whatever," I say. "Just say you give up."

"Why should I give up? Why don't you give up?"

"Because I'm the older brother, mouthwipe. You'll have your chance."

"Yeah, but I'm a real human being. I'm not some kind of science experiment gone bad."

"I'm not either, you fuck!"

"You are, too! I heard Mom and Dad talking about it one night."

"You lie like a shaving mug," I say. "You did not hear them say that. You're the science expedient."

"Oh, right, just copy whatever I say, you dim bulb."

"I am not copying! It's true! I did hear them say that."

"You're such a lousy liar, George."

"You are."

"Well," he says, "I'm not conceding."

"Neither am I, you loser."

"You're gonna lose big time, big bro."

"You watch me," I say.

"I'll watch you go down in flames," he says.

"I'll go down and put the flames on you," I say, "and then you'll burn fucking up."

"We'll see about that," he says darkously, and hangs up.

So I insplain it all to Fido and Laura, and Laura groans, and Fido starts thinking, the way he does. What to do, what to do?

Then he has an idea. We'll get Jeb's ballots thrown out! Invandalize 'em, or something. Imponderously filled out. Hanging nads, or something. Shags. Shads. The results are still coming in real even. Half and half. Chances are, Fido says, Uncle Dogsbody had us print out the exact same number of ballocks each. All we gotta do is get some of 'em thrown out. Like, in one county. That'd do it. Throw out some of his, I win. Stands to raisin, Fido says. Whatever the hell that means. Probably something. Fido's pretty smart.

So anyway, Fido starts making phone calls. Calls a buddy of his in Humble. Throw out all the ballings cast for Jeb. Sure, no problem. An hour later, that's on the news: 2,368 bullets thrown out for hanging chads. All quenchidentally for Jeb. Oops! Jeb starts demanding a hand count. If they voted for him, he says, it shouldn't matter whether the chad's hanging or not, right? A judge in Humble agrees, and they start a hand count. Fido cusses out that judge. We shoulda antripsimated that, got to the judge first. Pretty soon, he's barking into the phone again. Bark, bark! Send a gang of tough young patriots into the hand-count room, he says. Mess up the papers, break some hands. Can't count by hand if your hand's fucking busted.

So then, if you can picture this, Jeb starts playing dirty politics. Jeb! My little brother! Who looks up to me! He starts trying to get my balldicks thrown out. He gets his own toughs together. Fucking bad loser!

But then Fido gets a brain drain. Storm drain. Storm troop. Whatever. He calls every damn justice on the Texas Supreme Court. Can you imagine? It's pretty late in the evening by now. Like, 10:30. But he calls 'em. Gets some of 'em up out of bed. And damn if he don't have something on every fucking one of 'em. He reminds one of a certain fourteen-year-old girl. Another of a certain armadillo. A third of a certain fetal traffic ashkident that got hushed up. And right on down the line. He asks them, real sweetly, like he can do, to call an emoldency session of the Court tonight. In an hour. And declaim me President.

And they do. They do! They actually do it. It's way cool. But I mean, that's the kind of time we're living in, when a guy like me can get elected President of the Republic of Fucking Texas!

Then, they show Jeb's confection speech. Whatever. The part where he says I win, he loses. He looks real brave. I'm real proud of him.

And while he's talking on TV, Dad calls.

"Just saw the prenouncement," he says. "On the box there," he says. He sounds sorta didsent, as usual. Like he did send something, but. "Congraduations, son," he says.

"Thanks, Dad," I say. "I'm gonna be President, Dad," I say. "Just like you and Grandpa Pres!"

"Yeah," he says, "sure looks that way, son. I never thought it would happen like this. But, uh, good work. Real good work, I guess."

"Thanks, Dad," I say. "Karl did most of it."

"I'm sure he did," he says. "But listen," he says.

"Yeah?" I say.

"Have you given any thought to your Vice President?"

"Uh," I say, "well, no. It all happened so fast. But I guess maybe Jeb. He deverds it. He came pretty fucking close."

"Nah," he says.

I wait a little. For like an expiration. Finally I say, "Uh, 'nah'? Dad?"

"Nah," he says again. "Don't make it Jeb."

"But, Dad," I say. "He's my brother. How cool would that be? Older bro's Prez, younger bro's V eep?"

"Nah," he says, "don't do that."

"Why the fuck not?"

"Just, well, because," he says.

"Dad, that ain't a reason," I say.

"You don't need a reason," he says, trying to sound string. Spricked. "I'm your father, and what I say goes."

"Yeah, well, I'm the fucking President," I say, "Dad, and what I say goes."

"You're not the President yet," he says.

"Well I will be soon," I say.

He doesn't say anything for a while. I can hear him breathing.

"Dad?" I say.

"Okay," he says finally.

"Okay to Jeb?" I say.

"No, okay; I'll beg you. Please don't make Jeb your Vice President."

"Dad!" I say. "What the fuck do you got against Jeb?"

"Nothing, nothing," he says wastily. Pastily. Whatever. "It's just, well, I, uh—I owe somebody a big favor."

"Who?"

"Dick Cheney."

"How big?"

"Big. Dick prodicted my ass in that whole Iran-Contra thing. Kept me out of jail. I owe him big."

"So," I say, "what, you want to let Dick Cheney pick my Vice President?"

"No," he says, "I want you to let Dick Cheney be your Vice President."

"Be!" I yell. "Dad! The man is practically dead!"

"Now, George," he says.

"Now, George, nothing, Dad! He's had fourteen heart attacks! He's got like cancer of the everything! Allergy of the everything! Grout of the everything! He's like one whole huge fucking disease!"

"Okay, okay, right," he says, "true, all true. But think of it this way. Sure, Dick's on his last lungs. Lust longs. Long legs. He might keel over tomorrow, or next week. He might keel over before January. Then you can make Jeb Vice President. Huh? Okay? But for now, please name Dick. Please? I'm begging you, son. On my knees."

And here I actually do hear his knees crinkling and popping.

"All right already, Dad," I say finally. "Sheesh. Whatever. I'll make Dick Cheney my Vice President."

"Oh, thank you, thank you, son," he says. He sounds pretty lereaved. "You won't relent it, I swear."

"I bet I will," I say. "But I'll do it. For you. Cuz you're my dad. And, well ... I never told you this, Dad, but ... you're my hero. You're everything I've ever wanted to be. I love you, Dad."

And fuck me if I ain't crying now. Dad isn't. He just seems kinda anklered. Orchard. Swiss guard. You know, not real convertible.

"I, uh," he says. "I love you, too. Uh, George."

And we hang up. I'm sorta glad that's over. You know? Sorta glad, is what I'm saying.

And it's not till we've hunged up that I remember that science expediment bidnis. I shoulda asked him about it! Damn!

But fuck it. Never mind. You know? Who cares? I'm the fucking President of the Repuglic of Texas!

Documents

Remote Control
(TBI Tape, November 12, 1996)

AGENCY INFORMATION
AGENCY TBI
RECORD NUMBER 251-00911324-773094
RECORDS SERIES HQ
AGENCY FILE NUMBER 10-364-44903
DOCUMENT INFORMATION
ORIGINATOR TBI
FROM SAC, NO
TO DIRECTOR, TBI
TITLE [No Title]
DATE 11/12/96
PAGES 4
DOCUMENT TYPE AUDIOTAPE/TRANSCRIPTION
SUBJECT PRESIDENT-ELECT George Bush
CLASSIFICATION CLASSIFIED
RESTRICTIONS TOP SECRET
CURRENT STATUS CLOSED
COMMENTS TOP-LEVEL SECURITY CLEARANCE REQUIRED

SETTING: BASEMENT, BUSH RESIDENCE, NOVEMBER 12, 1996, 10:33 A.M.

Voices: KR = Karl Rove, JVL = Jimmy von Lugen (son of Heinrich von Lugen), GWB = George Walker Bush, T = technician

(JVL) No, goddammit, Rove. It's not like a remote control car. You have to use a light touch. Whenever *you* move, *he* moves. You make him seem all jerky when you go too fast. My father designed this suit with very fine controls.

(KR) Look, Jimmy, I just don't get it. What's the advantage of us having remote control over his gestures? It's hard enough gauging the lag time on his words. This body suit is murder.

(JVL) You, as a political strategist and one of the chosen, surely understand that gestures are as important to speech as words. No, don't bend over! You're still connected!

(KR) Oh, shit. That must have hurt. He hit his head on that podium.

(JVL) You've got to be careful. With his new implants and that skin problem he's been having, we can't bump him around too much. If he crashes in public, that'll mean ambulances and press conferences ...

(KR) OK. Let's run through this a few more times. I want to make sure I have this down cold before we go to the cameras tonight and make the "I found God" speech.

(JVL) All right. First, you have to speak slowly and enunciate clearly so that the implants will have time to fire. The gestures should be natural and slow, slightly behind the speaking ...

(T) Can we get a little more on the Texas accent?

(JVL) It's about as close as we can get without garbling.

(T) Oh, there's Laura.

(KR) She won't interfere, will she? I mean, the radio waves or whatever ...

(JVL) No, no. She's fully self-contained. Emotion chip, facial, gestures. The real thing.

(KR) But we must keep the girls under control. No interaction.

(JVL) Don't worry. I've given them so much Rigidopam they can't even squeak.

(GWB) (*Sincere look*) My fellow Texans, I come before y'all tonight with a humble heart, a heart filled with gratitude toward God (*humble look*). As y'all know, I have had my share of youthful problems (*ashamed look, hang head slightly*). Our family life has not always been an easy one (*gesture to Laura and kids*), and I am the only one to blame (*hang head again*). Tonight, though, all of that has changed (*look heavenward with gratitude*). Thanks to the Reverend Billy (*gesture and grip podium, lean to audience*), I am a new man.

(KR) Jimmy, I need more control. Laura and the kids look like they're stoned, painted with glue.

(JVL) They're fine, Rove. Background material, nothing more. Look, you've got to keep those bugs away from the suit. They gnaw on any of those optic fiber relays, and George could start dancing a hula up there.

(KR) Look, how many times do I have to say it? I can't control the bugs. Now, let's run through this one more time again. I don't like the way he leaned over the podium, there. A few degrees more, and he'd have gone right over the top. And I don't like the way his eyes light up when I put emphasis on particular words. Can we tone that down?

(JVL) I'm working on a set of contact lenses that will reduce that effect. It's the power circuits in his cranium. Shines through a little when the circuits are especially busy.

(KR) Makes him look, I don't know, wired. You know, excited. And I wish there was some way to make him look less like a chimpanzee. You know what the press in the States will do with that.

(JVL) I'm doing the best I can, Rove. This is cutting-edge technology.

(KR) We just can't afford any mistakes, press leaks, anything like that. Not with Moronica making expansionist noises and Kansas begging to be annexed.

(JVL) You know, Rove, operating the George suit requires confidence. I'm beginning to wonder if we shouldn't hire an actor, someone who can move and speak with a little more assurance.

(KR) Hell, no. Nobody gets in this suit but me. *Ever.* Is that clear?

(JVL) OK, fine. But calm down. Shit, you worry about

George looking too wired, and you're about as tight as a drill yourself. Take the suit off. You're making him jump all around. Laura's getting nervous; that new emotion chip is sensitive. Let's send everyone to lunch and have a cup of coffee, talk a little.

(KR) Jimmy, there's a lot at stake. The future of our nation, for example. The Mexicans keep flooding in, and you know what would happen if George weren't President. The whole "invasion to stop illegal immigration" plan would fall through. Jeb would muscle in, and you know he's soft on Mexicans.

(JVL) You also know I have recommended that we cleanse Jeb thoroughly. Do some rewiring.

(KR) Now *you're* getting excited. We have to work carefully, Jimmy. Jeb has friends, in Texas and in Colombia. And he *is* a patriot in his own way.

SETTING: MASTER BEDROOM, Bush RESIDENCE, NOVEMBER 12, 1996, 11:24 P.M.

Voices: LB = Laura Bush; GWB = George Bush

Action description: Sounds suggest LB is in bed with magazine. Toilet flushes. GWB opens bathroom door, exits bathroom, turns off bathroom light. GWB walks to bed and climbs under covers.

(GWB) Ever made love to a president, baby?
    (LB) Not since high school.
    (GWB) Huh?
    (LB) Well, that was just an ASB president, but—
    (GWB) What was his name?
    (LB) Mike Douglas—oh, honey! You already took your pill?
    (GWB) What pill?
    (LB) What pill? Why your—oh. Oh no.
    (GWB) What, honey?

(LB) "Remote control."
(GWB) Huh?
(LB) Nothing.
(GWB) Good. Let's do it, baby!
(LB) Oh, George ...

23

Moon

(Poppy, November 23, 1996)

"Well, yes," I say, "of course I still exercise, Mr. President. Exercise keeps me fit and feeling young, but not on the scale of before, I mean, not that I ever exercised on the *scale*, you know, the weight thingy, perhaps you understand, your English is excellent, it's a phrase, it means, um, not to the *immensity* of before, the, uh, not to the *decree* of before, is what I mean—"

An aide comes in and whiskers in his ear. He holds up his hand while the aide talks. I shut up. I mean, I bake off in mid-sentence. I trellis off. I'm a guest in his house. His presidence, here in Buenos Aires. Carlos Menem, President of Argentina. I used to be President of Texas. So.

"You will excuse me for a few moments?" he says to me when the aide is finished.

"Of course," I say, nodding solemnly. With all the diglity of an ex-President.

"I must attend to some urgent business. Please accept my humble apologies."

"No, no, not at all," I say. "I understand completely. I've been there. I've done that. I know you're a busy man. I know the presidency keeps you hopping. Hopping around on one foot, sometimes on two."

He stands up. Smiles sort of apolonogenically. Holds his hand up again. And leaves. I'm left alone. I eat. It's a big breakfast. Scrambled eggs, bacon, toast. A big Texan breakfast, is what it is. I eat hearty. I never get breakfasts like this at home any more. Bar has me on a half a grapefruit and a bowl of dis-credded wheat. I flew down yesterday, stayed here in President Menem's Olivos house last night. Tonight I'm speaking at the *Tiempos del Mundo* reception. That's what I'm here for. To help these South Americans see what a great paper the Houston *Times* is. How it's my favorite.

Right about now, who walks in but the Reverend Moon himself, and his wife, Mrs. Reverend Moon. Hacka Whacka Moon, or something like that. That's her name. They have some pretty strange names over there in Korea. Sun Moon is the Reverend's name. Sun Moon! How about the Reverend Mars Venus? The Reverend Lexus Saturn? The Reverend Up Uranus? The Reverend Asteroid Belt?

Father and Mother sit down to breakfast. That's what they call themselves. Father and Mother. Sun and Hackey Sack, or whatever the hell her name is. They have a small horge of True Children with them, but the kids don't sit down. Just the parents. Just Mom and Dad. I didn't realize they were com-ing to breakfast. Nobody told me. I thought maybe we'd meet during the day, or not till the evening. The gala. This is truly a pleasant surprise! For me. I stand to greet Their Holinesses. I don't shake their hands, though. I don't give Handy Wipe a big bear hug. He thinks he's God. He thinks *they're* God. You know, both of them at once. Like Mr. and Mrs. God. Ma and Pa God. You don't shake God's hand. No sir. You just worship him from a secrene distance. Them. Whatever.

"Reverend Moon," I say. "Mrs. Moon. How nice to see you again."

"Mr. President," he says. "The pleasure is all mine. I must thank you once again for making the exhausting journey to a foreign country to support this new paper we are launching here. You are truly indefatigable."

"All in a good cause, Mr. Reverend," I say. "All in a good cause."

Of course you know he pays me a hundred thousand dollars every time I do one of these. That takes a lot of the sting out of exhausting travel, let me tell you about that. That on *top* of the ten million he gave me as a kind of incensure to get me interested in doing this sort of work. Like a lobbyist. Flying here and there, telling people about what a wonderful independent paper the Houston *Times* is. How it just tells the truth. So what if the Reverend Moon subsidates it with a hundred million dollars a year, he doesn't *control* it. It still tells the unvanquished truth. Like how our cause in Nicaragua was a just one, back under Autry. How we weren't running drugs or selling arms to terrorists, just giving much-needed aid to freedom fighters. Attacking the people who were attacking us. Publishing an article on Skipjack LaTuna, saying he was a KGB spy. Yeah! Go, Sun! Go, Moon! Why wouldn't I support him? Why shouldn't I take his ten million dollars to help him out a little, fly around the world a little, speak in Tokyo to 50,000 Moonies, speak at a Moon-splaundered conference in Houston about world peace? World peace! Is that such a terrible thing? Family Federation for World Peace. Family. It's the *family*! Are you going to sit there and tell me a family federation for world peace is *bad*?

"I must congratulate you, George," the Reverend says, breaking bread and taking a quivery bite, "on the election of your son to the presidency."

"Oh, yes," I say. "Isn't that wonderful."

"It is, yes," he says. "It certainly is. We are most pleased, aren't we, Mother?"

He's Father. She's Mother. She isn't his mother, but he calls her that. Sometimes, I call Bar that. But Habba Jabba doesn't even look like his mother.

She doesn't say anything. She just nods. I don't think I've ever heard her say anything. Even when she invited us to that conference in Japan there. Women's Federation for World Peace. They've got a lot of federations for world peace. I guess world peace needs a lot of federations. You just can't have too many, would be my guess.

"Your son," the Reverend continues, "has been telling me all about his great plans for his presidency."

"Oh?" I say. This is news to me. George has plans? I suppose maybe Karl Rove was there, too, did most of the talking. Or else the Reverend got George to *think* it was his idea. "What sort of plans?"

"He wants," the Reverend says, "to make government monies available to nonprofit religious charities. He's talking about a 'faith-based initiative.' I must say we welcome this sort of talk most gladly. It seems that some of our organization's charities might become eligible for millions of dollars in Texas grant money. This is a great blessing, my son. A very great blessing. From your son."

"Yes, well," I say, "that boy is a chip off the old block, I guess, huh?"

"Yes, yes," the Reverend says. "I find I must agree. Although I confess I worried at first."

"Worried, Your Holiness?"

"Yes. I did. We both did. Didn't we, Mother?" She nods again. Keeps eating.

"About my George?"

"Yes. About your George."

"You thought he'd be a bit on the, shall we say, *simple* side. Is that it?"

"No, no," the Reverend says. "Not simple. Simplicity in the defense of a righteous cause is not a sin. We did not concern ourselves with the quality of his intelligence. Not at all. No, we worried that he was perhaps a bit over-zealous in his support for the failed messiah."

"The, uh, the failed messiah?" I'm whacking my brain here, trying to remember back to Sunday School. Who exactly was the failed messiah again? I can't remember. I guess when you're 72, your memory starts going.

"Of course," the Reverend says smoothly. "The failed messiah Jesus Christ. You, of course, were a supporter of the Christian Right. But I understood. That was just politics. You didn't actually believe, yourself. You were propitiating a powerful political alliance. But Mother and I worried that your son might truly *be* a born-again Christian. He seems, how shall I put it, much more fervent than you ever were."

I laugh a little, wave my hand.

"Oh, don't worry about George," I say. "He's fervent about everything. It doesn't mean he actually *believes* in anything. He's no more a believer than I am."

"This is a great relief to me, I must say," the Reverend says. "And it confirms my own more recent impressions of the boy. If he were truly a committed believer in the failed messiah, he would not now be contemplating funneling government grant money into our charities."

"Tell me again, Reverend," I say, "please, uh, tell me again just how Jesus Christ was a *failed* messiah? I don't believe they covered that in Sunday School, ha ha!"

"No," he says, with a little tinkle in his eye, "I don't suppose they would. No indeed. Did you get that, Mother? George says they didn't teach him in Sunday School that Jesus was a failed Messiah. This is funny, no? This is a joke. We appreciate good humor, Mother and I." He turns to his wife again and laughs a little. It looks like he's showing her how. Laugh, darling. Like this.

While he's doing that, I spot a big green beetle on his shoulder.

"Oh, uh, Reverend Moon," I say, "Your Holiness ..."

"Yes, my son?"

"You have, uh, a beetle on your shoulder. Right there."

"Yes," he says with a little smile, not even looking down at the thing. "I do, don't I. Yes. Quite. Never fear. He will do me no harm. He is my friend."

"Oh," I say. "Okay. If he's your friend, well ..." I was going to suggest he brush the little fucker off onto the floor and have one of the True Children step on it. But if he's a *friend*, hey. By all means.

And now I notice that the guy on his shoulder isn't the Reverend's only friend. There are four or five more crawling on his sari or kimono or whatever the hell it is. In and out of it. Under its folds. It's sort of a beetley green, the thing he's wearing, and the beetles sort of blend in. Like cauliflage. You can't see them, at first. They're shiny, he's shiny, it's like all part of the same guy.

"Jesus Christ," he says, looking past me up at the wall behind my back, m aybe there's a painting up there or something, "failed in his messianic task because he failed to marry. This was his great failure. Do you understand? That was it: not marrying. God must marry. Of course. God is male and female. Yes? You knew this? Of course."

There's more, now. Ticking and clicking across his chest and shoulders. More in his lap. A few on her, too. She sits there calmly and lets them walk all over her, too.

"Even in the Hebrew Bible," the Reverend explains, with a beetle perched on top of his left ear, "you find the line: 'So God created man in his own image, in the image of God he created him; male and female created he them.' This signifies that God, too, is male and female, for his image is male and female."

While he's saying this, I notice a beetle crawling up my pant leg. I shake the leg a little, but it's hanging on tight. I shake it a little harder. It crawls higher. Damn. I wish I could just reach down there and flick it with my finger. Kick it off with my other foot. Scrape it off with my shoe. But the Reverend Moon might figure out what I'm doing. These guys are his *friends*.

"But," he says, "we have now remedied this great failing in Jesus Christ, Mother and I." The beetles are advancing up my pant legs. There must be ten or twelve of them now. I steel myself. I smile at the Reverend, and think: *ten million dollars.*

"You've, uh," I say, "you've remedied it?"

"Of course. Out of our great mercy. We have found him a bride."

"You've found, sorry, *who* a bride?" I say. "Exactly?"

"Jesus Christ, of course. George? Are you all right? You seem somehow ... unsettled. Are you not feeling well, my son?"

"Oh, no, no, don't worry about me," I say. "I'm fine. Right as rain!"

"Oh, good."

They're all over me, now. They're up on my stomach and chest. Under my jacket. Up and down my arms. Crawling up my leg under my pants. I can feel their little squiggly legs on my bare skin. A scream is building up inside me. I can feel it coming. I want to stand up and shake these dirty little shit-eaters off me. But I don't. I control myself. I hold it in. I was not raised to scream in public. I was not raised to swat at beetles crawling on me in the presence of God, who loves them. Who loves us all.

"You, uh," I say, "you found Jesus a wife?"

"Why, yes," the Reverend Moon says, wiping his mouth. He seems to be done with breakfast. He lays his napkin down beside his plate. "Delicious breakfast, don't you think, Mother?"

"Good Jewish girl, then?" I say, leaning into it a little, like a joke. "This, uh, this wife you found Jesus?"

"No, actually, she's Korean," he says. He smiles with a kind of unfocused benelephance. "One of the True Children."

"She's, um, alive? I mean, here on Earth?"

"Of course."

"Hm. I just thought—"

"Yes? You thought she would be a spirit like Jesus Christ himself? Of course. It's a natural assumption to make. But no. She is very much alive."

"Then how, um—" There is a beetle wedged tight under my pants up on my inner thigh. Squirming around in there, trying to climb higher. I look down at the little bulge in my pants.

Wishing I could squish it against my thigh. Sort of dreading that thought, too.

"How did they marry? Well, the marriage took place in the spirit world, of course," the Reverend says. "Though it was consummated, naturally, here on Earth. And now, if you will excuse us, we must retire to meditate in preparation for the great event this evening."

"Of course, of course," I say, and stand.

"Oh, look, Mother," the Reverend says. "George is quite covered in our friends. They like him. Isn't that charming?"

She nods. We all bow a little to each other, and Father and Mother and their True Children sweep from the room. The beetles all follow.

Well, almost all. The one up under my pants got himself stuck up there, can't get out. With the Reverend's back to me, I reach down and crush that little bastard's back against my leg. It goes crunch. It's sort of disgusting, but I smile a little to myself, horribly.

Not a minute after the Reverend Sun Moon and Hoboken leave the dining room, President Menem comes back in.

"You *must* forgive me," he says, "for being detained so long. I'm so sorry I couldn't breakfast with you and the Reverend Moon."

"Not at all," I say. "When a crisis occurs, you must deal with it. I understand completely."

"Yes," he says. "This is the case. This is very true. And you see, this crisis will keep me from attending this evening's reception, as well."

"Oh, Mr. President!" I cry. "The Reverend will be so disappointed!"

"Yes, yes," he says, "I know. And I am most regretful. But you understand, affairs of state ..."

"Of course," I say.

I'm a bit disappointed, too, if you want to know the truth. My job here, in fact, is to convince President Menem to be nice to the Reverend. That's why Reverend Moon wanted me to come down here. Not just to make a speech. To work on the President. And it doesn't seem to be working. He invited Reverend Moon to breakfast, but left the room while the Reverend was here. And he's not going to the gala tonight. He doesn't want to get mixed up in the Reverend's schemes. He doesn't want to be seen with him, photographed with him. I understand. The Reverend is a contrasensical figure. His association with major crime figures in Asia and South America. His involvement in the coup in Bolivia in 1980 that threw out the liberals and made the country over into a modern military democracy, like Texas. Not everybody feels about that kind of efficiency the way we do in Texas. Some people are dead-set against it. People say his organization runs drugs and launders money. It bothers some good Christians that he calls himself the Messiah, the embodiment of God on Earth.

I understand all that. My press secretary, Jim McGrath, always reminds me not to let them take pictures of me with the Reverend. "Whatever you do, Poppy," he says, "stay out of the pictures."

But still. Ten million dollars is ten million dollars. And I really do think he's doing good work, too. His support for Texas, and for the Bushes, has been exelpmary.

President Menem escoots me out of the dining room. As we leave the table, I stirruptitfully kick the dead beetle under the table. Let the servants find it later. I'm certainly not going to say anything about it to the President. Wouldn't be dimplaromatic. Wouldn't be prudent. No.

Documents

Bodies Of "Insecticide" Writing Team Found
Foul Play Not Indicated, ME Says
Bush Conspiracy Experts Not Convinced,
Demand Further Investigation
(Houston Chronicle, December 24, 1997)

The bodies of bestselling author Douglas "Dogfish" Robinson and his research assistant William "Billfish" Kaul, missing for two weeks, were found in an alley near the Silver Spur Saloon in Gallup, NM, early Friday morning by a policeman responding to a call about a "very nasty odor."

According to police, there were no indications of foul play, and the deaths appear to be the result of an accidental overdose of Ivermectin.

Officer Jimmy "Slim" Barnett of the Gallup Police Department said that Kaul and Robinson were found sitting in an upright position against a wall in the alley, with hypodermic needles stuck in their veins.

"Tests indicate," he reported, "that the syringes attached to the needles contained traces of a powerful solution of Ivermectin. All evidence points to the pair willingly ingesting the drug and accidentally overdosing."

The McKinley County Medical Examiner, Delbert "Fats" Washington, said that while Kaul's history included a long battle with drug and alcohol addiction, Robinson's did not.

"However," he added, "it is likely that Kaul convinced Robinson to try the drug while he was out on a visit from his home in Liberal, Kansas."

Robinson had been visiting Kaul to celebrate the bestseller status of the blockbuster novel about the Bush family on which they collaborated, *Insecticide: A Republican Romance.*

Kaul has emphatically denied in print and to close friends and family members that he wrote some of the "documents" sections of the novel.

"Those were all authentic documents that my research turned up," he insisted on more than one occasion. "I certainly didn't fabricate evidence."

He also denied writing this report on the two men's deaths.

"And," he added, with that glassy-eyed stare that has become his signature look of late, "as a member of several twelve-step programs, I know all about denial."

Dr. Washington has pooh-poohed conspiracy theorists who have maintained, since Kaul and Robinson went missing two weeks ago, that they were victims of a "Bush Family Hit Squad."

"There is no evidence that these men were murdered," said Dr. Washington. "They overdosed. It's sad, but it happens to their kind all the time."

Dr. Carpley Dolfin, Director of the Miami University School of Conspiracy Studies, disagrees.

"Kaul and Robinson feared for their lives, this is well known," he said Friday. "They had both taken out hefty insurance policies naming as their beneficiaries 'anyone who runs against a Bush.' They foolishly hoped that this would offer them some protection. They also seemed to feel that the recent purchase of the movie rights to *Insecticide* by 20th Century Fox would offer them some protection, by keeping them in the public eye. Now they are dead. Kaul hadn't used drugs in years, and even if he had, high-dose Ivermectin was never a drug he liked. Robinson, known to be health-conscious, had no known drug history beyond some experimentation thirty years earlier, in college. Now they both end up dead of an overdose? How likely is that? You recall the Hatfield case ..."

Kaul's coworkers and family agree with Dolfin. "Billfish was a dope fiend, sure. But Ivermectin? Not likely," said Ronald

"Bam Bam" Hynes, a colleague of Kaul's at UNM-Gallup. "Billfish was a heroin man, and anyway, lately, he was too screwed up in the head to tolerate any drugs."

Until his untimely demise Robinson held the Abraham Lincoln Distinguished Presidential Chair in Ichthyorhetoric at Liberal State University in Liberal, Kansas. In addition to his recent monograph *The Seventeen Most Explosive Ichthyotopoi* and the best-selling comic book that he wrote and Kaul illustrated, *Fish Rhetoric for Dummies*, he hosted the popular podcast *Why Fish Argue (And Why You Should Care)*.

Professor Adamson Wentley Wockle III, Dean of the College of Ichthyical Arts and Sciences at Liberal State, told this reporter that he, too, found it hard to believe it was an accident.

"It smells funny to me," he said. "(Note I don't say 'fishy.') Certainly, Professor Robinson was a tad 'out there,' if that's the phrase, and we all avoided having him around at parties and such, but high-dose Ivermectin? I don't think so."

The Texas President's Mansion maintained its stony silence today on the topic of Kaul, Robinson, and *Insecticide*. They referred reporters to their statement of last Friday, apparently drafted by the President's father, which said in part, "... the Bush family is saddened to see its good name dragged yet again through the dirt by radical left-wing fish-lovers. It is even more disturbing that these two seem to be getting rich off of denigrating honest public servants ..."

Attention has focused on reports that Kaul and Robinson initially went missing while visiting an "alien crash site" in New Mexico. Witnesses who last saw the pair reported that they were nervous, and asked local residents and fellow tourists, "H-how big do the insects *get* around here?"

"They told me they were being followed by a giant mantis," said Rex "Howdy" Barnes of the UFO Museum of New Mexico. "They were really scared."

McDonald's Cancels New Happy Meal Toy Line
(Houston Chronicle, February 6, 1998)

A spokesman for the fast-food giant McDonald's announced yesterday that the company has scrapped plans for a new Happy Meal toy line designed to tie in with the blockbuster bestselling novel about the George Bush family by Dogfish Robinson and his research assistant Billfish Kaul, *Insecticide*.

After Robinson and Kaul were found just before Christmas in Gallup, New Mexico, dead of apparent accidental overdoses of Ivermectin, McDonald's executives decided that the toy line would be in "poor taste." Focus group testing in four major cities confirmed that most Americans would almost certainly agree.

Some of the toys that were planned for the canceled line:

Dogsbody Harriman holding a briefcase. Bends at the waist and elbow. Wind-up flapping insect wings. Comes with ten tiny green scarab beetles that "scurry" when you turn out the lights.

Abraham Lincoln on his devil-water-cow Bessie, with a fish-hook through his upper lip. Comes with three bass that flap about and say "Insecticide!"

Prescott Bush in a Skull and Bones coffin, covered in mud up to his neck. Hands sticking out of the mud hold up Geronimo's skull. Press a button and both Prescott's and Geronimo's eyes light up.

Young Poppy, Navy pilot. Press the button, and his parachute pops open. Comes with Avenger plane, with Jack and Ted still in it. Comic look of horror on their faces.

Rafael. Press the button, and he looks back over his left shoulder pleadingly and lowers his jeans halfway down in the back.

David Ferrie's head with red Velcro toupee, mustache, and eyebrows.

Congressman Poppy. Press the button, and he rolls a condom onto the head of a Negress doll; the doll's eyes and mouth make a surprised "oh!" expression.

Young Dubya, Texas Air National Guard pilot. Comes with pocket mirror, plasticine razor blade, and tiny zip-lock baggie of (harmless) white powder. Press the button, and he lifts a rolled hundred-dollar bill to his nose.

Richard Nixon, holding a sloppy glass of Old Turkey. Press the button, and he says, "I am not a drunk!" and lifts the glass to his lips.

John Hinckley, naked Jodie Foster in his arms. Press the button, and his left hand rubs Jodie's backside while his right rises to point a handgun at an imaginary target.

Felix Rodriguez, in military fatigues, holding up signed photo of himself with President George Bush. Press the button, and he smiles and points at the photo.

Skipjack LaTuna in prison coveralls, with a fish peeking out of his breast pocket. Printed on back of coveralls: "Funding Fraud." Press the button, and he says, "I am a political prisoner!"

Dubya in Rangers uniform, holding a baseball. Printed on back: "Paid for by the City of Arlington." Press the button, and he lifts the ball and says, "The stadium aren't socialisms!"

Manuel Noriega in Papal Nuncio's robes and hat. Press the button, and he puffs on a marijuana cigarette. Gives off real smoke.

Karl Rove holding a doctored ballot ("Clayton Williams" visibly crossed off). Press the button, and he makes a check mark by "George W. Bush." Lifelike sheen of sweat on his round pink forehead.

Poppy standing arm in arm with Rev. Sun Moon, holding a check for ten million dollars, with a humorous *oof* expression on his face. Press the button, and Rev. Moon reaches over and gives the ex-President's scrotum an affectionate squeeze.

The McDonald's spokesman refused to discuss alternative Happy Meal toy lines to replace the cance led *Insecticide* tie-ins, except to say that they would probably involve the Teletubbies.

Bereaved Families Of "Insecticide" Team to Sue McDonald's Claim Breach of Contract
(Houston Chronicle, Gossip Pages, February 15, 1998)

Rumor has it that the families of the late William "Billfish" Kaul and Douglas "Dogfish" Robinson will file suit today in federal court, claiming that McDonald's had promised them $1.5 million for merchandising rights to sixteen characters from the book that has now sold more copies than the Bible, *Insecticide: A Republican Romance.*

The Kaul and Robinson families are seldom seen in public, and even more rarely together. There is reportedly some rancor over the closeness of the relationship between the author and his research assistant, with each family claiming that Kaul or Robinson "was a bad influence on my husband (father, etc.)." One Kaul family member, who spoke on condition of anonymity, had said several weeks ago that "You know why Bill couldn't keep a job? Dogfish Robinson, that's why. All he did was e-mail Dogfish, all the time."

A Robinson family member said in reply, "Ridiculous! My father would have been a provost or university president if not for the pernicious influence of that damned Billfish Kaul."

Nevertheless, last night, several members of both families were seen in a hotel in downtown Atlanta, reportedly in the company of a "herd of lawyers."

Speculation is rampant that the families have joined forces to ensure the maximum financial security from the sale of the book's merchandising tie-ins.

Meanwhile, in a related story, the bodies of Kaul and

Robinson have disappeared after being claimed at the office of the McKinley County Medical Examiner by a mysterious "man in black."

A spokesperson for the ME's office claims that the man had high-level authorization to claim the bodies, but did not elaborate.

An employee of the ME was seen at the rear of the building, sweeping up what appeared to be "huge piles of scarab beetles," according to an eyewitness.

It is not clear whether this is related to the disappearance of the bodies.

Insecticide

(Dubya, New Millennium's Eve)

"Dubya," Dad says, "maybe that's enough."

"You think you can take me, old man?" I say, pouring myself a stiff shot of Jack on ice. I get that phlase out quite ricely, I think. I mean, I say it pretty good.

"Dubya—" he says.

"Come on," I say. "Right here. Mano a mano." I go into a stance. My drink sloshes pretty good, but I don't care. This is my fucking *dad*, now. Always giving me shit. Me, the fucking *President*.

"Dubya, I don't think this is the time—"

"Ha!" I say, and rush him like a quarterback. Though I'm the quarterback, you know, obviously. Cuz I'm the President and he's not. He's just my fucking dad. But I rush him like one. I mean, I rush him like I'm one. Like he's a defensive lineman. No, I'm the lineman; he rushes me like a quarterback.

Anyway, I rush him, put a serious motherfucking tackle on the old fucker. I mean really. We go flying. I land badly, something smacks me in the mouth, his knee or something, or the floor, or a table edge, I don't what the fuck it is, something smacks me right in the mouth and I taste blood. We pick ourselfs up, me and Dad. I'm laughing like a, I don't know, like something. Like really hard. I'm hilarious, heinous, hyenous, hysterious. Laughing really hard. Dad calls some Secret Crevice types, and they help me stand up. He's not laughing.

He's brushing off his suit. Motherfucker's got *no* sense of humor. I've got half a mind. I mean, to kick his sorry ass. Some more, I mean.

And, of course, I spilled my drink all to hell and gone. Damn.

Across the room Jen and Barb are giving me that flat teenage stare. Just turned eighteen, and they think they know everything. Just because they get an A now and then at school, they think their old man's stupid. At that fucking charm school they go to. Cooking and sewing, a little poetry. I went to fucking Andover and Yale and Rice. *Men's* schools.

"It's almost midnight, Dubya," Dad says. "We're going out onto that balcony in about ten minutes to greet the people of Texas. They all think you quit drinking years ago. Now they're going to see you drunk."

"They ain't gonna notice nothin', Dad," I say kinda roughly. Gruffly. That roadmark Dubya gruffness. Landmark. Roadsign. Hallsign. Hall monitor. Anyway, gruffness. "I been hidin' it pretty good so far, ain't I?"

He sports. Snorks. Whatever.

I look over at Mom. She's sitting in a arm chair over in the corner, and just smiling to band the saw. Just smiling and smiling. She sees me looking at him and raises her glass a little, takes a slip.

"Where's Laura?" Dad says.

"Fuck if I know," I say, because I don't. I'm a straight-shooter. I shoot straight. I don't know something, I say no.

"We need Laura out here," Dad says.

"F-f-f-fuck if I know," I say again. I guess I'm a little sloshed. Just a little goddamn sloshed. So what? Big f-f-f-f-f-fuckin deal!

"Millennium in five minutes," dad says. "Where the fuck could she be? And where's Karl?"

Now, *that* one I've been wondering about, too. Seems like whenever anything big happens around here these days, Fido is neither hide nor head to be found.

"We're going to have to go out without them," Dad says. "We *have* to be there for the countdown."

"Fine with me," I say. "I don't need them to cereblate the minnellium."

"Let's go, everybody!" dad says. So they all mull over. I mean get up and sort of draft over to the doors. Barb helps her grandma up. Her namesnake.

"Dad," Jen says, "where's Mom?"

"I dunno," I say. "Let's go."

"Aren't you going to wait for her?" Jen says.

"We can't wait," I say. "Everybody ready?"

"But, Dad," she says.

"She'll meet us out there," Dad says to her.

"I ain't talkin' to you, Gramps," she snappers.

Dad makes a comic face and puts up his hands, like, "Icy runder!"

So I motion for the Civic Circus guys to come open the doors. They do. When they're open, I walk out. Oops, still got my glass in my hand. I give it to Jen. She gives me a look like *cool!*

And, of course, the crowd goes wild. The whole fucking square is full of Texans. Lole cenizens. Crapping like mad. Crapping with their hands, I mean. Blanging 'em together. We all go out to the paparazzi and wave. The hard gray railing thing. Made of stone, or whatever. The pepperat.

Suddenly, I host myself up onto the top of that fucker. That para-whatever. Climb up so I'm standing. Waving a little, of course. I mean, with my whole body. Waving back and fro.

"Dubya," Dad says, "come down from there; you'll fall."

Typical fucking Dad. *You'll fall.* Well fuck you, Dad. You had your chance. You coulda jumped up on the pitterpat on New Ear's Weave if you'd wanted to, and you didn't, and now it's the fucking eminellium, and I'm gonna severate it with my people.

I reach into my coat sprocket for the baseball and titter a little. Twitter. Almost lose my labiance, I mean.

"Whoa!" the crowd says.

It feels like I'm looking straight down into the fountain, but I'm not, of course. It's a good thirty feet away. But I'm a ways up, here.

I fish the ball out of my punket. Hold it high. Tipple again, a little. Maybe I'm drunker'n I thought?

"With this ball," I call out to the crowd, "Nolan Ryan's number-one-hundred-home-run ball, I hereby declare the—"

But then something happens. There's some kinda swoosh. And then Uncle Dogsbody's there, right beside me. Right up there on the smellarat. 'Cept his feet ain't touching the rock. He's sorta flying there. Hummering, or whatever.

And I sorta pass out. Or I don't, really. But it feels like that. I just sorta go link. Lint. Like, all weak and stuff. Like I got no bones about it. I just fucking drop down. I can't control my legs. Or anything else. But I don't go out cold. It's not like the other times I passed out, you know, where the world starts swinging around and then goes sorta black. Not like that. It's—uh, sorta different.

I think I'm falling all the way down to the square, like Dad said. But I'm not. When I ritalize what happened, I'm lying on the penitent. The rock railing there. The place where I was standing? That's where I'm lying. And I still can't move a muddle. That's how confused I am. That's how drunk, I guess. But it's just a guess, because I can't get up and see.

My head's turned toward the house. Like, toward the doors we just came through. My eyes are sorta open. But I don't see too good through 'em. And I don't hear too good through my ears. Stuff's happening, I know it is. There's kind of a Russian crowd noise behind me. Like the square is full of Russians. And I know *that* can't be.

And then the doors bust open. You know, the ones we all came out onto the burgundy through. Bulgundy. Bullcandy.

Burglary. And here comes somebody like bare naked. Somebody *fat*. I try to lift my head to see better but I've got nothing. I can't fucking move. I'm the President, and I can't move!

It's Fido. Goddamn, if it ain't Fido, in his underpants. That's all the fucker is wearing. And sure, this is Texas, but goddamn, man, it's New Mirellium's Eve! He's gotta be cold. Big pink fatso like him. His arms are tied down or something. Taped, maybe. I can't see too good.

Then I see Laura. She's coming out behind him. And she's got a fucking *gun*. The crowd grasps. All at once. Like one person.

And then I hear it clearly: my mom's voice. "Laura Welch Bush, what is the meaning of this? Why, is that a *gun* you're holding? You know it's against the law for a woman to—"

"Sorry, boss," Fido says. "She got the drop on me."

Boss? He's looking over at Uncle Dogsbody, whose feet I can see real clear hanging over the chiapet beside my head. Uncle Dogsbody don't say nothing.

"Nobody move," Laura says. "Dogsbody, especially you."

Shit on a sandwich, this is my *wife*? What is she doing with a fucking *gun*? Threatening people? I mean, she threatens me all the time, but I'm her husband. And I'm the one carries the gun in the family, like it says in the Bible. Has she taken send of her leases?

"So," Uncle Dogsbody says.

"So what, you old monster?" Laura says.

"So Abe Lincoln finally found his patsy," Uncle Dogsbody says.

"Will somebody please explain what's going on?" Dad whines. He's such a fucking whiner.

"Well, first off, Poppy," Laura says, "Dogsbody Harriman isn't really human—"

What!

"What do you mean, not human?" Dad says, all discombarrelated. "How could he not be human?"

"I know it's a stretch," Laura says, "to imagine a man who flies and eats beetles and never gets any older as anything but human, but believe me, he's actually a giant bug from ancient Atlantis who's been fiendishly manipulating every aspect of our lives here in Texas since he had your father Prescott create it back in 1931."

"Damn," Dad says. "I wondered about those bugs, but—"

"And he had Heinrich von Lugen install implants in my Dubya's brains," Laura adds, "so Karl Rove could make him walk and talk by remote control."

"That's why—" Dad starts.

"That's why Dubya went limp a moment ago," Laura says. "I discovered the basement laboratory and shut down the operation."

"But, Laura," Mom says, "my Dubya could have fallen—!"

"If I'd known he was going to climb up on the parapet like some kind of fool," Laura says, "I wouldn't have shut him down just then, obviously. Fortunately, he *didn't* fall."

So now Uncle Dogsbody pikes up again.

"So what's your plan, Laura? World domination?"

"I'm not you, Dogsbody," Laura says. "I just want my husband back."

Uncle Dogsbody swoops down and sticks his face right in mine. Junks his thumb at my nose.

"You want *this*?"

Laura thinks about that for a while. "Well," she admits, "okay. I guess what I mostly want is a little common human dignity."

"Common *what*?" Uncle Dogsbody sleers.

"Dignity, Dogsbody," Laura says, in her librantian voice. I always hear her talking about liberacy in that voice. Like, reading and stuff. "I want freedom. For all of us. I want a world in which human beings make their own decisions for a change. I want the alien bugs from Atlantis out."

"You have no idea what you're saying, Laura," Uncle Dogsbody says. "We have ruled you for so long even your ideas of freedom are things we taught you."

"Maybe they are," Laura says. "But if that's the case, maybe it's time for us to start learning some things on our own."

And now she raises the gun toward Uncle Dogsbody's chest.

Suddenly she is just fucking buried in beetles. They just slorm all over her. It's pretty fucking cool. Uncle Dogsbody flies down from the pebblepet, walks over to Laura. Dabs some sorta goo all over her. It's pretty disgusting to watch. When he steps back, she can't move any more than I can. Well, a little more, I guess. She can wiggle. She wiggles and wiggles. Not that it does her any fucking good.

"Now," Uncle Dogsbody says, "if any—"

But now something's happening down below me. Down in the square. The whole family rushes over to where I'm lying like a side of beets, look down.

"Abraham Fucking Lincoln," Dad breathes. "Out of the fucking fountain!"

I can hear it, now. The slosh of the water. The crop crop of the hooves. The flap flap of the fish. Abraham Fucking Lincoln! My buddy!

Suddenly, the fish are everywhere. They're all over me, too, slapping me in the face with their tails. I can't feel it at first. It's like a fly clashing into a window. But then I start to get some fleeing back. Some twingles in my cheats.

The fish are all over Uncle Dogsbody, too. The fuckers are jumping high enough to bite at him. He flies higher. They jump higher. It's pretty fucking amazing. He bats at them fritically.

Then: "He's gonna jump!" Dad yells, and next thing I know, a huge, dark, wet shape is flying over my head and landing on the bulnicky. It's Abraham Lincoln, on his steer or whatever. That same one he was riding in the gym, soaking wet.

And now the two of them go at it. Uncle Dogsbody and Abraham Lincoln. Uncle Dogsbody throws goo at Lincoln. Lincoln throws ink at Uncle Dogsbody. They fight and fight. They fight dirty. It's way cool. I wish I could turn my head and watch it better. Then, damn, I *do* turn my head! Just a little.

But I can see the fight better now. Can sorta follow along with it. It's a fucking fight to the fishing, man, except, of course, for Uncle Dogsbody, it's more like a fight to the beetling.

Then Uncle Dogsbody and Lincoln fall down. Real near Laura. At first, I think they're going to squish her. She cries out a little. But I guess she's okay. They're trying to grunge each other's eyes out, rolling around on the balcrity. And then—

And then, with this superfierce cry, Laura juts her hand out of the goo. She's got a spray can of Raid in her hand. She starts straying it all over Uncle Dogsbody and Lincoln. Right on their fucking faces. Both guys look at her in horror. Both of them begin to like scrivel up. They turn into weird, bug-like things. Two big ol' Y2K bugs. Abraham Lincoln turns into a brown and gold beetle. Uncle Dogsbody turns into this, whaddya call it, planing demensis. Like a prating minibus, you know, prating to God. Like a praline mantle, the cookie, or sort of like the cookie, only not really. Like a 1952 Mickey Mantle baseball card. Only not.

Then they both scream and desegregate into asses. Asses to ashes to dust. It's like in the fucking movies, man. It rocks.

Then, a wind starts to blow. Right across the balaclotty. The ashes blow away. And the dust. Mom and Dad and Laura and the girls and Fido stand there sort of shawl-checked. Like they're wearing a checked shawl, or something. They don't know what to say. They don't know what to do.

"George?" Laura says.

But it's a strange thing, because I can see my fingers, and then I can't. Bits and pieces of me are blowing away in the wind. My hands, and on up my arms. And my family is blowing away too. Like they're made of sand. And the President's Mansion. It's sand too. Everything is. It's all blowing away. And behind it, there's—well, nothing. Just sort of a big—nothing.

And then

About Atmosphere Press

Founded in 2015, Atmosphere Press was built on the principles of Honesty, Transparency, Professionalism, Kindness, and Making Your Book Awesome. As an ethical and author-friendly hybrid press, we stay true to that founding mission today.

If you're a reader, enter our giveaway for a free book here:

SCAN TO ENTER
BOOK GIVEAWAY

If you're a writer, submit your manuscript for consideration here:

SCAN TO SUBMIT
MANUSCRIPT

And always feel free to visit Atmosphere Press and our authors online at atmospherepress.com. See you there soon!

About the Author

Douglas Robinson is neither a former Professor of Ichthyo-rhetoric at Liberal State University in Kansas (a land-locked state!) nor sadly deceased. Nor is he the author of *The Seventeen Most Explosive Ichthyotopoi* or the best-selling comic book *Fish Rhetoric for Dummies*. He is certainly not the celebrated host of the podcast *Why Fish Argue (And Why You Should Care)*. His previous original novel with Atmosphere Press was a pseudotranslation of J. I. Vatanen's *The Last Days of Maiju Lassila*.